"You liked that kiss," Cord said. "Just as you'd like it if you came to my arms now."

Diana felt herself go rigid. "You're forgetting this is a marriage in name only."

"I'll keep my part of the bargain. You leave tomorrow. But we still have this night." Cord moved closer, pinning her against the wall. Diana knew she should be furious—but the warmth of his body was so close, his hand deceptively gentle on her bare neck.

"Remember the taste of my lips?" Cord asked. "Wonder what it would be like to have me touch you again, to touch you all over? Who better to teach you the mysteries of love—and you are going to learn them, sweet, *soon*—than your own husband?"

Diana thought her marriage was a game—but now she knew she was playing with fire. . . .

THE
TURQUOISE
TRAIL

by
Susannah Leigh

AN ONYX BOOK

ONYX
Published by the Penguin Group
Penguin Books USA Inc., 375 Hudson Street,
New York, New York 10014, U.S.A.
Penguin Books Ltd, 27 Wrights Lane,
London W8 5TZ, England
Penguin Books Australia Ltd, Ringwood,
Victoria, Australia
Penguin Books Canada Ltd, 2801 John Street,
Markham, Ontario, Canada L3R 1B4
Penguin Books (N.Z.) Ltd, 182–190 Wairau Road,
Auckland 10, New Zealand

Penguin Books Ltd, Registered Offices:
Harmondsworth, Middlesex, England

First published by Onyx, an imprint of New American Library,
a divison of Penguin Books USA Inc.

First Printing, May, 1991
10 9 8 7 6 5 4 3 2 1

PUBLISHER'S NOTE
This is a work of fiction. Names, characters, places, and incidents either are
the product of the author's imagination or are used fictitiously, and any resemblance to actual persons, living or dead, events, or locales is entirely coinci-
dental.

I

St. Louis,
May 1846

1

H E   W A S , she decided, the most thoroughly objection-
able man she had ever seen.

A slight breeze blew up from the distant river, providing
a welcome hint of coolness to temper the heat of the late
Missouri spring. Alone in the shrubbery-secluded privacy
of a second-floor veranda, Diana Howard stared with curious fascination at the man who had just hitched his horse
to a post beside the main gate and was ambling up the walk
to the house.

It was not that he was exactly ugly. In fact, she had to
admit, "ugly" was the last word anyone would use to describe him. He was not tall, being as near as she could judge
from that distance about average height, but there was a
sense of size in his bearing, in the long, sure strides of his
gait. His hair, thick and curling halfway to his shoulders,
was almost blue-black, his eyebrows dark and straight. As
he turned and looked for a moment in her direction, taking
in the house with a careless glance, she saw that his eyes
were a deep, penetrating gray. Just enough showed of a
wide brow and high, arching cheekbones to make her wonder what he would look like if he shaved off the short, rather
bushy beard that covered the lower half of his face.

No, he was definitely not ugly—but there was something
about him. A kind of roughness that seemed almost calculated. As if, she thought, intrigued in spite of herself, he
knew the impression he created and was enjoying it. His
clothes were those of a typical frontiersman, like the crude
men she glimpsed sometimes on the street: trousers of some
heavy fabric, and a homespun shirt, tawny and loose and
vaguely flowing, with long, loose sleeves rolled to the elbows.

But on him the effect was different. The trousers were
definitely not tailored, but they fitted his lean legs well, and

the shirt molded itself to strong shoulders and a powerfully built chest, giving the impression of rippling muscles as he sauntered on again, apparently in no hurry to head for the side door, where people of his class could expect to be received.

The breeze picked up, catching a wisp of silvery blond hair and blowing it into Diana's eyes. She reached up distractedly and brushed it back.

Arrogant. That was the word for him. Utterly, insufferably arrogant! She could just imagine from that expression on his face—the insolent confidence of his bearing—that he fancied himself God's gift to women, though she'd have been hard pressed to picture herself falling for someone like that! Still, she supposed there were women who found conceit appealing. She noted, with rather more amusement than disdain, that he was headed, not for the side door after all, but the front.

If it weren't for the way he was dressed—and the fact that her stepmother had pointed him out the morning before as the wagonmaster her father had hired to lead his trading caravan to Santa Fe in a race against the U.S. Army, which was threatening to capture the territory and open the competition to everyone—she might almost have believed he was an aristocrat himself. Like all her maternal relatives, languishing in treadbare poverty in what was left of their fine Virginia plantations.

Like . . . Jordan?

Her mouth curved unconsciously as she thought of her devastatingly good-looking, very dashing secret fiancé. Hardly threadbare, Jordan. Like the man below, who had paused to gaze at the busy traffic on the Mississippi, far beneath the sweeping St. Louis hillside, her second cousin twice removed was slim and raven-haired, but otherwise, the two were worlds apart. For all his lack of funds, Jordan Crofte had never been anything but fashionably dressed. And utterly charming. Diana could close her eyes and see him—black-black eyes filling with lights of laughter . . . white teeth flashing beneath a mustache so thinly trimmed it looked as if it had been drawn in place . . . a long noble nose, echoing all those other long noble noses that always looked as if they had been tied with invisible cords to the heavens whenever he was around.

And, oh, that they certainly did turn up! She laughed

aloud as she thought of school vacations spent with the Croftes and the Davieses of Virginia, for her widowed father had had neither the ability nor the inclination to deal with a headstrong girl-child. How those blue-blooded noses tilted at the mere mention of the one black sheep in that otherwise impeccable lineage!

The sound caught the ear of the man below, and he turned, looking up. Diana eased back into the shadows, grateful for the thick veil of unpruned lilacs that screened her from his view, though she could still catch flickering glimpses of him through the gently rustling greenery.

She had been a child when she first became aware of her irrepressible cousin, though Jordan, nearly nine years older, had hardly known she existed. Then, unexpectedly, several months ago he had shown up at the latest of a long line of finishing schools, curious, as he put it, to "see how you turned out."

Judging from the flattering way he came back again and again, he had decided she'd turned out all right.

Indeed, it was because of Jordan's visits that she was home now, having been thrown out of her third prestigious and very expensive boarding school in as many years. Always before, her disgrace had been caused by some silly high jinks that might have been overlooked in a kinder environment. But this time, she had been caught running off for an evening of theater and God-knows-what with her cousin in Richmond, by an irate headmistress who had been "appalled, just appalled" at the scandal Diana had nearly brought down on the school.

Her father, who was even more appalled by scandal, had ordered her, not to Virginia as usual, but to the palatial estate she very much doubted he could afford on the affluent outskirts of St. Louis. Garland Howard was a man to whom outward appearances were important, and Diana knew she was in for more than the usual lectures. Not only was he socially ambitious, he had political aspirations as well, and his name was being bandied about as a replacement for one of the congressmen who had resigned to raise troops last year, in 1845, when the annexation of Texas made war with Mexico imminent.

He also had a new young wife, Rosalie, whose equally ambitious eyes were fixed, not on distant Washington, but the governor's mansion in Jefferson City.

Even a breath of scandal at this stage could spell an end to all their golden dreams. And there would be more than a breath when the *beau monde* found out that Diana was not only dallying with an unsuitable young man—whose escapades set whole parlors full of tongues wagging—but also planning on marrying him.

"Faith, an' isn't that the most beautiful man you ever laid eyes on?"

The voice came from behind, an oddly accented lilt. Diana turned to see one of several serving girls who had been imported from the British Isles because it was cheaper than hiring at home, and pleasanter, according to Garland Howard's views, than dealing with the blacks. Tisha, her name was, or Lisha—something silly like that.

"Beauty is as beauty does," Diana snapped, stepping past the girl into the beige-and-pink shadows of her bedroom, which opened onto one side of the veranda. If the man had heard her laughter a moment before, he could hardly have missed the girl's words. And Diana had the distinctly annoyed feeling that he was applying them accurately to himself! "You must learn to judge a person, not by pretty features, but the way he or she acts."

"Sure, I can't see much wrong with the way he acts, miss," Tisha or Lisha or whoever she was went on, unchastened. "Look how he walks. Haven't you seen the way he sort o' swaggers? Like it's he who owns the place, and not Mr. Howard."

Diana had indeed seen. "Swaggering is hardly a laudable attribute," she said, turning her attention to the wardrobe, which contained mostly leftovers from other visits, though Rosalie had added a couple of new gowns so she wouldn't disgrace them in public. "It's not the sort of thing that tends to recommend a man."

"It is if he looks like that."

Diana couldn't resist glancing back. The girl's already pink cheeks were flushed, setting off tumbled masses of golden curls, and her eyes glistened with unabashed interest. It suddenly occurred to Diana that while she had seen Tisha-Lisha with an occasional feather duster, she had never seen her do anything with it. Plainly the girl hadn't been hired for her skill at housekeeping.

Or her demure humility either, for the aproned blue-gray muslin outfit that looked modest on the other maids had been cut lower in her case, with the barest hint of white trim at the rounded neck, a cheap effect, heightened by the coy way she pulled it down her shoulders.

Why, she's here for my father, Diana thought.

She was not exactly shocked. Girls' schools were hardly places where tact ran rampant, and she had learned years ago that Garland Howard had a certain "reputation" with women, though she had assumed, naively, that that would end when he married Rosalie, who was just a few months older than herself, and a stunning, if somewhat flashy, red-head.

But some men never changed—or so she had heard. And, of course, her father had now been married several months. Maybe Rosalie was pregnant and delicacy required him to find some other accommodation and leave her alone.

"You seem to know a great deal about men," she said, aiming to sound disapproving, but letting her curiosity show. "Perhaps you are married? To someone back home?"

"Oh, no, miss—free as the wind, and like to stay that way awhile." She giggled infectiously. "You don't have to be a bride to know a fine-lookin' man when you see him. Or to have a bit o' fun. But I fancy you'll be knowin' that yourself, if even half o' what I hear is true."

"Oh? . . . And what do you hear?"

"Why, that you near run off with a handsome gentleman yourself. And got caught, they say, just in the nick o' time— and drugged back to that school near Richmond by the roots o' your hair."

Cheeky girl! Diana tried, but didn't quite manage to look stern. With all that bubbly laughter, it was hard not to like her.

" 'Drugged back' maybe, but not by my hair—roots or otherwise. Where did you come up with such a colorful story? No, no, don't tell me—I'm not sure I want to know. The gentleman in question is my cousin Jordan. We are, uh . . . good friends. But you're right, he *is* handsome. Much handsomer than that awful man you were drooling over just now."

"Then you *were* going to run off with him?"

"Only for an evening of entertainment. This happened in Virginia, remember." She wrinkled her nose in an imitation of snobbery. "Certain things 'aren't done' in Virginia."

"Ah, it must be beautiful. Virginia. I used to hear talk

of it sometimes, when I was a slip of a girl. It's where I thought I'd be going one day . . . but somehow it didn't turn out like that."

The strange accent was even more pronounced now, Killarney overlaid with something that sounded vaguely like a stab at upper-crust British. No, Diana longed to cry out, exasperated. It isn't beautiful in Virginia—if you're poor and pretending, and all your relations are so proud they'd starve before they'd tarnish their precious "heritage" with an honest day's toil. Not that they had any but the flimsiest claims to aristocracy, and those through kinship with her mother and herself. Why, the only one of the lot making money was a distant cousin in town, and he was almost as ostracized as Jordan because he dared to dabble, God forbid, in *trade!*

But the girl's voice was so wistful, her pale eyes so wide, Diana couldn't disillusion her.

"Yes, it is beautiful. The land is rich and red. You can smell it sometimes in the morning, and the hills are green, though it can be dreadfully tiresome in the country. But it's different in Richmond. You can have fun in Richmond if you're bold enough to go to the theater . . . and there are all kinds of fancy soirees they have to invite you to if your great-grandfather was the eighth Earl of Croftleigh. Perhaps when Jordan and I get married—*if* we get married—you'd like to come and work for us."

"Oh, wouldn't I just, miss. That would be the finest thing ever."

"Yes, well . . . ." Diana's voice trailed off. Rosalie might not object to her husband consorting with serving wenches, but she wasn't sure she wanted someone so pretty, and so obviously compliant, in her own home. It was not that she didn't trust Jordan. She did, of course, with all her heart—but there was no point setting temptation smack in front of a man! "We'll see . . . though I can't promise anything. But what are you doing here? Did you want something?"

"Oh, miss . . . I clean forgot. I was sent to fetch you—immediately. Your father wants to see you."

"Yes, I daresay he does," Diana replied dryly. She had avoided her father, except for dinner, when there were other people present, for the week she had been home. She had seen his manservant occasionally, or his confidential secretary, prowling the grounds, and she knew they were looking for her, but they hardly felt free to barge into her room with the door closed. ''I know what he wants, and I will see him—when I'm ready. In the meantime, I suggest that you tell him you couldn't find me, so he won't be angry with you for my recalcitrance.''

''Your re . . . calsitence?''

Diana suppressed a grin. It wasn't fair, using words the girl didn't know.

''My dreadful stubbornness . . . and I can be stubborn when I want. Just tell my father you tried. Tell him you knocked on my door, and when there wasn't any answer, you pushed your way right in . . . and I was nowhere to be seen.''

''But it wasn't him who sent me. It was Mrs. Howard mum. She said I had to do whatever your father wanted— and not dare come back without you.''

''Mrs. Howard *mum?*'' Now she placed that silly accent. Not British at all, but an attempt at Culture, with a capital C. ''Who on earth taught you to speak like that? Never mind, I know.'' Rosalie was extremely conscious of her *nouveau-riche* origins. Her father, like Garland Howard, had made his money in merchandise, only, unlike Garland, he hadn't married a veneer of respectability in the form of an English lord's granddaughter. ''Tell Mrs. Howard, then— Mrs. Howard *mum*—that you did your best. And I'm simply not in my room.''

''But, miss—''

''It's all right. She may carry on a bit, but she'll get over it. And it'll be the truth, in a way. I *won't* be here by the time you speak to her.'' She slipped out onto the veranda, eyeing the grounds below to make sure the man she had seen before was gone—probably at the front door scandalizing the servants!—and none of her father's toadies was in sight. ''I'm going out . . . for a walk or something. It's just too boring, staring at the same four walls.''

''You're . . . going out, miss? Dressed like *that?*''

The undisguised dismay in the girl's tone drew Diana's eyes down to the dress she had forgotten she was wearing. She had pulled it out of the wardrobe a short time before, curious to see if it still fitted—which it did, though not quite the same as a year and a half ago, when it had been part of her school uniform. The fabric was a figured chintz, soft blue on a pearl-gray ground, but so delicately patterned the colors seemed to run together, making it look at first glance like the blue-gray worn by the servants. Styled *en redingote*, with a row of buttons down the front and a rather low scoop bodice, it had looked suitably prim with a long-sleeved, high-necked white chemisette.

With nothing to speak of underneath, it had much the effect of Tisha-Lisha's outrageous costume!

"Yes, exactly like this," Diana said, amused, as she moved to the door. Poor fashion-conscious Rosalie. She'd faint dead away if she thought anyone might see her step-daughter dressed like this. "Don't forget. If anybody asks, you didn't find me. And you don't know where I am."

"Where *will* you be?"

"There, you see?" she said brightly. "You really don't know, so you won't have to lie."

She flitted through the door, laughing softly in the empty echoes of the hallway. She hadn't known herself where she was going until she found her feet heading toward the back stairway and recalled the semiclosed porch that served as a kind of good-weather parlor for the servants. It was small and rather dingy, and like everything else in the house not exposed to public view, meanly furnished, but at least it faced east, so it would hold the morning sun.

And no one would look for her there.

The stairs were deserted, and she hummed a little tune as she skipped down them. She wasn't expecting to run into anyone, least of all Rosalie—the whole idea was to avoid everybody—but if she did . . .

Impulsively, she reached up, loosening the neck of her dress, slipping it, just slightly, down her shoulder.

Which would bother her stepmother most? she wondered. The fact that she was clad like a servant? Or the fact that she looked so blatantly trashy?

2

CORD MONTGOMERY leaned insolently against an ivy-twined oak, where he knew he had to be visible to disapproving eyes that were sure to be watching from the house. It was warm, even in the shade, a day that promised summer heat by afternoon, and he ran his forearm abstractedly across his brow as he turned the scene that had just taken place at the front entry over and over in his mind with quiet satisfaction.

He had been every bit as clean as the flunky who had slithered the door open the prescribed amount and peered out with water-pale eyes. No, cleaner, he'd warrant—and his clothes were better pressed. But they were the clothes of a simple man, homespun fabric and natural dyes, and simple, homespun men did not call at a merchant's front door.

He had especially enjoyed the pinched expression on the fellow's features when he had been forced to go and find his master. And the supercilious smugness, a minute later, when he returned.

"You are over an hour early for your engagement," he had enunciated, pointedly leaving out the "sir" that would usually follow. "*Mr.* Howard will see you at the appointed hour. You will be received then. At the door *in the rear.*"

Easily done, Cord had informed him, or words to that effect. He would wait—on the grounds or in the garden, where he could have a look at the place. He's be back at the appointed hour. And he'd be back at the door he chose.

Flashes of movement showed on the river, and he turned to stare down at the vivid mélange of traffic that marked St. Louis as a bustling port. Haughty steamships, the queens of the river, held a steady course, while flatboats tumbled in their wake and tiny tugs darted in and out, jockeying for space on the crowded, rushing current.

Down on the waterfront, he knew, all would be raucous sound: boats pulling out, their great engines roaring and belching huge clouds of black into the sky; foremen on the levee barking out orders; roustabouts cursing and sweating side by side with slaves and the sons of slaves; shouts and bellows and masculine howls mingling with the ringing songs that eased the backbreaking labor and made the hours go faster. But here, it was a silent scene, and strangely unreal, the swirl of giddy color and boisterous noises muted by distance, until even the largest ships looked like toy boats bobbing on the water.

He had never been comfortable with towns, least of all towns like this. The San Antonio of his birth, nothing then, just a handful of settlers with not a dozen American faces in two hundred miles, was growing into his kind of place. A *villeta* with a focus and an earthy flair, everything radiating out of a dusty plaza at the heart, lazy with laughter and music well into the night, ranchos and haciendas stretching naturally into broad sweeping valleys and along the gently meandering brown river.

Here, everything seemed backwards. From necessity, he supposed, but the very trade that brought the city wealth and status destroyed its natural beauty. The levees should have been green and lush, broad, flat tops tempting lovers to promenade in the cool whisper of a summer dusk. But the earth was bare, tamped hard and rutted by countless feet, and crates and wooden barrels seemed to be everywhere, haphazardly stacked, in no particular order the eye could make out. An acrid smell of smoke and animals and sweat drifted up from the dirty water as wagons were loaded and unloaded with coal and slate, calico and corn, furs and harnesses and plows, coming and going from all directions.

The traffic generated by the river continued inland along narrow streets, Main and Second and Third, all choked with freighters' wagons, their creaking wheels underscoring the plodding hooves of oxen and mule teams. Crammed along each side was the commerce necessary to sustain all that activity, banks and hardware stores, insurers, druggists and wholesale grocers crowding the handful of old residences still left in town. Everyone else had moved up the bluffs and out into the hills, hygienically removed from the one thing that gave the town its special beauty and unique character—the river.

He would be glad enough when it was time to leave. And glad if he never had to see it again.

He shoved away from the tree, little prickles on the back of his neck telling him that eyes were still watching him. Whose? He had come an hour early on purpose, knowing that son of a bitch would never unbend enough to let him in. It gave him pleasure, imagining the man pacing back and forth in some parlor or study, cursing the upstart outside—and not being able to do a blasted thing about it!

He didn't like Garland Howard. He hadn't liked him the day he signed on, and he made his feelings clear. It amused him, perversely, to realize that he had made the other man dislike him equally in turn.

The intensity of his own reaction surprised him. He hadn't expected that. He had a job to do. He had expected to do it and get it over with, and not feel anything. Maybe one burst of satisfaction at the end, sweet or bitter, he did not know . . . but nothing until then.

Certainly not amusement.

He glanced up at the second floor, wondering which window was Howard's. Wondering—hoping—he was there looking down. Hoping he could read lips.

"I'm going to get you, you bastard," he mouthed softly. "I'm going to get you . . . and you're going to know it."

A long, shrill whistle sounded in the distance. A steamboat coming into port, drawing the coiled tension out of Cord's body as he looked down at arrogant, pristine whiteness, dominating the water. It was morning, the end of May, and the world around was gentle and at peace. Everything was as it should be. The time would come . . . the confrontation would come . . . but there was no point worrying about it now.

He could have shown up an hour late instead. The breeze was almost gone, the air hot and stagnant, making his beard bristle, and he half-wished he had not grown it, though he liked the rough way it looked. He had thought about coming late, but that seemed so predictable. People always came late when they wanted to set someone's nerves on edge.

Besides, early gave him an hour—for which he very definitely had something in mind. He loosened his collar to catch the coolness, aware as he did that he exposed dark hair curling up from his chest. He had heard an interesting

story or two in the short time he had been in town. Very
interesting. If, by chance, they were true . . .

Jamming his hands in his pockets, he started around to
the back of the house.

The porch was even quieter than Diana had imagined,
with not a sound coming through the windows or drifting
across the yard. The furniture was sparse, and old, with a
pronounced odor of mildew, but someone had made an effort to brighten up the place. Blue-checkered cloths, newly
washed and pressed, covered the tables, pansies peeked
cheerily out of cheap glass bowls, and a gilt-edged mirror,
albeit chipped, hung on one wall, where, until a moment
ago, it had caught and tossed back the morning sun.

Diana wandered over to stare curiously at her reflection
in the glass. Mirrors had been discouraged—though routinely smuggled in—in the many schools she had attended,
and the idea of standing boldly in front of one, not even
pretending to sneak, was still forbidden enough to be decidedly heady. Especially when her cheeks were faintly flushed,
and glittering flashes of green played with the blue in her
eyes.

Am I pretty? she wondered, pursing her lips slightly and
tilting her head to one side to study the effect. She supposed
she must be, for she looked almost exactly like the little
miniature she had seen once of her mother—the same delicate features, the same ethereal wisps of silver-blond hair,
the same startling aquamarine eyes—and she had thought
that her mother must have been the prettiest woman in the
world.

But "pretty" was a funny word, applied to oneself, especially when that self had always been taught that even the
thought was silly vanity. And no one had ever reinforced it
by uttering it aloud.

Still . . . she supposed she wasn't exactly homely. She
smiled subtly, trying to look worldly and mysterious, but
only succeeding in emphasizing her youth. She couldn't look
that much like her mother and not be at least moderately
attractive.

Not that she acted like her mother, heaven knew. She had
been told that often enough, in disparaging tones. Lady Alice had been sweet and gentle and obedient—except for the
one time she had defied her grandfather and married a hope-

lessly unsuitable man, a sin for which she had been promptly disinherited. The old earl, it seemed, was unforgiving, and none of his vast fortune had ever trickled to the shores of Virginia.

No, Diana definitely didn't act like her mother. She smiled raffishly, enjoying the effect in the mirror. She was planning an "unsuitable" match too, but with her father living so close to the edge, there wouldn't have been much for her to inherit anyway—even if Rosalie didn't provide him with a passel of other heirs.

And certainly her mother would never have dressed like this!

The laughter she had been holding back burst out at the disreputable picture she presented. The gown was even worse than she had thought. It fitted all right, but what had fitted loosely once was snug now, particularly in front, where she had grown quite a bit the last year or so. Her bosom was not exactly full, but it was high and nicely rounded, and her shoulders were looking quite silky, especially with the neck of the dress lowered like that.

What would it look like if she tugged it just a little farther—like a ball gown in a ladies' book? Or, considering the fabric and style, something worn by a housemaid with more than housemaiding on her mind?

She reached up to try the effect, but never had a chance, for suddenly a hand came out of nowhere, catching hold of hers. She barely had a second to take everything in. A naked forearm, lightly covered with dark hair . . . the smell of something mannish . . . a rough-shirted male chest filling the glass behind her. Then she was being drawn up and turned around, and a mouth was coming down on hers. Hard.

Her gasp of surprise was drowned in the force of that wildly unexpected assault. Numb with shock, Diana let her head fall back, too startled to resist. She had been kissed before—Jordan had not been her first teasing brush with passion—but she had never been kissed like this. Those had been boyish lips, impudent or tentative, depending on the will behind them. This was a man's mouth, bold, demanding, sure of what he wanted. And what he wanted, apparently, was *her*.

Incredibly, arrogantly, he pursued his attack, assuming her welcome, not asking, but taking as he ravished her

mouth thoroughly with his lips, his tongue, the entire force
of that utterly masculine being.

And Diana, caught off-guard, was unable to halt the tingling sensations that stirred deep within her. Was not even
sure she *wanted* to halt them.

Horrified, struggling to summon her stunned brain into
focus, she wedged her hands against his chest and shoved.

"Sir . . ." she cried weakly, still too confused even to
see him properly. But it was barely a whisper, caught low
in her throat, and she heard him laugh in response.

"What, protests, my pretty? It's too late for protests. You
would not have kissed me like that if you were unwilling."
He pulled her close again, his lips seeking and finding the
base of her neck, tickling her with the hair that covered his
face, evoking responses everywhere at once, all over her
body. "Mmmmm, I think I'm going to enjoy this, Irish. . . .
And I think you are too."

"Sir!" Her voice was stronger now, ringing with the indignation that should have been there before, and a hint of
fear too. As she pushed him back again, she recognized the
man she had seen earlier on the lawn. He was even more
arrogant than she had imagined. "What . . . what do you
think you're doing?"

"I think, Irish, I'm introducing myself to you." He
grinned, a slow, rakish leer. "And I think, unless I'm very
much mistaken, you're liking the introduction . . . for all
that you've suddenly turned prim."

"Irish?" Diana gaped at him, her mind, still hopelessly
muddled, grasping irrationally at the one thing that stood
out. "I don't much care for your idea of an introduction
. . . and I don't know why you call me 'Irish.' I haven't a
drop of Irish blood in my veins."

"No?" One brow went up, but he did not seem the least
put off. "Only your temper, eh? You do look more English,
I admit . . . and I had expected a mop of gold, not silver.
But some things at least"—he let his eyes run down her
figure, sliding over shoulders that were much too exposed,
coming to rest with calculated impudence on the faint cleavage above her rounded neckline—"are exactly what I was
looking for. And, by the way . . . I know you were lying."

"Lying? *Me?* What on earth are you talking about?"

"Why, your claim that you didn't like my introduction,
of course. You liked it, little miss Irish-or-no. You liked it

very much . . . and by God, so did I.'' His hands were on the neck of her gown suddenly, one at each side. Before Diana could react, before she even knew what he was doing, he had pulled it open, popping little buttons with a clatter all over the floor. His breath came in a long, low hiss when he saw that she had nothing on underneath.

Helplessly Diana stared back at him, too caught up in the expression in those piercing gray eyes even to move. Why, *why* hadn't she at least worn a light chemise, the way she had always been taught? And why wasn't she running away?

Then it was too late, and his mouth was challenging hers again, hungrily, his hands even hungrier as they cupped and caressed her breasts with the confidence of a man who was sure of the woman he was with. For a single dizzying instant Diana was tempted to let him go on, curious, eager to see what other emotions he might conjure up to go with the jumble of hopelessly confused ones that were already swirling through her.

No! she thought frantically, forming but not uttering the word, for his lips were too persistent, too enveloping, too— God help her—tempting. Desperately she realized that this was her last chance to resist. Reason returned, cold hard reason, and with it a fear more intense than anything that had passed before.

Not fear of him, but of herself—and the wanton abandon he seemed to have awakened.

Raising her foot, she jammed the heel down on his instep. When he stiffened with surprise and pain, she raised her hand, striking him smartly across the face.

"How dare you, sir? How dare you come into my home and treat me like this? How *dare* you?''

"Why, you little witch . . .'' His eyes narrowed, jaw tightening as he stood his ground, struggling with an onslaught of his own conflicting emotions. She was a beauty, all right, everything he had expected. By God, she was a beauty! She had inflamed his senses until he could hardly think straight. But no one had prepared him for this little game she was playing.

He didn't mind games. He even liked them sometimes. Especially when lips were soft and full . . . and delightfully enthusiastic. But he liked to know the rules.

"How dare *you* kiss me like that, and then play prudish?

A kiss like that is a promise, sweetheart. Hell, that one was
a sacred vow!''

"Oh!" Diana began to tremble so badly she was sure he
had to see. She was aware of the warm air on her breasts,
aware of her own nakedness, that her dress was hanging
loose. But she was paralyzed with fright and fascination,
and she didn't dare even the slightest movement for fear it
would set him off again. "You caught me unaware. I . . . I
didn't know you were there until you grabbed me! How was
I supposed to know you were going to kiss me? I couldn't
have stopped you if I wanted to. . . . And I didn't make any
promises!''

"Didn't you?" he said coolly, his eyes all the while raking her with searing heat. "Ah, but I think you did. You
might not have been able to stop *my* lips from kissing you.
But you could have stopped your own lips from saying: Yes,
yes . . . more . . . more.''

His voice was brittle with sarcasm, but there was something else too. A longing he recognized more than she, and
he knew suddenly that he had to have this woman. From the
moment he had touched her, the moment he had first felt
her tremble in his arms, he had been lost to anything remotely like reason.

The moment he had touched her, hell! The moment he'd
seen her primping coquettishly in the mirror, biting her lips
to make them inviting and red. He had known then that he
had to possess her, no matter what it cost.

And it was going to cost plenty.

"So that's the game, is it? You really *didn't* take to my
introduction. Passion is fine . . . and I guess you like it all
right . . . but other things need to be discussed first. Like
maybe my name? Cord Montgomery, at your service,
ma'am." He swept her a mocking bow. "And why I came?
Why, to see you, of course. . . . And do I have cash rattling
around in my pocket? Oh, yes, ma'am, I do.''

"You want to talk about . . . *cash?*" Diana gaped at him,
disgusted. This man was a total stranger. He didn't even
know her. He had come in and seen her dressed like a servant—and just assumed she was a whore! "You think I'm
going to sell myself? To *you?* For cash?''

"Cash, gold, jewelry . . . you name it. You got my interest, you boosted the price. Just like you intended. What

do you say to fifty dollars? That's a hell of a lot for a chit like you.''

"Fifty dollars?" Diana spat out the words contemptuously, too angry even for common sense. "You don't look like a man who could spare fifty dollars."

The answering gleam in his eye told her instantly she had made a mistake. She should have kept up her protests, pretended she hadn't even heard that degrading allusion. She took a step backward, frightened as he followed with a stride of his own. For the first time, it occurred to her that she might not be able to talk her way out of this. It was going to be hideously embarrassing if she had to rouse her father and the staff!

"So that *is* it," he said, drawing just the conclusion she had feared. "I should have known. If I'd been dressed in fancy clothes, we wouldn't be having this little conversation. Fine. Cash in advance . . . how's that? Fifty dollars? A hundred? Come on, Tisha, you know damn well—''

Tisha? Shock ran through her as the truth dawned at last. He hadn't thought she was just any servant. He thought she was Tisha, whose reputation had obviously gotten about! And hanging around on the servants' porch, dressed the way she was—could she really blame him? "My God . . . you believe I'm Tisha."

He leaned back slightly, studying her with a look that was not the least nonplussed. "And you're not?"

"No. My name is Diana . . . Diana Howard. My father is Garland Howard, the master of this house! And the man who hired you to lead his wagon caravan down the Santa Fe Trail into Mexico. If you want to keep your job, I suggest you apologize—and get out of here!"

She had expected him to look horrified, even, despite his colossal ego, shamefaced. But he only stared for a moment, gray eyes filling with something distinctly unpleasant. Then he threw back his head . . . and laughed.

"Nice try, honey. And a pretty name it is, too. *Diana* Howard. Elegant and aristocratic. Do you really think I'm fool enough to believe the daughter of the house runs around in patterned chintz? And practices enticing expressions in front of a mirror?"

"But I *am* Diana Howard!" she cried, furious with him for putting her in such a ridiculous position. But with the strange, unexpected, bewildering sensations that were surging through her—and all those dainty buttons scattered over the floor—she was more anxious than ever to avoid a confrontation. "This is an old school uniform. I . . . I was just trying it on. It goes with a long-sleeved chemisette, which I don't have anymore. I only wore it in case . . . in case I ran into my stepmother, Rosalie. Because I knew it would annoy her."

There was just enough embarrassment in that spate of words to lend credence to her protests. Diana didn't know whether to be relieved because he seemed to believe her, or even more furious. Far from looking contrite after the ferocious way he had savaged her innocence, he actually seemed amused, the swine!

"Ah, well . . . I reckon I'll just have t' keep a rein on my animal urges," he drawled, his voice perceptibly rougher now that he knew who she was. "And here I thought we were gettin' along just fine. But shoot, ma'am . . . I don't hold all that breedin' against you. Every pretty little filly's gotta be broke sooner or later. I'd be mighty happy, if you changed your mind, to oblige."

Diana gasped. Really, the man was intolerable! She had thought he was conceited before, when she had glimpsed him from the veranda. She hadn't guessed the half of it!

She was so angry, she had completely forgotten that she was still standing half-dressed in front of him. He seemed to remember at the same instant, for his eyes dropped, pointedly taking in her dishabille.

Or perhaps he was reminding her of it!

She drew her hands forward to pull the dress together, but he stopped her.

"Here, let me do that, ma'am." Swiftly, expertly, he arranged the fabric, fastening the buttons that still remained, hands lingering insolently on her breast in ways that sent shivers down her spine. "There, now, that's better. You just hold it"—he took her hands and pressed them against her breast—"like that. No one'll notice anything . . . unless they look close. You wouldn't want to go traipsin' around the house all disarrayed like that. . . . Or would you?"

The rakish lilt to those last words drew Diana back to reality. "Certainly not," she snapped, fighting to regain her poise. "I'm leaving now, and I'll thank you not to follow! I don't want to scream. I'd hate to have to scream. But I will if you force yourself on me again."

"With all due respect, ma'am"—he grinned—"I don't think you know nothin' about forcin' . . . yet. Though, as I said, I'd be glad to oblige."

"Why, you . . ." Diana caught her breath, sensing he was determined to have the last word, and knowing he probably would. Mustering what little was left of her pride, she turned, managing somehow not to look back as she swept with what she hoped was a show of indignation out of the room.

Precious heaven, what had happened to her in there?

She paused halfway up the back steps, safely out of sight, so weak her knees felt as if they were going to give way. What in the name of all that was holy could she have been thinking of? He was a horrible, despicable man—she had loathed him on sight—but he had taken her in his arms, and she had fairly melted with pleasure!

He had accused her of responding to his arrogant kisses, and he was right. She *had* responded, not just to his kisses, but to his hands, to his male body hard against hers, to the terrible, fascinating innuendos in his eyes.

Curiosity. She could have understood that. She had never encountered a man like this before, and never would again. Naturally she was curious. But there had been more than curiosity in her reactions. She had *liked* what he had done.

Thank heaven she was going to be here only a few days!

She brushed these disturbing thoughts out of her mind and concentrated on what lay ahead. Just time enough to settle things with her father, and that would have to be soon. The wagon train was scheduled to leave any day now. Garland would be gone, and everyone with him, even silly, snobbish Rosalie.

And she would never have to see this Cord Montgomery again.

She would have felt considerably less complacent had she been able to see the expression on the face of the man she had just left. Cord Montgomery was still grinning as he stood alone in shadows that deepened to an illusion of coolness as the last of the morning sun left the porch.

So . . . Garland Howard's daughter. And a hot-blooded little thing, beneath that porcelain-pretty silver-and-aquamarine facade. She protested now . . . but protests intertwined with passion had a way of evaporating into languid afternoons and long candle-scented nights.

He had been as eager as anyone to get out of here. It was he who had been pressing hardest to leave. Now it occurred to him it might be worth his while to stick around a couple of days. He wouldn't mind getting to know the lady better.

And if that bothered her father . . . well, as his cousin Johnny always said, there was more than one way to skin a cat.

This time, as he jammed his hands in his pockets and headed around the corner of the house, he was whistling.

3

"HAVE YOU SPOKEN to her yet?"

Rosalie Howard's shrill voice penetrated her husband's concentration as he stood at the parlor window and stared out at spring-green leaves on the tall oaks that lined the drive. It was not her usual manner of speaking, but this was the third time she had asked the question, and she was getting impatient.

Garland turned wearily. "No, I haven't spoken to her. But I will as soon as I find the minx. I sent my man around again half an hour ago. Apparently she's up to her old tricks, hiding in her room with the door closed. I don't know what you expect. You haven't had any better luck yourself. . . . Didn't you tell me Tisha couldn't find her when she went to look this morning?"

"So she said when she got back. Unless of course your daughter bribed her. I suspect Tisha would do quite a bit for money." Rosalie sighed, hating the quarrels with her husband that seemed to have gotten even more frequent since the willful Diana had come home. "Though I tend to believe her this time. She was practically shaking when she had to tell me she'd failed. She was afraid you'd be angry. I don't think the girl likes you very much, Garland."

"I really don't care whether she likes me or not." Striding over to the only comfortable chair in the room, he took up his paper. The subject of his daughter was beginning to get on his nerves. God knew, she wasn't the least like her mother, for all that the resemblance was so uncanny sometimes it jolted back memories he thought he had forgotten. Alice had been a docile little creature, sugar-tongued and hungry to please, though the one thing he had really wanted from her was the one she hadn't been able to give—her grandfather's fortune. "As for Diana, she can't stay in her room forever. Sooner or later, she has to come out and face the consequences of her behavior.''

''There isn't much time left—we were scheduled to leave days ago—and you know this is important.'' Rosalie had taken the place her husband vacated at the window, but the yard outside was empty and nothing caught her eye. ''We don't dare leave things until we return. That unfortunate entanglement with her cousin might have ruined everything if you hadn't caught it in time.'' She turned back petulantly. ''You'll find she comes down freely enough when you're not around. Why, she even went for a ride with me—and stared disgustingly at that man you hired, that Montgomery person, who happened to be passing. He really is odiously conceited! And she shows up at the dinner table when she wants to flaunt herself in front of guests.''

''Yes,'' he remarked dryly. ''She is unfortunately lovely, isn't she? I can see it's a trial for you, having her around.''

Rosalie flushed. ''I'm not jealous of your daughter, Garland. What a spiteful thing to say!''

''Of course you are, my dear. And not irrationally.'' Rosalie was striking enough, a tall, voluptuous redhead with a vivid complexion and intriguingly catlike yellow-brown eyes. But petite, ethereal Diana was a beauty. ''Under other circumstances, I might rather have enjoyed this rivalry between my wife and my daughter. It really *was* amusing, the way you two tiptoed around each other at the wedding. But right now, I have other things on my mind. I'll take care of Diana when I'm ready.''

There was enough finality in his tone to warn Rosalie to drop the subject. She had already learned that her husband could be unpleasant when he was annoyed.

''I still don't see why you insist on taking me with you, Garland. It's going to be such a long, nasty trip . . . and I could accomplish much more here. Think how nice it would be to come home and find the servants trained and the household running smoothly. I could even redecorate the parlors and the dining room. Everything is embarrassingly out-of-date.''

''Decorating costs money, especially with your extravagant taste. And money is something we don't have . . . *yet*. I expect I'll turn a pretty profit, from both my ventures—enough to finance a campaign and still have something left for the parlors—but until then, we aren't exactly wallowing in wealth. But then, I don't have to remind you of that, do I?''

"No, no, of course not." Garland had made it clear that he was extremely disappointed in her in that respect. Her father, wanting to arrange as advantageous a marriage as possible, had let it be inferred that she came from money, when in fact he was as close to financial ruin as his son-in-law.

But then, Garland had represented himself as a man of means too, and it seemed to her, with a considerably younger bride, he had gotten the better of the deal! Though that, too, was something she had learned not to discuss.

"I wouldn't have to decorate anything," she went on, putting into her voice a hint of the coyness that had worked so well in the early weeks of their marriage. "I could just sit quietly, waiting for you . . . not spending a cent at all. Not even on clothes. It would be so much better for me. All that jouncing and prairie air is sure to be hard on my health. Especially considering my . . . well, you know . . . my 'condition.' ''

"Your 'condition' is perfectly natural, my dear," he said, impatient with the self-conscious delicacy she used in alluding to her pregnancy. Certainly there was nothing else delicate about Rosalie. "I can't imagine you sitting around quietly, any more than I can imagine your not buying any clothes. Besides, you're healthy as a horse. We aren't going to be roughing it. There'll be a cushioned seat to ride on, and a comfortable tent at night. And, of course, I expect to provide a personal maid. Tisha perhaps . . . yes, I think Tisha would—''

"Tisha?" She forgot for a moment how much he hated being interrupted. "But . . . the girl is *hopeless,* Garland! The worst of all the maids. Why, she's quite cheeky sometimes . . . and she doesn't know a thing about hair! Or taking care of clothes.''

"She'll learn. The others did. And she's newly arrived enough not to, uh . . . not to be overreliant on creature comforts. She'll adapt nicely to the situation. I really don't see what you're fussing about. Pioneer women have babies all the time without half this whimpering and carrying on.''

"Yes . . . and some of them die too," Rosalie retorted with an unaccustomed show of spirit. "Or lose the little ones. You'd be dreadfully upset if that happened. Remember how pleased you were last month when I told you I might be carrying your son?''

"Yes, well . . . I suppose I was," he conceded. The thought of a boy-child had puffed his vanity briefly, a left-over, he supposed, from the days when he wanted a son so desperately from Alice. But he found, once the novelty wore off, that he was bored with the idea, just as he was growing bored with Rosalie.

He had honestly enjoyed his young wife at first. She had been surprisingly enthusiastic when she came to his bed, and both his vanity and his body had thrived on her very flattering responses. But responsiveness in a woman had never held Garland Howard's interest long. If a willing body was what he wanted, he imported another little blond from Scotland . . . or a sloe-eyed brunette from the south of England. No putting up with whims and demands. And no whining when he got tired of her.

Rosalie was watching him intently. "And you aren't now?"

"Yes, yes, of course I am. I'm just too busy to deal with this nonsense. Naturally, every man wants a son. But he doesn't look forward to nine months of, uh . . . unavailability on the part of his wife."

"Oh." Rosalie blushed again, a deep crimson. She had not expected to like being married to an older man. She certainly hadn't expected to like what happened when the curtains were drawn and the door shut behind them at night. But she had. She had liked every unexpected touch and intrusion into her body—she liked it very much—and she missed it desperately. What a pity her mother had been wrong when she warned Rosalie not to expect a respite from "things" just because she got pregnant. "But honestly, Garland, isn't that all the more reason for me to remain at home? I mean, if we can't do anything anyhow . . ."

"No. My mind is made up." He rustled his newspaper pointedly, bringing the conversation to a close. He was no more pleased than Rosalie with the arrangement, but he wasn't about to leave someone of her lusty inclinations at home. The scandal his daughter had caused was enough. An unfaithful wife would spell *finis* to his political ambitions. "I don't want to hear any more about it. Don't you have some last-minute things to attend to? Instructions to the staff perhaps . . . ?"

"But, Garland—"

"I said I'd speak to Diana, and I will. That should please you. You did come for that, didn't you? Then . . . Ah!" He looked up as a man appeared in the doorway. "Yes?"

"A word with you, Howard?" The voice was deep and drawling, Missouri with hints of something farther south.

"Certainly, Ryder, certainly. Rosalie was just on her way out, weren't you, darling? You know how it is with women. So many details to fuss over. Take your time, my dear, take your time. . . . What? No peck on the cheek for your husband?"

"Yes . . . of course." Rosalie was conscious, as she went over and touched her lips to the stubbly cheek her husband presented, that Ryder had not taken his eyes off her. She had known him all her life—he had been a teenager when she was a baby—and she had never liked him. As long as she could remember, he'd had a way of stripping women visually. Not secret and seductive, as it might be with another man, but open and intentionally insulting.

Garland watched, amused, as his wife slipped past Ryder into the hallway, eyes pointedly averted.

It seemed, after all, that Rosalie did have some sense. Ordinarily she simpered all over the place if a man even looked at her.

"Have you always had such a way with women?" he asked dryly.

Ryder grinned. "I have exactly the way I want. When I want. Women are there to be used . . . if a man's smart. Not the other way around. Though I will admit there's one little lady who's roused my interest. I wouldn't mind being a mouse in the corner when she finds out what you have in mind. I don't suppose you've had a chance—"

"No, no," Garland cut in testily. "I've been round and round the thing the last half-hour with my wife, thank you. I'm all talked out on the subject."

If Ryder noticed the older man's rudeness, he didn't let it show. Easing his body onto a straight chair, he stretched lean legs out in front, crossing them carelessly at the ankle. His full name was William Ryder Jr., but he had dropped the "junior" years ago, even before his father died, and no one ever called him by his first name.

"I understand Cord Montgomery's been here," he said

evenly. "Your man greeted me at the door with the information. Made quite a stir, did he?"

"He came an hour early," Garland grumbled. He folded up the newspaper and tossed it impatiently on the floor. "Didn't even pretend he'd made a mistake. That man takes a special delight in being obnoxious."

"And you let him cool his heels the full hour . . . and received him twenty minutes late. Bad move, Howard. Real bad. He wanted to rile you, and you let him see that he did. You should have thrown everything aside and ushered him in with a smile and a handshake." He chuckled. "That would have thrown him."

"The hell it would. Nothing throws that s.o.b. Even my wife things he's 'odiously conceited' . . . though I daresay she means it differently."

Ryder, remembering the reputation pretty Rosalie had been acquiring when her father got smart and locked her up in the evenings so he'd have a virgin bride to offer, was inclined to agree. He might have had a try at her himself, if he'd been interested in the obvious type.

"What did Montgomery have to say?" he ventured, steering the conversation into safer channels. "Is he still champing at the bit to get to Independence and make sure the outfitters have the wagons ready so there won't be any delays when we finally get there?"

"No." Garland looked vaguely troubled. "He seems to be changing his tune. In fact, he thinks we ought to hold off, for a few days at least. What with Congress declaring a state of hostilities against Mexico, and Kearny's forces already on the march to Santa Fe, he thinks the traders'll be held somewhere along the trail anyway. They won't let us go ahead for fear our wagons will fall into enemy hands. It might be better for a bunch of 'greenhorns,' as he puts it in that nasty twang of his, to wait in comfort in St. Louis."

"The devil, you say! He's the one who's been pushing all along. To make sure we don't get stuck someplace—or if we do, we'll be the first wagons in when the U.S. flag goes up over conquered territory."

"Well . . . apparently now he thinks it's too late." He eyed the other man thoughtfully. "You don't agree?"

"Maybe. But if there's a chance in a thousand, we've got to take it. And Montgomery knows that. I wonder . . ." He jumped up, pacing back and forth restlessly, like a cat in a cage. "It's dangerous waiting. Damn dangerous! Santa Fe isn't the only piece of land we've got our eyes on. Zachary Taylor and his men are already over the Nueces, pushing the border of Texas down to the Rio Grande. That's what escalated this into a shooting war in the first place! Once he secures the territory, settlers are going to come streaming south from San Antone."

"I know, I know." Garland nodded. "Streaming" wasn't exactly the word he would have used, considering the vastness of the Texas frontier. But even half a dozen could make things damned awkward. "It's settled, then. Sit down, blast it. You're making me uncomfortable. Montgomery leaves for Independence tonight, whether he likes it or not. It'll take a few days to get loaded and make sure the teamsters know what they're doing. By that time we'll be there ourselves."

Ryder stopped pacing, but he didn't sit. "Are you sure you can trust him?"

"Hell, no." Garland leaned back, laughing as he ran his hand through thinning gray hair. "I'm sure I can't, but there's not much I can do about it. The man knows wagons, he knows the territory—he speaks the language a damn sight better than that pidgin you call Spanish. Unless I want to take on a Mexican, what choice do I have?"

"A Mexican might be better."

"No!" He half-rose in agitation, then forced himself back onto the cushions. "I don't want a Mexican—I won't *have* a Mexican! They all look the same, the little black-haired bastards. Nothing to tell who they are or where they're from. You don't know what you're getting with a Mexican."

"You don't know what you're getting with this man either. I tell you frankly, Howard, I don't like him." Ryder rested his hands on the back of the chair, leaning forward, lips thinning into a hint of a leer. "He reminds me too much of myself. I never feel good about a man who reminds me of myself. Like as not, he'd stab you in the back."

"Would he?" Garland studied him coolly. There *was* something very like Montgomery about this man, at least physically. An inch or so taller, but otherwise they were about the same build, with the same jet-dark hair, the same gray eyes, the same rugged cut to the features, though Ryder was clean-shaven, his skin appearing more swarthy than tanned. They even had similar drawls, but Montgomery's was clearly Texas, while Ryder showed traces of his mother's Mississippi.

"Oh . . . he would."

"And what about you? Do I need to worry that you're going to pull a knife when my back is turned?"

"Me? Now, why would I want to do something like that?" He uncoiled his body from the chair back and sauntered over to the door. "Just because you screwed my daddy out of his share when he was fool enough to join up with you fifteen years ago? And you're planning on screwing me the same way now?"

"Your father and I were partners on that first caravan to Santa Fe—which we approached, incidentally, with equal naiveté, expecting to come back with wagonloads of turquoise and Mexican gold. The precious little we got from our trading venture was split down the middle. Fifty-fifty."

"The legitimate trading maybe, but there's more than one kind of 'commerce.' You came back with enough to make you a rich man for a decade and a half."

"Why not? The planning was all mine. The brains, the daring . . . the risk! Your father had very little to do with it. He was handsomely rewarded for minimum effort."

"*Luck,* not planning! Blind luck. And the risks were equal!" Ryder's eyes flashed, dark gray, almost black, anger showing for a second through his customary reserve. "Only you were tough, and Daddy was weak, so his reward was a paltry ten percent. The same paltry ten percent I'm supposed to lick out of your hand like a hungry hound!"

"That's ten percent more than he had before. Can I help it if your daddy ran through the money like water? Lucky for you—isn't it?—he died seven years ago, or there'd have been nothing left for you to inherit."

"You had ten times as much, and it only took you twice the time to get to the same place!"

"There, then, you see." Garland's tone was cool. "All you have to do is be double the manager your daddy was with money, and we'll be even. And I'm not offering ten percent of a fortune this time. I'm offering ten percent of *two* fortunes, which goes a way toward soothing pride. It isn't every man, friend Ryder, who gets two fortunes offered to him on a shiny silver platter."

The other man's eyes narrowed, squinting from the doorway.

"You're very sure of yourself, Howard. You're not afraid that knife's going to start looking mighty tempting?"

"Not as long as I have a certain little paper in my possession. Which makes us the perfect confederates. I can't double-cross you because I need you to get what I want. And you can't double-cross me because you'd wind up at the end of a noose."

He paused, smiling unkindly.

"What a pity that poison took so long to act. I guess maybe you didn't know better . . . or maybe you didn't have a chance to get what you wanted. Anyhow, your daddy had plenty of time to write a nice long note, telling just how badly you wanted what was left of his money . . . and what you were willing to do to get it. If it hadn't been found by an old family retainer, the sheriff would have had it long before this. The handwriting's a little shaky, his being so weak and all, but I imagine it could be verified by an expert."

"I imagine. . . . How did you persuade old Alfred to part with it, anyway?"

"How do you think? Oh . . . and, Ryder."

"Yes?"

"In case you're considering overwhelming me somewhere on the trail and taking it by force, I'd better warn you—I won't have it with me. It'll be nice and safe with someone I trust, who'll have instructions to open it up and take a peek in the event of my untimely demise. If I were you, I'd keep a finger or two crossed for my good health."

"I'm not worried about you, Howard." His face relaxed, easing almost to amusement. "You're too mean to die. Yeah, money does woof, doesn't it? Poor greedy old Alfred."

"I had a feeling you'd see things my way."

"Yeah . . . ten percent of a pair of fortunes does look better than a hangman's noose. Especially when that ten percent comes with some very interesting possibilities. Well, I guess you'll be getting ready for that chat with your daughter." He grinned suddenly. "Feisty little thing, isn't she?

Garland hesitated. "Very feisty. But I know what I want, and I'm aiming to get it."

"So am I, friend . . . so am I."

As it turned out, Garland had his chat with his daughter late that afternoon, though not through any efforts of his own. Diana had finally decided it was time to get things settled and stop avoiding the inevitable. After all, she reminded herself, bolstering up her nerve, what could her father do to her? She loved Jordan and he loved her, and that was all there was to it.

Besides, after her unsettling encounter this morning, from which her senses were still reeling, she was determined not to spend a minute longer than she had to in her father's house.

Garland Howard was in the room he liked to call his study, although except for a mass of papers half-piled, half-strewn across a paneled desk at one end, it gave more the appearance of a masculine parlor. He had been living off the money brought back from that first Santa Fe venture, with occasional caravans sent out over the years, and had never developed either an inclination or a head for business. But he was inclined toward politics, and politics required at least a show of sharp-eyed industriousness, so the desk was never empty, and shelves of philosophical and economic treatises lined the walls.

Diana found him in an overstuffed chair at the far end of the room, a half-empty brandy snifter in one hand, a fat cigar in the other.

"I think it's time we had that little talk you've been itching for, Father," she said as she came over to stand directly in front of him. "I'm beginning to pity your manservant, prowling around the yard all the time looking for me. And poor little Tisha. She was scared to death when she had to tell Rosalie she couldn't find me in my room."

"So . . ." Garland raised his eyes somewhat tentatively to peer at his daughter. "You bribed her to lie for you."

"Not bribed. Bullied. I told her flat out I wasn't jumping to your orders. Come, Father, what did you expect the poor thing to do? Drag me to your study by force?"

"She could have told Rosalie—or me—that you were in your room, and let us decide how to handle the situation."

"Nonsense. You'd only have taken it out on her. Besides, what good would that have done? I'd hardly have sat around waiting for you to come and fetch me. . . . But all this is beside the point. You wanted to talk to me, and I'm here. Let's talk and get it over with."

Garland grunted as he bit down on the end of his cigar. In spite of himself, he had to admire the minx. She was more than feisty, she was bold enough to try to best him on his own terms. He found he was beginning to enjoy the conversation, especially knowing, as he did, who was going to win.

"I called you home, daughter, as you are well aware, because accounts of some highly unacceptable behavior reached my ears."

"Unacceptable?" She tossed her head contemptuously, setting fair curls bouncing around her face in a way she knew made her look like a little girl. "Let's at least use the right word. 'Scandalous'—isn't that what you mean? You're such a hypocrite, Father. You're not the least bit worried about whom I've been seeing or what I've been doing. You're only upset because some prissy schoolmistress caught me and mouthed it all over Richmond."

"Very well, then . . . 'scandalous' will do." Garland laid the cigar in an ashtray on the table beside him, uncomfortably aware that he was losing control of the conversation. "Your behavior alone would have caused scandal enough. But the young man you chose . . . ! Have you no wits at all? This cousin of yours, this Jordan Crofte, is an idler and a scoundrel. Worse, he's a gambler who's rumored to have stolen from his own father to support his wastrel life! I daresay he's good-looking enough, and oozing with charm, but looks and charm don't put food on the table, young lady. Or pay for all those fancy clothes you're used to."

Jordan is more than good-looking, Diana longed to shout back. He is excruciatingly handsome . . . and charm gives sustenance to the heart. But such arguments were sure to get her nowhere, and she had sworn not to let herself be drawn into a word match with her father.

"You know how it is with rumors," she said instead. "Jordan *has* lived unconventionally, I'll admit that. He has a way with horses and dice . . . and, yes, before you try to throw it in my face, I suppose women too. But he's young! He's been sowing his wild oats. Now that he's fallen in love with me, all that has changed. He's ready to settle down."

"Even if I believed that—which I don't—I could not countenance your relationship with him. It's much too late for pretty changes of heart."

"It's never too late, Father."

"In this case, yes, I'm afraid it is. The young man already has a tainted reputation. To allow him even the most casual association with this family would be disastrous. As you know, I'm interested in a career in politics—''

"Which you are quite ready to put ahead of your daughter's happiness."

"Which I am ready to further in any reasonable way." His temper rising, Garland gripped the snifter in both hands. "Do stop bouncing like that! You look like one of those little birds on the lawn. Naturally, I have no intention of sacrificing my family for my ambitions, but neither do I intend to cater to a spoiled child who thinks of nothing beyond her own immediate pleasures. I forbid you to see this young man again. I don't expect you to listen, but—''

"And reasonably so, Father." To his surprise, she took a seat opposite him, tucking her feet up as she had when she was a child. Obviously, she had come prepared for everything he had to say. Or she thought she had. "Because I'm *not* going to listen. And I'm not going to obey. You might as well prepare yourself for the worst. Not only am I going to *see* Jordan again, I'm going to marry him!"

"Ah?" A faint tic showed at the corner of his mouth, but otherwise his face remained impassive. "What makes you think I'd give my blessing to that?"

"I'm not asking for your blessing. Or your permission. I'll be eighteen in a few months. You can't stop me then."

"Can't I, my dear?"

"Don't think you can buy Jordan off, Father, or scare him away with threats! That might work with a lesser man. But not Jordan. We've already talked it over, and we've decided we're going to stand firm. And if your precious political career goes down the drain, that's just the way it is!"

She braced herself for the explosion to follow. But if anything, his face appeared even calmer, with only a glimmer of something in his eyes that made her slightly nervous.

"You are going to be married," he said quietly. "But not to Jordan Crofte. I've arranged a more suitable match. The wedding will take place in a few days. Before your stepmother and I leave."

"In a few *days?*" Diana gaped at him, startled in spite of herself. She was not surprised that he was trying to foist an unwanted husband on her. Indeed, she had expected something of the sort. But she was surprised at the boldness of his timing. "Who is this paragon of virtue you've persuaded to take on a bride with only a few days' courtship?

I can just imagine what he's like! Do I know him? Have we met?"

"Once or twice . . . more or less in passing. As for the courtship, it isn't necessary. He knows, of course, that there won't be any love at the beginning. Being a reasonable man, he doesn't expect it. His name, by the way . . ." He hesitated slightly, watching for her reaction. ". . . is Ryder. The son of my former associate, whom perhaps you remember. There are mutual reasons why an alliance between our families is desirable. You will be the bond that cements us, so to speak. And of course, he isn't exactly throwing away his manhoond. You aren't unattractive, you know."

"Oh, sweet heaven . . ." Diana half-whispered the words, shocked at last. Now she recognized the glimmer she had detected in his eye. *You're not unattractive, you know.* . . . Was that really her father talking? And . . . *Ryder?* She could place him only indistinctly in her mind, but the association was unpleasant, a tallish man, handsome in a way, with dark, brooding, arrogant features.

Unaccountably, her thoughts flashed back to other dark, arrogant features, and she remembered vividly the man she had encountered that morning . . . and the disturbing sensations that had set her blood boiling. Instinctively she knew she would never feel like that about the man her father had picked out for her.

"Why, I'd sooner marry that Cord Montgomery you hired to lead your wagons into Mexico!"

"I don't recall having offered the choice, my dear. Now, if your little tirade is over, perhaps you're ready to look at things sensibly—"

"Sense has nothing to do with it!" she burst out, then, unexpectedly, started to laugh. Sense had *everything* to do with it! Here she was, determined to keep her head, and the first time he caught her off-guard, she flew into a senseless tizzy.

"It's no use, Father. You can talk about this marriage all you want, but how do you propose to get me to agree? I suppose you could lock me in my room . . . only if I didn't get out by myself, Jordan would come and rescue me. Or you could shackle me in irons and drag me to the altar."

"Oh, I don't think I'll have to resort to anything so melodramatic. You're used to expensive finishing schools and a very nice allowance. How many girls you know have an allowance like that? You've no concept of what it's like to go without luxuries, to say nothing of the necessities! As you pointed out yourself, you're very nearly of age. You wouldn't expect me to go on supporting an adult child who has nothing but contempt for my authority.''

Diana stared at him almost pityingly. ''Are you saying that you'd cut off my *allowance.*''

''I'm saying just that.''

''And you think with no money, I'd have nowhere to go? That no one would take me in?''

''Surely you don't believe all those impecunious relations took care of you holiday after holiday with no reimbursement?''

''No, I don't suppose they did . . .'' Lady Alice's family had been kind enough, true to the traditions of hospitality that were so deeply ingrained in Virginia, but she had always had a sense that they never truly liked her. Perhaps because of her mother and the man she had run off with. Or maybe it was her own hoydenish high spirits. ''But you haven't heard a word I've said, have you? I don't need anyone to take me in because I already have someplace to go. I'm in love. I'm going to be married! Jordan will give up horses and dueling, and even get a job, if he has to, to support me. I didn't expect an allowance from you. I wouldn't accept it. *Jordan* wouldn't accept it.''

Garland raised the glass to his mouth, lips tightening as he contemplated his daughter, curled up like a cat on the couch. What had been entertaining before was becoming distinctly irritating. She was so sure of herself.

''Jordan Crofte would accept anything it pleased him to accept. Don't flatter yourself he'd want you for a wife if he thought you came a pauper.''

''But he does. He knows all about my mother, and how she was cut out of her grandfather's will because she married you. He's the one who told me about it. And you can't think he expects me to inherit anything from you? That would be stupid, Father! As a matter of fact, he thinks you won't be able to support your new wife and the family you'll probably start.''

Garland bristled. The word ''stupid'' cut too close to let pass, and he felt his gorge rising. He wasn't enjoying the interview anymore, but he was going to enjoy the way it ended. He was going to enjoy very much watching all that cocky pride deflate in front of his eyes.

"Haven't you wondered at all why your impetuous lover hasn't come to rescue you before this?"

"No-o-o-o," Diana lied. She had, in fact, wondered. They had agreed, when she came home, that Jordan would leave her here for only a few days at most.

But then, Jordan had a way of finding poker games in the most unlikely places—and maybe it was just as well. He had always been lucky at cards. This way they'd have a stake for their new life together.

"No, of course not! I'm not the least bit concerned. I know I can count on Jordan. He'll come soon enough . . . when the time is right."

"He won't come soon *or* late. Jordan Crofte won't ever come for you again."

"You mean . . . ?" Diana felt the first twinges of doubt in her stomach. "You *did* buy him off?" But, no! That was impossible. Jordan wasn't like that. Jordan wouldn't trade love for cash. "I don't believe you! You're lying! You could never buy a man like Jordan!"

"I could . . . and I would. But I didn't have to." He fixed her with his eyes, hard and glittering, waiting for the response that was sure to come. Call him stupid, would she? "Jordan won't be coming . . . because he's dead."

Dead? The whole world seemed to turn upside down. Diana reached out, but there was nothing to catch hold of. Everything was reeling, the room careening so wildly she couldn't get her bearings.

Jordan couldn't be dead. He *couldn't*. She loved him so much. But then she looked at her father's face, the petty, mean triumph in his eyes, and she knew that he was.

"He's really . . . *dead?*"

"Killed, as suits a man of his proclivities, in a barroom brawl. In the midst of a lively game of chance. Over an ace up somebody's sleeve, I understand. The word came last week, while you were still on the train from Richmond."

It was so like her brash lover, Diana did not even question it. This was exactly the way a man like Jordan would die. The way a man like Jordan would *expect* to die. But, oh, how could her father look like that? So smugly self-satisfied—because he had won and she had lost.

He's glad, she thought bitterly. He's *glad* Jordan is dead

and I'm bleeding inside. He doesn't care about another man's life. He doesn't even care about his daughter's tears. All he cares about is himself. And his damn political career!

"Well, Father," she said, when she could trust her voice again, "it's nice you're so pleased. Because if you thought there was talk before, when I was merely sneaking out for a night at the theater—it's nothing to the scandal you're going to face now."

She paused, just long enough to make sure he was listening.

"Jordan may be dead . . . but I am carrying his child."

4

DIANA would never know how she got through that long, terrible night. The house all around was deathly still, not a board creaking, not a breath of wind rattling the heavy shutters on the windows.

All she could think was that Jordan was dead. She would never hear his velvet-soft voice again, the teasing music of laughter that seemed to caress her ears. She would never feel the smoothness of his hand on her cheek, never smell the faint aroma of tobacco lingering on his fingers, the musky fragrance of the hair oil he favored. She would never again fall asleep with the scent of magnolia drifting through the windows and dream of the man who was going to fill her life with joy.

Whatever had possessed her to throw out that bold taunt to her father?

She stared numbly at the wall, dull and shadowy in the faint light of a single candle. She was not pregnant with Jordan's child. Their relationship had never progressed to such intimacy, though he had tried, heaven knew, to get her to give in. She wished now she had. She wished with all her heart she had known everything, shared everything with this man she loved so much. She wished she *were* carrying his child. At least then she would have a part of him to keep and cherish forever.

But she wasn't. That was just something she had thrown out in spite. A childish response. He had been so smug and self-satisfied, her father—hurting her almost as much with his callousness as with his words—and she had lashed out, longing to hurt back.

Now she was going to pay for it.

She drew up her legs on the old rocker where she was sitting and wrapped her arms around them. She had been a fool, thinking she could hurt him. He'd be angry, yes, and he might worry for a while. But the only one who was going to get hurt was her.

If Garland Howard had been anxious to marry her off before, he was going to be doubly anxious now. To Ryder if he was still agreeable—or someone even more loathsome, who'd be willing to take "damaged goods" for a price.

And he wasn't going to be too particular how he went about it.

Diana was to find out the next morning exactly how right she had been. It was still early, but sunlight was peeking through the cracks in the drawn draperies. This time, Garland came to her room himself, not bothering with intermediaries as he gave a perfunctory rap and swung the door open.

If he noticed that her eyes were puffy and she was wearing the same outfit she had had on the afternoon before, he did not mention it.

"I'm sure you realize," he said stiffly, "that it's more imperative than ever now to find you a husband. Fortunately, Ryder is not squeamish about such things. In fact, he professes a slight preference for a wife with 'experience.' The wedding will take place as soon as arrangements can be made."

"No." Diana was so tired, she was hardly aware of what she was saying. "Don't you know I'm grieving, Father? Don't you know the man I love has just died? . . . Don't you know I will never, *never* take anyone else in his place? Not even to save you the embarrassment of a bastard grandchild!"

"Watch your language, young lady. And I suggest you don't make rash statements. I think, when you've had time to consider the matter, you'll realize you don't have a choice. I'm going to make you a little proposition, and I don't believe you'll turn me down."

Diana looked up dully, her throat suddenly dry. "What kind of . . . proposition?"

"Simply this. I will send you anyplace you choose—so long as it's far enough from St. Louis not to occasion gossip—and you can wait in comfort to give birth to your baby. Assuming, that is, you're a married woman. If not, I'm afraid you're going to have to come with us on this trading trek into Mexico. By us, naturally, I mean your fiancé and me. He is actually quite enthusiastic about it.''

"You can't mean . . . ?'' Diana shuddered. "But what *good* would that do? You can make me miserably uncomfortable. You might even jeopardize my . . . my pregnancy. But you still can't make me marry this man!''

"I don't think you quite get the idea, my dear. From my point of view—don't you see?—it really doesn't matter. You can change your mind and be married, just in time, by some priest in Santa Fe . . . or you can stubbornly refuse, and the child will be born in obscurity, far from St. Louis. Either way, I come out ahead. And, of course . . .''

He had started toward the door. Now he stopped and turned.

"It will be a long trip. Rosalie is going to have a tent of her own. Her maid sleeps in the wagon. Similar arrangements will be made for you. . . . Whether you have the tent to yourself, of course, will depend on your fiancé.''

Diana shivered. The implication in those words was all too clear. She sat alone in her room for the rest of the day, remembering what he had said and hating her brain for being so numb. Tisha tiptoed in with a steaming bowl of soup about noon; but seeing the look on Diana's face, she tiptoed out again without a word.

Intolerable. That was the situation her father had maneuvered her into. Utterly intolerable. And it didn't help to realize that her own foolish lie had made things a thousand times worse. Now her father was more determined than ever. She could give in to him, the way he wanted. She could marry a man she didn't even like and hope against hope that somehow things would work out before he came back from Mexico.

Or she could continue her defiance and suffer God-knew-what on the trail.

The next days passed in an emotional fog. Diana felt as if she were sleepwalking, cutting off feelings because they were too painful to endure. Somehow, she managed to stand up to her father, though she was aware that that was less courage than the fact that she was simply too dazed to focus. She was also aware that there were ministers and judges on the frontier, and the final decision would not be made until the wagons were ready to roll out.

She was barely conscious of the details of their departure,

made rather hastily the next morning, since there were no more wedding plans to hold them in St. Louis. Later she would not even remember the jolting carriage ride, crammed between crates and trunks, over rutted streets to the levee. Nor had she more than the vaguest sense of the long, uncomfortable steamboat voyage to Independence, and that a sense primarily of the grief and fear that swept over her in alternate debilitating waves.

It was only after she had been in Independence for two or three days that she finally began to pull out of the hazy semidusk that seemed sometimes as if it were going to surround her forever.

Everyone, she had to admit, went out of the way to be thoughtful, even strangers. The hotel was jammed to capacity. Cots had been set up in the halls and men were sleeping on couches in the parlors, even on the floor—this was the season traders and adventurers set their sights westward, and Independence was a terminus for both the Santa Fe and Oregon trails—but waiters always seemed to find a place for them at the long tables in the bustling, raucous dining room. And an extra morsel of succulent veal always appeared on her plate, or a handful of wild strawberries, as if they had seen her pallor and were coaxing her to eat.

Garland himself was, if not exactly considerate, at least less authoritarian, as if he sensed it was only a matter of time and he would have his way. Oddly enough, neither he nor Ryder—who had been keeping his distance, thank heaven, though leering unpleasantly out of the corner of his eye—seemed unduly concerned about the baby, and to her relief, the subject was not mentioned. The hired hands, most of them grizzled veterans of the trail, whose names were still a jumble in her mind, made a point of doffing their hats when they saw her, though she could have sworn some of them had never tipped a brim to a lady in their lives.

Even Cord Montgomery seemed to have dropped his mocking arrogance. He had made one ribald comment when he first saw her, a pointed allusion to their previous encounter—then penetrating gray eyes had taken her in, turning thoughtful suddenly, quizzical, and he had gone out of his way to be almost courteous since then.

It was amazing, the mystique sorrow gave a woman, she thought late one afternoon as she stepped out onto the crowded porch everyone insisted on calling a veranda in front of the hotel. If her grief hadn't been so new and raw, she might almost have been amused, the way everyone was treating her.

Not even Rosalie, who had to know everything, could bring herself to be spiteful. In fact, she had taken to stopping by Diana's room several times a day, ''to see how you're getting along,'' she said. And when she couldn't persuade her stepdaughter to come shopping, she ordered a number of garments herself, which she considered suitable for the trip, and brought them back for Diana to admire.

A gust of wind blew across the street, driving thoughts of Rosalie from her mind. It had rained off and on, and the streets had been muddy yesterday, great gobs of brown spattering onto the wooden decking. But today everything had dried considerably, and freighters with their massive wheels, and plodding oxen, and lean, rawboned horsemen stirred up a fog of dust that hovered in the air.

Independence was not particularly pretty to Diana's eyes, but had circumstances been different, had the pain and dread not been growing in her heart, she would probably have been fascinated by the teeming throngs and rough, throbbing traffic that swelled the streets and spilled out over the walkways.

This was above all a frontier town, weather-grayed storefronts providing a backdrop for all manner of men: traders, like her father, with their conservative black jackets, and scouts in fringed buckskin; slaves and free blacks and paleskinned mulattos, and Indians with long greasy hair, looking and smelling of camps on the plains. Diana gaped in spite of herself as a group of them passed, Kansas or Kiowa in dirty white blankets and cast-off denim pants, just close enough so she could make them out, but not so close they were threatening.

In the midst of all those robust faces, she was surprised to pick out the startlingly pallid features of a number of invalids, some with mufflers wound around their chins, halfway to their noses, though the day was arm. It was a moment before she recalled that the prairies were renowned for their curative powers.

It seemed to her brave and a little touching, all these young men with their consumptions and their liver complaints, leaving the safety of their beds to dare the wilderness in one great adventure that would cure or kill.

Like me, she thought suddenly, intrigued by the comparison. The ills of their bodies and the wounds of her heart, all brought to the vast open plains for the winds to cleanse, the sun to heal.

Only, unlike her, these invalids weren't going to have to worry about sharing their tents with a man who had considerably more than healing on his mind!

She took a tentative step toward the street. It was not especially pleasant on the crowded wooden veranda. The early-June sun baked the boards and brought out a distinct aroma of sweat. But it occurred to her, as she hesitated a moment at the edge, that it might be even more unpleasant on the street.

"Begging your pardon, ma'am. You look like you don't know whether you're coming or going."

Diana looked up to see a friendly face under a shock of sandy hair grinning at her from the saddle of a sturdily built bay.

"You're right." She laughed. "Mr. . . . Blake, isn't it? I'm getting a little bored with the view from the veranda, but I'm not sure I want to get tangled in that madness on the street."

"Yes, ma'am . . . *Randall* Blake." He dismounted and stood, reins loose in his hands, beside the hitching post in front of the hotel. "Your father kindly took me on as an assistant wagon master, though I can't say I've the experience for the job. And 'madness' is a good description. But it doesn't look quite so chaotic from the back of a horse."

"No, I don't suppose so." Diana placed him now, a young West Pointer, a lieutenant—from North Carolina, she thought—who had turned in army blues to try his luck with one of the large trading caravans. "You get a different perspective, looking down on things. From where I stand, though, it's rather intimidating."

"I'd be pleased to escort you around . . . if that isn't too forward. Your father has a number of excellent horses at the livery stable down the street. Montgomery—the wagon master—picked them out himself and likes to see them exercised."

"Thank you, that's very kind. But I don't think . . . Not today."

He was looking at her curiously, his eyes almost the same

sand tone as his hair. "You don't like to ride, Miss Howard?"

"Oh . . . I love it! I used to drive everyone wild at school. I was always sneaking out and making off with one of the horses—bareback! But I . . . I don't feel like a ride today. It *is* getting rather late."

"Yes, ma'am. I understand. . . . I'm sorry. It really was presumptuous of me. I only thought you might like to have a look at the town."

"It wasn't presumptuous at all. And do stop saying 'ma'am.' Call me Diana . . . or maybe 'Miss Diana' when Father or Rosalie is around. But no 'ma'am.' And certainly not 'Miss Howard.' Even the servants don't say that."

"I'd be happy to, ma . . . Miss Diana." He smiled self-consciously as he swung back into the saddle. "I'm Randy to my friends. . . . I hope you'll return the favor. And if you ever find yourself looking for an escort, I hope you'll think of me." His face reddened as he raised his hand to the brim of his hat and realized he wasn't wearing one. "Well, so long. You take care."

"You too," Diana called after him, smiling to herself as she watched him pick his way through the Conestogas and dearborns that clogged the streets. She had seen him only once or twice before, briefly, but even then it had been clear that the young man had more than a passing interest in his employer's daughter.

Any other time, at any other place, she would have been flattered by his attentions. Randy Blake wasn't exactly handsome, but his boyish features had a way of twisting into a crooked smile, and there was warmth and eagerness in his eyes. Diana found herself trusting him, almost instinctively. She liked the young man's soft-spoken manners, his thoughtfulness, the gentle, respectful way he looked at her.

Only this wasn't another time or another place. She sighed as she looked back at the doorway, bathed in shadows now that the sun was at an angle. This was here and now, and she had been putting off her problems too long as it was.

Even if she hadn't just lost Jordan, even if her heart weren't dead to feeling, she wouldn't have had time to indulge in a playful flirtation with Randall Blake. That nasty little proposition of her father's required all her concentration.

And she was beginning to realize more and more that he had been right. She really didn't have a choice.

What on earth had she thought she was going to do?

She went back into the hotel, hating the crowds that left no secluded corner, even in the ladies' parlor. Run off and start a new life for herself? Somewhere her father couldn't find her? That was a laugh. She didn't have so much as a dollar left over from all those school allowances. And with no useful skills, how could she hope to make a living? Why, she couldn't even manage decent needlepoint, much less sew a straight, serviceable seam.

As for those relatives in Virginia . . . well, Father was right there too. Even if she had the money to reach them, they wouldn't be likely to take her in. And where else could she turn?

Heading toward the stairway, she started for her room. It was a tiny, stifling chamber, and she hated it, but at least she'd have some privacy there. She supposed her great-grandfather must have made some provision for her in that infamous will of his. The money for all those fancy finishing schools must have come from somewhere.

But even if he had . . . She paused halfway up the stairs, more discouraged than ever. Knowing how he felt about his only granddaughter, her mother, she could just guess how much he'd left! About enough to provide for her upbringing. For the things *he* considered necessary. That would hardly include enabling a disobedient child to run away!

She could have wept as she reached the upper hallway and found it unexpectedly deserted. A moment ago, she had wanted nothing so much as to be away from everyone. Now the silence and the empty shadows only reminded her how terribly alone she was.

There *wasn't* anything she could do. She realized that with a sudden cold clarity. She had been running away from the truth for days, trying to hide by putting things off.

But there was no more putting off, now that it was almost time to leave. There was no place left to hide. She couldn't set out on her own. And she couldn't let her father take her with them, and put her in a tent by herself . . . and wonder if he was bluffing, or if that man really was going to be free to use her as he chose.

He had won. She knew that, with the first rational thought that had crossed her brain since she learned of Jordan's death. Her father had won, with the terms he knew she could not resist.

At least he had offered one small shred of hope.

She started toward her room, then hesitated, turning the other way. At least this unwanted marriage would buy her some time. They would be gone for months, and she would be someplace safe. Anything could happen in months.

"I do wish you'd stop all that fussing and get ready." Garland Howard's voice was petulant as he addressed his wife's reflection in the mirror of the small dressing table. "There's nothing wrong with your hair. Tisha did a perfectly presentable job."

"She did not. All these curls look dreadful. They're five years out-of-date!" Rosalie frowned at her image in the harsh light from the window. The first few days, she had almost enjoyed being in Independence. With the crowded conditions at the hotel, they had been forced to share a room—and a bed—and she had been pleasantly surprised to find that her husband's scruples did not extend to dark midnights with a warm, willing body beside him. But last night, he hadn't come back, pleading crises at the camp, where the wagons, already loaded, were kept under guard, and she had a feeling he was going to do the same thing tonight. "I don't know why you insisted on bringing that girl with us. She's next to useless."

"Not exactly . . . but that isn't worth arguing about. We're hardly going to a formal event. There won't be anyone in the dining room to impress. I've noticed it's impossible to get an adequate meal if you don't arrive when they begin serving—unless, of course, you happen to be my daughter. The choicest portions never seem to have run out where Diana is concerned."

"You know, Garland . . ." Rosalie turned toward her husband, a long-handled silver brush poised for an instant in the air. "I can't help feeling sorry for her. She looks so pale, I'm really quite worried."

"The only person you ever worry about is yourself. You've never shown the least sympathy for any woman prettier than you. Why all this sudden concern for my daughter?"

"I don't know . . . it just seems so sad. Loving him like that, and losing him . . . and then learning she's carrying his child. I must say, you've been very good about it. Why, to look at you, one would think you weren't bothered at all.''

"I'm not."

"You're . . . not?" Rosalie laid the brush down and swiveled around to face him. "Really, Garland, sometimes I don't understand you at all. I would think you'd be beside yourself. Because of the scandal."

"Scandals can be averted, my dear . . . or hushed up. Or lived with, if necessary. Some things are more important. For instance, the terms of Croftleigh's will."

"The earl's will? Now I really don't understand. What does Diana's grandfather's will have to do with the remarkable way you're accepting this baby she's going to have?"

"Her great-grandfather," he corrected, bending down to adjust his black silk cravat in the mirror. "*Alice* was his granddaughter . . . and his only heir. Imagine the old misanthrope's dilemma when he went to disinherit her and found no one to leave his fortune to. All he could do was place everything in trust for whatever children she might have. According to the terms of his will, boys were to receive their shares outright on reaching majority. Unfortunately, having a sensible skepticism for a woman's ability to handle business affairs, he decreed that girls' shares would remain in trust, to be administered by attorneys until they married and the responsibility could be turned over to their husbands."

"I know all that," Rosalie broke in, resenting the way he had sometimes of treating her as if she didn't have a brain in her head. "You've told me often enough how bitterly disappointed you were when the only child Alice presented you with was a girl."

"If it had been a boy, everything would have been different. I would have kept a boy with me. I would have trained him over the years, molded him to my way of thinking. There are millions at stake, dammit—millions! Enough for a man to live like a king. Enough for *ten* men to live like kings! We would have worked things out together, my son and I. We would have forged an empire for ourselves."

Passion raised his voice to an alarming pitch, ringing through the room. "Well, you didn't have a son," Rosalie reminded him hastily. "You've had to make other arrangements, which aren't all that bad. There's no point—"

"No, I didn't . . . but fate has a funny way sometimes of

turning things around.'' He went over to the door, laughing harshly as he leaned against it, one hand resting on the knob. ''The old earl was not only dictatorial, he was downright sadistic. The thing goes on for generations! My son— if I'd had one—could have done anything he wanted with his fortune. He could have squandered it or hoarded it and disposed of it in a will of his own. But my daughter's trust remains in perpetuity. Whatever is left when Diana dies will go to her children—divided up exactly the same way.''

He was laughing again, softly, almost to himself. Rosalie stared at him.

''Sometimes I really *can't* make you out, Garland. I honestly don't see what's so funny—''

''Of course you don't, my dear. Of course you don't. I didn't expect you would. Come on, now, your hair looks even curlier than it did before. No, no . . . don't pick up that damn brush again. Let's go. We're late enough as it is.''

Pulling open the door, he gestured her out with an abruptness Rosalie dared not ignore. Neither of them glanced over their shoulders as they hurried down the dimly lighted hall to the staircase. If they had, they might have glimpsed a shadowy figure pressed against the wall, barely daring to breathe for fear they would notice.

Diana had been there only a few minutes, but those few minutes had been more than enough. She had just arrived, ready to swallow her pride and capitulate, when her father's raised voice had come through the door.

''. . . *the terms of Croftleigh's will.*''

She had stopped at that, pressing her ear shamelessly against the door, not even caring when passersby shot her looks of amusement. By the time Garland Howard finally got his wife out of the room, she had heard enough to set her brain reeling.

Her great-grandfather *had* provided for her in his will. Not the pittance she had imagined, to take care of her upbringing, but his entire fortune. Millions, if her father hadn't been exaggerating. And she would have absolutely no control over it!

Indignation flooded through her as she realized how little respect the old earl had had for her, even before she was born! If she'd been a boy, none of this would be happening. A boy would be looking forward now to taking charge of his own resources. Young men, it seemed, were deemed suitable to control their destinies. But she, a woman, would be dependent on lawyers or husbands for the rest of her life!

That was why her father had been so eager to marry her off. She dared to breathe again, trembling as she pushed away from the wall. Not because of any scandal. Not because he was worried about his precious political ambitions. He wanted to make sure she had a husband of *his* choice. A husband with whom he obviously had some sort of arrangement.

And that was why he'd been so wildly furious when he learned of her passion for Jordan. He'd been afraid news of their engagement would get out, and lawyers would appear from somewhere to tell them the true terms of the will. That was why he'd rushed her out of Richmond. And why he'd looked so smugly satisfied when he informed her of the timely coincidence of Jordan's death.

Oh, God help her . . .

Anger turned to despair as the reality of what was happening began to sink in. He was never going to let up on her now. He *hadn't* been bluffing when he'd told her that Ryder would be free to come to her tent. He would overlook nothing, stop at nothing, to force her to give in. Somehow he and this disgusting man had gotten together, and they were going to control her.

And through her, the fortune her great-grandfather had left.

She started slowly down the hall, a kaleidoscope of thoughts spinning around in her head, one spilling over the other. She had been wrong before. She *wouldn't* be safe. Not anywhere. She might have a few months' respite while they were gone, but it would be just that. A terrifyingly brief respite.

They would keep after her, even if she agreed to marry him. They would hound her, torment her, give her no peace until she had produced the male heir that would guarantee all those millions in perpetuity.

Unless . . .

A group of men passed, brushing against her in the narrow hall, but Diana barely noticed as a sudden bold thought flashed across her mind.

Unless . . . she already had a husband!

5

FLICKERING RAYS filtered through the smoky glass of an old tin lantern hung high on one wall, bathing the livery stable in an eerie half-light. Diana drew a deep breath to steady herself. Shadows turned the stalls and corners into fathomless caverns, but her ears picked out an occasional rustling like the scraping of a hoof or the swishing of a tail. The familiar smells of hay and horses and unvarnished wood reminded her of other nights, when she had sneaked out for long moonlit rides over the hills.

Only she wasn't going for a ride tonight. And there was more at stake than a tongue-lashing or expulsion from another school.

She ran her hand nervously down the folds of her skirt, feeling the smoothness of *mousseline de soie* that had never been worn before. The gown was one her stepmother had chosen, a vibrant apricot pink that should have overshadowed her fragile coloring, but brought out highlights in her cheeks and accented her eyes instead. It was a little too tight, for Rosalie had misjudged her size, clinging where it should have hung, and the pointed bodice plunged a little too low to be modest on someone with high young breasts.

But modesty was hardly what she needed now. She peered into the darkness at the rear of the stable, where the faint outline of a door was barely distinguishable. She had already tried being modest once that night—and all it had gotten her was humiliation!

She cringed at the memory of those embarrassing moments. She had been dressed much more simply—in a blue sprigged-cotton crepe, becoming, but almost childlike with its wide lace collar and matching blue cashmere mantle—when she had accosted Randall Blake in one of the parlors and persuaded him to take a stroll with her in the sunset coolness of the veranda.

Of all the men she had met or seen in that town, Randy was the only one she was inclined to trust. She didn't know him well, of course—she had been very aware of that as they stepped out into the dusk. But then, she didn't know *any* man well, and at least he seemed kind and decent. If she had to take a husband of convenience, it might as well be him.

As it turned out, Randy was *too* decent. Miserably, Diana was forced to admit that at least part of what had followed was her own clumsy fault. Afraid to be honest, she had skirted the subject instead, reminding him coyly that, except for her father, she was totally unprotected, and the thought of a long journey in the company of foul-mouthed mule skinners and rawhide-ragged frontiersmen was so intimidating, it nearly made her swoon. Naturally, things would be different if there were a husband to look out for her. . . . And, of course, she had money of her own, so she wouldn't be a burden . . .

She had almost felt guilty, the pleasure in his eyes had been so genuine when he had realized what she was getting at. Obviously he cared for her sincerely, and he was flattered that she would consider him as a marriage partner. But his sense of honor had been honed to a sharp edge in all those years at West Point. He would speak to her father, he had told her—gladly. He was *eager* to speak to her father. But he wouldn't consider eloping without his consent.

Too late, Diana realized that she had gone about it all the wrong way. She had tried to appeal to his chivalry. She had thought she could tell him the truth later, when the marriage was a *fait accompli*. And, of course, he would be too much of a gentleman then to take advantage of her.

She should have appealed to his senses instead. Diana stood alone in the silent stable, quietly assessing the scene that could not be replayed. She should have worn the apricot-bright gown, with its none-too-subtle appeal, and drenched herself in exotic perfume filched from Rosalie's dressing table. She should have quickened his heart and stirred his pulse until he could no longer think what he was doing.

She should have implied everything, *promised* everything—given it if she had to. Anything was better than allowing that slime Ryder to come to her tent.

Well, she wasn't going to make that mistake again. She glanced at the door, still closed, though she thought she detected noises behind it. With Randy out of the picture, there was only one man she could imagine bold enough to defy her father. And that man, she had been told, spent his nights at the stable so he would be on hand to look after the horses.

She wouldn't, of course, promise *him* anything. And she certainly wouldn't deliver! But she was going to have to be more direct than she had with Randy. Greed—that would get him. Greed, and cleverly worded arguments.

And with a man like that, a glimpse of bosom and a whiff of French perfume couldn't hurt.

Bracing herself, she stepped over to the door and knocked.

If she could have foreseen the expression on Cord Montgomery's face when the door swung open, she would never have had the courage to come. Golden lanternlight shimmered from behind, backlighting bearded features as he stood in the doorway and stared out at her. Not a flicker of surprise glinted in those smoke-gray eyes.

Coolly, almost nonchalantly, he took in everything about her. The softness of her hair, left to spill silvery and abundant over her shoulders . . . the way her dress draped itself, half-hiding, half-revealing the ripening lines of her bosom . . . the hem that was a fraction of an inch too short.

Why, it's almost as though he expected me, she thought. She shuddered as it occurred to her that there might be another reason why he bedded down in the back of a stable rather than camping with the rest of the men on the outskirts of town. No doubt he was used to receiving women visitors in the middle of the night.

And judging by the arrogant smirk that was beginning to show beneath that bush on his face, he thought she, like the others, found him irresistible and hadn't been able to stay away.

"This is not what you think," she said stiffly.

"No, ma'am?" Skepticism crooked one brow as he glanced pointedly at the empty stable behind her. "I reckon it's just my nasty mind. Can't image what would give me a vulgar idea like that." The drawl became more pronounced as he shook his head in mock confusion. "Couldn't be the way that pretty dress sorta follows where you go . . . or the fact that it's a little late for a social call."

"I don't make calls in stables, Mr. Montgomery." Diana

swept past him into the room, regretting her impulsiveness
the instant she saw that it contained a narrow bed and very
little else. She was aware of papers strewn across a rough
gray blanket—inventories for the caravan, she supposed—as
she turned hastily to cover her confusion. "Nor do my social obligations extend to people like you. I have come on
a matter of business."

"Ah . . . business." He followed her into the room,
shutting the door behind him. Diana was acutely aware of
how hard and male his body was as he leaned indolently
against it. "And here I was, thinkin' you weren't int'rested
in business proposals from me. You made it clear, last time,
you didn't want my, uh . . . cash."

Diana felt her cheeks burn crimson. The man was impossible. He knew she was uncomfortable, and he was enjoying it! "I still don't want your cash. I didn't come to
discuss *that*. And I'm certainly not interested in any proposals you might make. Quite the contrary. I'm here to propose something to *you*."

"Now, that *is* intriguing. Care to sit down?" He swept
the papers toward one side of the bed, grinning when he
saw her reaction. "No? You won't object if I do? Okay, you
got my interest. What do you have in mind?"

"I . . . I want you to marry me."

He had just been sprawling back crudely on the bed. Now
he sat up, staring at her—at a loss for words, she'd wager,
for the first time in his life.

"What?"

"That isn't exactly how I meant to say it, but . . . yes. I
need a husband. I need a man with the backbone to stand
up to my father. A man without too many compunctions to
get in the way. And I need him now. It seems to me, Mr.
Montgomery, you match the description."

"I'm not afraid of Garland Howard," he agreed, glancing down at his hands. The drawl was almost gone now, as
if he had affected it before only to mock her. "And, no,
when it comes to him, I don't suppose I do have any compunctions. But, charming as you are, sweetheart"—he looked
up again, wickedly—"and sore as the temptation may be to
pursue the obvious blisses you offer, I'm afraid . . ."

"Don't be ridiculous! I'm not offering anything of the
sort! I told you, this is purely a business proposal. I need

your name on a marriage certificate, for which you'll be handsomely paid. After the ceremony, we don't ever have to see each other again. In fact, I insist on it. Certainly we wouldn't *live* together. You can go anywhere you choose. I couldn't care less. *I* will be on a train headed back east.''

Cord leaned forward, elbows on his knees, eyeing her curiously. ''If you don't want my virile body in your bed . . . or my dazzling repartee in your drawing room . . . what *are* you looking for?''

''I . . .'' Diana caught her breath, wishing there were some other way—*any* other way—out of this. ''I think I'd better tell you the truth.''

''That might be a good idea.''

She began hesitantly, trying at first to convey the general idea without giving too much away. Then, seeing his face close up, and remembering the mistakes she had made with Randy, she decided on complete honesty. Once she'd started, everything came spilling out. Nothing was held back, not even the awful pain she had felt when she learned that Jordan was dead . . . or how close she had come to buying time for herself by agreeing to marry Ryder. How she *would* have agreed if she hadn't arrived at her father's door at precisely the moment he was clarifying to Rosalie the terms of her great-grandfather's will.

''So you see,'' she concluded, ''the only way I'll ever get them to leave me alone is by marrying someone else. I don't know how much money is involved. My father said 'millions,' though he was probably exaggerating. But there has to be thousands—*hundreds* of thousands! I'll give you half of whatever it is if you help me.''

''Half of 'whatever it is.' What a generous offer. And all I have to give in return is my freedom.''

''In name only.'' The irony of his tone was not lost on her. ''In reality, you'd be free to do anything you wanted. As I told you, this would be a marriage on paper. No demands—or expectations—on either side.''

''No *expectations?* Ah, but I'm the sort of man who always has expectations . . . especially of pretty girls who preen in front of mirrors. I wonder, if that's really what you're after, that you didn't approach someone else with this little 'proposal' of yours.''

''I did,'' she admitted. ''But he . . . he had compunctions. I wouldn't be here now if I had anyplace else to go.''

"No . . . I don't suppose you would." His features turned thoughtful. "Has it occurred to you, little girl, that you might be jumping from the stewpot into the fire? What's to prevent me, once we're married and I take control of your fortune, from keeping it *all?* Not just the half you offered?"

"I wouldn't let you. I . . . I don't know much about legal matters, but I'm sure there are ways to annul a marriage if the attorneys are clever enough. From what I've heard of my great-grandfather, he hired only the best. If you try to renege, you'll end up without a cent. And anyway, I *know* what will happen if I marry Ryder. With you, at least I stand a chance."

"You seem to have everything all worked out." His eyelashes dropped down, shadowing his face as he stared for a moment at the floor. He had seen Ryder around, and disliked him intensely, wondering what there was about his ex-partner's son that attracted Garland Howard. Now at least his curiosity was satisfied. "But I'm afraid you made one small miscalculation. I don't want—or need—your money. Perhaps, if you had something else to offer . . ."

"Something *else?*" Diana was extremely conscious of the way he was looking at her, almost touching, physically, with his gaze.

"You didn't come dressed like that, and reeking of perfume, to stir my gentlemanly instincts. Playing with fire and hoping to win? Or did you have something else in mind? Your lips did show a delightful enthusiasm on the servants' porch in St. Louis. If money won't tempt me, you might offer to follow that ceremony calculated to frazzle any bachelor's nerves with a night of ecstasy beyond my wildest imaginings."

"I'd rot in hell first!"

To her surprise, he threw back his head and laughed.

"At least you're honest. What a refreshing surprise! Beautiful women aren't usually so candid."

" 'Stupid' is more like it," she said ruefully, hating herself for letting him goad her into losing her temper. "I should have agreed—and let you try to collect after the wedding!"

"I'm not a fool, Diana. I would have known what you were up to, and I wouldn't have taken it kindly. Besides, your instincts were right. Honesty is a trait I appreciate—particularly in lovely ladies. I like to see it encouraged."

"You mean . . ." She watched him warily, not sure if he was playing games or if he really meant what he seemed to imply.

"I mean, I would be pleased to marry you."

"Just like that? No more discussion? No negotiations?"

"Just like that."

"But . . . *why?*"

He laughed again. "Don't overplay your hand. Maybe I was only pretending to disdain the money. Maybe there's a gallant cavalier hidden under this rough exterior, and I can't bear the thought of a damsel in distress . . . or maybe I just don't like your father, and I'm looking forward to the expression on his face when he finds out I've stolen his daughter."

"And his daughter's fortune?"

"And her fortune." He got up, not coming closer, but the room was so small he was almost touching her. "I'm not the marrying kind, so a 'wife on paper' isn't an undue hardship. I don't suppose you've taken care of the arrangements? The wheres and whens of this little rite? No, I thought not. Well, then, I suggest you get back to the hotel before your father figures out you're gone, and leave the details to me."

He stepped over to the door, passing so close Diana could feel his breath on her exposed neck and shoulders.

"Unless, of course," he said as he opened the door and moved to the side, "you're having second thoughts. Unless you were secretly hoping for a little more, uh . . . discussion. The negotiations *could* be continued."

"I told you before—"

"I know." His eyes glinted with amusement. "You'd rot in hell first."

Cord Montgomery stared moodily into his glass, catching elusive flashes of gold in the amber-brown liquid. Saloons in that crowded frontier town were open round the clock, but it was heading toward dawn and the rest of the tables were empty. Only a handful of hardened drinkers were propping themselves up along the bar. Somewhere down the street, men were brawling. He could hear their shouts in the back of his consciousness, but here it was so quiet the scraping of his glass sounded unnaturally loud when he pushed it away.

God, she was a pretty little thing. In spite of himself, his mind drifted back to the girl who had paid him such a surprising call a few hours before. There was something strangely haunting about her beauty, evoking raw masculine responses, playing on the male need to feel strong and protective. Sheer innocence perhaps . . . the illusion of fragility in daintily chiseled features and pale wisps of platinum hair, in lips that were a little too round and fantastic, in wide, ingenuous turquoise eyes.

Innocence cloaked in garish orange. That absurd dress! It ought to have looked tasteless and tawdry. Yet somehow, on her, it mingled poignant reminders of extreme youthfulness with a tantalizing promise of maturity, and he had been aware then, as he was now, with a renewed throbbing in his groin, that he desired her.

He was a fool. He tilted his head back, draining the contents of his glass. A damn fool. There were half a dozen other, sensible ways he could have reacted when she told him about that infernal trust her great-grandfather had set up.

He couldn't have left her to Howard's mercies, of course— or that bastard Ryder's. That would have been unthinkable. But a few well-placed inquiries would have located the firm of lawyers handling her trust. He was going to have to do that in any case once they were married. No doubt the lawyers were every bit as efficient as Diana, in that transparent show of bravado, had maintained. They would have seen that she was properly protected. And if a husband had been deemed necessary, they could have found one a hell of a lot more suitable than Ryder.

Or Cord Montgomery.

His lips twisted in the faintest hint of a smile. But that, of course, would have cheated him out of the look on Garland Howard's face when he found out who his new son-in-law was. He pulled a slim black *cigarito* out of his pocket and rolled it absently on the scarred tabletop. And the undeniable pleasure of seeing Howard's lovely young daughter at least one more time. Did she remember, he wondered, that wedding ceremonies always ended with a kiss?

He raised his glass, intending to beckon to the bartender. As he did, he caught sight of a dapper man with a broad-brimmed beaver hat and generous mustache standing in the doorway.

"Cousin Johnny." He waved the man over, shoving one of the chairs out with his foot. "I thought you left yesterday afternoon. Didn't you tell me you were on your way out of town?"

"I was, dear boy. I was." He lounged long-leggedly in the chair, tipping back his hat to reveal a shock of auburn hair, untinged by gray despite the fact that he was twenty years his cousin's senior. "But the best-laid plans, you know. I could hardly disappoint a lady, now, could I? Particularly one as charming as . . . Well, never mind. It was only a slight delay. I'm off at the crack of dawn."

Cord snapped his fingers at the bartender. "Don't you think you're cutting things a little close, coz?"

"Close is my middle name. I've never liked gambling on sure things. At any rate, I've a fast horse and a neat way of dodging trouble. Don't you worry about me, boy. I'll get where I'm going in plenty of time. But what about you? Brooding alone in a saloon at four in the morning, contemplating the world in a whiskey glass, is more my style than yours."

"If it were you, it would be bourbon. And actually, I was contemplating my future." He grinned suddenly, taking an empty glass from the bartender, who had just ambled over, and sending him back for Kentucky's finest instead of the whiskey he had brought. "In a way, I'm sorry you won't be hanging around. It might amuse you, watching your baby cousin hauled up in front of a preacher to say his I dos."

"You're getting married?" The other man's expression did not change, but his shoulders stiffened almost imperceptibly. "I didn't know you were acquainted with any of the beauties in town. May I ask . . . who's the lucky lady?"

"Garland Howard's daughter. The lovely, very devious Diana."

"Garl . . . Damn!"

"My sentiments exactly. Come, cousin, a toast." The bartender had just set a full bottle on the table and shuffled back into the haze of stale smoke over the bar. "And don't look at me like that. I'm not leading her down the garden path. The lady knows the score. Hell, she proposed to me herself. 'Purely business,' as she put it. . . . But you're not filling your glass. Here, let me do it for you. I've never known you to turn down bourbon. Here's to nuptial bliss, whatever the hell that is. And to other things, more sweet."

John Montgomery did not drink, but continued to stare at him, half-curious, half-concerned. Cord, sensing he needed time to adjust to news that had to be disturbing, turned back to the bar, catching the eye of one of the men standing there.

"Slim . . ."

The man who materialized at the table, on remarkably steady legs for someone who had spent several hours in a saloon, was the antithesis of his name. Short and barrel-chested, he gave a squat, solid impression, not fat, but burly, like a man used to brawling.

"Yeah?"

"I've got a little job for you. . . . You've met my cousin John?"

"J. J. Montgomery, at your service." The hat slid back a little farther, the face beneath restored to its customary equanimity. "Pleased to make your acquaintance, Mr. . . . ?"

"Yeah."

"Not an inventive conversationalist," Cord said with a sidelong glance at his cousin. "But a good man to have in your corner. I want you to keep an eye on a certain young lady, Slim. Your employer's daughter. Diana Howard."

"Aw . . . I don' know." Slim's features twisted into a grimace, his face taking on a ruddy hue. "I ain't no good with women. I don' never know what ter say w'en they're around."

"I don't want you to say anything. Just be your usual scintillating self. All you have to do is slouch around the hotel. In the dining room when she's eating, on the veranda when she takes some air, in the hall outside her room at night. Anyone tries to get near her—*anyone!*—they mess with you first. I'm not expecting trouble, but I don't want to take any chances. It's worth a hundred to me . . . and it's just for a couple of days." He crinkled a greenback temptingly. "Starting now."

The two men watched as Slim crumpled the bill into his pocket and headed for the door, moving with strangely cat-like strides. John Montgomery waited until he had gone, then turned to his cousin.

"I don't like the sound of this, Cord. Are you positive you know what you're doing?"

"No. And I don't like the sound of it myself . . . but I'm

going to do it anyway. So all you can do is wish me well and drink to my health.''

''I take it there's no affection between you and the lady?''

''Affection?'' Cord laughed harshly as he jabbed the unlighted *cigarito* between his teeth. ''No, I wouldn't exactly call it that. Lust, on one side at least—maybe the other. But affection? Hell, no.''

There was enough bitterness in his tone to bring concern to the other man's eyes again. The bond ran deep between these two. They were more brothers than cousins, and despite the difference in their ages, friends.

''Hearts heal, boy. Time changes things. You may find a lady you want to marry one day, and it's going to be damned awkward, explaining that you already have a wife.''

''Not likely.'' Cord struck a match, illuminating impassive features in a sudden flare of gold as he lit the *cigarito* and took a deep drag. ''There's only one woman I ever wanted to marry. You know that, cousin. And I couldn't have had her anyway.''

He picked up his glass suddenly, breaking the spell with a grin.

''You're not the only one who doesn't like to gamble on a sure thing. And pretty Diana Howard is the least of my gambles right now. . . . What do you say? To my health?''

''To your health.'' John Montgomery touched his glass to his cousin's, knowing there was no arguing with him when he got like this. Besides, what was there to argue about? Things couldn't get any riskier than they already were . . . and he *had* heard the girl was a beauty. ''And the future.''

Cord raised one brow, appreciating the irony in the other's voice.

''To the future.''

The wedding was to take place in the front room of a small cottage several miles from town. Diana had not seen Cord since that eventful night at the stable, but he had managed to slip her a message, through a stocky man who appeared at her door, telling her when the ceremony would be and where she should meet the carriage he would send.

She had thought she was calm enough when she put on the same modest blue cotton crepe she had worn for her embarrassing confrontation with Randy Blake and slipped around the corner of the hotel. But now, as the hired coach rolled to a stop between rows of pink and white flowers, she felt her stomach contract.

Am I doing the right thing? she thought fleetingly. *Am* I jumping from the stewpot into the fire? But then she remembered that the alternative was to perform this same sacred ritual with the man her father had chosen, and she forced herself out of the carriage and up the path to the door.

Her first thought was that she must be early. The only other person in the room was a stranger, a compactly built man in an extremely well-tailored black broadcloth jacket and pearl-gray trousers hugging slim male legs. He was half-turned away, his beardless jaw and nose strong in profile, his deeply tanned skin setting off thick raven hair, long, but fashionably cut, curling behind his ears and onto his collar.

Just as she was wondering who he was, and whether she ought to be alarmed, he turned. And out of those sun-bronzed features sparkled eyes of startling gray.

"Mr. . . . Montgomery?"

His mouth was fuller than she had imagined, wide and sensuous, the upper lip faintly bowed. Now it was curving at the corners.

"I think, under the circumstances, you might call me Cord. And you needn't stare at me with flattering astonishment. Did you expect me to come to my own wedding unshaven, in a rawhide jacket with spots on the sleeves, smelling of hay?"

"I don't know what I expected," Diana murmured, embarrassed, but unable to take her eyes off him. It occurred to her, idiotically, that he really was quite handsome, and dashing—as if anything so frivolous mattered at a time like this! "Do wagon masters always travel with ascots and beaver hats in their baggage?"

"Fortunately, Independence boasts an excellent haberdasher, and quite a fine tailor, too, who by sheerest coincidence happened to have a bolt of broadcloth suitable for the occasion. But here . . . this is the minister coming toward us through the garden, and his wife and two daughters, who will act as our witnesses. Shall we step out and greet them? I've always had a fancy to be married in the sunshine."

When she didn't respond, he took her hand and tucked it under his elbow.

"Smile nicely, now. And try to cling to my arm like a dutiful bride-to-be."

Diana did not have to try. The lump in her stomach had broken up into butterflies, and her knees were so weak, she couldn't have stood without support. The minister was peering at her benignly from behind gold-rimmed glasses, plying her with questions—her full name, how old she was, where and when she had been born—and somehow she managed to keep her head enough to add a few months to her age when she answered. Then it was Cord's turn, and she heard the same mild voice asking if that was his given name or if it was short for something else.

"Just 'Cord' will do fine," he replied in his deep baritone, with a hint of the drawl she had come to know so well, and suddenly the ceremony was beginning.

A bouquet of flowers, pink and white like the ones lining the drive, appeared from somewhere, and Diana clenched it in one hand while Cord grasped the other with surprising firmness. As if in a fog, she heard the words spoken, the vows repeated, her voice as well as his, though she didn't know where it came from, and a slender gold band was sliding onto her finger.

She was only vaguely aware of the moment the minister stopped speaking, vaguely aware that eyes were watching, twinkling, faces smiling expectantly. Then Cord's hands were on her shoulders, turning her around, sliding down her back, and she realized he was going to kiss her.

He can't, she thought helplessly. He can't! But his lips were already touching hers, not the modest little peck at the edge of her mouth that would have been appropriate, given the situation, but a hard, roguish, thoroughly knowing kiss, as arrogant as that first time, when he had thought she was a whore—and as frighteningly compelling.

Diana tried to resist, but her knees were jelly again and she couldn't move. It would be too hideously embarrassing, with everyone watching! And besides, something in her own lips didn't want to resist. Burning and treacherous, they parted beneath that unexpected onslaught, longing, not for him to stop, but to keep on, probing and challenging, scouring her mouth with his impudent tongue.

She was numb with shock when he finally released her, the sound of his voice a throaty chuckle in her ear.

"You must forgive my wife," he said to the accompaniment of appreciative laughter. "She's so overcome with passion for her bridegroom, I'm afraid it's left her quite speechless."

The mockery in his tone jolted Diana back to reality. Furiously she glowered at him, speechless enough for the moment, though hardly from passion. How dared he? she thought as he took her arm and guided her out to the waiting carriage, the minister and his women following behind with giggles and congratulations. How dared he take advantage of the fact that she couldn't resist him in public? How dared he kiss her like . . . like some possession he had bought and owned!

"You are a dreadful, disgusting man," she hissed as the coach pulled down the drive and they were finally alone.

"Agreed," he said easily. "But at least I'm not boring. Now, turn and wave, sweet . . . one last smile on those pretty pink lips. The minister's gone, but the ladies are still there. We wouldn't want them to suspect the truth."

"I don't care what they suspect! They can't do anything anyhow. It's all over. No one can do anything now."

"No, I suppose not . . . but still, I think we'll swing past the camp instead of heading back to town. The sooner your father learns the jig's up, the sooner he's going to stop his scheming. Besides, as I believe I mentioned before, I'm looking forward to the expression on his face."

The expression on *his* face? Diana's temper flared again. He had stirred her emotions, leaving her in a turmoil, and now he was talking about her father! "You really are a . . . a pig!"

"A *pig?*" To her consternation, he seemed to enjoy it. As if she had just handed him a compliment. "And why is that, pray tell?" He draped his arm carelessly across the back of the seat—almost, but not quite, touching her. "Because I dared to kiss you on the lips? . . . Or because you liked it?"

"You didn't kiss me on the lips. You kissed me *in* the mouth. And I didn't like it. I hated it! It was sickening."

"No . . . it wasn't sickening . . ." He moved his hand, just barely grazing her shoulder, not quite letting himself smile when he saw how hard she pretended not to notice. "You did like it, Irish," he went on, taunting her with the name that had to bring back memories. "You liked it very much. Just as you'd like it if you came to my arms now and let me kiss you again . . . with no one watching this time. There's the fire of a woman beneath those ladylike manners they taught you at finishing school. You just haven't figured it out yet. . . . Or what to do about it.''

Diana felt her body go rigid. His voice was caressing, teasing, playing games he knew she couldn't handle.

"You're forgetting yourself, sir. This is a marriage in name only. I told you I planned to go east immediately, and you agreed. You have no rights to my lips . . . or anything else."

"I'll keep my part of the bargain. I've already booked passage, as a matter of fact, and arranged a chaperone. You leave tomorrow. . . . But tomorrow isn't until *after* tonight." He settled closer on the seat, pinning her against the wall. "You'd be surprised how long—and sweet—a night can be."

"Are you suggesting . . . ?" Diana broke off, confused. She ought to be furious—she knew she should—but the warmth of his body was so close, his hand deceptively gentle on the bare skin at the neck of her dress.

"Why not?" He pitched his voice low, forcing her to lean forward to hear. "You *did* enjoy that kiss . . . as you enjoyed it once before, when I caught you so ungallantly off-guard. Are you remembering the taste of my lips . . . the feel of my hand on your breast? . . . Wondering what it would be like to have me touch you in other places . . . with other parts of my body . . . ?"

Cord was conscious of the softness of her next to him in the carriage, the smell that emanated from her hair, the rise and fall of her bosom as her breath came in little gasps, and what had begun as teasing became earnest with the urgent aching in his groin.

"What would it hurt, Irish? We *are* married. Who better to teach you the mysteries of love—and you *are* going to learn them, sweet, soon—than your own husband?"

"But . . . ." Diana gazed at him with troubled eyes. "You said before . . . you were going to send me away tomorrow . . ."

"I'm not asking for forever, love . . . nor am I willing to give it. I'm only asking for one sweet, beautiful, incredible night." He laughed softly, half to himself, realizing a second before she did that he was not going to get it. "Every bridegroom deserves a wedding night. And every bride."

"Oh." Diana felt as if he had slapped her in the face. She knew she was being foolish, she knew it was irrational—she had set the terms of their relationship herself—but just for one instant she had dared to hope he truly wanted to be her husband.

But all he wanted was to use her for one night—and discard her in the morning!

"You really are a pig."

She turned away, aware of a strange sense of disappointment when he did not try to hold her back, but removed his hand and slid to the far side of the carriage.

I wanted him to stop me, she thought helplessly. I wanted him to reach out and take me in his arms. I *wanted* him to force me to kiss him again . . . and forget everything else.

She stared unseeing at the passing landscape, at fields shivering with knee-high grasses and trees whose names she did not know fringing streams in the distance. She realized suddenly, with intimations of a maturity which had never come to her before, that her feelings for this man were not the superficial feelings of a young girl for a handsome stranger who had caught her eye.

He had not been wrong before. She *had* liked his kisses. She had never felt that way when Jordan kissed her, never longed so completely to surrender, never yearned for the sweet terrifying secrets his lips seemed to promise. If she had, their relationship would not have remained so innocent.

She stole a glance at Cord Montgomery out of the corner of her eye. He was looking straight ahead, seemingly unaware of her, his profile even stronger than it had appeared when she first saw him clean-shaven in the minister's parlor. He's more than handsome, she thought, filled with a sudden inexplicable sadness. There was power in those intensely masculine features, and vitality—and excitement—and it tore her heart apart to think she might never see him again.

This was the man she wanted. This, and not Jordan, whom she had thought she loved so passionately. Jordan had been laughter; Jordan had been adventure and fun, and she had thrilled to the forbidden appeal of his charm. But the hurts of her heart had already begun to heal. This was a man her heart could never forget, and she would have given every cent of her great-grandfather's fortune if he could come, hat in hand, to call on her, the way men called on women they fancied.

"You don't care about me at all, do you?" she said quietly.

There was a strange look on his face as he turned. "If I didn't, I wouldn't have let you draw away from me just now. I do care . . . but not the way you want. Not the way you *think* you want."

Diana looked off again. The fields gave way to more fields, beginning to take on the color of prairie wildflowers, the trees and stream banks to more trees and stream banks. She was aware that she was being perverse. She had asked him for help, and he had obliged her. She had told him, emphatically, that this was to be a marriage in name only, and he had agreed. She had said she wanted to go east, and he very thoughtfully had arranged it. She ought to have been grateful.

But she was more miserable than she had ever been in her life.

It was just dusk as they pulled into the camp. Most of the men were scattered, quieting oxen that had been set to the yoke for the first time, or stretching broad sheets of canvas across the arched bows of newly painted wagons. Garland Howard was standing alongside a temporary fence, speaking with Randall Blake, who seemed to be doing something to the rails. A short distance away, Ryder lounged against one of the posts, tight black pants and a black shirt giving him the unsettlingly feral look of a panther at rest.

Randy looked up at their approach, and Diana—remembering the scene that had passed between them—and knowing he was just waiting for word from her to speak to her father—wished fervently he were someplace else.

"What in blazes?" Garland started over, scowling as he caught sight of his daughter on the seat of the open carriage. "I thought I told you to stay in town. You'll be in the way here. And who—?"

He broke off as the man beside Diana swung down to the ground and turned to face him, features breaking into a slow grin.

" 'Evenin', Howard." His voice took on strains of Texas again—probably to annoy her father, Diana thought. She noticed he seemed to turn it on and off at will.

"The devil, you say! You're dressed mighty fancy for a hired hand."

"I reckon," Cord drawled wickedly. "For a hired hand." Everyone had stopped working, faces from all directions watching curiously. "But just the right duds for a bridegroom. Say hello to your new son-in-law . . . Pop."

The expression on Garland's face was everything Cord had hoped for. Even Diana forgot her trepidations as she stared in fascination. Ryder, surprisingly, seemed unconcerned, almost amused, as if this were just a little setback. But Garland turned ashen, then a deep florid purple, and all he could do was sputter incoherently for several seconds.

"You bastard!" were the first words he managed to spit out. "You damn filthy bastard! What the hell do you think you're doing, sneaking off with my daughter behind my back? . . . Don't you know she's underage? I'll . . . I'll have you in jail. I'll dissolve the marriage—"

"She'll be of age," Cord cut in calmly, "by the time you get the thing to court. *If* you get it to court. I reckon there's some lawyers back east—in Richmond, is it?—would have a few things to say about that."

The color drained out of Garland's face again.

"You know."

"I know . . . and she knows. Did you think she was such a fool, Howard? But, of course, she's your daughter . . ."

"Damn you!" Garland gaped at him, hating this man who stood so smugly in front of him—knowing he'd been outwitted and that there wasn't a thing he could do about it. But at least he could stick the knife in, once, and twist it around. "I should have known. There's only one thing that would induce someone like you to make a laughingstock of himself. And you will be a laughingstock, Montgomery. Marrying a woman for her money is one thing. It's something else to take on another man's brat."

"Another man's brat?"

Something in his voice caught Diana's ear. A faint wariness, and just for a second she couldn't figure out what was going on.

"Didn't she tell you?" Garland's eyes took on a nasty look. "By God . . . that's rich! She's pregnant, Montgomery. My sweet, innocent-looking daughter is going to have a baby—and it sure as hell isn't yours!"

Diana felt as if someone had kicked the air out of her.

That silly lie! She had forgotten all about it. With everything that had happened these past days, it had completely slipped her mind.

"I really don't care." Cord's voice was calm, but she could feel tension in the hard body leaning against the carriage. "Your daughter's innocence—or lack of it—is no concern of mine. Ours is not a conventional union, as you are well aware. I don't care how many children she bears. Or how many fathers they have."

But he does care, Diana thought miserably, as he turned away from the coach, making it clear that she was going to take the long ride back to town by herself. He cared terribly. Not because she was pregnant. Not because of any innocence she might or might not have lost, but because he had been caught off-guard—and everyone knew it. Because he had been embarrassed in front of the others.

Cord Montgomery was an intensely proud man. She settled back in the carriage, struggling desperately to hide her dismay. She had already learned that in the short time she had known him. And proud men did not like being made into "laughingstocks."

Even if she told him the truth now, it would be too late. He would think she had done it on purpose, set him up to play the fool.

If only she had warned him . . . if she had just remembered, and had the sense to *tell* him . . .

She rested her head against the high seat back, wearily closing her eyes as the driver guided the carriage into the gathering darkness. She had felt so close to him that afternoon. She had wanted to feel even closer. She had hoped that someday they would meet again, and things would be different.

A silly daydream perhaps, something that could never be, but now the dream was shattered. Now she was going to have to go back east, as she had claimed she wanted, and pick up the pieces of her life and start again.

6

"**I** ASSUME you realize this changes everything."

Cord's voice was brittle as he stood in the small hotel room and faced the woman who had been his wife for the last four hours. Diana, huddled on the edge of the bed, could only look back at him, searching miserably for some shred of compassion behind the anger in his eyes.

"I know I made a mess of things," she said, bitterly aware that there was nothing she could do. If she let him go on believing she was pregnant, he would hate her for tricking him into marrying him. But if she admitted she'd been lying all along, he would hate her even more for letting him walk into that humiliating scene at the camp. "I'm sorry, the way it turned out, but—"

"It's a little late for 'sorry,' sweetheart. I don't give a damn what you did, or why—or how justified you felt at the time. The past is over. I can't do anything to change it. But I've got a healthy concern for the future. Naturally, this means all bets are off."

"All bets are . . . off?" Diana eyed him nervously. Hadn't he told her father it would take months to get an annulment through the courts—and was he really willing to give up the fortune he professed to disdain?

"We had agreed to go our separate ways after the ceremony," he said curtly. "Obviously, that will be impossible now. Instead of sending you off with a chaperone—who would no doubt have proved inadequate—I'm going to have the rare privilege of bringing my pregnant bride with me to Santa Fe."

"Oh." Diana felt a moment of sheer relief. He wasn't casting her out after all. "I was afraid you meant . . . But why would you want me with you, Cord? I thought you despised me."

" 'Despise' is a mild word. And 'wanting' is hardly how

I would have expressed it. But I'm afraid the rather peculiar terms of your great-grandfather's will leave me no choice.''

"The will?" Somehow, that was the last thing she had expected him to say.

"Surely you haven't forgotten the unique conditions that separate girl children from their brothers. You seemed quite put out about it when you told me. What do you suppose is going to happen if this child you are carrying turns out to be a boy?"

"I don't see . . ." She broke off as it occurred to her suddenly what he was getting at. She *did* see. Lawyers would continue to administer a daughter's inheritance if anything happened to her. But a son would have considerable assets in his own name. "You mean, you think my father might . . ."

"I mean I think your life is in danger. Garland Howard would stop at nothing to get control of old Croftleigh's estate. And that little deception of yours—"

"I didn't deceive you . . . exactly."

"You weren't straight with me, which is the same thing. That little deception put me in peril too. Give birth to a boy, and my life will be worth about as much as yours. So you see, I have to take you with me, not just to protect your hide, but my own as well. Your father may not be the brightest man in the world, but it isn't going to take him long to figure out that he would be the logical guardian if, say, the boy were an orphan."

"Oh . . . my God." Diana stared at him. Was that why Garland had been so complacent about her impending motherhood? "I . . . I didn't think . . . it didn't even *occur* to me . . ." She had thrown out that foolish taunt just to spite him, never realizing what far-reaching consequences it might have. "It was stupid of me to lie like that."

"It was more than stupid," he said, misunderstanding. "It was despicable. I've no doubt you *didn't* think. All you saw was what you wanted—and you set out to get it. And the devil take anyone who got used in the process. I don't like being used, lady."

"That's not altogether fair," she started, but he would not let her go on.

"And I don't like being lied to. Honesty is the only virtue that counts, as far as I'm concerned. You could have 'slipped' a dozen times, with a dozen different men, and I'd

have understood—but I don't understand self-serving lies!''
He laughed harshly. ''Did I tell you, that night in the stable,
how impressed I was with your spirited honesty? That will
teach me to fall for wide-eyed innocence. Innocence, hell!
You're about as innocent as I am.''

He started toward the door, then whirled to face her.

''If there's one thing I hate more than a lying little witch,
it's a lying little witch who asks me to protect her—and then
puts *my* life in jeopardy.''

Diana gasped at the terrible anger that seemed to vibrate
through every taut muscle in his body. ''But surely you can't
believe . . .'' she said weakly. ''I mean, I know my father
would do a great deal to get his hands on my inheritance.
But you're talking about your *life*. And mine! You can't
believe he would actually kill me.''

''Maybe not.'' The rage seemed to cool somewhat, but
his jaw was grim. ''You *are* his daughter. He might have
qualms when it comes to you. But deaths are easy to fake,
and if you didn't cooperate, he could have you locked up
someplace for the rest of your life. That would leave only
one parent—one *legal* parent—to deal with. And he sure as
hell would kill me.''

There was enough conviction in his tone to tell Diana he
meant what he was saying. And she couldn't be sure he was
wrong. She knew so little about her father; she had seen
him only a few times in her life. All she knew was that he
was grasping and arbitrary, and he had never, as far as she
was aware, given a thought to anyone but himself.

Would a man like that be capable of murder?

She glanced up at Cord, still standing at the door. The
real lie was one he knew nothing about, and she realized
unhappily that she was going to have to tell him. It would
be horribly embarrassing—he would be even more contemptuous when he found out what a fool she had been!—
but he had a right to know his life wasn't in danger.

''You don't understand—'' she began, but got no further,
for there was a sharp rap at the door. Cord, who was closest, lifted the latch.

Ryder stood grinning on the threshold.

''I hope I'm not interrupting anything,'' he said with a
leer that implied the opposite. ''I don't usually call on newlyweds, but given the circumstances, I thought you might
not mind.''

"Uh . . . no." Diana got up and went over to stand beside her new husband. "No, that's all right . . ."

Cord cut in sharply, "What do you want, Ryder?"

"Just to offer my congratulations. And to show there are no hard feelings." He extended his hand. "You make a handsome couple. Dark and fair . . . that's something I've always fancied."

His eyes lingered on Diana, making her take an unconscious step closer to Cord. He's looking at me as if I belonged to *him,* she thought, shivering. As if my marriage to someone else is just a minor nuisance he's going to have to work out.

Cord must have sensed it too, for she felt his body stiffen. "I don't shake hands with the likes of you, Ryder. You already know where I stand. You knew it when I refused to sign you on as assistant wagon master after your boss tried to shove you down my throat. Now, if that's all you came for . . ."

"Oh, that's all . . . for now." A slow grin came over his face as he ran his hand through thick dark hair, cut in almost the same fashion as Cord's. "And Howard is my partner, not my boss. If I wanted the job, I'd have had it. . . . Well, I'll be saying good night."

"I'm leaving myself." Cord extricated his arm from Diana's hand, which had somehow become tangled around it. "I wouldn't want you getting the wrong idea, Ryder, so we'll just head out together. Mrs. Montgomery and I have a purely business relationship . . . with no room for fun and games. You can go back to your 'partner' and report that."

Diana sank down on the edge of the bed after they were gone, trying not to remember the insultingly personal way Ryder's eyes had made free with her body. No matter what happened, no matter how disastrously things turned out with Cord, she couldn't regret anything that had saved her from marrying that man. She couldn't imagine *him* stepping out of her room and quietly closing the door.

It was a moment before she even remembered that she hadn't had a chance to tell Cord the truth. The unexpected interruption had driven it out of her mind. She started toward the door, intending to go after him, then hesitated as she realized Ryder might be lingering in the hall.

Besides, there'd be plenty of time in the morning. Cord would probably be back with the first light—if not earlier—

to berate her again for her treachery, and she could speak with him then. Morning would be soon enough.

But in the morning, she didn't have a chance, nor in the days that followed. Not only did Cord refrain from coming to her room, he seemed to be busy all the time, riding to and from the camp, conferring with tradespeople and teamsters, and taking care of so many details at once, he never had a minute to himself.

Diana had not realized how complicated it was, arranging for one extra person, especially when that person was a woman and the wagon master's wife. There was a carriage to be chosen, and a saddle horse for her to ride when she got tired of jouncing on the padded wooden seat, a custom-crafted tent and suitable furnishings—even an entire new wardrobe, for Cord had taken one look at the outfits Rosalie had picked out and pronounced them "utterly preposterous." She couldn't have gotten him off for five minutes by herself, even if she'd wanted to.

And, in truth, she wasn't sure she did. She steered her new horse out of the livery stable into the early-June sunlight, keeping a firm hand on the rein as one of the last of the traders' caravans passed on its way to the Kansas border. He was just the sort of mount she favored, a spirited palomino, barely more than a colt, and skittish, but full of mischief and fun to ride. Not exactly appropriate for a grueling journey, but that late in the season, little horseflesh was available, and the handful of reliable geldings Cord had picked out were already spoken for.

She had honestly intended to level with him. She *would* level with him—but would it really hurt to keep things to herself a little longer? Until they were well under way? He was only bringing her along because he thought she was pregnant and he had to protect her. If she told him now, she'd be left behind.

Wagons rumbled past, heavy wooden wheels a foot wide and man-height in diameter, spewing up a swirl of yellow-ocher. Diana stared at them in fascination. Massive Conestogas, three tons of weight, gouged into the road, obscuring the tracks of a dozen stolid oxen, yoked in pairs. Teamsters swaggered beside them, greenhorns making their first trip and crusty old-timers with gray hair and tobacco-stained beards, cracking their whips to put on a show for the crowds that never failed to materialize when one of the great trains set out.

Interspersed were the lighter dearborns, drawn by mules, with a high seat for the driver in front and canvas stretched taut over bows of Osage orange. Side curtains were open now, but they could be drawn later to provide protection from the sun, and privacy for traders who might use the wagons as sleeping quarters on rainy nights.

Everything was so new, Diana could almost smell the wood and wheel grease. Pristine white covers billowed like seagoing sails in the wind. The gears were freshly painted, a vivid blue; the boxes displayed scenic panels on gaudy grounds of red. Some even had names, as diverse and fanciful as the men who steered them into the sunset. The *Constitution* and the *Prairie Witch,* the *King of Romany* and *Las Tules* and even poor ill-fated *Marie Antoinette.*

And they were all going west. Diana felt a stab of envy. All cutting across sprawling prairies mantled crimson and gold with wildflowers; all stopping at night on the banks of sycamore-studded streams, braving storms and flash floods and attacks by savage, whooping Indians.

Temptation rose with the dust, twining around her heart. Like half the girls her age, she had read and reread Josiah Gregg's spellbinding *Commerce of the Prairies,* falling asleep with it at night, dreaming of exotic worlds beyond the pale of civilization, and thinking how unfair it was that men had all the fun.

It seemed such a great adventure. She could feel the sun reflecting off the earth, the hot alkali wind biting into her cheeks. She could smell the coffee simmering on the fire, taste the first eye-opening sip on a chilly morning. She could see the faint outline of purple mountains, capped with snow, as they grew more distinct day by day on the horizon.

"That's the last of the big caravans. All the major traders except your father are gone now, though we'll probably catch up with them at Council Grove." Randall Blake pulled alongside her on his own horse. Diana made a point of continuing to stare after the train. She had seen Randy only a few times since her hasty marriage, and he was much too polite to say anything, but she knew what he had to be thinking.

"They do look wonderful, don't they? I hadn't imagined the wagons would be quite so big. Or so dazzlingly white."

''Enjoy the illusion while you can. Those 'dazzling' covers will be brown and bedraggled long before they reach Santa Fe, and the wheels will have fallen off so many times, they'll be tied together with buffalo hide. The glamour is all at the beginning.''

''I don't care. It still looks exciting. I've always wondered what it would be like to experience life on the trail.''

''Well, I guess you'll find out,'' he said rather stiffly. ''I thought maybe you were going to stay behind, but it looks like you're coming along.''

''Yes,'' she said noncommittally, ''I guess I am.''

Was she? She stayed where she was for some minutes after Randy had gone and the caravan was a cloud of dust in the distance. It would be such fun, and really, there was nothing for her here. When Jordan died, she had thought her life was over, and in a way it was. The life she had always known—the friends at school, the forbidden forays to the theater—seemed empty and unappealing. But the lure of the west caught her imagination.

And of course . . . Cord would be there.

Not that she cared about that! She pulled the reins sharply, causing the horse to rear. Holding him steady, she started back toward the stable. Cord had made it clear that he wanted as little to do with her as possible. And that was just fine as far as she was concerned!

There had been a few brief moments, in the confusing aftermath of their wedding, when she had fancied there might be something between them. But now, forcing herself to think rationally, she realized she had been silly. She had only been intoxicated by his very expert kisses. He had drawn her out of the numbing shock of Jordan's death, had taught her that she could be attracted to a man again, and for that she was grateful.

But intoxication wore off, and sobriety returned.

No, she was not the least bit tempted by Cord Montgomery. She didn't care if she never saw him again. But just once in her life, she wanted to do something bold and wildly different. Just once, before she settled down and grew old in a rocking chair in front of a window somewhere, she wanted to surrender to the call of adventure.

And she was going to do it.

II

---

*East from
Independence,
June 1846*

7

THE SUN had settled low on the horizon. Deep rays of gold highlighted spring greenery that spilled in tumbled cascades down the steep banks of the creek. Diana slid the first few steps, then looked back, laughing as she caught sight of a small black face quivering with indignation.

"Lawdy, Miz Mon'gomy, you doan 'spect me ter go down *there*. They's snakes there, sho' as my name's Effie. Ah cain't see 'em, but Ah knows they's there."

"Not with all that screeching. If there were, you'd have scared them off!" A brisk wind blew in fits and starts, refreshing after the heat of the day, and Diana was feeling pleased with herself for having followed her instincts and come with the wagon train. "Come on. Don't be such a ninny. There are wild berries all over the place. They'll be perfect for dinner."

"If they ain't snakes, then they's bahrs. Ah done hear 'bout bahrs, Miz Mon'gomy. You ain't gon' ter ketch Effie messin' wid no bahrs."

Diana laughed again. The girl sounded so genuinely terrified. "You might make me believe there are little green snakes slithering through the undergrowth. But bears are great huge creatures, Effie. You won't find a grizzly hiding under a strawberry leaf. Oh, all right. Stay if you want. Just fetch my bonnet—I left it over there on the bank."

"Yas'm, Miz Mon'gomy. Ah's off, Miz Mon'gomy." She scrambled away, so obviously eager to get out of the dreaded descent that Diana could only shake her head. Effie had been an unexpected gift from Cord, not because it was appropriate for a wagon master's wife to have a personal maid, she suspected, but because Rosalie had one—and he seemed to take pleasure in annoying her father.

Certainly the girl had been an extravagance. Cord had had to buy her from an unscrupulous Mississippi slave

trader, and then offer wages, too, since he insisted on giving
her her freedom.

And all for precious little! Diana thought as she watched the
girl search for the bonnet, which was right under her nose.
Except for a surprising ability with hair, Effie couldn't seem to
do anything. But she was an amusing little creature—about of a
height to come up to Diana's nose—and lively enough to be
entertaining when she wasn't working herself into wide-eyed
states over snakes and bears and fearsome "wile In'ians."

"Well, I expect you're as useful as you can be, Effie,"
she said as the girl came scurrying over with the bonnet.
"And I think you might just call me 'ma'am.' It comes a
little easier off the tongue. Besides . . ." She hesitated,
aware that it wasn't the garbled pronunciation that bothered
her, but the uncomfortable idea of sharing a name with a
man who so obviously resented her. "It's much more . . .
What on earth is that?"

She broke off as a long trail of dust appeared on the horizon. Effie followed her gaze calmly.

"Jest sojers. Dragon sojers. They rode pass befo', wen
you was in the tent seein' ter yo' clothes."

"And you were procrastinating so you wouldn't have to
help. Never mind—did anyone say what they're doing here?"

"Not 'sactly. I hear one the men tell they's dragons, gon'
ter Santer Fe. Mist' Hahrd, he doan seem ter lak it much.
Or Mist' Mon'gomy."

"No, I don't suppose they do." Diana remembered having heard talk of a military expedition to Santa Fe that might
ruin the season for the traders. Now she wished she'd listened more closely. "I wonder if this means we're going to
be held back. . . . Well, there's no point worrying about it.
You stay here, Effie—and keep a sharp eye out for bears!
I'm going to see if I can find us some dessert."

She half-stepped, half-slid down the slope, trying not to
jump when she heard a faint rustling. In truth, she had no
more idea than Effie if there were snakes. This was her first
night on the trail. The freighters with their ox teams had
started out three mornings earlier, but Garland Howard and
his womenfolk, enjoying a last brief taste of real beds and
restaurant cooking, had just caught up that afternoon in the
swifter mule-drawn dearborns.

By the time she reached the bottom, her skirt had already
snagged several times on the prickly vegetation. It was one

of the practical garments Cord had chosen, a simple indigo cotton, and relatively comfortable without the petticoats she had removed the instant she arrived in camp and saw her tent already erected. With it she had selected a pale blue India muslin spencer, buttoned down the front, also practical, since Cord had issued orders to the tailor that nothing white was to be allowed.

He had also insisted, to her horror, on outfitting her with several pairs of men's denim trousers. Diana had agreed only because she was too embarrassed to argue in front of the haberdasher, and because it had suddenly occurred to her that she hated being confined to a sidesaddle. Now, as she tucked her skirt up at the waist, baring several inches of shin, she was thinking that pants might have other uses besides riding astride.

"Wat you doin', girl?" Effie was so shocked she forgot herself. "You cain't show yo' lags lak that. Decent folk doan go round hef nekkid."

"Don't be a goose, Effie. The snakes and bears won't mind." She kicked off her slippers and waded into the water. To her delight, bright patches of red showed thick on both sides. "I've never seen so many strawberries in my life. There must be thousands! What a plump, juicy pie we'll have."

"You knows how ter make a *pie?*"

There was enough awe in the girl's voice to bring a faint smile to Diana's lips. Indeed, she did not know how to make a pie, and she rather suspected Rosalie and Tisha didn't either.

"Or maybe strawberries and cream." She scooped the fattest berries into her bonnet, aware of nothing but the lull in the wind and the lazy buzzing of the bees as she filled it to overflowing. She had nearly finished when Effie gave a yelp of alarm.

"*Oh!* Miz Mon'gomy . . ."

"What is it, Effie?" She straightened up, taking care not to drop any of the berries. "Did you spot a bear?"

"Not exactly a bear, ma'am."

Randall Blake's soft southern tones drifted down the sunshine-drenched banks. Diana laughed as she slipped muddy feet into her shoes.

"The way Effie's looking at you, you might as well be. We were just taking a walk—every bone in my body aches after riding all day in the carriage—and I couldn't resist these heavenly strawberries.''

"It's not a good idea to wander off without telling anyone." Randy came partway down the grade, extending a hand to help her. It was he who had remained behind to escort them from Independence, but he had been on his horse, she in a dearborn, and they had spoken barely six words to each other. "Fortunately, Slim—one of the men— saw you and mentioned it. I was tending an ox with a bruised shoulder. I had to leave him to come and find you."

"I'm sorry." Diana snapped the words, irritated less by the scolding than by his rigid formality. "I didn't realize I was putting anyone out. No one explained the rules to me. I suppose you're going to tell me Effie was right and there really are bears and snakes in this gully."

"Bears are the least of your worries. They're more afraid of you than you are of them—unless you have the bad luck to come between a she-bear and her cubs. And snakes aren't a big problem around here." He pulled her to the top, where his horse, a sturdy gray gelding, was contentedly nibbling the tips of fresh shoots of grass. "There aren't any rules. Just common sense. A lot of people are moving around now. Soldiers heading west, traders and their crews . . . adventurers looking for action and not too particular about where they find it. It isn't wise for a lady to wander off by herself."

"I *am* sorry," Diana said, somewhat more contrite. "I really didn't mean to cause any worry. I guess I just didn't think anyone would notice I was gone. Effie . . ." She beckoned to the girl, who was watching openmouthed, hoping fervently that this pleasant-looking young man with the sand-colored hair would talk her impetuous young mistress out of future walks in the wild.

"Yas'm."

"Take these berries back to camp. Run along, now, don't dawdle. And don't spill half of them on the way."

She turned back, hesitating as she saw how intently Randy Blake was watching her. She couldn't know that the exertion of climbing had turned her cheeks a beguiling pink—or the effect the wind created in fair curls tousled almost childishly around her face. But something in his eyes made her aware of how she looked, and she realized suddenly that her skirt was still tucked up, leaving her ankles bare.

No wonder Effie had been so alarmed when he appeared on the bank! Unhitching the fabric, she dropped it abruptly, talking rapidly to cover her embarrassment.

"I'm sure someone will be able to do something with them. The strawberries. . . . I picked them for a pie, but then it occurred to me I don't know *how* to make a pie. I suppose somebody must. The cook maybe. . . . Is there a cook?"

"Of sorts." Randy made an effort to keep his mouth straight. She looked so young, her confusion was so charming, he couldn't help remembering the way he had felt when he spotted her on the veranda of the hotel in Independence. "Wagon trains always have cooks, though the most you can hope for is decent stews and biscuits, and maybe coffee that isn't too vile in the morning. You count yourself blessed if they don't have a stash of liquor hidden at the bottom of one of the flour barrels. Most of the men learn to cook in self-defense. Some of them are pretty good. There's an old skinner, Slim, who makes a kind of crustless pie with a doughy thing on top. He invented it just for wild berries."

"It sounds delicious," Diana said as Randy took the horse's reins and they began to walk side by side toward the camp. "I was afraid we'd have to eat them plain—or with cream. If there *is* cream. I don't even know if we have a milk cow."

Randy nodded. "Montgomery—that is, your husband—got one when he found out . . . well, when he heard Mrs. Howard was expecting. He thought she ought to have fresh milk."

He finished awkwardly, stuffing one hand in his pocket, and Diana, who knew perfectly well he wasn't thinking of Rosalie, felt her heart sink. If he kept on being too polite to speak his mind, and she kept on being too cowardly, there were going to be an awful lot of uncomfortable silences between them.

"Randy . . ." She waited until he had stopped and was facing her, then forced herself to go on. "You must think I'm terrible."

"Uh . . . no," Randy began gamely, but was spared the discomfort of going on by a soldier who had just come around a grove of elms and was reining to a stop beside them.

Diana listened with half an ear as the rider inquired about

the wagon train, which was just settling down for the evening, and Randy answered frankly, telling who they were, what plans they had, and where they were heading.

"He's a lieutenant," he told Diana after the officer had gone and they were walking again. "Seemed like a West Pointer, though I didn't recognize him. He's probably with the First Dragoons. Ben Moore's men. And before you're too impressed, the reason I know all this is that there are just two companies in the area—Moore's and the Missouri Mounted Infantry. I could tell this fellow's a dragoon by the color of his uniform."

"I thought all uniforms were blue."

"They are, but the facing is different. Yellow for a horse soldier, green for the mounted rifles, red for the artillery, light blue for foot soldiers, orange for dragoons. You see what extraordinary information we former soldiers carry around in our heads."

Diana saw what he was doing, and just for an instant she was tempted to go on walking and chatting and forget what she had started before. It would be so much easier to accept Randy's generous chivalry and leave the painful words unsaid. But she liked this young man, and she knew she had used him shabbily.

"You didn't answer me before," she said softly. "*Do* you think I'm terrible?"

He stopped to look down at her.

"I thought maybe you'd changed your mind about asking."

"I thought so too . . . for a minute. But I didn't. I want to know. And you're still evading the question."

"No . . . I don't think you're terrible. I think what you did was wrong, but I understand. You felt you needed a husband. You *did* need a husband—but you should have been honest. Even if Montgomery married you for money, like your father says, he ought to have had the truth about the child. I saw the look on his face when he found out. He was angry. I would have been too."

He was more than angry, Diana thought, shuddering. "And if I'd been honest with *you*—would you have wanted me? Never mind, I don't expect an answer to that. But you're right. I did have to have a husband—only not for the reason you're thinking. If I hadn't found one on my own, my father was going to force me to marry Ryder."

"Ryder?" Randy made no attempt to hide his shock. "The man's an animal! He may dress like a gentleman, and speak like one, but he's more akin to the wolf or coyote. What kind of father . . . ?" He broke off, shaking his head. "But I'm being unfair. Naturally, he was worried about you. He wanted to see you settled, and he wasn't thinking—"

"Oh, he wanted to see me settled, all right. But he most certainly *was* thinking. You see, I'm an heiress—and control of my fortune went directly from attorneys to my husband the day I wedded. My father had a considerable stake in who that husband was."

"Are you saying he would have made you marry *Ryder* just to get his hands on your inheritance?"

"I'm saying precisely that. Cord Montgomery didn't marry me for my money." Diana smiled wearily. "I married *him* for it. And for whatever little peace of mind I have. They would never have left me alone until I gave in."

Randy was silent for a moment, pondering the unexpected ugliness in what she had just told him. "I wonder," he said at last, "that it didn't occur to you to marry the father of your baby."

"I couldn't. He's dead."

"I see."

They covered the rest of the ground to the campsite in silence. Fresh wheel ruts and large patches of earth tamped almost bare gave mute testimony to the many caravans that had passed before, but the Howard party was far enough behind to have the area to itself. Small bands of oxen, turned loose to forage, were scattered around the overgrazed plain, lean, wild-looking beasts with long horns that spoke of Texas origins. Some were still in yoked pairs, but most ranged freely, showing an occasional touch of whimsy, like a horn that had been painted red, or a bit of blue cloth tied to a tail.

They had nearly reached the wagons, which fanned out haphazardly in several directions, when Randy stopped to look down at her. Mules and horses had been tethered at intervals on thirty-foot ropes, and the sound of mallets rang as the last wooden stakes were driven into the ground. Here and there, voices rose sharply, feisty old-timers disputing their staking ground with newcomers who hadn't learned the rules.

"I still think what you did was wrong," he said quietly. "But I *do* understand. And, Diana . . ."

"Yes?"

"You were wrong about me too. If you had told me the truth, I would still have wanted you. I'm sorry you felt you had to lie."

He was smiling gently as he left. Diana, recalling the regret that showed in those kindly features, felt a pang of her own. Had she been wrong not to trust him?

She started toward the central area, where the cook wagon was already bustling with activity. A pungent odor of coffee wafted over the dust and animal smells, the wheel grease and leather, tobacco and sweat, that formed the predominant scent of the camp. Randy would have been wonderfully sympathetic if she had told him the truth, and understanding, as he had been today. But he would still have insisted on doing the honorable thing. And honor, for a man like Randy Blake, would have meant standing up to her father, face-to-face, everything out in the open. He wouldn't have known how to fight dirty if he had to.

No . . . she had done the right thing. The only thing she could. She had turned her fate over to Cord Montgomery, a man who knew how to temper honor with pragmatism.

The camp had been set up in several well-defined sections, as if intentionally separating the men from the traders, and the traders and their women from each other. Diana noticed for the first time that her tent had been pitched in a fairly central area, while Rosalie's was off to the side, well away from everything else. For her father's convenience, she supposed—if he felt the urge to slip in in the middle of the night.

The two dearborns, in which the maids bedded down, were also separated; Diana's, with Effie, was conveniently close to her tent, while the one that sheltered Tisha had been placed in a shadowy space under a grove of elms. Diana, remembering her previous suspicions, felt a moment's queasiness, then brushed it aside. What her father did with his nights was his own business. And what Rosalie tolerated was hers.

Several small fires had been lighted, for they were still in an area with relatively abundant wood, and there was a distinct nip to the twilight air. Cord was standing beside one of them, thumbs looped casually through his gunbelt as he leaned back, listening but not saying anything while Garland and Ryder carried on a conversation with the young lieutenant who had ridden by before.

Had there ever been a man more intensely masculine? In spite of herself, Diana felt her eyes drawn to him. His body, in leg-hugging trousers and high black boots, was as lean as the Texas longhorns, and as powerful. Ryder, beside him, glanced back for an instant, and she was struck once again with how similar they were, these two men with their black-black hair and gray eyes and sinewy male muscles. Both exuded a primal, almost bestial aura, yet one evoked the compelling arrogance of wild mustangs and cats that prowled the soaring peaks, the other the sly craftiness of things lurking in dark wooded nights.

Rosalie, apparently, had spotted the men too, for she sauntered closer, not curious to overhear the conversation, Diana was sure, but because the lieutenant with the high cheekbones and wide clear eyes was exceptionally good-looking.

What a silly, vain creature! Diana felt immensely superior as she turned away. It was one thing to carry on a flirtation with a young man who was falling all over himself to get your attention. It was quite another to wiggle your body in front of someone who hadn't even noticed you were there.

A new scent piqued her nostrils, something sweet and tangy coming from a smaller blaze, a few feet from the cookfire where the coffee was brewing. As she approached, Diana spotted steam rising from a blackened pot, tended by a stocky man with a round face and broad barrel chest. Apparently this was "Slim," for those were definitely strawberries she smelled, and that had to be a cobbler crust on top.

She was not the only one who had been drawn by the sight of this undomestic-looking figure in leather chaps and a dusty bandanna poking and prodding the coals under his culinary creation. On the other side of the fire, a copper-skinned man of indeterminate age and almost total nudity was watching the proceedings in unblinking silence.

Diana laughed out loud. Here, clearly, was one of Effie's "wile In'ians"—and, if she was going to be honest about it, one of the fierce, whooping savages who had sent chills of anticipation down her spine. Either Josiah Gregg and all those other chroniclers had exaggerated, or things had changed on the prairies. It was still going to be an adventure—and doubtless there was some element of danger—but she wasn't quite as brave as she liked to fancy.

"You find the sight amusing, madam."

Cord's voice in her ear made her jump. She hadn't realized he had left the others and come to stand directly behind her. Nor had she realized that she would be quite so conscious of the unsettling masculinity of his presence.

"Yes . . . well, no, not the sight exactly. More myself. The only Indians I've ever seen were in Independence—at a nice safe distance. I thought they'd be wildly primitive on the plains. You know, bodies streaked with war paint and tomahawks dripping blood. I certainly didn't expect to find a warrior in front of the fire, tamely watching some cowboy cook up a pie."

"He's a Kaw—or Kansa—Indian. One of the tamer tribes. They're harmless enough . . . but I wouldn't leave anything lying around if you want to see it again."

"Oh." Diana bristled at the edge of sarcasm in his tone. "Naturally, I don't know anything about the various tribes. The others aren't so harmless?"

"Not by a long shot. The Kaw give us trouble occasionally, or the Osage—they're sly enough to try to get away with a mule or a horse, especially at night, when they think someone else will be blamed. But the real menace comes after we pass Council Grove, which we'll be reaching in six or seven days. That's where we start running into Kiowa and Pawnee."

Diana shivered in spite of herself. "Are they dangerous?"

"Not unless you let down your guard. I've heard of men riding off by themselves and not coming back, but generally even the Pawnee are cowards if they're not cornered. They rarely attack a man unless he's alone and separated from his six-shooter. The Apache, who range south of Santa Fe, are a different story. Apache are mean enough to lay an ambush out of pure spite. And the Comanche . . ."

His voice trailed off as he glanced back at the place where the lieutenant was still talking to Garland Howard. Ryder had gone off someplace, and Randy strolled over to join them.

"Let's just say I hope you don't ever have a chance to find out what the Comanche are like. Of all the tribes on the trail, they're the one the others consider most treacherous. And the only one they fear."

"It sounds like you're afraid of them yourself."

His jaw tightened. "Fear is a stupid emotion. I don't believe in it. It cripples you when you need your wits. But I have a good healthy respect for what the Comanche are capable of . . . and if you come within a hundred miles of one, I hope you do too."

"I'll keep that in mind," Diana replied, hating the way he deliberately made her look foolish for her spontaneous burst of laughter. This was her first time west of Missouri. How could he expect her to know about Indians? "I saw you talking to that young officer over there. The dragoon lieutenant. Is he one of Ben Moore's company on the way to Santa Fe?"

If she hoped to impress him, she was disappointed. He didn't even seem to notice her astuteness. "And points beyond. The 'Army of the West' under Colonel Kearny—General Kearny now—consists of sixteen hundred regular and volunteer troops. Once they raise the American flag over Santa Fe, they'll be heading on to California, maybe Chihuahua. That's Lieutenant Thomas. Paul Thomas. He just gave us the official word. No traders are allowed into those territories until they've been secured. There's some talk that they hope to take Santa Fe without a fight, but we could be stuck cooling our heels for months."

"Are they going to stop us here?"

"It doesn't look like it. They're letting us go on, at least to Council Grove. Some of the caravans may camp there, where it's more comfortable, but I'm for pushing to the banks of the Arkansas, or Bent's Fort if we can. I want to be close to the border when the territory opens up."

Diana watched him curiously. "Why is that important?"

Cord's eyes narrowed as he looked down at her, choosing his words carefully. "I want the other trains to be eating our dust when we roll in. Not just to Santa Fe, but farther on. Once the United States takes over, it's going to be a whole new game. There's a lot of money involved in this venture—but only if we get there first. When the place turns American, so many wagons will come in, they'll have to pave the roads."

"Is there really that much at stake in a trading venture?"

"On this trip, yes."

"But . . . why does that matter to you? I've already of-

fered you half my fortune. You can have more if you want—
I don't care. Surely that's enough.''

''I told you,'' he said coldly, ''I don't want your fortune.
I want *this* fortune, and I'm going to get it.''

Diana clamped her teeth down on her lower lip, exasperated. Just for a second, he had been talking to her like a
human being. Now his voice was dripping with scorn again.
Plainly, she had wounded his ego—though it was just as
plain he didn't give a fig about hers! Out of the corner of
her eye she saw that young Lieutenant Thomas had finally
noticed Rosalie. The other men had left, and he was fussing
with his stirrup, pretending something needed adjustment
so he could get a better look.

''Someone ought to tell him she's a married woman!''

''He's just looking,'' Cord said, coolness dissolving into
a decidedly unpleasant amusement. ''You can't blame the
man for that. If looking—and lusting—were a crime, the
jails would be full.''

''I *don't* blame him. He probably doesn't even know she's
my father's wife. But she does, or ought to! Look at that!''
Rosalie was bending over the fire, not for warmth, but because shimmering flames set highlights dancing in the folds
of a gold silk gown and intensified the brightness of her hair.
''She's preening in front of him like . . . like a peacock!''

''A peacock is a male . . . and the way your stepmother
is preening is distinctly female.'' Gray eyes glittered with
mockery, echoed in the faintly curving corners of his full,
sensuous lips. ''Does it bother you so much that your father
married a young, attractive woman?''

''You find her attractive?''

''I do. Very. Any man would, don't you think?''

''I really wouldn't know,'' Diana lied. Rosalie *was* pretty,
but it was a trashy, obvious prettiness. Pregnancy gave her
a provocative appeal, her waist still slim, her breasts swelling to a size it was impossible not to notice, her hips distinctly womanly, and Diana hated her suddenly, not for the
infatuation in the lieutenant's eyes, but for the way Cord
was looking at her.

''I think she ought to remember she's about to become a
mother,'' she blurted out, ''and not behave like a hussy.''

''Ah,'' he drawled annoyingly. ''And you, of course, are
in a position to judge another woman's character.''

''That's not fair!'' Diana choked back the urge to startle him with the truth about her supposed dalliance with Jordan. It had taken just one day in a dearborn to get her here—it would take one day for him to send her back. And no doubt he would, too! "I made a mistake, and I'm paying for it. Dearly. But the"—she gulped on the words—"the father of my baby loved me and wooed me, and made me love him too. I would never have flaunted myself in front of a stranger. I certainly wouldn't have given him reason to believe I was ready to . . . to offer what married women usually reserve for their husbands. And that *is* what she's doing."

"Maybe," he agreed. "You made a mistake . . . and lied about it. At least your stepmother's honest about what she is. You might stop thinking of yourself for a change and show a little compassion."

"Compassion?"

"She's married to an old man who has no use for her except as an ornament at his dinner table. Or maybe an occasional plaything in bed, though I doubt even that if I'm right about the little serving wench who's got every man in my crew detouring past her wagon. Before you're so quick to judge, try looking at things from her point of view. And remember, you're not without impurities yourself. Good evening, madam."

Diana watched, trembling with anger, as he went over to Rosalie, spoke a few words, then impudently, deliberately, introduced her to Lieutenant Thomas. It didn't help in the least that he was partly right. Rosalie had been almost pleasant these past days—and it couldn't be easy, being the wife of a man like her father. But she had absolutely no morals, and less taste, and the comparison stung, even if Cord did think he had cause.

She started back toward the tent to brush her hair and put on something warmer. Things were obviously going to be more complicated than she had imagined when she decided to come along on this adventure. She had made her peace easily enough with Randy, but Randy was generous, and even though she had hurt him, quick to forgive. It was not going to be so easy making peace with Cord Montgomery.

And if he kept on acting in this patronizing, insufferable, arrogant way, she was not sure she wanted to!

8

THE FAMILIAR CRY of "Catch up" . . .
"*Caaatch* up!" swept with the dawn wind across the plain
as the camp came alive in a flurry of activity. Rough-clad
teamsters, their beards brown with tobacco, plunged into a
milling throng of cattle, struggling to pick out "wheelers"
and "leaders," "swings" and "points," through the swirling dust. Even experienced veterans had trouble identifying
their teams, and the most enterprising had found ways to
mark their oxen, with paint or ribbon or bits of colored rag.
Soon a clang of harness bells joined the wild cacophony,
and jangling yokes and iron chains mingled with the braying
of the mules and the whooping and cursing of the men.

Cord could feel the dust in his nostrils as he sat on a
powerful blood bay and squinted into the dizzying jumble.
A few of the more troublesome pairs were still yoked, as
they would be for some weeks, but most had been unfet-
tered for the first time, and this was the test of how well he
had chosen his crew. Once they were organized, and men
and animals knew each other, he would expect every hand
to have his team in harness in twenty minutes.

"Whoa, Lance! Steady there." He laid a hand on the
bay's neck. Most wagon masters favored mules, or at least
a less skittish gelding, but he liked the stallion's spirit and
speed. "Hold it, boy. Nice and easy."

His eye picked out a young mulatto, Aaron, and in spite
of himself he smiled. The boy was green, but game. He had
caught a burly wheeler by the horns and was manfully trying
to turn it toward the wagons. The animal, its bruised shoulders remembering the weight of the yoke, was pulling just
as hard in the other direction.

The boy almost had him when the ox broke away suddenly, leaving nothing to grab but the tail, which Aaron did
with more valor than wisdom. It was only a second before

he was flipped head over heels in the dust, narrowly missing a trampling as he leapt to his feet again.

Thank God he hadn't started the boy on the mules. If he'd tried that trick with a mule's tail, he'd have nothing to show but a hoofprint on his hindside—when he landed about four states from here! He was going to be all right, young Aaron. He had gotten hold of the horns again, a good grip this time, and was easing the brute over to where one of the older teamsters was waiting to slide it under the yoke.

"Things are looking good." Ryder drew up beside him on the mule he rode while working. His personal mount was in the remuda with the others. "That young Kentuckian isn't taking hold, and it looks like we might have a bottle problem with one of the teamsters. But there's enough man-power to cover if they take French leave."

Cord nodded. He didn't like Ryder, but the man knew his way around a wagon train. "What about that ox with the strained shoulder?"

"Doesn't seem too bad this morning. It's a little tender, but he took the yoke without too much complaining. One of the wheels on wagon three is wobbling. Probably just be the way it's made, but it wouldn't hurt to check it out."

"I'll do that." Cord threw a speculative glance at the lighter wagons, Garland Howard's sporty rockaway and three dearborns—two for the women, one for the maids and luggage—which were hitched and ready to go.

"You might want to change your mind and send the mule teams ahead. They make better time, and it would be more comfortable for the fairer sex not riding in everybody's dust."

"I'm sure the 'fairer sex' will survive," Cord replied dryly. "I may rearrange things later, but right now I want the faster vehicles in the rear."

"Can't say I blame you . . . wanting the little lady where you can keep an eye on her." Ryder's mouth twisted in a slow, unpleasant grin as he shoved back a broad-brimmed black hat ostentatiously banded in silver. "If something like that were mine, I wouldn't let it out of sight either."

"Well, it isn't yours." Cord glared at him coldly, fighting back the bile that rose to his throat. "Let's get something straight, Ryder. Whatever claims you had on your partner's daughter ended when she married me. And for the record,

this is strictly an arrangement of convenience. I have no
desire whatever to keep an eye on the 'little lady.' ''

"So-o-o . . .'' Ryder drawled out the word, making no
effort to hide his amusement. "You *are* sweet on her. I had
wondered. Well, so long, boss man. I'm just going to have
another look at that wheel.''

He rode off without waiting for instructions, without even
asking permission, and Cord felt his temper seethe. It was
the order he would have given, and Ryder knew it, but there
was deliberate insolence in his manner.

He forced his eyes back to the boy, Aaron, who had both
wheelers hitched now and was going for the rest of the team.
It was stupid, letting that comment about Diana get under
his skin, but the man had a way of riling him. Ryder was
by far the ablest member of the crew—by rights, he should
have been assistant instead of the inexperienced Randall
Blake, but Cord was glad now he had followed his first
instinct.

It was midmorning by the time the wagons were ready to
roll. Cord gave the call himself—"Stretch out!"—in a clear
baritone, and wagon after wagon joined a long line to snake
slowly through the blowing gold-green grasses of the Kansas prairie.

Cord felt a little thrill, as always, when he watched one
of the mighty trains pull out. Forty freighters first, still white
enough to gleam in the sun, creaking wheels punctuated by
the sharp *crack-crack* of the whip as oxen leaned into the
yokes. Next the dearborns, and Howard's affected little
rockaway, wedged between the luggage carrier and the cook
wagon. Finally, the herds of support animals—the working
mules and pleasure horses, the *caballado,* or "calf-yard,"
with its several dozen extra oxen—leaving a trail of yellow-
ocher in the cloudless blue behind.

The last man and mule had gone when he flicked the reins
and began to ride slowly up the line, eyeing every vehicle
as he passed, paying particular attention to wagon three.
Ryder had a sharp eye. Problems with wheels were to be
expected later, when the dryness of the plains caused
shrinkage, but this one looked as if it had been improperly
constructed. Apparently Garland Howard had been cutting
corners.

Cord frowned. An occasional wheel on an occasional

wagon wouldn't make much difference. But if it went further than that, there was going to be trouble.

Ordinarily a wagon master spent much of his day ahead of the caravan, scouting out the road and searching for signs of trouble, while his assistant followed in the rear to watch for stragglers and teach greenhorns the ropes. But here, where the trail was well marked, the men unaccustomed to working as a unit, he gave the road only a cursory glance and turned back to make sure everything was all right along the line.

Almost against his will, his eyes sought out Diana's wagon as he passed. She had crawled over the barrier in front and was perched half-in, half-out, trying to engage the driver in conversation. Since the driver was Slim, who distrusted women only slightly less than mules, he wished her luck.

Poor Slim. If he couldn't work with horses, he wanted a team of oxen. Mules and women were taken on only as a favor to the boss man. He was going to earn a fat bonus before the trip was over.

Randy Blake was holding his own when Cord finally reached him. He might be inexperienced, but he learned quickly and his instincts were good. He had already solved one problem with the cook wagon, averted a stampede of mules, and somehow managed to quell a quarrel between two old skinners. After that, a mere flash flood or raging dust storm would be child's play.

"I'm going to take Aaron off the wagons and send him back," Cord told him. "If you need me for anything, he can carry a message. I have better things to do than check on a man who obviously knows what he's about."

"Thanks," Randy said, flushing at the praise.

"Don't thank me." Cord raised the reins, holding them poised for a second. "A man earns his own responsibilities on the trail."

Diana had grown tired of trying to interest Slim in conversation by the time Cord got back, and was walking beside the wagon, darting occasionally into nearby fields to catch up a handful of wildflowers. For all his resolves, Cord found himself slowing his horse to keep pace. She looked so childlike—the minx!—and so preposterously innocent, those little blue blossoms cupped to her nose. If he hadn't known better, he would have thought she was as pure as a little girl, unsullied by a man's hands, and utterly inexperienced in the ways of love.

But the lips that had parted eagerly under his, and the child growing in her belly, spoke differently.

Something hot and urgent throbbed in his groin, and he hated himself for the longing that surged through his veins. She had lied to him. She had lied and used him—and hadn't given a damn as long as she got what she wanted! A man would have to have his brain examined, getting mixed up with someone like that. But when did a man's brain have anything to do with what went on in the lower parts of his body?

Rosalie's carriage passed next. She leaned out petulantly, looking bored and uncomfortable until her eyes lit on him with hints of the same seductiveness that had sent silent invitations to the lieutenant the afternoon before.

Cord was struck, as he glanced from her to the lithe figure in the meadow and back again, by the contrast between the two women. Rosalie, all vivid color and voluptuous curves, her full breasts spilling over the side of the carriage, crying for a man's hands to scoop them up . . . Diana, slender and silvery, nothing but a tinge of color in her cheeks until she looked up and you were caught in the drowning pools of those eyes.

Of the two, Rosalie ought to have been the most provocative, but it was Diana that his eyes kept seeking. Diana that he watched as the wind tugged her skirt, blowing it against her legs, clinging. A glimpse of ankle showed, slim and pale, and he found himself imagining the whiteness of her shins, her knees . . . the lean, shapely curves of firm young thighs . . . the soft nest of downy hair where her legs joined her body . . .

"Damn you for a fool, Montgomery," he muttered, digging his heels into the horse's flanks. He was conscious of the hardness of his body pressing into the hard leather of the saddle as he trotted toward the front of the train. What was it Cousin Johnny used to say? That western saddles were made with horns to remind a man he was a man.

Those prissy English fox hunters in their "pink" jackets didn't need them, he always said. But a randy western cowboy without a saddlehorn would be riding around all day with something else sticking out in front of him.

He didn't stop until he had pulled well ahead of the long

line of wagons. Even then, he paused only briefly to scan the road that stretched out, empty, to the horizon. He was still conscious of the saddle pressing uncomfortably against his swollen manhood. Bitterly conscious of his inability to control the reactions of his own body.

He wasn't in love with her, God knew. He didn't even *like* her. He only wanted her because he couldn't have her. And he couldn't have her because he wasn't about to go crawling to some tent in the middle of the night and play stupid courting games with a woman who had lied to him! He'd be even more of a fool, giving in to his desire, than he was for feeling it. A man had to have some pride.

Only . . . His mouth twisted wryly. Pride didn't do a hell of a lot for the way a man felt in the saddle. He turned to the side, veering off the road to search for someplace with wood and water for the noon break. He had a feeling this was going to be a long trip.

A damn long trip.

Arid days on the trail shaped themselves into a pattern that Diana soon came to recognize. Dressing in the chill half-light of predawn, on the road by six-thirty or seven, eight or nine if the oxen had to be rounded up. Stopping around eleven, "nooning" it was called, a respite for men and animals from the full heat of the sun. Then on again in three or four hours, traveling sometimes until late in the afternoon, sometimes until sunset.

Nooning was an especially important part of the day. A good wagon master chose his spot with care, for cattle that had been well grazed and watered were less likely to wander at night. It was also the time when the crew took their chief meal, and Diana cast more than one envious glance at the wagoners' fire, where the sound of ham sizzling in an iron pan mingled with male camaraderie and boisterous hoots of laughter.

It was their fifth day on the trail, and she was lounging on a buffalo robe beside the dearborn, a lace-edged parasol propped up for shade. Effie had just gone to pick up lunch, and she was sprawled out with a pair of pillows, staring at waves of heat on the horizon and thinking how much more sensible denim pants were than skirts that had to be tucked around one's legs and watched every second in case a breeze came up.

''That sho' is one *fat* rug,'' Effie said, wriggling bare toes through thick buffalo fur as she brought back a plate of grilled bread and salt meat, with the inevitable tinned vegetables and milk Cord insisted be part of her diet. ''That Mist' Mon'gomy, he knows how ter take care o' his wimmen. All Miz Hahrd got is a blanket, an' you kin feel a blade o' grass raht t'rough it.''

''Yes, he does make an impression, doesn't he?'' Diana quipped sarcastically. Effie's eyes were fixed pointedly on a piece of salt beef, and she stabbed it with a fork and held it out. She was beginning to realize that the girl was not as flighty as she seemed. Playing dumb was a good way to get out of extra work, and besides, white folks seemed to expect it. ''But I think he has it in mind to impress my father, not me. Everything Rosalie has, I have to have too, only more and bigger—and fancier. If she weren't along, I probably wouldn't even have a carriage.''

''Well, she is—an' you do,'' Effie said practically. ''Wid nahs fat cushions, lak Miz Rosalie ain't lak ter see, an' a tent what doan leak . . . an' plenty o' buf'lo robes. Doan seem ter me it makes a whole lot o' sense worryin' w'ere it comes from.''

Diana looked at her curiously. With no rain so far, Effie couldn't know whether the tent leaked or not . . . unless she had been talking to Cord. In truth, he had provided for her quite extravagantly. Her carriage was much finer than Rosalie's, her tent almost luxurious, her practical pants and cotton skirts supplemented by a number of surprisingly pretty gowns for evening.

For all his protests, Cord Montgomery had obviously wasted no time getting his hands on her money. Though she had to admit, he seemed to be spending it mostly on her.

They started out again about three in the afternoon, Effie riding in her mistress's carriage, for Tisha had been complaining bitterly about being treated ''like a darky.'' And Effie was complaining almost as bitterly about Tisha's fancy airs—''lak she think mebbe she a lady herse'f!''

Ordinarily, Diana would have taken Pal—her name for the new palomino—for a frisky canter, but she had ridden him most of the morning and felt like a walk. A shallow creek ran between steep banks a few yards from the trail, and she scurried down to follow it.

The stream cut away from the rutted wagon track in

places, twisting through sere banks, with only an occasional scrubby tree, but the sound of hooves and groaning wheels told her she was on course. The air was warm and lazy, the distant clamor of the caravan so low she almost had the feeling she was alone in the world, when she heard something behind her.

More curious than alarmed, she turned. Cord was sliding down the bank, dark features even darker than usual.

"What the devil are you doing here by yourself? I have enough trouble watching for stray mules. Do you think I'm going to ride by your wagon all the time to make sure you're in sight . . . and drop everything if you're not?"

Diana dug the low heels of her boots into the ground and glowered back at him. "Frankly, it didn't occur to me you'd mind if you didn't have to see me for an hour or so." All the good feelings of a moment before evaporated in a burst of irritation. He had already let her know, in no uncertain terms, that he didn't care about her. What business did he have ordering her around? "You did say we wouldn't run into hostile Indians until after we passed Council Grove. And I'm not afraid of snakes."

"The only snakes you need to worry about here are two-legged ones. The rattlers come later—and they warn before they strike. This isn't the grounds of your daddy's fancy St. Louis estate. The last thing I need is some damn fool woman meandering off without telling anyone—"

"I've already had this lecture. From Randy Blake, though he expressed himself a little more courteously. And I didn't *meander* off. I told Slim where I was going and what I'd be doing. And I mentioned the matter to my father when I passed his carriage."

Her father? Cord drew in a sharp breath. Apparently she had forgotten why she was here—though he had to admit she was probably safe enough until the baby was born.

"You told Slim?" he muttered gruffly. "And he said it was all right?"

Diana flashed him an impudent smile. "I don't think he liked it . . . but he couldn't do much about it. To object would have required an entire sentence. Maybe two. Slim never says more than 'Yeah' or 'Nah' when a lady's around, and then only if he's backed into a corner."

"So you figured you'd use that to manipulate him?" Cord tensed his mouth into a hard line, less annoyed by the pretty

duplicity of her smile than his own startlingly intense reaction. Too many nights with a blanket alone on the hard
ground were beginning to get to him. "Is that your tech-
nique? Find a man's weakness and work on it? What was
mine? An overinflated sense of my own *manhood?* It
worked, didn't it? Fluttery lashes and big wide eyes . . . the
picture of helplessness and truth. *Truth?* Hell, lady, I don't
think you'd recognize the truth if it bit you on the nose."

"Don't you?" Diana tried to brush past him, but the bank
was too slippery and she slid back. His hand was on her
arm suddenly, strong fingers gouging into her flesh. The
masculine smell of horses and leather and sweat was in her
nostrils. "I'm not quite as deceitful as you make me out. I
never intended to lie to you . . . I never *wanted* to lie. I
. . . I just didn't mention every little thing—"

"You didn't mention *one* thing—because you were afraid
you wouldn't be able to use me if you did. You were afraid
I'd back off and say 'no deal,' and you'd have to find some
other sucker to give your child a name."

No! Diana longed to cry out. She hated this ugly bitterness between them, hated the things he had to be thinking—
with good enough reason, if they were true. *No, I didn't
tell you about the baby because I forgot . . . and it didn't
matter anyway!* They were five days from Independence.
Was that too far to send her back?

"You keep talking about how *I* lied. How *I* used *you.* But
you aren't any more honest with me."

"What the hell are you talking about?" His eyes darkened warily.

"Ow. You're hurting me." Diana tried to pull away, but
his grip was too tight. "I mean, you're playing at being
wronged. As if this were a real marriage, and you had some
right to expect fidelity. This is strictly a cash arrangement—
which you don't seem to mind as much as you claim. How
dare you demand 'honesty' about my past? You have a past
of your own you've never bothered to mention. Or is that
because you're a man, and passion makes you 'strong' and
'virile' . . . and a woman with the same feelings is a slut?"

"That has nothing to do with it," he grumbled, caught
off-guard by the argument he would have admired under any
other circumstances. "*My* past doesn't include a baby I expect you to raise as your own."

"No, but I'll bet there are plenty of other unsavory details. Your manner toward women isn't exactly chivalrous. You grabbed me from behind—remember?—the first time you saw me. You didn't ask how I felt. You didn't *care*. Nor did you care when you kissed me at the wedding, knowing full well I'd be too embarrassed to slap you in the face. And you accuse *me* of using you?''

"All right, lady, you want honesty, you'll get honesty." Both hands were on her arms now, daring her to move. "I do have a past, and it does include women, but I've always been open about my feelings. If I desire a woman, I let her know. And I don't pretend it's anything else. You're the worst kind of liar, sweetheart. You don't just lie to me . . . you lie to yourself. I *did* ask how you felt. Not in words, but I asked. And you answered." The pressure of his chest was a hard distraction against her bosom, too vulnerable without a chemise beneath her shirt. "What you said was: I want *this.*" He half-lifted her so she was standing on her toes. "I want you."

"Oh." He was so close she could feel the rhythmic flutter of his breath on her lips. "I . . . I didn't . . ." She tried to make her mind work, but everything was a muddle. "I didn't even know you were there . . . that first time. You came from behind—"

"And the next time, in the minister's garden? Ah, but you were embarrassed, with everyone there." He was toying with her lips, almost but not quite touching. "What about this time?"

"This . . . time?"

"I'm not behind you this time. And there's no one watching." He released her arms slowly, hands lingering just a second, then letting go. "Turn and run, if you can, Diana. Say no to me . . . if you can."

He was not holding her any longer, physically, but the spell of his eyes was more than she could resist. Run, Diana told herself helplessly, you *have* to run—but somehow she couldn't.

His mouth came down gently, with an unexpected tenderness that took her breath away, and suddenly her own mouth was parting and his tongue was becoming reacquainted with the warm moist secrets within.

She did not even recognize the little whimpers that came from her throat, nor was she aware of a deep answering groan as Cord lost control and pulled her hungrily into his arms. His mouth turned savage, urgent now, demanding where only seconds before he had been sweetly cajoling. His hands were sliding down her back roughly, claiming each slender, yielding curve, cupping her buttocks, drawing her to the throbbing heat of his groin.

Diana went rigid as she felt something against her belly. She had been sheltered, but she was not naive—she had heard enough from the older girls at school to know what that was . . . and what he wanted to do with it.

"No . . ." she whispered, but it came too late. His hands were caressing her, slipping under the fabric, touching her— inside. There was something fascinating about that hard, very masculine part of him, threatening, but tantalizing, and her body moved of its own accord, arching closer.

Hair tumbled over her shoulders—had he pulled it out of its pins or had it come loose by itself?—and his fingers were finding and unfastening the row of tiny buttons on the front of her blouse. Diana felt the fabric fall open, felt the provocative roughness of callused fingers skillfully evoking responses, felt hardened nipples leap into his palm.

Is this what it's like? she wondered dizzily. Is this what it is to desire—and be desired by—a man? Is this what it is to finally become a woman?

But just as she was sure nothing could keep them apart, just as she was sure she was about to know the sweetness and pain of love, he pulled away. She was conscious first of a warm breeze on her bosom, then of gray eyes gazing down at her.

"So you see, you *were* lying. You did want me to kiss you."

Diana could only stare at him. Was this part of the game, a teasing interlude to prolong the anticipation? Or didn't he want her at all? Had he been making fun of her in the cruelest way possible?

She would never know, for just at that moment a series of shouts came from somewhere nearby. As the sounds drew closer, she made out Cord's name and realized that one of the men had come looking for him.

And if he hadn't, her humiliation would have been complete—one way or the other!

Cord reacted first. Muttering an impatient oath, he pushed her away, shoving her around so her back was to the slope. Her fingers were trembling so badly, she barely managed to do up the buttons on her blouse before a sound of running footsteps reached the bank. Turning, she found herself staring into the startled eyes of the mulatto boy, Aaron.

If she hadn't been so embarrassed, the look on his face would have been priceless.

"I . . . I'm sorry, boss," he stammered as he skidded to a stop halfway down the sandy grade. "I didn't know you was here with the missus. I didn't mean to interr . . . to . . . Aw, shoot! I got worried—Mr. Blake got worried—when we couldn't find neither of the women. He said I'd better come an' look for 'em. I didn't know Miz Montgomery was with you."

"That's all right, Aaron," Cord drawled dryly. "It's just as well you came when you did. That is, uh . . . no wagon master should stay away from his train too long. Wait a minute. You said *both* the women were gone."

"Miz Howard is missing too. I wasn't worried 'bout Miz Montgomery—Slim said she told 'im where she was goin'—but then the other one started walkin' too. She kinda fell behind, and hasn't nobody seen her for a while."

"I see. Well, you escort Mrs. Montgomery back to her wagon. I'm sure you can manage without me, can't you, dear?" His voice was brittle, and Diana sensed he was angry, though whether at her or himself, she could not tell.

"Yes . . . of course."

"Good." He turned his attention back to Aaron, as if he had forgotten she was there. "Tell Blake to ride on ahead and scout a campsite. You take over Mrs. Montgomery's wagon—it's time you learned to handle the mules—and send Slim up to help. I'll keep an eye out for stragglers and look for Mrs. Howard."

Cord waited until they had gone, then started up the hill toward the place where he had looped Lance's reins over a jagged stump. Sweat poured down his face, stinging his eyes and saturating the bandanna around his neck. He knew—as Diana could not—that he hadn't been playing games. He had taken her into his arms, not to teach her a well-deserved lesson, but because he had been unable to hold back his own overwhelming urges.

If the boy hadn't come along when he had, he would have thrown her on the arid earth, torn off those absurdly provocative trousers, and buried the last of his resistance and self-respect inside her.

He found the bay and mounted in an uncharacteristically jerky motion. Damn! She was becoming an obsession. A stupid obsession he couldn't afford. He should have taken the time to find himself a woman in Independence, a nice compliant tart with nothing more on her mind than cash and good times. Maybe if he had . . .

He headed Lance toward the edge of the bank, staying close so he could see down into the shallow gully. His was a male body, with strong male needs—normal needs—that had too long been denied. He was ready for a woman. Every muscle, every nerve, every instinct cried out for a woman's embrace.

But that woman wasn't going to be Garland Howard's lying daughter.

Rosalie was a half-mile down the bank. Perched disconsolately on a rock beside the slender trickle of water, she stared with annoyance at the broken heel of her slipper.

It had hardly been made for walking. She didn't know what had possessed her to try, but Diana seemed to be having so much fun flitting around the fields, and the wagon seat had been so hard. Besides, there was nothing else to do.

She looked up at the sun, a nasty red-orange ball sinking to the horizon. It was so boring sometimes, she wanted to scream. Garland hardly spoke to her anymore. He rode in his own carriage all the time, and hadn't come to her once at night—though she had hoped at first, when she saw where the men were pitching her tent.

But the hopes never materialized, and she was lonely and miserable, sick to death of the heat and dust—and now she had gotten herself lost! Well, they would just have to come and find her. She supposed they would eventually. They could hardly expect her to walk over rough terrain with her shoe like that, and her feet so sore they were beginning to blister.

She untied the kerchief from around her neck—a bandanna, that darkly arrogant wagon master had called it when he gave it to her—and dipped it in the water. A little rivulet of sweat was running down the front of her dress, and she sighed with relief as she loosened the top buttons and dabbed at her cleavage.

She was just beginning to feel better when she had the uncomfortable sensation that someone was watching.

Looking up, she saw Cord Montgomery standing not twenty feet away. White teeth showed almost wolflike through slightly parted lips as his eyes ran slowly down her body, making no effort to pretend he hadn't noticed—and wasn't obviously responding to—her dishabille.

Oh, God. Something cold and sickening ran down her spine as she caught a glimpse of herself in the smoke-gray mirror of those eyes—her bodice open halfway to her waist, her breasts full and heaving in little gasps of panic, skin milk-pale where the sun never touched it. But with the fear came another, unexpected sensation—a sharp stab of pleasure at the admiration in his eyes—and she realized, horrified, that he had seen it.

She clutched her bodice, trying to pull it together. But he had already covered the space between them.

"Leave the dress alone," he said roughly. "You have beautiful breasts, and you know it. . . . And you know I want to see them." His fingers were busy as he spoke, undoing the rest of the buttons, slipping the thin chemise off her shoulders, gripping her wrists when he had finished, so she couldn't pull away. "And you know I'm going to want more."

His eyes were devouring her, insolently making the rounds of first one swollen breast, then the other, reveling in the voluptuous femininity that was emphasized by her condition. His tongue flicked out, unconsciously, wetting his lips.

Like a snake, Rosalie thought, shivering. Sinister and deadly—but exciting too—and she could almost feel it on her breast, licking, teasing the nipple.

"You can't do this," she said, her voice so feeble she could barely hear it herself. "You mustn't." *She* mustn't. She had never been with any man but her husband—and he had satisfied her! It would be the worst kind of sin, committing the act with another.

"Ah, but I can . . . and I must. And so must you." His hands were on his belt, drawing her eyes to the hard mass that stretched the front of his trousers taut. Then he was unbuckling it, and still she could not tear her gaze away. "You looked at me when I rode by your wagon, Rosalie

. . . and you wanted me. The invitation was in your eyes. You want me now.''

"I . . . I was just flirting." She stared helplessly, trying not to look as he released the hard rod of his manhood, trying desperately to think of something to negate the frightening reality of his words. "I always flirt. But I . . . I'm a married woman . . . and I'm expecting a child. You wouldn't want to hurt the baby.''

"I've taken pregnant women before. I know how to be gentle. I will be gentle with you, Rosalie. But I *am* going to have you.''

He was forcing her back, pinning her down on the ground. Wild with fear and self-disgust, Rosalie raised her hands, doubling them into fists to pound against his chest. But somehow they were clutching instead, clawing at his shirt, opening it, while he tugged her skirt over her waist in a hunger that was now mutual and all-consuming.

He had not lied. He was gentle as he penetrated her. But Rosalie was not even aware of it. All she could feel was the hardness of him, the deep thrusting motions, quickening and intensifying, until every corner of her need and loneliness was filled, and she abandoned herself to the sheer pleasure of his lovemaking.

Only later, when he retreated from her body and she was empty again, did the loneliness come back, and the shame. Remorse flooded over her like a vast tidal wave, sweeping everything away as she realized suddenly what she had done.

"I'm not like this," she wailed miserably. "You think I'm an awful harlot . . . but I'm not. I've never been with a man before . . . except my husband." She blushed suddenly, deep crimson hinting at memories too delicate to mention. "You took advantage of me! I was alone and I'm not very strong and you . . . you *made* me do it!''

"No one made you do anything." Amusement gave his rugged features a raffish look as he dampened the bandanna in the stream and wiped glistening beads of sweat from her breast and belly. "And you are *exactly* like this. Which is nothing to be ashamed of, incidentally. You're a woman, with a woman's instincts and a woman's sensual responses. That's nothing to apologize for.''

Rosalie eyed him cautiously. He sounded sincere—those could almost have been compliments—but everything in her extremely rigid upbringing had taught her to believe that men felt differently about women who behaved as she just had.

"I'm not supposed to respond. I . . . I'm not married to you!"

"And I'm not married to you." The cloth was no longer cool, but strangely warming as he continued to rub her body, touching her—everywhere—with an ardor that seemed odd in a man who had just finished with her. "You don't hear me apologizing for anything that went on. Quite the contrary, I'm inclined to gloat. Judging from your reactions, I performed manfully."

"But you don't love me!" she burst out. "You don't even pretend to."

"I don't like pretending. It's a waste of time. People get hurt when you pretend." He stretched out, his body lean and very male beside her. "I *don't* love you, Rosalie . . . but you don't love me either. You gave in to my disgusting advances without one kick or yelp because your body craved the warmth and strength of a man. And I made love to you, sweet hypocrite, because my body craved a woman. Now, shall we battle some more—and I can coax you to yield, or bully you, or force you, if you prefer? Or shall we get down to the business both our bodies crave?"

Rosalie gasped. "You want to do it again?" She could not keep her eyes from drifting down. She half-expected to find him teasing. But to her astonishment, he was hard, and quite unexpectedly large.

He saw her reaction and laughed. "You're married to an old man who spends too many nights in the servants' wagon. Though he must have more life in him than I thought, to bring a flush to those lusty cheeks. What you need is someone who's young enough to take advantage of your very considerable charms."

"I . . . I don't know what you mean . . ." Rosalie tried not to concentrate on his words. She had seen Garland around that trollop Tisha's wagon, but she hadn't wanted to think about it. "I don't see what difference age makes . . ."

"Well, then, I'll have to show you."

He eased his weight on top of her, pressing her down. The soil was gritty against her back, which was naked now, for somehow he had managed to undress her completely. Rosalie sighed as she felt his hands touching and caressing her, preparing her for his entrance.

It was wrong, what she was doing. She knew it was wrong. But it was wrong what Garland was doing too . . . and he had no right to expect fidelity if he wasn't ready to give it.

Then he was inside her, and there was nothing else. Just the hunger of two people who needed but didn't love each other, joined for a moment in sweet forgetfulness.

It was sunset when they reached the spot where the camp had already been set up. Cord had placed Rosalie in front of him in the saddle, and she could feel his strong masculine arms reaching around her, as she knew he could feel every female curving of her body. They had stopped once, with no shelter but waist-high grasses, and made love again, but she could feel the renewal of his desire jabbing impudently into her back.

She tried to look cool as she slipped out of the saddle and hobbled on her broken heel across the empty space in the center of the camp. But every move she made, every subtle inflection of her body, was the sultry languor of a woman who had just been made love to, and thoroughly satisfied. Cord, watching, knew that every man had to have seen. And guessed.

His eyes sought Garland Howard, who was standing next to his carriage, fussing with something on the door.

I've just had your wife, you bastard, he told him, waiting for an answering flare of rage. *I pulled her down in the dirt, without any niceties, and took her like she's never been taken before.*

But there was no anger in the eyes that looked back at him. Only weariness and relief. So, Garland was bored with his wife, as she was growing bored with him. Apparently he didn't even care if her adulteries were a public spectacle.

He threw a glance at Rosalie's tent, barely visible behind a massive freighter at the side of the camp. A nice discreet distance. The irony of it did not escape him. Garland Howard had had his wife's tent placed in an isolated spot so no one would know he wasn't fulfilling his husbandly duties. Now that same isolation would serve as a mask for her lover's visits.

And he *would* be going to her.

He turned his horse toward the outskirts of camp to check on the herds. He would hold her in his arms and whisper endearments if she needed them, and make love again and again. Tonight and tomorrow . . . and every night . . . until his body was so sated he no longer thought of the nymphlike figure who even now must be watching from the door of her tent.

One way or another, he was going to get rid of that damned obsession.

9

A FAINT GRAY haze seeped over the edge of the horizon, dissolving the last dusty remnants of moonlight. Drawn out of her tent by a pungent aroma of coffee, Diana groped through the shadows to the cook wagon, where a fire was spitting yellow sparks into the air. She was finding, rather to her surprise, that she liked the first chill of morning, when the world was just beginning to stir and the sun had not yet put in an appearance.

She was not alone when she reached the fire. The men must have been restless—perhaps apprehensive, though they were still this side of Council Grove—for empty cups had been scattered here and there, and hard-faced cowhands were finishing the last scraps of salt beef and biscuits left over from supper.

A couple of them nodded—an old mule skinner named Nate and the boy, Aaron, who was always friendly—but most kept their eyes pointedly steered in other directions. Plainly, Diana thought as she poured a cup of coffee and hunkered down to savor the heat and bitterness on her tongue, the trail was a man's world, and any woman who ventured too close was asking to be invisible.

She was just draining the last dregs when a moon-faced man appeared.

"Good morning, Slim," she called out, tempting fate.

" 'Mornin', miz," he rumbled back, red-faced.

Diana tried not to smile. It was a compromise, two words instead of his usual one, a token of the improvement in their relationship that had begun when she insisted on learning to drive the mules. Aaron had proved hopeless at the task—tangling the harnesses within minutes, and expanding his vocabulary in the most amazing ways—and she had decided to take things into her own hands. Clearly the boy had no talent for mules. And just as clearly, someone had to learn if Slim was ever to have a break.

He had not exactly been thrilled. Dealing with mules and a woman at the same time was not his idea of a pleasant way to spend the day, but neither was expressing his opinion in words. So he had set his jaw in a grim line, sat beside her on the front seat, folded his arms across his barrel chest, and waited for her to make a fool of herself.

To his surprise, and her own, she had done well. She had always had a firm hand with horses, and she quickly learned that half the battle was holding the mules steady, showing them who was boss. One eye was always on the road, watching for ruts and potholes, the other glued to the harnesses so she wouldn't make Aaron's mistake.

By the end of the afternoon, even Slim had had to concede she was good, and the lessons that followed had included several exchanges which almost passed for conversation. Diana glanced over at him now. He was finishing his coffee as he watched the first of the teamsters head out to round up the oxen.

"Looks like we're going to get off to a good start for a change," she ventured.

"Looks like it," he growled.

Diana was grinning as she went over to the luggage wagon and dragged out the bulky western saddle Cord had given her for Pal. *Three* words. That was something of a record.

She lugged the saddle down and carted it awkwardly to where Pal was still grazing at the end of his tether, though most of the animals had been unstaked. At first, the men had taken care of everything—saddling the horse when she wanted to ride, currying him when she was through, bringing him back to the herd—but driving the mules had given her a new sense of independence, and she took pride in pulling her share.

Besides, keeping busy was a good way to take her mind off what was happening between Cord and Rosalie.

A dull, sick feeling knotted in her stomach as she gazed over at Rosalie's tent, standing alone at the edge of the camp. It was not that she had actually seen Cord slipping in or out. But she *had* seen the way he had looked that day he brought her stepmother back on the front of his saddle.

Not, of course, that she cared. Theirs wasn't a real marriage. It didn't matter in the least what he did.

She hoisted the saddle on the palomino's back, startling him with the abruptness of the motion. He gave a faint snort, and she ran her hand down his neck. She and Cord had a purely business relationship. What he did beyond that was none of her concern!

Adjusting the saddle, she snapped the cinch deftly under the horse's belly. She knew now that he *had* been playing games that afternoon by the stream. And no doubt laughing himself sick at how easy it was to get her to respond. She tightened the cinch with a jerk. If he had transferred his attentions to Rosalie, so much the better. She didn't need the confusing way he made her feel, the sudden spurts of warmth that ran through her veins every time those smoky eyes settled on her.

Let Rosalie worry about it! It was her problem now.

She reached for the bridle, then realized to her annoyance that she had left it in the wagon. She had just started back when she sensed something wrong in the fields.

Turning curiously, she scanned the area with her eyes, but all she could see was oxen milling around, exactly where they belonged. The terrain had grown drier, the grazing less abundant, and it was not uncommon for them to take "French leave," drifting back to the place they had found food and water the night before. Cord had had to send men after them several times, delaying their starts so badly that they would not reach Council Grove until tomorrow.

She was about to head for the wagon when she felt it again. Nothing tangible—just a prickly sensation on the back of her neck. She had been on the trail just long enough to have developed a sixth sense, and her head tilted unconsciously, nostrils flaring, as if sniffing the air for a clue.

It was a second before she realized. Several of the oxen were strangely nervous, hooves pawing the earth, eyes rolling back in their heads. Any second now, they were going to stampede! And if they did, the others would follow, and the mules and the remuda, and they would lose a full day of travel!

Instinctively she raced over to the horse, one hand unhooking his tether while the other reached for the reins. Her foot was halfway to the stirrup when she remembered he was unbridled.

Her heart sinking, she looked back at the cattle. Their restlessness was so clear now, there could be no mistake.

By the worst kind of coincidence, most of the men were on the far side of the camp. Only two were close enough to see what was happening, and they would be as helpless as she, for they were on foot.

It was then that she noticed a mule a short distance away, already saddled, though no one was around. Without stopping to think, she ran over and vaulted onto his back. She had never paid any attention to the oxen—she had no idea how to handle them—but she knew she had to try. No one else could get there in time. If disaster was to be averted, she was going to have to do it herself.

Guiding her mount over to the oxen, she gripped the reins hard, the way she had learned while driving the team. At least he seemed steady, not balky, like the other mules she had worked with. Mercifully, he seemed to know what he was doing, because, God help her, she did not.

Fear rose from somewhere deep in her throat, cold and hot at the same time, as she saw them begin to move in unison, changing from individuals into one great surging mass. Once they became a herd, it would be impossible to stop them.

Instinct taking over, she picked out one that seemed to be the leader and started toward him. She could not have said why. She only knew that if she wanted to stop the others, she had to stop that one. If he went on a rampage, they were sure to follow.

Pressing the mule forward, she tried desperately to force him out in front, hoping to slow the beast until some of the men could get there. The dust was rising in choking puffs—she could hardly breathe, but she had no time to tie her bandanna over her mouth—and it was all she could do to hold her seat on the rough-gaited mule.

He seemed to have a will of his own. No matter how she tried, he refused her commands, holding stubbornly to the side of the steer, which was beginning to break from a trot into a run. Diana's pulse quickened as the thud of hoofbeats turned to thunder on the earth.

He's afraid, she thought helplessly. The ox is so massive, he's afraid, and I'm not going to be able to control him! Then she realized that he was pressing closer, and she understood suddenly what he was doing.

He was trying to turn the steer to the side! Whether by instinct or training, he was edging its head around, arcing its path so it would run itself out in every-contracting circles.

And it was working! Diana's eyes were smarting. She could hardly see, but she could feel him turning, and she knew she had won. The ox was turning—and the others were following!

Suddenly everyone seemed to be there. Through swirling dust, the golden rays of sunrise illuminated lean, hardened features under floppy-brimmed felt. Slim was there on another mule—apparently he hadn't had time to get to the horses either—and young Aaron and Randy Blake.

Cord appeared out of nowhere, drawing up abruptly beside her. Instead of nudging her aside, as she half-expected, he reined his mount in, backing her up, and Diana's heart soared as she realized he was allowing her the triumph of finishing what she had begun.

Her face was streaked with dust and sweat when they finally got the oxen quieted and the men began to sort them into teams. Pulling off her bandanna, she didn't even notice how grimy it was as she mopped it across her brow. Everything was still chaos, but it was organized chaos now, men and animals working together, as if nothing had happened and they were anxious to get on the road. Diana laughed as she saw one of them—an old teamster the others called Deadeye—trying to manage the frisky Pal. Apparently she had commandeered his mount!

Her throat was so dry she could not speak—every muscle in her body screamed with pain—but she had never felt so alive in her life. She had been tested, as only men were usually tested, and she had not been found wanting.

The crew went back to their chores as soon as the animals were yoked and in place. They were used to emergencies and didn't let anything throw them for long. But they found excuses to circle occasionally, giving a nod or a grin—or a rare tip of the hat—to let her know they had seen.

Slim said it for them all.

"You done good, missus," he told her. "*Real* good."

Diana felt a surge of exhilaration. He accepted her. It was a small thing, that spontaneous speech, but it had not come easy, and she appreciated it. They all accepted her! For the first time since she had set out in her prim indigo skirt and stylish cotton spencer, these men accepted her.

She was no longer on the outside. She belonged.

* * *

Diana was quickly to discover that that optimistic assumption was somewhat naive. The west was still the west, men were still men, and ladies stayed in their place. It was not that the crew didn't like her—they stopped to chat sometimes, or point out interesting things along the way, and generally treated her as a kind of mascot—but conversation still ground to a halt when she strolled over to the wagoners' fire, and didn't start again until she was gone.

Obviously, one madcap ride on muleback into a herd of stampeding oxen was not enough to break down barriers it had taken generations to build.

She tilted back the man-style hat that shielded her face and squinted down at the sweeping vista beneath her. They had reached Council Grove—the last outpost of civilization—late the afternoon before, and struck camp on an isolated hilltop, well above the sea of waving grass that stretched west as far as the eye could see.

And well above the masses of other traders who had chosen to camp on the plain. Diana stared in fascination at the bustling scene at the base of the hill. Council Grove had gotten its name because it was here that the agents who surveyed the road—Sibley and Mathers and Reeves—had met with the Indians and worked out a treaty. She doubted they would recognize it now. What had once been wilderness might almost have been a town, the individual camps were crammed so close, one against the other. Except the "buildings" were wagons and tents, the streets dirt paths worn down by the comings and goings of men and horses, oxen and mules, even an occasional dog.

A strip of timber ran along the edge, half a mile wide and verdant with oak and walnut, ash and hickory and elm. The waters of a stream glittered invitingly, frothing white in places, with soap foam, as men jockeyed for space to wash their clothes and lay them on the rocks to dry. Beyond, oxen and mules spread into the grassy meadows, grazing idly or lolling in the shade of large leafy trees.

Diana spotted a number of blue coats among the men coming and going from the stream. The soldiers had been here when they arrived and were still conferring with the traders, but two caravans had pulled out that morning, so apparently they weren't going to be held back.

She scanned them curiously to see if she could pick out

Rosalie's young lieutenant. It was hard to tell at that distance, but two or three tallish ones had their hats at a jaunty tilt. If he *was* here, if he and Rosalie got together—

She broke off abruptly, angry with herself for letting the thought sneak up on her. What Rosalie did—or Cord, for that matter—had nothing to do with her. He was an attractive man; there was no denying the idiotic way her heart leapt into her throat when she saw him, and apparently he was attracted to her too. But at least *he* had the sense not to pursue the attraction!

She strolled back to the camp, which had been laid out in a circular pattern on the hilltop, wagons shaped into a makeshift corral with openings at both ends. If she couldn't join in the camaraderie of the men, at least she was on friendly-enough terms to see what they were doing.

The camp was lively with movement and noise. Though they were to be there for several days, no one was idle. Some of the men were herding animals in and out of the corral, taking them down to graze on the lusher pasturage below. Others must have been felling timber, for Diana could see branchless trunks being dragged up the slopes and stripped of their bark. A metallic clang of hammers rang out, punctuated by occasional whinnies as horses were shod, wagons repaired. Here and there, she spotted men cross-legged on the ground, cleaning rifles and molding bullets, for they were coming into a region of game.

Curious, she ambled over to where Randall Blake was squatting, half-beside, half-under a massive freight wagon, apparently lashing one of the newly hewn trees to the underside.

"What on earth are you doing?" she called out over the sound of hammering, which was even louder here. "Surely we're not going to drag that heavy thing all the way to Santa Fe?"

Sandy eyes lit with pleasure as he looked up and saw her. "Not unless we're exceptionally lucky. This is the last place to get hardwood. From now on, it's all piñon and scrub. When axle trees give, and tongues snap under pressure, we'll be glad enough we laid in a supply for repairs."

"But it looks like you're stowing them under *every* wagon," Diana protested, looking around at the activity that seemed to be taking place all over the camp. "Are we really going to need that many?"

"And more, especially with these vehicles. I don't say your father was cheap exactly—maybe he didn't know any better—but we've had trouble with a couple already, and we're badly overloaded. My guess is, near the Arkansas, we'll start leaving a trail of merchandise behind."

A trail of merchandise. . . . Diana found herself laughing later as she thought about it. It made such an odd picture. She could almost see it—bolts of brightly colored gingham, red and gold and blue, and wooden spice chests and shiny copper pots, all lined up on a parched, empty plain!

"I don't suppose it ever actually happens," she said somewhat wistfully as she stopped to watch Deadeye rub some foul-smelling grease into one of the harnesses. "I mean, there's a lot of money invested in a trader's cargo. I can't imagine anyone just jettisoning it along the way."

He looked up, lively eyes reminding her that his nickname was said to come from his prowess at the business end of a rifle. "Happens all the time," he said cheerfully.

"But surely the traders—"

"Ain't got no brains, the lot of 'em. They pack four tons o' tobacker an' taffety in a wagon's only made t' hold two, an' they think they're gonna git twice the money. They don't." A chuckle came through the brown-stained gray of his beard. *"They git nuthin'!* The wagons break down, an' they have t' leave it behind."

"But some of these men have been going down the Santa Fe Trail for years," Diana persisted. "The first time, they might miscalculate. But after a while, they ought to have more sense."

"Sense an' greed don't mix. An' most of 'em got more o' one than th' other. The farmers, now, they's the worst. You see four-posters sometimes, jist settin' there on th' Oregon Trail—an' big black cookstoves with nuthin' round but the bleached bones o' oxen been driven too hard. But you see plenty you shouldn't on the Turquoise Trail too. You take them men down there." A shot of tobacco arced out in the direction of the camp-city below. "Mebbe four, five of 'em got any sense at all. Mebbe ten—an' then not much. Not like your husband. He's worth the lot of 'em."

"Uh, yes . . . I daresay." Diana could feel him staring at her. She knew the men respected Cord, but most of them had been there when Garland Howard accused him of marrying her for money—and all of them had to know which tent he was sleeping in. "You called this the 'Turquoise Trail,' " she said, changing the subject. "It doesn't look turquoise to me. Green and yellow would be more like it. Or maybe yellow and brown, the way things have been looking."

He chuckled again. "It'll be more brown later. Won't see green till we hit Colorady, an' ain't a whole lot there. They call it the Turquoise Trail 'cause that's what ever'one thinks he's gonna find. Ever' dang-blasted fool sets his foot on this road, the first time, he's got a head full o' fancy stories. Thinks he's gonna find Spanish gold lyin' in the streets, an' Indian silver, an' great chunks o' turquoise."

He made a contemptuous sound with his lips.

"All he gits fer his trouble is a heap o' dust an' some dirty little hovels. Ain't no more riches there fer the takin' 'n anywhere else. Them few what made their fortunes did it the hard way. They carted wagons across the plains an' sold goods fer what they could git . . . an' come back near empty an' started again. The only treasure on the Turquoise Trail is the sweat o' honest work. And the only man gits it is th' one knows what he's doin'."

"None of the stories are true, then?" Diana asked, a little disappointed. Naturally, she hadn't expected gold in the streets, but . . . "Not even *one?*"

"Well, mebbe the legend o' the Mexican silver," he conceded.

"The Mexican silver?"

"Happened fifteen, twenty years ago. 'Bout the time your paw took his first caravan t' Santer Fe. The Mexicans was fightin' each other then. They's always fightin'—cain't jist have a revolution an' git it over, like civ'lized folks—an' they needed the silver fer some troops. Fella name o' Vargas was in charge. A real patriot, they thought—th' only one they trusted. They say he loaded eight, mebbe ten wagons at the mines in Chihuahua an' was headin' up to' join with th' army somewhere south o' San Antone."

He paused, eyes twinkling as he made sure she was listening.

"Didn't never git there."

"You mean . . . the silver was stolen? He was waylaid by bandits?"

"Might o' been. There's plenty o' *bandidos* in those parts'd kill ya fer the fillin's in yer teeth. But it wasn't never seen agin . . . an' Mexican silver comes in bars, with marks on 'em, so they'd be easy t' identify. Could o' been melted down, o' course, but that ain't the way o' bandits. An' this fella Vargas *was* seen. A week later. In San Antone.''

"Oh." Diana's eyes widened as the possibilities occurred to her. "You think he made off with it himself?"

"Mebbe. Mebbe not." Deadeye took a thoughtful chaw on his tobacco, sending another brown arc through the air. "Mebbe he didn't have a chance. He got the bars hid, all right, somewhere in the hills, but even the drivers didn't know where. He'd got rid of 'em first, all but one—and that one met up with a couple o' Comanche before he could talk. Some folks think Vargas was done in by his cronies. Some think he got hisself caught by *bandidos* tryin' t' git back t' the silver. Some think he jist plain died o' shame an it's still there waitin' fer the man is smart enough t' find it.''

Diana was fascinated in spite of herself. This was exactly the kind of story she had wanted to hear.

"You say all this happened around the time my father made his first trip to Mexico?" A sudden unexpected thought jolted into her mind, though common sense told her it was wildly improbable. "Has he heard the legend, do you think?"

"I reckon. Ever'one has. Folks like t' talk sometimes, speculatin' on what it'd be like, diggin' up all that silver. I reckon they'll be all over the place with their picks an' shovels soon as the territory turns American.''

As soon as it turned *American?* The same thing Cord had said, in somewhat different context! Just for a second, the thought didn't seem quite so wild. That would explain what bound them together, these two men who obviously detested each other. And why they were in such a hurry to get where they were going.

But that was preposterous. Even as the suspicion took hold in her mind, Diana realized how silly it was. The story was just a story, after all—it probably wasn't even true.

And even if it were, how could Garland Howard, with no interest in anything Mexican—and not a word of the language—have stumbled on secrets that had eluded heaven-knew-how-many fortune hunters over the years?

It was, in fact, so silly, that she nearly forgot about it.

Early in the evening, the sounds that drifted across the camp told Diana that the men were gathering by their fire.

She had just stopped to warm her hands at another, smaller blaze when she noticed Cord standing by himself, staring at something with a curiously intent expression.

Turning, she saw Rosalie half-leaning against the luggage wagon, a faded crimson gown highlighting the faintly guilty flush on her cheeks. Next to her, bending solicitously so he wouldn't miss a one of those honeyed words, was a tall figure in a blue coat and trousers.

So Lieutenant Thomas *was* here.

Diana tensed as she looked back at Cord, every muscle in her body bracing for the savage rage she was sure she would see. But to her surprise, he seemed almost detached, thumbs hooked loosely through his belt, lips curling, not so much in scorn as amusement—as if he were enjoying the tender scene!

He's so callous, she thought helplessly. Women don't mean a thing to him. He doesn't have any *feelings*. Not even for someone with whom he's been intimate. He can watch her flirt with another man—he can know she's probably going to have an affair with him—and he doesn't feel a *twinge* of regret.

Her eyes drifted back, drawn by a fascination she could not control. Why did it bother her so much, the way Rosalie was behaving? The dress was the only one she wore in the evenings now, the only one that still accommodated her thickening waist—neither she nor Tisha had any skill with a needle—and it clung disgustingly, accenting everything on a body that was already much too obvious.

And Lieutenant Thomas was falling for it, the fool! He was practically tripping over his feet in an effort to play the chivalrous swain, as if this were some lady he was courting, not a silly hussy who was married to another man!

Diana's lips must have been puckering with disdain, for there was an edge of laughter to the voice that broke into her thoughts.

"Still judging your stepmother, I see."

Diana whirled around, bristling as she saw Cord's features twist into the arrogant mockery that always made her see sparks.

"I'm surprised to find *you* taking it so calmly. I know you don't care about her, but that colossal ego of yours must be bleeding buckets. It can't be pleasant, watching your mistress drool over another man. . . . Or are you going to deny you're sleeping with her?''

The amusement drained out of his face. "I'm not going to deny anything. Or confirm it. What I do with my life is no business of yours. You asked for my help, as I recall, and I gave it—though you pulled a few nasty tricks in the bargain. I should think that would satisfy you.''

"It *is* my business, if you insist on making it public. I don't care what you do. It doesn't make a whit of difference to me *where* you spend your nights! But do you have to make sure everyone knows about it?''

"Ah? So that's it. You want to preserve the proprieties.'' He seemed to relax, almost smiling as he moved closer to the fire, his hard masculine body accented by the primitive brightness of the flames. Diana had the uncomfortable feeling that he knew perfectly well she didn't care what anyone thought. "Why is it improper for me to be seen in the company of a lovely lady—while you spend half your day cavorting with Randy Blake? If people are going to talk, wouldn't they as soon talk about one as the other?''

"I . . . Why, I don't *cavort* with Randy Blake! I don't even flirt with him. We go for rides together. He's nice to me, but we're just friends. And I'm certainly not sleeping with him! That makes the difference.''

"Not as far as propriety is concerned. No one has actually *seen* me with Rosalie. All anyone can do is guess. And no one has peeked into your tent in the middle of the night to make sure Randy Blake isn't there. If you wanted to be proper, my dear, you shouldn't have gone for all those long, chummy rides. And you sure as hell shouldn't have gotten yourself pregnant!''

"Why, you—!'' Diana bit her tongue, so angry she almost came out with a few words that would have proved her lack of propriety once and for all. Why did he have to be so maddening? Why couldn't he, just once, try to understand? And why was he so disturbingly attractive? "You're a fine one to talk! You haven't got one decent bone in your body! Don't tell me it was all selfless generosity that prompted you to rescue an heiress by marrying her. . . . And what *are* you doing with my father? There must be dozens of traders who'd pay more for your services! I almost believe the two of you are after the Mexican silver.''

"The Mexican . . . silver?'' He drew in a sharp breath,

but his face remained impassive. "What do you know about that?"

"Just what Deadeye told me." She stared at him curiously, wondering for an instant if she had hit on the truth. "He said it was stolen from some Mexican patriots—they were using it to finance their revolution—and then it was lost . . . and people have been looking for it ever since."

"And you think . . . what? That this 'colossal ego' of mine is challenged by the idea of succeeding where everyone else has failed? . . . Or that I'm a common thief?"

"Well, not common exactly." She forced herself to meet his gaze. "But yes, I do think you'd take something if you wanted it badly enough. And I don't think you'd worry too much who held the legal title."

"Then you don't know the first thing about me, madam." Coldness alternated with a flash of fire in his eyes. "I did *not* marry with an eye toward your inheritance, no matter what you believe. And I would not steal . . . But dammit, woman!" He pulled off his hat, tumbling dark hair on his brow as he slapped it brusquely against the side of his pants. "I didn't come here to quarrel. I came to apologize—which is not one of my favorite pastimes. And to give you a present."

"A . . . present?"

"I dropped it off at your tent. I don't think you'll have any trouble finding it. But . . . what is this? My present appeals . . . but you're not interested in my apology. What a mercenary little creature."

In spite of herself, Diana felt her lips turn up at the corners. It was hard, when he was being amusing like this, and thoughtful, not to like him. But his moods had a way of changing, and she wasn't sure she wanted to be drawn into his web again. "I'm afraid, if apologies are in order, I have to be first in line. I had no right to jump all over you before. Or to glower at Rosalie. I guess . . . well, it isn't very nice, but I guess I was jealous."

"Jealous?" One brow went up, not unkindly, but the implication was clear.

"Of the lieutenant, of course," she said hastily. "What did you think? He's very handsome, and it's obvious he admires Rosalie. I was just being childish because I don't have anyone to fawn over me."

"You have young Blake," he reminded her gently. "And

half the men in camp, though they don't express themselves quite so gallantly. The lieutenant *is* handsome, and he seems a decent sort. But he's not very bright. They make a good couple.''

"Well, then . . .'' Diana's ill will dissolved in a rush of good humor. She didn't dislike her stepmother. In fact, when she wasn't thinking about how Rosalie spent her nights, she almost felt sorry for her. "I wish her well. I hope they run off and live happily ever after."

"I don't suppose that's in the cards. Rosalie's pretty, but she doesn't have any spunk. The most I could wish for her is . . .'' An early widowhood? He caught himself just in time. The man *was* Diana's father. "A comfortable life. And it's I who jumped all over you. Not literally, of course . . . pleasant though the prospect might be.''

Diana sensed the teasing in his tone. "I think we're getting back to apologies again, and I'm intrigued.''

"I daresay you are,'' he replied dryly. "You're not going to let me off easily, are you? Very well, then. I misjudged you, Diana. I made some assumptions I shouldn't have. I thought because of who you were—and some of the things you had done—you were going to be a spoiled brat and make everyone's life miserable. I was wrong.''

"Indeed?'' This was even more intriguing than she had expected. "You may go on if you like—I don't mind hearing more. Not spoiled *and* not a brat?''

"Not a brat, anyway. You don't snivel when it's too hot, or whine when it's cold, and you pitch in and do your share. If anyone else had been master of this train, you'd have had a word of appreciation before now. Especially after the way you stopped that stampede almost single-handed. Of course . . .'' He paused, a rakish look coming into his eye. "You were a damn fool, rushing in like that. You didn't know the first thing about what you were doing—''

"Every greenhorn has to start somewhere.''

"Greenhorns at least have a little coaching. You could have gotten yourself killed. When they told me where you were, I thought I was going to have to come and scrape you off the ground.'' His voice took on a sharp note. Diana was surprised to see a line of sweat on his upper lip. "I swear, if you ever pull a trick like that again, I'll take you over my knee and spank you. But just this time, I have to agree with Slim: you done good, missus. Real good.''

Diana was still basking in the unexpected praise as she started back toward her tent. Things were definitely looking up. She might still be an intruder in that all-male world, but at least the men were willing to chat with her now and then. And Cord was actually being friendly.

It occurred to her that friendship with a man like that might be a lot safer than anything else he had to offer.

She was so engrossed in her thoughts, she completely forgot about the present Cord had promised. But the present had no intention of letting itself be overlooked. Diana heard it even before she saw it. A constant, bewildered, helpless, indignant yelping.

A dog?

She stood in front of the tent staring at a medium-size bundle of wriggling fur tied to a rope that had already become hopelessly tangled, and wondered whether she ought to be amused or exasperated.

He was not, heaven knew, a prepossessing beast. He couldn't have been more than a puppy, and his coat was a mangy yellow and tan. But he looked, beneath that quivering timidity, as if his tail was itching to wag.

At least he'd be company.

Diana squatted down, extending a hand to coax him over. He stopped barking, but pulled back, cringing unexpectedly, and she sensed that he had been abused. She was trying to think of a way to win him over when she noticed that someone had left a can with dinner scraps and a few dry biscuits soaked in bacon grease.

It seemed Cord Montgomery had a heart after all.

10

THE LAND grew increasingly hostile as they left Council Grove. Whole days passed sometimes without a glimpse of a tree, and lunches, and even suppers, were frequently crackers and cold ham, for firewood was scarce.

This was Indian country, the domain of the Kiowa and Pawnee, and the wagons traveled in a tight line, all but Garland Howard's rockaway, the leader now, choking in the dust of the vehicles ahead. There was little danger of daylight raids, but stragglers ran the risk of being cut off, and animals had to be watched so they didn't wander away. Dry alkali winds alternated sometimes with devastating rains, great blinding sheets of water that halted all movement and swelled creeks to rivers, rivers to rushing white torrents.

But mostly it was dry.

Diana ran her tongue across her lips, imagining a big glass of icy well water as she reined in her horse. But water was rationed, and the meager portion she'd receive with her noon meal would be gritty and tepid. Dust lined her lashes, yellowing them slightly and giving a hazy look to the landscape.

"Come on, Buddy," she called. "Here, boy . . . come on, now. I don't want you up there!" Heat brought out the snakes, and piles of rocks on either side were rife with nests of rattlers. Sometimes they came down to sun themselves on the road, and a sharp popping of gunfire sounded occasionally as men in the lead cleared them off. *"Buddy!"*

The dog cocked one mismatched ear and looked disappointed, but came loping back. "Buddy" was hardly the name she would have picked—"Scruffy" would have been more like it—but that was what he'd been called by the old scout who had picked him up with a broken leg in some hovel on the Missouri frontier, and he seemed to recognize it.

Besides, as Cord had pointed out, it went with "Pal."

Surprisingly, Buddy was turning out to be a sociable beast, though he didn't like men, and only occasionally tolerated a scratch behind the ears from Rosalie or Effie. He was strictly a one-woman dog, and from the first grease-soaked bite of biscuit, that woman had been Diana. If he had a fault, it was that he was becoming quite possessive and growled at any man who came close.

"Here we go, boy. That's it. Good Buddy. . . . I'll race you to the wagon."

The caravan was just coming to a halt as they got there. They would be nooning again without wood or water, but it was too hot to go on. Their midday breaks were longer now. It would be five or six before they started again, traveling well past nightfall, midnight if the moon was bright.

As she reached her wagon, Diana saw that the curtains were open, though the sun was scorching on the padded slab where Effie was seated. At night, Cord drew the wagons into a broad oval, corralling the animals inside, with guards posted to watch for Indians, but at noon he was content to tighten the line and make sure the herds were supervised.

The look on Effie's face was so miserable, Diana almost felt guilty. It really was hard on her, this long, hot, dusty journey, but there wasn't much anyone could do about it now.

They had been two men short when they left Council Grove, one an old drunkard who had been too soused to roll out with the rest, the other a gangly, eager-faced lad hungry for the green hills of Kentucky. And one woman— for the homesick Kentuckian had taken Tisha with him.

Briefly Diana had thought that her father would be driven to his wife's tent again, and she hated herself for the little surge of anticipation she couldn't quite control. Every time she thought she had come to terms with her feelings for Cord, something happened to confuse her again.

But instead of turning to Rosalie, Garland had set his sights in another direction, and she had caught him one afternoon studying Effie with a speculative took in his eye.

She had been shocked—and surprised. Effie was a sweet-looking girl, if somewhat plain, and *cafe-au-lait* coloring hinted at indiscretion in her background. But Garland had always despised blacks, ranking them in his warped scale somewhat lower than the brown-skinned Mexicans. She couldn't believe he would even *think* of something like that. And she certainly couldn't permit it.

Swallowing her embarrassment, she had gone to Cord and told him what she feared. To her relief, he had not laughed, but seemed to take her seriously.

"I wouldn't permit it myself," he agreed, "if I thought the girl was being forced. But the camp is swarming with people. We're on alert, especially at night. A cry for help wouldn't go unheeded. I think we have to let her make up her own mind, Diana. She's not a child. Despicable as it might be, the choice is hers."

"*Choice?*" Diana's mouth dropped open. How could anyone be so dense? "I spent too many holidays with relatives on a plantation to believe that. *Their* morals might be rigid, but everyone isn't so particular. All up and down the river, black girls gave birth to babies the color of Effie all the time. And they didn't do it by choice!"

"Effie's not a slave, Diana," he reminded her patiently. "She's a servant. I bought her freedom myself. She got the papers before we left. And she's *my* servant. She doesn't take orders from Garland Howard."

Diana refrained from reminding him that Effie was actually *her* servant. She had bought her, or at least her money had.

"That's all very pretty, but do you really think a piece of paper will make Effie stand up to my father? She's been a slave all her life, Cord. She has a slave's mentality. She's used to doing what she's told. Maybe she's even been told to do *this* and given in for fear of reprisal. You can't expect her to change overnight."

He shot her a look of surprise. "I hadn't thought about it that way. All right, I'll have a talk with your father. . . . No, that would only make things worse. I'll have a talk with the girl. She's a sharp little thing when she's not playing dumb. She'll listen to me, if I have to spell it out in excruciating detail. And I'll make sure her wagon is pulled close to your tent at night. Buddy can bark for two as well as one."

Cord was as good as his word. She had no idea what he said, but Effie stuck to the wagon after that, never venturing anyplace she wasn't visible, not even closing the curtains.

He had also, apparently, told Aaron to keep an eye on

her, which brought out the boy's protective instincts and was turning him into quite the gallant. Diana didn't know if it was a sly move on Cord's part, or just a coincidence, but Effie had definitely dropped her flightiness, and there was a new light in her eyes whenever Aaron was around.

"All right, all right," Diana said, laughing as she reined up and saw the question quivering on the girl's lips. "Go and find your young man. I saw him three or four wagons back, and he didn't look busy."

"Yas'm. I sho' will. Thank you, ma'am."

"Go for a walk if you want. There's plenty of time. But don't stray away from the wagons. If there aren't Indians, you'll step on a rattlesnake!"

And don't, whatever you do, hold hands, she thought with a grin as the girl scurried away, hips swinging unconsciously, setting dust-streaked gingham adrift round her ankles. I don't want to have to worry about your reputation too!

"Not bad. Not bad at all. I like 'em lithe and lean." Ryder's eyes lingered insinuatingly on Diana as she tied her horse to the wagon and dipped into her pocket for a sugar lump. The mangy yellow cur was romping beside her, jumping up and down for attention. "Look at her, Howard—see how she moves. Always a lady, even in those pants . . . but not *too much* of a lady. Who'd have thought anything so pretty would come out of your loins?"

Garland grunted as his eyes reluctantly shifted to the line of wagons behind them. It was hot, and he hated moving. He had been lolling in the rockaway, trying to find a comfortable position, when Ryder had come up to annoy him.

"She takes after her mother," he grumbled grudgingly. "Alice was very pretty, but she had no fire. Bland as milkwater."

"Didn't care much for your first wife, did you?" Ryder made the question deliberately provocative as he bit the end off a cigar and stuck it in his teeth. He was rewarded with a flicker of annoyance before the other man gave it up as too much work.

"No, I can't say I did. It was amusing at first, the way she catered to me, but I tired of it soon enough. Alice was extremely docile. I can't abide docile women." In spite of himself, his eyes continued to follow his daughter, so like her mother in appearance, and yet so different. If Alice had had more spirit . . . "I might have liked her better," he conceded, "if she'd come with the money I expected."

"The money you married her for?"

If Ryder was looking for another rise, he didn't get it. "Damn right—but she came with only the clothes on her back!"

"Like your second wife? You did think Rosalie was provided with a handsome dowry, didn't you?"

"Yes, well . . . her father put one over on me there. I thought he had a nice fat bankbook, and it was just a list of creditors. But then, he thought I was rolling in it too. We put one over on each other, for all the good it did either of us! Rosalie is docile too. No gumption. Spend enough money on her and give her what she wants in bed, and you wouldn't hear a whimper out of her."

"I see why you preferred the other one—the Irish maid with the impudent tongue, which she no doubt knew how to use in other ways too. If I had a choice, I'd have slept in the wagon instead of the marital tent myself." In fact, he *had* slept in the wagon, several times, while Garland snored through the night, and found to his delight that Tisha did indeed know a number of quite remarkable tricks with her tongue. That she had not always liked what he did in return was, he suspected, a good part of why she had deserted her rich patron and run off with a penniless Kentuckian. "She *was* a tempting wench, and prettily put together. . . . Or maybe you like it when pregnancy fills out the hips, and breasts swell like overripe melons."

Garland grunted again, closing his eyes. The conversation was beginning to pall. Rosalie was hardly his favorite subject, or Tisha either. Except for an occasional mild twinge of annoyance, he never even thought about her anymore.

Ryder watched with distaste as the older man rearranged himself on the seat, one eyelid twitching where a fly had landed on it. He was letting himself go fat. Pockets of corpulence settled in his cheeks and neck, in the puffy rounds under his eyes, and his belly slopped over his belt.

Fat men disgusted him, especially the old ones. They reminded him of his father, of the softness and ugliness, the weakness that had been etched in every one of those sagging wrinkles. He had just sat there, a fat, helpless old man, watching everything fall apart, letting himself be used and discarded, like yesterday's trash. He had complained, he had wept, but he had never had the backbone to stand up and demand what was his. And his son had watched, and hated him for it.

And let the hating show.

He clamped his teeth on the unlighted cigar, tasting the strong, slightly sour tobacco in his mouth. He had let the hating show—but if he hadn't, Garland Howard wouldn't be so sure of his blackmail, and he wouldn't be here now.

A burning sensation between his legs reminded him that the daughter was still there. He looked around to see Diana standing in a meager patch of shade. The dog had gone, and she was alone, glancing up at the dearborn, as if she were considering a nap.

The aura of sensuality that always surrounded her was heightened as Ryder imagined her inside, twisting restlessly on matted-up quilts, perspiring like a horse that had been ridden too hard, unable to sleep in the heat.

"Now, that's one sweet picture. You have a hell of a daughter, Howard. I like hot-blooded women . . . and that one's temperature is sizzling. She might have a husband, but he's not taking care of her. She's going to be nice and ready when I crawl into her bed."

"Are you mad?" Garland's eyes snapped open. "Whatever chances you had went up in smoke when Diana figured out what was going on. If she couldn't stand the idea of being your wife, she sure as hell isn't going to become your trollop. Why do you think she arranged that marriage with Montgomery?"

"A marriage of convenience, my friend. And who said anything about a 'trollop'?"

"You bet it was a convenient marriage! Damned convenient—for him. There's a convenient little paper, all signed and sealed in Independence. It'll stand the test of scrutiny."

"I wasn't thinking of disputing the marriage." Ryder's lips twisted, his expression unfathomable, yet sly. "I was thinking . . . the trail is hard on a man. Many who go down it don't come back. Now, if one of those were Cord Montgomery . . . if he were to meet with an unfortunate accident . . ."

"You *are* mad. You think you can take on Montgomery?"

"I'm going to have to take him on sooner or later. The

man is a hired hand. He's well paid for his services, but he's going to want more when the time comes. If the solution to that little dilemma turns out to be permanent . . . well, the lady is going to need another 'protector.' ''

Garland squirmed, suddenly not liking the idea of turning his daughter over to this man, though he wasn't sure why. ''You're a greedy son of a bitch. We stand to make a fortune from this trip, without Diana's money. Isn't that enough?''

''Not as greedy as you. I only stand to pick up ten percent—*if* we hit paydirt. You're looking at the other ninety, and you wouldn't mind a little extra insurance yourself. Don't tell me it hasn't occurred to you that the child she's carrying might be a boy.''

It had. Garland closed his eyes, shutting out the other man's face. He had been thinking of little else since the idea first came to him. But that brought up the problem of Montgomery again, which he didn't want to have to deal with. And, of course, something would have to be done about Diana.

It wasn't that he had any affection for the girl. He never had and never would. But a kind of grudging admiration had come over him lately. It intrigued him, the way she handled herself, the way she tried things women weren't supposed to try, the way she fought for what she wanted, and he liked the idea that she was his.

Not that that would stop him. Nothing stopped him when it came to money. He would do what he had to. But he didn't have to think about it now.

''Why don't we just get where we're going,'' he said, ''and see what we find? It's too damn hot to worry about things that might never happen.''

He tilted his head back, mouth falling open. Ryder's lips curled with contempt as he watched. Flies were all over his lashes now, so thick they looked like kohl. The old fool, he'd go blind before he got back to St. Louis.

If he got back.

He was laughing under his breath as his eyes returned to Diana. She was in the carriage now, leaning out to pull the curtains closed. So she *had* decided to take a nap.

He found himself wondering what it would feel like to be shut up in those stifling shadows with her, to see that creamy body naked . . . what it would be like to do the things he had done with Tisha in the still of night when she couldn't cry out . . . and whether she would dislike it as much.

The heat had intensified, even in the last half-hour. Cord could feel the weight of it pressing on his chest as he crossed an open stretch of land to where the mules were grazing. The constant barking of the dog cut through an almost unnatural stillness. Nothing moved but flies and mosquitoes, and an occasional twitching tail, as every man who could be spared stretched out in the shade of the wagons.

Bad and getting worse, Cord thought with a quick glance at the sky. Great banks of gray had covered the sun that morning, but it was clear by ten, and beastly hot again. Even now, clouds were massing in the north, clinging like giant fungi to the horizon, but the air was stagnant and deathly still. There would be heat lightning soon if this kept up.

He knew he ought to get some rest himself. A man could run only so long on coffee and willpower. The animals were going to be thirsty tonight, everyone's nerves on edge. He'd need his senses if Indians were around.

But he was too restless to sleep.

He headed for one of the mules, who'd been limping slightly that morning. Sleep brought dreams, and his had been disturbing of late, all tangled up with silvery-fair tresses and sweet smells, like wildflowers and perfumed soap. Blast the woman! He thought he'd gotten her out of his mind. He had, for a while, but the feelings were beginning to come back. The unsettling yearnings.

He was conscious as he walked past Rosalie's wagon of eyes staring at him. He didn't turn, but he knew they were there, and he knew they were troubled and questioning.

"You never come to me anymore," she had complained that morning when she managed to get him alone for a few seconds. "We used to be together every night. Sometimes you even slipped into my wagon at noon. Now I hardly see you."

"That's not true," he had said somewhat guiltily. He knew it took all her courage to confront him like that. "I came to you the night before last. And it wasn't for a casual chat."

"Yes, but you only stayed until . . . You only stayed a few minutes. Then you went away again. Are you seeing her too? Is that it? Is that why you've lost interest in me?"

Her? It was a second before he'd realized what she meant.

"I haven't been with anyone since the first time we possessed each other—and I don't expect to. The responsibility for every man and animal on this wagon train is mine. We're in Indian territory, with hardly any water and damned poor pasturage. I have to be alert at night, not indulging myself in feminine arms.''

It had come out a shade too slick, but she hadn't challenged him.

"Then you do still want me? You'll come to me again?''

"I expect I will, darlin' . . . I expect I will.''

And no doubt he would. He found the mule he wanted, and cut it out from the herd. A man's body was a contrary thing. He could spend months on the trail, but let a woman come into the picture, and a week without lovemaking was intolerable. He would go to her, and they would use each other briefly, but she wouldn't satisfy his needs—any more than he satisfied hers. Afterward, she would lie alone in the darkness, thinking not of him, but of a young lieutenant who found excuse after excuse to ride out of his way and see how they were doing.

And he would be thinking of . . . What? Pale strands of silver spilling across the dark, sweat-matted hair on his chest? Pink lips parting to receive the urgent passion of his kisses?

He jammed a bit in the mule's mouth and tied it to a wagon wheel. Dammit, she wasn't even his type! She wasn't at all like the woman who hovered, vaguely, somewhere on the edges of his dreams. Like the black-haired, stately, serene beauty he imagined would one day fill his life.

Like . . . Carla.

Carla. He froze for a second, the leather thong still in his hand, then jerked it tight. He hadn't thought of her for months. She was a part of him, of his soul, his flesh, every breath he took. She always would be. But like his breathing, she had become an unconscious instinct.

Carla. . . . All the emotions came back, sweet, bitter, raging. She had been his first love . . . his *only* love. He could still see her, the way she had looked that first afternoon. The blouse she had been wearing, flowing and white against amber-gold skin . . . the jeweled comb in her hair . . . the jet-darkness of thick curling lashes. She had been gathering roses and had pricked her finger on a thorn, showing a tiny drop of red.

He could remember everything. Every single detail. And he felt again, just for a second, the love that had swept over him then, complete and unquestioning.

He bent abruptly, taking care as he forced the animal's hoof upward. No stone that he could see, but the area was tender. The mule would have to be shod, a nasty job. Only Nate could handle it, if he was willing.

How old had he been then? Thirteen? Fourteen? He had felt so helpless when they brought him, orphaned, to the house of the uncle he had never known. Helpless and vulnerable—and because of that, his young chin had jutted out, his eyes flashing sparks of defiance. His parents had died a short time before, and he remembered being filled with a wild, uncontrollable, irrational anger—as if somehow it was all their fault. As if they had abandoned him on purpose.

His uncle had seemed to understand. He was a tall man, strong enough to be gentle, and he had not tried to force him. But his aunt—his mother's sister—had held out her arms, and he had drawn back, afraid that she would smother him with love. That she would expect him to love her back.

Then Carla had come into the room. Carla with her roses and her little drop of blood.

It had been a hopeless passion. Even then, he had known it. They were first cousins, and she had been nearly five years his senior. His love could never have been requited. But he had not minded. His own love had been enough, and he had begun to hope, to dream, to come alive again, bit by bit.

Then she had left him too.

His heart contracted as the anguish came back. *Black hair, floating on the water.* . . . It had haunted his dreams for months, for years. He thought he had finally driven it away, but here it was, as vivid as ever. Shimmering black, swirling in the current, catching the reflection of the sun, clinging to her arms and shoulders as they pulled her from the water.

They had told him, weeping, that she had been shamed, that a man had used and discarded her cruelly . . . that she had not been able to face the humiliation of a child out of wedlock and had taken her life. They had told him all sorts of things he hadn't understood, and that wouldn't have mattered if he had. All he knew was that Carla had left him, like everyone else he cared about.

She had made him trust her, *love* her, and then she had left him alone.

He had vowed then, with all the tenacious fervor of an adolescent heart, that he would never let himself trust anyone again. Never let himself love.

Perspiration stood out on his forehead, cold even in the heat, as he dragged himself back to the present. His uncle had died soon afterward, his aunt a few months later, and then he had really been alone.

But he had been fifteen then, and able to take care of himself. He had his father's land, and something from his uncle, and he didn't need anyone. He had learned not to need. And he had damned well learned never to open his heart to the hurt of caring.

Now here he was, fifteen years later, longing for a wisp of a girl who was carrying another man's child.

The sweat was pouring from his body, drenching his clothing, by the time he finally untied the mule and signaled one of the men to come and get it. He felt utterly drained, as if every ounce of strength had been sapped from his body. Maybe he *would* lie down for a while. He thought he could sleep now.

He had just started toward a shady spot under one of the wagons when he noticed that the dog, Buddy, was gone. He had been nipping at the heels of the cattle a moment before, making a nuisance of himself. One of the hands must have chased him away.

Better go find him, Cord thought, casting an eye at the nearby rocks. If Buddy tangled with a nest of rattlers, he wasn't likely to come out on the winning end. The dog had formed a strong attachment to his mistress these past couple of weeks, which was just what Cord had hoped. But Diana was forming attachments of her own, and she'd be heartbroken if anything happened to Buddy.

It was even hotter in the back of the dearborn, where Diana drifted in and out of a hazy half-sleep. The drawn curtains had been a mistake. What little air still moved was shut out, making the temperature soar like the inside of a bake oven. But at least she could peel off her shirt and lie half-naked, sweat glistening in a translucent layer over the nipple-peaked hills of her breasts.

Dreams came and went, disjointed and confusing . . . as elusive as the sleep that never quite drew her into its embrace. Cord's face . . . she could see Cord's face . . . moody and mocking, as it had been that afternoon by the stream. She could feel his presence beside her in the shadows, hard and hungry and tantalizingly male.

Was that his hand, brushing damp curls from her brow, lingering a moment, as if to test her response? So real . . . it felt so incredibly real. She sighed as the hand moved gently, now feeling the pulse at the base of her throat, now following the curve of her shoulder.

Her body arched closer, seeking the illusion, and a soft unconscious moan slipped from her lips. She had denied him so long, tried to will away her feelings, but now her mind, half-drugged with sleep, could resist no longer.

Then the hand landed on her breast, and her eyes flew open.

Ryder's evil grin was leering down at her. No dream, but reality. One knee was bent, the other black-booted leg half-dangling out of the wagon as he poised above her in a position that left little doubt of his intent.

"*You?* What the hell are you doing here?"

The language slipped out, learned from years of hanging around stables. Ryder's grin widened. His tongue darted out, running along the edges of his teeth.

"I always knew you weren't a lady. Well, never mind . . . I'm no gentleman myself."

"Obviously not!" Diana struggled to clear her sleep-groggy mind. "You've made your point. Now get out!"

"Not till I've given you what I came for. What we both know you want." His lips were parted lewdly; beads of saliva clung to the corners. "You were almost begging for it when I touched you. You were making little whimpering noises."

Nausea flooded over her. The closeness of him was sickening, the body heat in that stifling place. What had she done with her blouse when she took it off? "You're awful! *Disgusting!* I never gave you any reason to believe I was interested. If I was crying in my sleep, it was . . . it was because I was . . . hot and uncomfortable . . ."

She was groping for the blouse, but he saw it first and tossed it out of reach.

"Those weren't the whimpers of a lady who's uncomfortable. Those were the little bitch sounds a woman makes when she wants a hard one in her. You've had it before . . . and you're panting for it now."

Diana gasped, sick with fear as she realized he believed what he was saying. He actually believed it!

She knew she was being irrational. He couldn't hurt her—all she had to do was cry for help—but just the threat of him, the grossness of his hovering body, was so repulsive, it was all she could do to keep from swooning.

"Do you seriously think I'd *willingly*—"

"Shit, honey, I don't think it, I know it! You practically thrust your hips at me before, you were so eager."

He ground down on her, making sure she felt his erection, savoring the shudder than ran through her body. He wouldn't do what he wanted to her now. He'd give it to her the way he knew she'd like it, make sure she was ready for more tonight. Once, she might cry rape—but twice, and she wouldn't be able to protest. Then he could do anything he wanted.

"Spread your legs, honey," he said hoarsely. "You're gonna love this."

The fear was more than fear now. It was sheer terror. Diana writhed to the side, struggling desperately to get away. She tried to scream, but she saw what she was doing. His hand was over her mouth, hard, suffocating, and she couldn't make the sound come out.

Damn him! Damn this vile, hideous wretch for what he was trying to do to her! She could hardly breathe—he was choking off her air, making her head spin—but she fought with every ounce of strength in her body. If she could just get free, just for a second . . . if she could sink her teeth into his hand . . .

But she never had a chance, for he let go suddenly with a muffled curse. Almost simultaneously, Diana heard an angry snarling.

Stunned, she looked down to see Buddy's jaw clamped like a vise around his booted ankle.

"That damned dog . . ." Drawing his other leg up, Ryder aimed a kick at the animal's head. Just at that moment, a hand came from nowhere, grabbing him roughly, jerking him out of the wagon.

Snatching her blouse, Diana held it over her breasts as she peered out. Ryder was sprawled in the dust, Cord standing over him, glowering down with the blackest rage she had ever seen.

"You goddamned filthy son of a bitch! I ought to kill you with my bare hands." But it was not his hands that threatened, but the heel of his boot, neatly positioned over the other man's Adam's apple. "What the hell do you think you're doing with my wife?"

Ryder's eyes flashed blue-gray fire, but he held back, waiting prudently until the pressure let up. Wriggling out from under, he slapped the dust off his trousers almost coolly.

"Your wife of *convenience*, as you have been at considerable pains to point out. You don't want her, and you haven't been a model of decorum yourself. I shouldn't think it was any of your business what she did. Or with whom."

Cord faced him silently for a moment, a throbbing vein standing out at his temple. "Everything that happens in this caravan is my business. I'm still the wagon master. Any woman who travels with us is under my protection. And any man who forces himself on her answers to me."

"Oh, so you think I was *forcing* her? You think this little romp was against her will?" Ryder's expression changed subtly. He's enjoying this, Diana realized, sickened. He finds it amusing! "Against the dog's maybe . . . but not the lady's. She liked what I was doing. She liked it just fine. And I liked what she was doing back."

For an instant it looked as if Cord's fist was going to smash into his face.

"You think I'm fool enough to believe that, Ryder?"

"What's the matter, boss man? Your ego can't take it? You think she ought to be lying around pining for you while you're off screwing the stepmother? . . . I'd watch it, if I were you, Montgomery. I'm still part owner of this train. I can get rid of you anytime I want."

Cord's face hardened. Diana shivered as his eyes moved slowly, fixing her with a long, unblinking, speculative look. He *can't* believe it! she thought helplessly. He can't believe those awful, disgusting lies!

Then his eyes were back on Ryder. "Not if you want to get to journey's end," he said with quiet control. "I know the territory, I know the language. You can't make it without me. You're the one who's expendable."

"Not if *you* want to see the end of this little venture. If I pull out my wagons now and throw in with the competition . . . well, I don't think you want to see that happen."

Diana looked from one to the other, not quite sure what they were talking about, not caring at the moment. She only knew that Cord's jaw was set, and she had the terrible feeling that the doubts the other man had planted were germinating in his mind.

"Get the hell out of my sight, Ryder," he said wearily. "And stay out of it. You can talk to me about business, but I don't want to hear from you otherwise. I don't even want to know you're here. Mess with me again, I *will* kill you. That's a promise."

His eyes dilated, darkening almost to black as Ryder slithered away, catlike on the balls of his feet. Only then did he turn back to Diana.

She sensed the question in that penetrating gaze.

"I . . . I was asleep," she said hesitantly. "I didn't know he was there. He must have crawled in without my realizing. I just . . . I opened my eyes, and there he was . . ."

"You don't have to do this, Diana." Cord's tone was strangely formal, but not unkind. "You don't owe me any explanations."

But she wanted to explain. She couldn't bear what he was thinking, especially since it was partly her fault. She *had* given him cause to believe she'd been sullied at least once before. And her lips had responded—three times now!— when he kissed her.

"I thought I was dreaming. He must have put his hand on my hair, or maybe that was part of the dream. At least I felt a hand on my hair, and . . . it was so gentle . . . But it wasn't a dream! It was a nightmare. The worst nightmare you can imagine! If Buddy hadn't been there—"

"Shhh, love," Cord cut in, so intent on soothing her that neither of them noticed the unintentional endearment. "Shhhhh. It's all right. Buddy *was* there, and nothing happened. That's a hell of a watchdog." He threw an appreciative glance at the still-alert dog at his feet. "I like your style, Bud old boy."

The canine eyes that glittered back were filled with anything but admiration.

"I'm not sure the feeling is mutual," Diana said with a weak laugh. "I think Buddy was planning on amputating Ryder's foot . . . which would have been an awful mess with no doctor around."

"There are doctors with some of the other caravans," Cord replied dryly. "As a matter of fact, a number of traders were in medicine before they turned to commerce—but I'm not sure I would have sent for one for him." He paused, looking thoughtful. "I don't think Ryder'll try anything again, but just to be on the safe side, I want Effie in your tent at night. You can watch out for each other. And keep Buddy inside."

An unexpected thought occurred to Diana. "That's why you got him, isn't it? So I'd have protection."

"The idea did cross my mind. Especially when I found out he didn't like men."

"And Effie? I wondered why you insisted on bringing her along. She's absolutely hopeless—at everything except arranging hair! I thought it was because Rosalie had a maid, and you wanted to show up my father, but that wasn't it at all. You didn't want me left alone. But *why,* Cord? I thought you hated me. When you heard I had lied—"

"My God, Diana, I never hated you. I was angry, I admit. I hated what you had done, but I didn't hate *you.* Certainly I didn't wish you any harm. Surely you know that by now."

He saw the confusion that misted her eyes, and smiled, but inwardly, so she wouldn't see. If only she knew how far he was from hating her. She looked so innocent, so vulnerable, sitting there with her blouse held up, shielding her small young breasts.

What would she do if he eased it out of her fingers and tossed it aside. If he climbed in beside her and pulled her back on the rumpled blankets that covered the floorboards?

"Ah, Diana . . ." His hand stretched out. Just to touch her, he told himself. On the cheek. Just the lightest touch. But he would never know for sure, because a set of fangs appeared suddenly, bared, backed up by a menacing growl.

He started, then burst out laughing.

"Good dog, Buddy." He withdrew his hand slowly, cautiously. "That's a good boy. You protect your mistress from everyone . . . even me."

He was still laughing as he sauntered away, leaving Diana to pull herself together in the wagon.

"Especially me, old boy. *Especially* me."

11

THE AIR was still again an hour after dusk. The last of the clouds had blown past, and a full moon cast deep blue shadows across the plain. The silence was so heavy, Cord felt he could almost reach out and touch it.

Everyone always talked about the calm before the storm. No one ever said anything about the eerie calm that came after.

His eye ran over the landscape, assessing the damage. The violence had been swift, the devastation so complete it looked as if a marauding army had passed through. Trees were down everywhere, some cleaved in two by bolts of lightning, others torn from the earth, lying like prehistoric beasts on their sides, massive root structures jutting jagged-edged into the sky.

There were two kinds of men: the kind who hated storms, and feared them, and looked for someplace to hide—and the kind who reveled in the challenge. Cord had always been one of the latter. There was something awesome and exciting about nature at its most savage, a wildness that made a man feel more alive and showed him who he was.

No, there were *three* kinds of men, he admitted grudgingly. Garland Howard has been frightened out of his wits. His skin had turned pasty, eyes glittering like little beads in a sea of puffy pallor, but he had worked beside the others, fighting back his fear.

It was the first time Cord had had the slightest admiration for him. It made him uncomfortable somehow, these little surprises. Who would have thought the man had hidden resources of courage?

Not like his daughter, though.

Cord laughed aloud, enjoying the brittle sound on the crisp air. Diana had been magnificent. She should have been terrified. Women turned into flighty butterflies at the first sign of a storm. She should have been cowering in one of the wagons, like Rosalie and poor little Effie, a blanket clutched over her head.

But not her! The memory surged through him, a keen physical sensation. The rain had been fierce, drumming the earth, drowning out everything but ear-splitting claps of thunder, and lightning flared in great forked streaks. Violent gusts of wind had caught her hair, streaming it out like banners around her, lashing it back, sometimes with the force of a whip, but she had grabbed one of the lead yokes of oxen and held her own with the teamster on the other side.

He had had one bad moment when he had seen her glance toward a nearby cottonwood, thinking she intended to shelter them there. But either she knew better, or the teamster did, for they had turned to a shallow gully instead, bullying them down a second before the lightning he had feared demolished the tree. He had not had time to dwell on it, for a crew was struggling with one of the wagons, laboriously sliding it down the slope, and he had scrambled over to help.

The storm had lasted only an hour, perhaps two—time was impossible to judge in that madness of heart-stopping, hammering noise—but when it was over, a litter of wagons was splayed across the earth. Mud-drenched canvas and broken wheels . . . trunks split open . . . massive wooden crates . . . bolts of calico and satin, unwound by the wind, their gaudy colors incongruous, like a trail of wounded tropical birds.

Five wagons lost, Cord guessed—with a good part of their merchandise. Maybe six or seven. Bad, but it could have been worse. Some of the cattle had stampeded in terror, but they were still in yoke, and men had been sent to find them.

Ryder came toward him on foot.

"Strictly business, boss," he called out, holding up one hand with only a hint of sarcasm. "I'll take you on some other time, but right now I'm too dog-tired to fight. Dead-eye spotted the missing oxen. They're in a ravine about half a mile back. I sent Slim to help him bed them down. No point trying to get them back tonight."

"What about the wagons? Had a chance to count them?"

"Five smashed, five more with damage, though we might be able to salvage a couple. With a little reloading, we ought to get most of the goods to Pawnee Rock. We can sell the excess at a loss—if the other traders weren't hit too bad.''

''And if their wagons are sturdier than ours,'' Cord replied glumly. He had known it meant trouble, those damn shortcuts Howard had taken.

''They are. I posted men along the gully, two shifts, half the night each. Haven't seen any sign of Indians, but that doesn't mean they aren't around. I'll take the first watch. You can spell me.''

Cord did not remind him as he strode off, cocky despite his exhaustion, that he hadn't waited for orders. He was too weary himself not to appreciate efficiency. Ryder knew what he was doing, all right. He'd have made a damned fine trader, if he'd been inclined toward honest work.

Cord slid down the bank to where the wagons were arranged, moon-brightened billows of canvas, like schooners lined up in port. Time enough to worry about getting them out in the morning. One of the freighters had been wedged under a slight overhang, and he saw Randy Blake pause beside it, stooping to speak to someone beneath.

Diana? He scowled unconsciously. That relationship shouldn't be encouraged. The boy was plainly infatuated and was bound to get hurt. But at least he'd found shelter for her and was seeing that she took care of herself.

Cord located the supply wagon where he kept his bedroll and extra clothes, and pulled out a dry shirt and pants. There were a thousand things that had to be done, details that needed to be worked out, arrangements to be made, but his thoughts kept drifting back to *her*.

He stripped naked in the moonlight, muscles rippling, skin tingling in the faint breeze that had just come up. God, but she was incredible! He had just caught a glimpse of her after the storm. Her eyes had been shining, her head tilted up, nostrils flaring like a Kentucky thoroughbred scenting the air, and he had known as he looked at her that the expression on her face mirrored his.

There had been no fear in her, as there was none in him. There had been no time for fear. She felt only the sheer exhilaration of having dared the storm and fought back—and come out a winner.

He was proud of her. He had no right to be. He had had no part in building her character; nothing that had happened tonight had had anything to do with him. She was not his

wife in anything but name. But he was proud, and he felt
an urge to tell her so.

He grabbed a dry blanket and headed impulsively for the
freighter. Holding it in one hand, he braced the other against
the rain-slippery side and leaned down.

"You done good, missus," he said. "Real good."

Diana looked up, surprised at the sound of his voice. She
was nestled on a pile of blankets at the far side of the wagon,
next to the overhang, which offered partial shelter.

"I thought you told me if I ever played teamster again,
you'd take me over your knee and spank me."

Cord grimaced. "I told you quite a lot of things. Is your
memory always so keen?"

"Only when you want me to forget." She managed a
tired smile. "Tell me something you'd like me to remember,
and see what happens."

"Why do I have the feeling you mean that?" Cord squatted down where he could see her better. Rays of moonlight
cut obliquely into the cavern under the freighter. Someone
had given her a man's shirt, two sizes too large, and a pair
of trousers, which she had secured with a pink lace sash.

"You look like a rag doll," he said, amused, but uncomfortably aware that baggy pants and rolled-up shirt sleeves
did nothing to diminish the supple sensuality of her body.
"Was that the best you could manage?"

"You mean my fine new wardrobe?" Diana laughed,
shaking back damp curls that clung to her shoulders. "Yes
. . . Randy lent them to me. The luggage wagon tipped over
when they brought it down the slope, and my trunks ended
up in the mud. It'll be days before everything's dry again—
to say nothing of clean!"

"Do you think that's wise? Not the clothes, the friendship
with Blake. You've been seeing a lot of him."

"I suppose so, but what's wrong with that? We don't go
for rides anymore, if that's what you mean, so no one can
talk." She paused, a sudden tilt to her head giving warning
a second before she said, "Don't tell me you're jealous!"

"Jealous? Of course not. Why would I be jealous?" It
was such an alien emotion, Cord might have been tempted
to laugh if he hadn't sensed some truth in it. He had no
right to be jealous of Randall Blake, any more than she had
a right to look askance at what had happened between him

and Rosalie, but there was a decidedly undignified feeling in the pit of his stomach every time he thought of them together.

"No, of course I'm not jealous. I was thinking of the boy. It isn't fair to him. He's head over heels in love, you know. You're tormenting him cruelly."

She looked up solemnly, like a little girl, her eyes the color of forest pools at midnight. "I don't mean to. There's nothing between us. Randy knows that. And there never can be. Maybe he likes my company."

"I'm sure he does, and I don't blame him. But it must be tearing his heart out. Go easy on him, love."

This time he heard the endearment, and strangely, it embarrassed him. He was not used to feeling awkward with women. He was conscious suddenly of the blanket hanging over his arm like a waiter's towel, and he offered it stiffly. Blake had brought blankets too, but she had arranged those on the ground to absorb the wetness.

Diana took it and draped it over her shoulders. Something tugged at Cord's heart as he saw that she had buttoned the shirt up wrong, one button off. Like a little girl again.

"So you really aren't jealous," she said. "What a pity. I *had* hoped."

"Why? So you could dangle my heart in your collection?"

"No. Because it would mean you forgive me."

"For what? Braving the storm with the men? Helping to get the oxen to shelter? Not crying when your clothes ended up in the mud?"

"No." Diana laughed, surprised at how easy he was making it. He had to know she was speaking of more than the storm that had just ended. "For not having been altogether honest when I asked you to marry me."

"Ah, that. Well . . . yes, I suppose I forgave you a while ago. You were very young, and you must have been frightened. Your father gives the impression of weakness, but he makes a formidable enemy. I might have done the same thing myself, under the circumstances."

"You might?"

"I might . . . but I would have been wrong." He reached out, then thought better of it and dropped his hand back to his thigh. "You didn't have to lie to me, Diana. I would have helped you anyway. I enjoyed thwarting your father,

and I wouldn't have minded about the child. I *never* minded
the child. It was the lie I hated.''

''But you seemed so angry . . .'' She hesitated, recalling
the look that had come over his face, the terrible controlled
rage. ''I thought your pride was hurt, finding out like that,
in front of the men—''

''Good God!'' The words exploded out of him. ''Do I
really give that impression? I *am* proud, Diana, but my pride
is secure enough not to care what anyone thinks. I was angry because you lied to me—perhaps, too, because you
didn't trust me—but I realized when I cooled down that you
had your reasons. A lie with a reason isn't quite the same
thing.''

A lie with a reason. . . . Diana looked away, painfully
aware that the real lie between them was one he didn't know
about.

She very much doubted he'd consider it a lie with a reason!

''I wonder that you dare to come so close,'' she said
lightly. ''Aren't you afraid Buddy will sink his teeth into
you?''

''Not likely.'' He was laughing as he smoothed out one
of the blankets and sat beside her. ''Your furry friend is
considerably braver with would-be attackers than thunder-
claps. All I could see of him was a pair of enormous eyes
glowing out of the back of the cook wagon. He didn't take
the bone I tossed . . . but he didn't growl at me either.''

He lapsed into silence, and Diana, enjoying the moment,
did not try to speak. They were not touching, but she was
acutely conscious of the warmth of him beside her in the
darkness.

Without looking, she knew he was watching her, and she
realized that they had reached a turning point in their relationship. The anger was gone, the sparring, the need to
drive each other to arm's length. He respected her, and she
was finding to her surprise that she respected him. He liked
her, and she liked him. He desired her.

Tell him, a little voice prompted. *Tell him now . . . before
it's too late. Tell him the lie without a reason, and pray that
he'll understand.*

But they had been so close tonight. Closer than ever.
Closer than she had dreamed possible. The bond was still
so fragile . . .

Soon, she promised herself. She would tell him soon. She would *have* to tell him soon. But not tonight. Not until their feelings had a chance to blossom and grow.

Something moved outside, and she looked around, grateful for the distraction.

"Was that Deadeye?"

Cord turned, but whoever it was had gone. "Probably Nate. They're about the same size. Deadeye and Slim are with some of the oxen."

"But it looked like he was carrying a rifle. Surely the men aren't standing watch. The animals are so tired they can barely move, and I can't imagine Indians prowling on a night like this."

"The animals *are* tired, though they're restless still, and jittery. But don't underestimate the Indians. They know we're as exhausted as our livestock, and likely to get careless. There's nothing they'd like better than to run off with some of the horses. And maybe a scalp or two."

Diana shuddered. "Kiowa?"

"Or Pawnee. They're about the same when it comes to making trouble. Most of the traders are a little more leery of the Pawnee, but Kiowa have been known to set up their tepees with the Comanche. You don't do that without picking up a few habits."

Something jogged Diana's memory. "*Nasty* habits?"

"Extremely."

"You talked about the Comanche once before. You told me you had a healthy respect for what they can do."

"I ought to," he said grimly. "I was their guest for a while."

"You were . . . their *guest?*" Diana stared at him curiously.

" 'Captive' is the usual word. It's not an uncommon story, unfortunately, though mine has a happy ending—of sorts. They raided our ranch when I was a boy. The hands had gone to a fiesta in San Antonio, and I was alone with my parents. It was only a small war party, not a dozen men, but it looked to me like all the devils had come screeching out of hell."

He paused, as if to catch his breath, then went on matter-of-factly.

"My father was killed instantly. Comanche take only women and children. My mother . . . well, savages are not

gentle with the females they capture. I was forced to listen
to her screams for many hours before she finally died. They
took me with them from camp to camp for several weeks,
until my cousin learned where I was and came with the
ransom. Cousin John was always a bit of an adventurer. He
took me to the home of an uncle, where I remained until I
was old enough to be on my own.''

His voice was utterly devoid of expression. Diana listened, fascinated. She had never heard anyone speak like
that before. No inflection, no variation—nothing at all.

''How old were you?'' she asked quietly.

''Thirteen. Thirteen years old. It is an impressionable
age.''

Thirteen? She couldn't even imagine it.

''It must have been awful for you, Cord. I'm so sorry . . .''

''Don't be.'' He seemed to pull himself together, as if
sensing her horror and shock. ''It was a long time ago, and
I was one of the lucky ones. I got out before it was too
late.''

''You mean . . . they *killed* the others?''

''Occasionally. But, no—that isn't what I meant.'' His
voice turned hard again. ''Comanche make their captives
into savages, like themselves. They teach them to kill and
torture and rape. More than one has been too ashamed to
return to civilization. Once a man has committed unspeakable acts—or a boy—once he has buried his knife in the
chest of an innocent rancher, or pinned an unwilling woman
screaming to the ground, it is hard to walk among his peers
again.''

He stared out into the blackness of the night. What is he
thinking? Diana wondered as the moonlight stroked his face.
For a moment, they had seemed so close. Now it was as if
he were a million miles away. What was going through his
mind? Memories? Sensations? Feelings he thought he had
left behind?

He looked a little like a Comanche himself. Features
strong, sharp-edged, immutable, as if they had been chiseled out of stone. Wind-tousled black hair hanging halfway
to his shoulders. There was something raw in him, un-
tamed, like the stark rawness of the prairies he knew so
well, the craggy rawness of the mountains beyond. Not arrogant, as she had thought at first, but fiercely independent.

Wild with the wildness of the savage who rode bareback, whooping across the plains.

Was it just the memories that lingered? Or had that strange, cruel world touched him more deeply than he cared to admit?

Then he turned, and his face softened, and his voice, and whatever she had sensed before was gone.

"You are looking at me very strangely."

"I was wondering what kind of man you are."

"I wonder myself sometimes."

He swayed toward her, and Diana thought for an instant he was going to kiss her. So near . . . She lowered her eyes, but she could still feel him watching. He was so near. She could almost feel his hand on her chin, almost feel him tilting it upward, almost feel the bruising force of his mouth.

But he did not move, and she sensed that he was waiting for her. Not taking this time, but asking, and all sorts of conflicting emotions tumbled over each other until she didn't know what she wanted.

It would have been so easy if he had forced her feelings. If he had pulled her into his arms and quickened her senses, leaving her breathless and giddy. She had never been able to resist him—she would not resist now in the darkness under the wagon. . . . Only he wasn't making it easy. He was asking her to decide, not with her body, but with her mind and her heart.

"What kind of man *are* you?" she whispered softly. "Harsh or generous, tender or mocking, thoughtful, stubborn . . . maddening?"

He seemed to sense what she was thinking. "I am all those things . . . and more. But I'm not sure you want to know."

Then he *was* kissing her. His mouth was brushing hers, so lightly she could barely feel that tender pressure. There was no violence in him now, none of the male arrogance that had assaulted her before, no lewd insinuations, only a terrible, frightening, aching gentleness.

Her own mouth followed, searching, her body drawn on invisible strings, hungry to close the space between them, yet afraid too . . . still afraid. If only he would pull her hard against him . . . if only he would free the sensations that were screaming to burst out.

All reason was gone now, drowned in the compelling

sweetness of his kiss. Only feelings were left, no conscious thought, or she might have recognized the moment when desire crossed the bounds to love.

It was he who pulled away, still gently.

"I think it's time for me to go and see how the men are getting on."

Go? Diana could only sit there, stunned. It was like a splash of cold water in her face.

"You don't . . . want me?"

A harsh laugh seemed to tear out of his throat. "Don't *want* you? My God, Diana, I know you're young, but what do you think has been going on these past weeks? I haven't exactly kept my lusty inclinations a secret . . . at least I didn't think I had."

The words trailed off, husky and barely audible. Everything Diana had sensed before, every mood, every passion, seemed to be coming together, all at once.

His voice was a caress when he spoke again.

"Don't you know, Irish, if I stay, I'm going to lay you down on that blanket and make love to you?"

"Would that . . . ?" Her breath caught somewhere deep in her chest. Was that really her voice, coming from far away? Was she really saying, "Would that be so wrong?"

It was truly a question. She was still not sure, still not ready, but she knew suddenly that she wanted to be persuaded.

And he knew it too.

"It would, for you," he said gently. "For me too . . . but, yes, it would be very wrong for you."

"Would it?"

He started to laugh again, softly.

"If you're going to dress in men's shirts, love, at least learn how to button them."

His fingers moved down the front of her shirt, unfastening the buttons deftly, drawing the coarse fabric open. Moonlight gave a bluish cast to ivory-pale skin, highlighting the subtly rounded curves that rose and fell with each rapid breath, darkening the slender arcs beneath. She couldn't see his face—it was all in darkness now—but she could feel the intensity of his longing, as she knew he could feel hers.

"Ah, Irish, Irish . . . you have a lovely body. It was made for a man to worship." He bent toward her, slowly, almost languidly, teasing first one nipple, then the other, with the same gentle mouth that had kissed her before. He was not touching her in any other way, he made no other move, but the aching swelled in her body until she was sure it must burst.

Then suddenly he was closing the shirt, fastening the buttons again.

"I do want you, Diana. God help me, I want you more than I have ever wanted any woman in my life. But I want you to be happy. And your happiness can't be with me, love. It can't be with me."

12

WAVES OF PAIN washed over her, surging to an almost unbearable crescendo, easing back again, like giant combers crashing against the shore, then ebbing out to sea.

Diana tried to force her mind to focus. A tunnel . . . she was in a dark tunnel that seemed to stretch on forever . . . something bright at the end . . . a small round light, but she couldn't get to it.

Cord? . . . She could hear voices, *his* voice, greatly muffled, as if from far way. Cord, concerned, caring, questioning, calling her name again and again . . .

Then the pain was back. A terrible throbbing that seemed to split her head, and every muscle in her body hurt as darkness closed in around her again.

It was lighter when at last she drifted back to semiconsciousness. The tunnel was gone, and she was out in a meadow. She could feel the warmth, smell the sharp, pungent aroma of grass. Her eyes were closed, but she sensed the light through them. Her head still ached, her arms and legs ached, even her bones seemed to ache, but the terrible debilitating pain was gone.

A meadow?

Everything came back suddenly, pictures flashing in split-second clarity. The shimmer of sunlight, a beautiful day for a ride. Pal flying through knee-high grasses, hooves barely touching the ground, mane streaming like liquid gold behind. Cord's voice calling something she couldn't hear.

She hadn't even seen the prairie-dog town. All those quaint little faces hidden in the grass—the hole invisible until it caught the horse's slender leg, and he was falling with a shrill whinny of pain . . . and she was falling with him, hurtling with one sharp stab of fear through the air.

Then her head struck something, and pain seared through her shoulder as everything went black.

Cord . . . ?

She mouthed the word, a small, silent plea. Hands appeared from somewhere, resting on her forehead—cool, soothing, efficient—and a voice was speaking. Only it wasn't Cord this time. It was another voice, older, heavily accented . . . somehow reassuring . . . .

Diana opened her eyes.

Not a meadow at all. She was in her own tent, with its familiar sloping walls and the funny circular table that had been cut to go around the pole in the center. A man was sitting beside her, a stranger with light hair and bushy whiskers and a manner that somehow made her feel safe.

He was still speaking, softly, the words coming together now in a French-sounding accent. He was, he told her, a doctor, who had been traveling with one of the other caravans when Cord sent a frantic messenger to fetch him. His name was Masure and he was from Belgium, but he had lived some time in this country, and she was not to worry about anything. She was going to be all right.

He kept saying the same thing over and over, assuring her that no bones had been broken, no damage done when she hit her head, but there was something funny in his voice.

"You're . . . sure?" she said weakly. "There's nothing you're not telling me? I . . . I didn't break anything?"

"No, no, nothing broken." The words were comforting, but his tone was somehow wary. "The skull, it is extremely hard. It is designed to protect the brain. And the bones of young people do not break themselves easily. You see, your mind is clear already. And you can wiggle all your fingers and toes."

Diana did, testing first her hands and feet, then her arms, her legs. There was a certain discomfort, especially in her shoulder, but everything seemed to be working. She was embarrassed to feel something warm and moist between her thighs, and she realized, startled, that her monthly bleeding had begun.

She was so irregular, it had hardly occurred to her she was overdue. If anything, it had been a relief, not having to hide a condition that was incompatible with the lie she had been telling. What a time for it to arrive!

She looked up self-consciously, trying to think of something to say. But the doctor's questions had changed, still

gentle, but probing, and extremely personal. At first, she
was puzzled; then suddenly she understood.

They had told him, of course, that she was pregnant. And
if she was showing blood . . .

That was what he had been getting at. All those pointed
questions, the guarded looks, the slightly sad reluctance.
He was offering her, though he couldn't know it, a way out
of the dilemma that had been troubling her for weeks.

She was not altogether proud of herself, but she grabbed
at it.

"My baby?" she said with a quaver in her voice.

His expression was regretful but firm. "You are young.
There will be, for you, other children. You must look to
your blessings. You are strong. You are healthy. You have a
husband who loves you very much. He has nearly worn the
ground down from all that walking back and forth in front
of your tent."

"Then . . . I *have* lost the child."

The tears that welled in her eyes were genuine, if not for
quite the reasons he assumed. He gave her hand a fatherly
pat.

"It is God's will. Perhaps it is for the best. One never
knows in these cases. Perhaps the child was not strong
enough. You must learn to accept . . . and go on with your
life."

Diana let the tears roll down her cheeks, relief mingling
with shame and a rather disturbing realization that, in order
to get out from under one lie, she had had to tell another.

But at least, she thought with a little sigh which the doctor misinterpreted, this was a lie she couldn't get caught at.

Everyone was kind. They remained in camp for several
days, no question now of keeping up with the other traders,
who were well on the way to Bent's Fort. Effie turned almost efficient, waiting on her mistress hand and foot, and
the men went hunting every morning for antelope and hare
and wild grouse to tempt her delicate appetite.

Diana, whose appetite was in fact ravenous, though she
managed with some restraint to pick at her food, had the
good grace to feel guilty. A few months, even a few weeks
ago, she would have relished the game, playing her part to
the hilt. But the willful young girl who had rolled out of
Independence on an impulse and a lie was a young woman

now, with a heart and a conscience, and she hated deceiving people who cared.

Even Rosalie went out of her way to be kind. Appearing in the tent late one afternoon, she thrust out a bunch of wildflowers, odd purplish things with fuzzy green leaves.

"I'm so sorry. I know how awful this is for you. I . . . I wish it had been me."

Diana was too shocked even to feel the nettles as she took the bouquet. "Don't say that, Rosalie. Don't even *think* it. Nothing's going to happen to your little one. He'll be fine!"

"I know, and I am grateful. I didn't mean that I don't care about my baby. I do. Terribly. But . . ." She struggled, searching for the words. "You loved the father of your child. He filled your life with joy."

"Oh." Diana was uncomfortably aware that she had completely forgotten about Jordan and the childish infatuation she once labeled love. The only man who had any place in her thoughts now was Cord Montgomery.

"But it's different for you, isn't it?" she asked gently. "Because you don't love the father of *your* child?"

Rosalie flushed. "I could have loved him—I *might* have loved him—if he'd let me. I really am sorry," she murmured as she headed for the open doorway. "It *should* have been me. It would have been better. For everyone."

Diana gaped after her. As long as she lived, she didn't think she would ever understand people. Rosalie's child had been conceived with a man who treated her abominably, and now even her lover had deserted her to pace an anxious path in front of someone else's tent.

Rosalie should have been breathing fire and spitting venom. Instead her sympathy seemed genuine.

But it was Cord who was kindest of all. Cord who was there for her from the beginning . . . Cord who brought steaming cups of tea for her to sip, Cord who sat patiently at the side of her bed and coaxed her to try a little solid food, Cord whose surprisingly gentle hands wiped her brow over and over with a cool perfumed cloth.

She would have loved the attention if the worried expression on his face hadn't made her feel guiltier than ever.

"You're glad this happened," she lashed out perversely. "That's why you're being so nice. You didn't want to get stuck with another man's bastard, and now you won't have to."

The color drained from his swarthy tan. "You don't mean that, Diana," he said quietly.

"I do. You can't deny it! This child would have had your name. The precious Montgomery name—and he wouldn't have been yours. You didn't want that."

"I didn't," he admitted. "But I would have accepted it. I was angry. I've already told you that. I also told you there was no animosity in my heart toward the child. I would never have blamed him. Or her. And I would never rejoice at the death of an innocent unborn."

He slipped out of the tent, leaving her alone to feel petty and rather foolish. She had not been angry at him, but at herself. She hated having to lie again, though in truth, she didn't see what she could do about it. Besides, this lie canceled out the other. It would all be over soon, and she could take the doctor's advice and get on with her life.

She resolved to begin by being pleasant when Cord returned, and sweet-tempered, and show him how grateful she was for his kindness.

But somehow she forgot when she saw the kettle he was carrying, with a basket balanced on top.

"What on earth is that? It smells vile."

"Vile, indeed!" He sounded pleased, as if he approved of her show of spirit. "Is that my reward after hours of sweating over a smoky cookfire? Be careful, woman. You might hurt my feelings."

"You mean you prepared that—whatever it is—yourself? The wagon master turns his hand to *cooking?*"

"Actually, I'm quite good at it." He set his burden on the table and lifted the pot lid with a dramatic flair. "Over an open flame, that is. Put me in a kitchen, and I'd probably get lost on my way from the chopping block to the woodstove."

Diana wrinkled her nose as the odor grew stronger. "I detest chicken soup."

"It isn't chicken. It's fresh prairie partridge, with herbs and tinned vegetables. I know, I know—sounds dreadful, but I don't think you'll find it half-bad. Here, then, be a good girl and give it a try."

He dished a portion into a tin cup and held it out. Taking a tentative sip, Diana found to her surprise that it was really quite tasty. She spooned up a chunk of partridge, taking care not to gulp too heartily.

He was more than kind. He was gentle and considerate and compassionate. When he was like this, a tender friend—almost a lover—she could detect nothing of that brash, sarcastic, mocking rogue she had encountered on the servants' porch.

But the rogue was there. She knew he was, even though she couldn't see him, and suddenly she felt inexplicably frightened.

"I don't think I want any more." She handed back the cup, nearly empty, with a bit of broth in the bottom.

"That wasn't so awful, now, was it?"

"No, but . . . Cord?" She looked up suddenly, an unpleasant thought coming into her mind. "What . . . what happened to the horse?"

"The horse?" His back was to her as he busied himself at the table. Diana could hear the sound of the lid being replaced, followed by a slight rustling. "Oh, you mean . . . Pal?"

She did not miss that a split second's hesitation.

"Oh, my God—he broke his leg!" She could see it all again. The sun shining on a golden mane, neck arching up, head lifted as if to defy the wind. He had been so beautiful and so frisky, and she had ridden him so hard. "You had to shoot him. I heard a whinny . . . I remember that . . ."

"No, no, nothing like that." He turned, his expression oddly careless, as if he had barely heard what she said. "Look what I have here. Slim and Nate went berry picking. Together. An unheard-of compliment, which I hope you appreciate. It's the first time those two old skinners have agreed on anything. . . . And stop letting your imagination run away with you. Pal is going to be fine."

"I don't believe you."

He lowered the bowl so she could get a look at the berries, deep red, with a scant portion of cream, which was all the cow was giving these days. "What's this? You're calling me a liar?"

"I heard that catch in your voice."

"Yes, well . . . there is something I didn't want to tell you." He sat on a three-legged stool by the bed, balancing the bowl on his knees. "Pal's leg wasn't broken, Diana, but he suffered a bad sprain. There was no way he could have kept up with us. Fortunately, a small party came by, heading east. They're going slowly enough to nurse him along. He'll find a good home with them.''

"He's gone?" Diana was embarrassed to feel the sting of tears in her eyes.

"I'm afraid so. I'm sorry. It couldn't be helped."

"But he *is* going to recover? He won't be lame or anything?"

"I don't think so, but it doesn't matter. He's not headed for the racetrack, love . . . just a safe refuge."

"Oh, Cord, it was my fault!" The tears came out, rage and regret running in hot streams down her cheeks. "It wouldn't have happened if I hadn't been so stupid! I shouldn't have charged into that meadow . . ."

She was weeping for the horse she loved, the graceful, spirited animal she had hurt and nearly destroyed, but Cord did not know that. To him, she appeared to be weeping for the child, and the intense protective instincts that had long lain dormant burst in his heart. She was so young—and so beautiful—to be hurting so much.

"It wasn't your fault, Diana. You're new to this country. You couldn't have guessed—"

"But I should have!" The tears had subsided, but there was still a film over her eyes, blurring his image and making it shimmer. "I know about prairie-dog towns. I've seen them before. I should have realized—"

"You couldn't have, sweet. The grass was too tall. Only an experienced frontiersman would have sensed the danger. I don't blame you for this—I blame myself. If I had kept a closer eye out . . . My God, Diana, if anything had happened to you, I would never have forgiven myself!"

He leaned forward, eyes strangely bright as he took her hand. Diana felt the calluses on his fingers, the warmth that seemed to flow from his veins into hers, and she realized for the first time, consciously, that she was in love with this man.

That was what had frightened her before. Because it really *was* love this time . . . because her heart, once committed, could not be taken back again.

"Nothing did happen to me. You heard the doctor. I'm fine.''

"You lost the baby," he reminded her. There was sadness in his voice, and Diana wished suddenly that she could tell him the truth. She *longed* to tell the truth, but she was afraid of losing the tenderness between them, and after all, he never needed to know . . .

"There will be other babies. Someday. I'm still very young. I can have lots and lots of babies if I want to."

"But not with your handsome second cousin."

"No." Diana heard the question in his tone, and she knew what he was asking. "No, but perhaps that's for the best." She met his gaze as openly as she could. "I didn't love him, Cord. I thought I did, but I didn't. He was flattering and fun, and I was truly sorry when he died. But I stopped mourning long ago."

Cord sensed she was telling the truth, but somehow there was no comfort in the knowledge. She might not be mourning her lost love, but her heart had to be breaking for the child. He took the bowl over to the table and busied himself with a clatter of lids and utensils.

"You don't seem interested in the berries. I'll leave them in case you change your mind. It's going to be cool tonight. The cream will last awhile."

As he turned, he was surprised to detect a healthy glow in her cheeks. Her hair was loose and rumpled, a pale spray spilling over her shoulders, half-hiding slender young breasts beneath that lacy thing she was wearing. Luminous turquoise eyes were wide and somehow trusting.

She looked so lovely. God . . . so lovely. He longed to take her into his arms and comfort her.

"I *would* have accepted the child," he said stiffly. He was not tall, but he looked like a great bear of a man as he stooped to keep his head from brushing the sides of the tent. "I never intended anything else. If I had, I would have disavowed the marriage at once. I may be proud of my family name—I *am* proud of it . . . I come from a proud heritage—but I am not too possessive to share it with a child. He—or she—would have been raised as mine. Unconditionally."

Diana was silent as she sat and watched him, and tried to keep from crying.

Once again he misunderstood.

"I am a hard man, and an obstinate one. I am rough sometimes, and demanding and inflexible, but I am not a monster. I would have seen that the child was cared for. And you."

* * *

It was dusk when Cord emerged from the tent. The day's work was over. The men were relaxing by the fire; the sounds of their voices drifting over the vast emptiness of the plain. Somewhere, Buddy was barking. Scrounging, he supposed. Still fearful of men, but hungry enough to approach.

What in God's name had possessed him, lying like that about the horse? It was not the sort of thing he usually did. But she had seemed so vulnerable—the pain had been so fresh—he hadn't been able to add to her anguish.

There had been no sprain. No small party heading east. The animal's leg had been shattered, and he had had to put it out of its pain.

He turned his back on the camaraderie by the fire. It had not been one of his proudest moments. He had never learned to handle it, having to shoot a horse. It was, to him, an unnatural, wasteful act, and there was always anger associated with it. But this had been different. This time he had felt an almost savage fury as he raised the gun and aimed.

As if somehow it had been the horse's fault. As if the terror he had felt when he saw Diana hurtling through the air—the terror he still felt as he recalled those anxious hours waiting for the doctor—had come, not from God or fate or sheer bad luck, but from this beautiful animal he was about to destroy.

It hadn't helped.

Beads of sweat stood out on his forehead as he crossed the wagon-ringed corral where the oxen were beginning to bed down for the night. He had felt only confusion and shame as he stared down at that carcass on the ground and realized, for the first time in his life, that he had taken pleasure in killing.

He was vaguely surprised to find himself in an area where an open-air carpenter's shop had been set up, with tools and precious scraps of lumber. He hadn't understood until he got there where he was going. Or what he had to do.

He chose a likely pair of boards and began, awkwardly, for his woodworking skills were minimal, to fashion them into the rough form of a cross. It was the only thing he could do. The only way a man who had spent most of his life in the rugged society of other men could express the grief and anger and helplessness that would not fit into words.

He had seen them often enough, weathered gray markers at the sides of dusty wagon ruts. The graves of men, for the most part, far from the homes they had left behind, the families and friends who would never know where their loved ones were buried.

But there were women too, for Mexican traders sometimes brought their wives, and the trail was hard on women. And an occasional sad little marker: "Juanito Herrero, Tres Años, Que Dios Haya." Or: "Infante García, 1 Mayo 1834– 2 Mayo 1834."

His hands worked deftly now, warming to the task. The edges were chiseled clean, the surface sanded. He would have raised this child. There had never been any question of that. Raised him generously, not grudging his true parentage, not even remembering it after a while. He would have been a father, like his own father in the days before a Comanche raiding party had put an end to his childhood. There would have been warmth in his heart again, and laughter. And love.

He stared down at the blank cross, realizing suddenly that he did not even know what to inscribe on it. It had been too early to tell whether the child was a boy or a girl. It was just a loss—more anonymous even than Baby Boy García, who had died too soon to have a name.

A boy. He would have liked that. He would have taught him to ride, and taken him on his first pony to explore the ranch outside San Antonio. He would have gone hunting with him, and fishing, and had long man-talks beside the fire on dark, still nights like this, with the wolves howling in the distance.

Yes, he would have liked a boy.

Or a girl. . . . The chisel began gouging into the wood, moving with a will of its own. What would she have looked like, this little girl who would have been his daughter? A miniature of her mother, all pink and silver, bubbling with laughter one minute, blue-green eyes flashing fire the next?

Oh, God. The pain twisted like a knife in his gut. Anyone could be a father to a boy. But a girl needed tenderness.

He had not realized, until he finished, what his hands were carving on the marker. The darkness was impenetrable. He had needed the lantern to work by. He needed it now to see what he had written:

Baby Montgomery
July 19, 1846

Baby *Montgomery*. He understood then what his heart had
known all along. He had wanted this child. Not accepted,
but *wanted*. Somewhere in the last long weeks he had come
to think of it, not as Jordan Crofte's offspring, but as his
own. And he had wanted it.

"You *are* a fool, my friend."

He made his way outside the circle of wagons to a site
that was somewhat sheltered by an outcrop of rocks. How
often had he called himself that since he met the pretty
woman who now bore his name? The word had never been
more appropriate.

God help him, he had wanted more than the child. He
had wanted the woman, and the marriage, and the life that
went with such things. The normal, comfortable everyday
life of normal, everyday men.

The life that could never be his.

He jammed the cross into the ground, hard. No random
puff of wind would blow it away. That life had been lost to
him the day the Comanche slaughtered his father in front of
his eyes . . . the long, terrible night he lay in a filthy camp
and listened to his mother scream . . . the bitter-chill morning he looked into an icy stream and saw raven tresses on
the water.

There were things yet to do. Plans that had already been
made. And those plans did not include a wife sitting prettily
by the hearth and the sound of children's voices drifting
through the window.

Diana found the marker late the next afternoon. It was
her first time out since the accident, and she was dressed
like a lady again, in a blue skirt that skimmed the top of
her slippers. As she stood and read those painstakingly
carved words, little tendrils of something cold and uneasy
twined around her heart.

It was his way of telling her he was mourning too. It was
not just her pain that touched him, not the agonizing loss
he thought *she* had suffered, but his loss too. His pain. He
was grieving . . . as he believed she was grieving.

Only his grief was real, and hers was a sham.

"I would have made a good father," he said as he slipped up beside her.

What could she reply to that? What words could possibly make up for what she was just beginning to realize she had done?

"I know," she said simply.

"I might not have been much of a husband. I *wouldn't* have been much of a husband. Even if . . . if things had been different . . . I'm no good at the kind of gentleness a woman needs. But I would have been a father to the child."

And he would have, Diana thought unhappily after he had gone. The sad little marker looked strangely lonely in a broad sweep of sun-dried grasses. All the tender instincts he had been at such pains to hide would have made him the kind of father she had only glimpsed on rare summer visits with friends.

If things had been different, he had said. But what he had meant was: *if we were really married.* It was the first time he had referred to their relationship as anything but a ploy to thwart her father. Something was happening between them, some new closeness they were both reluctant to acknowledge, and Diana sensed in this dark, enigmatic man a need to cherish, as she sensed in herself a deep hunger to be cherished.

Not good at gentleness? What could have been gentler than his hands on a brow racked with pain? The soothing sound of his voice, caressing her in and out of consciousness? No one had ever been gentler in her life, or kinder. Or more compassionate.

And how had she repaid him? She turned away from the marker, trying to ignore the queasy feeling in the bottom of her stomach. By lying—and continuing to lie! It seemed a shabby way to begin this new friendship, or whatever it was destined to be.

The sky was washed with crimson, deepening to purple as she headed back toward the wagons. Night fell quickly on the prairie, and a fire had been lighted, glowing red and gold in the darkness.

Everything should have been perfect. Buddy bounded out to meet her, and she laid a hand absently on his head. Things couldn't have been better if she'd planned them that way. She'd gotten out of having to confess the truth, her father and Ryder had had the last of their hopes thoroughly dashed, and Cord was finally beginning to look at her with tenderness in his eyes. She ought to have been beside herself with pleasure and relief.

Why, then, were those funny little doubts nagging at the back of her mind?

III

Bent's Fort,
late July 1846

13

AFTER ANOTHER LONG, hot, almost unbearably dry stretch of trail, Bent's Fort finally came into view on the twenty-ninth of July, a Wednesday, late in the afternoon.

Garland Howard, in the lead carriage, grunted irritably as he leaned back against dust-stained cushions and squinted into the sun. It was an ugly place. It had been ugly the first time he saw it; it was even uglier now, with yellow light soaking into high adobe walls until they looked like some freak of nature jutting out of the soil.

"Hardly a promising sight." He turned to the woman beside him. "If you think it's bad now, wait till you get inside. They water the dirt floors a couple of times a day, but it doesn't keep down the dust, and livestock squeal and defecate all over the place. I don't suppose you'll find it exactly pleasing."

"No, I don't suppose I will." Rosalie kept her eyes fixed on the fort, perhaps a mile in the distance. "But then, we won't be there long, will we?"

"That depends on the soldiers, my dear." A hint of amusement twisted the corners of his mouth. "Surely you noticed all those camps we've been passing the last hour or so. You seem to have an eye for gentlemen in blue jackets. I very much doubt we'll be allowed to go on until the fate of Santa Fe has been settled. It might be a few days, of course . . . but then, it might be weeks. Or months."

A faint shudder ran through her, and his pulse quickened unexpectedly. He had been more than a little annoyed when Montgomery had commandeered his wife's dearborn for some of the goods salvaged from the storm and put her in with him, but the arrangement was turning out to have certain advantages.

He chuckled under his breath. Proximity was taking its

toll. He had ended up in her tent last night—more a reflex than anything, not because he really wanted her, but because there were certain needs that had to be satisfied.

She had surprised him. For the first time, she hadn't opened her arms with her usual pathetic gratitude. She had actually drawn back—that affair with the young lieutenant must have progressed to the delicate stage—resisting her own impulses as much as his.

She had not succeeded, of course. Rosalie would never succeed at anything like that. But the cry that had been torn from her throat at the appropriate moment was a cry of anguish, not pleasure, and it had excited him. He liked a woman to fight.

And he liked her to lose.

"It's going to be crowded at the fort. Half a dozen of the big trains will be in, God knows how many stragglers, and we're probably the last comers. As I recall, the rooms for boarders are extremely limited."

"I'm sure they'll find space for us."

Garland laid a hand on her arm, fingers puffing out where the rings had gotten too tight.

"I'm sure they will, my dear. I'm sure they will."

For Diana, riding on the high seat of the luggage carrier a few paces behind—her own wagon had been pressed into service with the others—the fort was not ugly, but almost majestic in an oddly primitive way. Soaring into the sun-blazoned sky, high adobe walls and corner bastions, perhaps thirty feet tall, gave it the romantic appeal of a medieval castle. Just for a moment she could almost see knights at the east-facing entrance, lances drawn to protect damsels within as the long, sweet cry of a trumpet heralded the approach of sunset.

The illusion lasted only an instant. Looking around at the military encampments that surrounded the fort, Diana could not imagine anything less like a fairy tale. Tents seemed to be everywhere, and horses; there were odd little structures built of tree limbs for shade, and laundry flapping limply in the dust.

It looked like Cord hadn't been exaggerating when he told her the Army of the West consisted of sixteen hundred regular and volunteer troops!

"Do you think we'll have to stay here long?" she asked. Cord was on the seat beside her, the reins in his own hands, for he had sent Slim ahead to help Randy Blake guide the caravan to the fort. Ryder, thank heaven, was doing a temporary stint as assistant wagon master far to the rear.

"I doubt it. We're the last to arrive, on the heels of most of the army, it appears. The general is due at any time—he might be here already. My guess is that he's planning on marching his men out again almost immediately."

"What about us? The traders?"

"We'll probably be allowed to follow at a comfortable distance. They think they're going to take Santa Fe without a fight, but there'll still be delays. A week or two to secure the town, and God knows how long after that, while the military makes up its mind whether to go to California or Chihuahua or both."

Randy confirmed most of his guesses a short time later when he rode back to check on last-minute details.

"You'll have to go the rest of the way on foot. The fort is too crowded to keep the wagons inside, even the animals. I could only make arrangements to board some of the horses. Kearny arrived a little while ago. They say he's moving on in three or four days."

He turned to Diana. "That's General Kearny," he explained. "Stephen Watts Kearny, the commander of the Army of the West. He's predicting that the Stars and Stripes will fly over Santa Fe within a month."

Diana saw his eyes light up, and for the first time she wondered if he regretted the career he had left behind to seek his fortune in trade. She was also aware of the way he was looking at her, and she remembered, rather guiltily, that Cord had said he was in love with her.

"It sounds like you agree." She climbed down from the wagon, welcoming the chance to stretch her legs.

"Yes, ma'am. The Mexicans are fighters, but they can't stand up to us. Besides, they had the fight kicked out of 'em in Texas. We'll be in Santa Fe before you know it. California too." His eyes grew brighter, and Diana had the uneasy feeling that he might have rejoined his former comrades if he weren't still hoping. "But I'd better get back and see about camp. I found us a good space—just outside the gate. We'll be able to get the animals inside if there's any trouble."

Twenty minutes later they were striding into the fort, Diana feeling small and very protected with Cord beside her.

The walls seemed even higher here, rising up as if to envelop them. There were doors along the sides, but the center was open, an expanse of unpaved earth broken only by a well in the center. Probably ninety feet square, maybe a hundred, though it seemed larger, for it was bustling with noise and color and movement.

Diana had expected to find primarily men in that isolated outpost, and certainly there were many: frontiersmen in fringed rawhide, their faces lean and leathery as they cut through the crowds; cowhands in faded denim pants lounging against doorposts at the side; traders clustered here and there in little groups, black broadcloth jackets almost brown after weeks on the trail. But there were a surprising number of women too, in gaily colored outfits that she supposed were Mexican, with flared skirts and great quantities of gaudy jewelry, and startlingly low bodices.

She stared in frank fascination as one of them passed on her way to the well, a waterjug balanced on greasy black hair. And she thought she had seen scandalous necklines at the theater in Richmond! The woman was not young, nor was she beautiful, but she moved with a swaying grace, and her blouse plunged to reveal most of an extremely ample front.

Cord, surprisingly, didn't seem to notice—or perhaps he was being discreet as he joined a group of traders a short distance away. Left to herself, Diana took advantage of the moment to explore her new surroundings.

The doors on the sides led to a series of rooms, some apparently private, for men came and went, and an occasional woman, shutting them off again. But the others were public, and as Diana peeked in, she quickly discovered that this compact space supported a surprising amount of activity.

One room appeared to be a parlor, though there was no furniture, just cushions arranged along the walls and a table with a water pail and dipper. Diana spotted several men, traders by the look of them, chatting and smoking. A sloe-eyed woman, dressed in what appeared to be the customary manner, blithely ignored them as she combed her hair, rubbing in some rancid-smelling oil. There were also a dining hall, a kitchen from which pungent aromas were beginning to emanate, a smithy, a small store, an icehouse, a room with a dilapidated billiards table, even a barber shop—an extremely popular establishment, judging from the line of scraggly-looking men waiting to get in.

Diana stood almost in the center of the court and smelled the dust and spices, horses and tobacco and sweat, and thought how amazing it was to be among people again. The place was filthy, but it was alive. The floors were dirt, the buckets in the corners overflowing, and men spat on the ground, but there were chickens squawking and donkeys braying, pots clattering and stirrups jangling; somewhere a child had started to wail, and women were laughing, and men scolded and quarreled and bragged.

She should have hated it. Any other time, she *would* have hated it. But after weeks of vast empty plains, with nothing but the howling of the wolves at night and the sounds that drifted back from the wagoners' fire, it seemed like a little bit of heaven dropped to earth.

Cord did not exactly share his wife's enthusiasm for the fort. Coming out of one of the rooms on the side, where he had just finished making some rather hasty arrangements, he took her arm and guided her toward a staircase to the second floor.

Crowded places had always had an unpleasant effect on him. It seemed a suffocating, indecent way to live. He never minded the sweat of labor; that, at least, was honest. There was something obscene about the stench of men's armpits under black jackets on hot days, rooms too carelessly cleaned, too many mouths exhaling in a limited space.

His distaste was only heightened when he saw the small chamber that had been allotted to them.

It was no worse than he ought to have anticipated. He ran his eye around the room, taking in a long, corridorlike space with a bed jammed against one wall and about six inches to squeeze past to the table and chairs under the window. He had already been told that they'd had to double up and triple people up some of them strangers in beds smaller than this to make room for the two married couples in the How-ard party. And naturally, the better of the rooms had gone to the trader, not his wagon master.

It occurred to him that perhaps that had been an exaggeration. He didn't see how a bed could be smaller than this. It would have accommodated one person comfortably enough, provided he didn't get the urge to turn over in the middle of the night. For two, it was an impossibly snug fit, especially when one was a warm, supple female, the other a man whose masculine parts were already beginning to respond.

Diana made her way over to one of the two chairs wedged between the table and the wall and sank down with a weary smile.

Had she noticed the size of the bed? Cord wondered. Probably. It was inescapable. But perhaps she hadn't realized quite what it meant.

"Sorry about the cozy quarters," he said. "I'm afraid there's nothing else available. We were lucky to get this."

"Oh, it's not bad. A bit close, but I expect it'll do."

"You do understand," he said rather stiffly, "that you'll be sharing it with me."

"Oh." A flicker of surprise showed in her eyes, though she didn't look quite as alarmed as he might have expected. "I thought . . . I just assumed you'd stay with the wagons."

"No," he replied simply. He had thought so himself, briefly. But all the major traders were here, men she would encounter again in Santa Fe, and a husband spending his nights elsewhere would put her in an extremely awkward position. Besides . . . "There are too many people for Buddy here—I'm leaving him in camp—and Effie will be bunking with the *domésticas* in the servants' quarters. Ryder has apparently decided to throw his bedroll under one of the wagons, but I don't trust him to be on the right side when they lock the gates at night, so it looks like you're stuck with me."

She seemed to take it in stride. In fact, her lips turned up again, almost an impish look.

"Well, then . . . it *is* going to be cozy, isn't it?"

They had dinner in the room, partly because it was more convenient, partly because Cord knew it would occasion exactly the kind of gossip he hoped to avoid if newlyweds were to appear in the crowded dining room.

The meal was simple and heartily prepared—chicken in a spicy red sauce, toned down for *gringos,* but still explosive with little flecks of *chile,* and fresh warm tortillas. Cord poured two glasses of beer and shoved one across the table at Diana.

"Sorry. There wasn't time to fetch any milk from the cow."

And just as well, he thought, suppressing a grin as he

watched her roll up a tortilla and scoop out a portion of chicken and sauce. Milk was fine for quenching thirst, but it had very little use when it came to putting out fires!

He rolled his own tortilla and waited for the inevitable reaction.

But she only gasped slightly, took a long swig of the icehouse-chilled beer, dipped the tortilla in again—a little more gingerly this time—and declared that she thought she was going to like it once she got used to it.

The little vixen. Cord was aware of a decidedly unsettling admiration, warming more than the blood in his cheeks. She knew he had been teasing, and she had gotten the better of him! He looked across at her—an illusion of fragility in pale blue muslin, her hair piled in a careless billow on top of her head, for she had not bothered to send for Effie—and thought how far she was from everything she had ever known, and what a good sport she was being.

He also thought that the blue dress had been a mistake. He had chosen it himself, along with most of the other garments she wore in the evening, but the color had a way of accenting and deepening her eyes, and the rather mature styling reminded him that she was not a girl anymore, but a woman.

It wasn't going to be easy to lie beside her all night and pretend she wasn't there.

"You are aware, I hope," he said as he retired to enjoy a slender black *cigarito* with some of the men, and give her a chance to undress and slip into bed, "that you have nothing to worry about when I get back. We will only be sharing a bed because there isn't room for a blanket roll on the floor. Naturally, I don't intend to take advantage of the situation."

"Naturally." She glanced up through surprisingly dark lashes. "You've always shown *great* restraint when we were together. You'd never, say, take advantage of finding a lady alone in an isolated ravine. Or kissing her in front of the minister when she couldn't object."

Damn her. In spite of himself, Cord felt an urge to laugh. She looked like such an angel—until he caught that devilish glint in her eye.

"I haven't always been a perfect gentleman," he admitted. "But neither have I been a complete cad. You've had a terrible shock, Diana. Your body is still recovering. It could

cause you irreparable damage to be with a man again so
soon. I would never do that . . . to any woman. Especially
to you.''

The silence was almost eerie after he was gone. Sounds
drifted through the half-open window—the court was going
to be noisy most of the night—but inside, the quiet was so
deep Diana could hear her heart beating.

He cared for her. He had as much as told her he cared.
He was only holding back because of the ''miscarriage,''
because he thought he might hurt her.

Would it be a good idea to tell him, after all? She forced
the thought out of her mind as she turned the lamp down
and began to remove her dress. The unaccustomed beer was
making her giddy, and it was hard to keep things straight.
She wanted to tell him, since she couldn't bear lying, but if
she did, he would be angry, and that could ruin everything.

Surely a lie that kept two people together was better than
a truth that tore them apart.

Diana was in bed when Cord returned, the lantern still
burning on a low flame on the table. Her eyes were closed,
but her breathing was shallow, and he couldn't tell if she
was awake or asleep. She was wearing some sort of filmy
thing, white, with lace at the throat and wrists. Fortunately,
the night had turned chilly and the blanket was nearly up to
her chin, only one slender arm sticking out.

Cord looked down at her for a moment, hating himself
for the things he was thinking, then went over to the table
and began to undress.

He considered for a moment wearing his clothes to bed,
at least his Levis, or maybe a pair of drawers. He frequently
slept fully dressed on the trail, where cattle could stampede,
Indians attack at any time. But blast it all, this wasn't the
trail! He slept nude in bed, and he damn well wasn't going
to change his habits just because some slip of a woman was
lying beside him, her perfumed hair spread all over his side
of the pillow.

He was a man, after all. He wasn't some bull in a breed-
ing pen! A man had needs, passions, normal bodily reactions. But a man had a mind and a will to control them. He
didn't have to mate indiscriminately every time his private
parts throbbed! Cord turned toward the lamp, tugging his
belt off and slapping it on the table as he started to unbutton
his shirt.

The noise caught Diana's attention. She opened her eyes drowsily, realizing for the first time as she saw Cord's back in the lanternlight that he had returned. She started to murmur a greeting, then saw his shirt slip down, exposing one bronzed arm, then the other, and the sound disappeared in her throat.

Every ounce of common sense warned her to close her eyes, to pretend she was asleep before he got to his pants and started to undo them too. But every curious instinct tempted her to keep them open, and curiosity won. She lowered her lashes just enough so she wouldn't be caught if he looked around suddenly, and continued to watch as his hands moved toward his waist.

She had seen the upper part of the male torso unclothed before. All those Indians along the Missouri frontier had been nearly naked, except for dirty rags tied around their waists. And the teamsters occasionally removed their shirts on sultry afternoons when they thought she and Rosalie weren't around. But she had never seen a torso like this.

Fascinated, she let her eyes run along his shoulders, feeling how wide they were, almost as if she were touching them, tracing the bulging muscles that continued down his arms, lengthening and rippling across his back. There was a sense of lithe power, almost catlike, in the bronzed, tapering lines that flowed to his waist.

Then his trousers fell, and her eyes followed, almost hypnotically. Firm buttocks, hard, but perfectly molded— shadows caressing sinewy valleys—gave way to long, lean thighs and the legs of a man in superb physical condition.

Lean and primitive, she thought, mesmerized. Man must have looked like that at the dawn of time when he ranged the prehistoric plains and competed with jungle beasts for food. Diana was surprised to notice that the tan lines were faint, even around his midriff, and she realized with a forbidden tingle that he must have frolicked like the Indians, naked in icy streams, perhaps even across the fields.

Then he turned, and every other thought vanished as she caught sight of the hard, dark, extremely large rod protruding from the front of him. If he hadn't been looking away, he would have seen her eyes snap open just for a second before she closed them again in shock.

The older girls at school hadn't been lying. They had said that that part of a man was enormous. But surely they couldn't be right about what he was expected to do with it. It seemed a physical impossibility. And yet . . .

She caught her breath, trying not to let him hear as she felt that hard male body slip into bed beside her. And yet, there had been something strangely compelling about it, frightening, but exciting too, and new feelings stirred within her. Feelings that had been awakened before by his kisses, reemerging now, making her head spin.

She lay in the darkness, waiting, half-afraid he would turn and take her in his arms, half-afraid he wouldn't . . . and disappointed when he did not.

Cord was acutely conscious of the soft warm body pressing into his back as he settled on his side and struggled to fall asleep. When he finally managed, it was as much from sheer will as exhaustion, though the day had begun early and he had gotten little rest the night before. Even then, the awareness of her did not vanish. If anything, it heightened, forming into disturbing, sensuous, highly erotic dreams that tormented his sleep and left his body bathed in sweat.

The lantern was still sputtering on low when he woke an hour later. His swollen manhood ached with urgency, still hard—or hard again from dreams—and he realized groggily that it was rubbing against a muslin-covered feminine thigh. Diana? He barely managed to stop his arms as they reached out to twine around her.

Angrily he turned away, cursing the bed for being so narrow he couldn't lie on his stomach. That would tame his rebellious erection!

Dammit all, what was wrong with him? He was acting like a boy—some green adolescent lying around fantasizing about delights that were never going to be his.

He punched his fist into the pillow. Diana stirred beside him, and he struggled to relax. It had been years since he had lain in bed like this—*years!*—dreaming of a woman he couldn't have. Take them or forget them, that was his motto. Either way, he didn't lose any sleep over it.

Only he couldn't take her . . . and he couldn't forget. Groaning softly, he held his body rigid, feeling the hard edge of the bed dig into his side as he forced himself back to sleep.

The next time he woke, he discovered to his disgust that he had rolled over again. Her nightdress had come up—she must have been sleeping restlessly too—and this time it was bare flesh that tempted and tortured his manhood. And this time it was too late to stop his arms, for they were already around her, hands intimately cupping her breasts.

He tried to pull back, but there was no place to go on the bed. Diana murmured something in her sleep—was she dreaming too, the same sweet, erotic yearnings that tortured his own sleep?—and curled up in his arms, her body heat turning the sweat on his chest to steam.

So easy. . . . It would be so easy to give in to his urgings. To just do the deed and have done with it . . . and worry later why he couldn't.

"Shhhh, love." He drew his hand back, resting it a moment on her thigh, silky skin making his fingertips tingle. "It's still the middle of the night. I didn't mean to disturb you."

But she only cuddled closer.

"Ummm," she murmured again, sleepily molding her body until it shaped itself to his. "Cord . . ."

It was not a question but a plea. The murmurs had turned to little cries, unconscious sounds that might have frightened her had she been fully awake. He shouldn't have poured all that beer. What had he been thinking? She wasn't used to alcohol. She had gulped freely to ease the heat of the chilies. Now she was clinging too heavily to sleep, unable to distinguish dreams from reality.

He let his hand rest on her hip, not drawing the sheer fabric down, but inching it slowly upward. He had let this go too far. He had held her in his arms, caressed her God knew how long—in God knew what ways—before he woke. He had aroused her, as he himself was thoroughly aroused.

He couldn't do anything about the aching in his own groin, dammit! But at least he could help her.

"It's all right, love," he whispered softly. "It's all right. I'm going to take care of you."

His hands were surer now. He slid the gown up just a little farther, cradling her buttocks as he eased her into the crook of his arm, fingers finding the sweet, warm, moist lips in that nest of downy hair.

A shiver ran through her, not shock, but anticipation, and her legs were spreading apart . . . as if she knew what he was doing.

And, of course, she did know. Cord grimaced wryly. She was not inexperienced. Why did he persist in trying to make

a virgin out of her? She had spread her legs at least once
before, for at least one man, who had gone a hell of a lot
further than Cord was going tonight.

He was surprised at the jealousy that surged through him.
She could never be his first experience; he had no right to
expect to be hers. He didn't *want* to be hers. He worked his
fingers deftly, caressing, manipulating—ignoring his own
excruciating desire as he felt her respond, thrashing wan-
tonly on the bed, moaning out loud now, all inhibitions lost
in a blur of longing and dreams.

She's asleep, he thought, amused and surprised and
strangely excited. Responding, but still asleep. The beer had
taken its toll. He had the feeling he could possess her completely and she would not even know it had happened.

Diana *was* asleep, but it was a fitful, dreamy sleep,
haunted by sensations that seemed to come, then slip away.
She almost had them, almost understood, then everything
turned fuzzy again and she seemed to be lifted on feather-
light winds that floated her off. There were no pictures in
her dreams. She could not see Cord's face, she could not
see anything, but she sensed he was there. And she knew
he had something to do with the strange new things she was
feeling.

Reaching. She seemed to be reaching. She was only haz-
ily aware of the burning that began deep in her belly, somewhere between her legs, radiating outward until her entire
body seemed to burst into flame. She was reaching for
something, but she didn't know what it was. She only knew
that she wanted it, desperately, urgently, every corner of
her being stretching, groping, aching for release.

Then his fingers found that one special spot, and suddenly it was there, everything she had hungered for, and it
seemed so right, so natural, as she convulsed, quivering, in
his arms.

Her eyes opened briefly, wide and ingenuous, as if reality
and dreams had come together for an instant, and she was
bewildered by what she found.

"I had no idea," she murmured, her voice surprisingly
coherent, "that it would be like this." Then she was asleep
again, still quivering, but lightly, her head cushioned trust-
ingly on his chest.

Cord found himself looking down at her, his bewilder-
ment at that moment matching her own. She sounded so

naive—everything seemed so new—it was hard to believe
this was not an introduction to love for her. But she had
done all this before, had felt these same sweet, stabbing
emotions . . .

Or had she?

The thought jolted him upright. Easing her back on the
bed, he strode over to the window. The courtyard was still
now; even the chickens had given up their squabbling and
were roosting in the shadows. Damn that bastard, Crofte!
He hadn't even taken the time to give her pleasure! He had
used her for his own needs and finished with her . . . and
left her wondering what it was all about.

He jerked his pants from the chair and tugged them on,
forcing his uncooperative member inside, where the stiff
fabric would keep it in line. It would have been the easiest
thing in the world to please her! Beneath that porcelain-
pretty coolness flowed the warm red blood of a passionate
woman. A few sweet kisses as prelude, a little restraint
along the way, and she wouldn't have been surprised by her
dreams tonight.

But all that son of a bitch had thought of was his own hot
prick! He had gotten what he wanted and hadn't given a
damn about her.

Well, that wasn't going to happen with *him!*

He kicked one of the chairs out and sat, turning the light
up as he took a blank sheet of paper from his knapsack and
searched for pen and ink. She had been used by one man.
She wasn't going to be used by another! He'd spend half the
night with the wagons from now on. That wasn't unreason-
able—they were his responsibility; no one could talk about
that.

And if he caught an occasional catnap, a couple of hours
a night, who would gossip? They knew where he was spending the rest of his time, and they wouldn't expect him to get
much sleep.

He glanced down, startled to see that he had been scrib-
bling. He had taken the paper out mostly as a distraction,
but he saw now that he had sketched the rough shape of a
map.

Imaginary for the most part—everything was guesswork
now—but he was surprised to see how detailed it was. Taking up the pen again, he scratched out a couple of X's. More
guesses. He'd do better worrying about business than the

little blond curled up in his bed, smiling faintly, as if she were pleased with herself.

Would she remember in the morning? he wondered. Or would she think it had all been a dream? And did he want her to?

He forced his eyes back to the paper. Good guesses? He thought so. Good enough to have something to go on if Garland Howard pulled a double cross at the last minute. That was just the sort of thing a bastard like that would do.

But then, wasn't that what he was planning himself?

14

"Ah, yes, the Mexican silver. You Americans are all alike."

Esteban Olivares leaned back against a pair of inadequate cushions and surveyed the small group that had gathered in the parlor. He was a sociable man. He liked talking, and he liked having an audience. This was an eminently satisfying one. The usual traders—Davy, Harmony, Glasgow, a Magoffin brother—along with some surprising additions in the person of Garland Howard and the son of his former partner.

And the women. Olivares' dark eyes lingered curiously on the very pregnant redhead, so silent in one corner . . . the exquisite little blond, whose head had snapped up at the mention of the silver. Ladies rarely accompanied the American traders; now they had been included in two parties, though only the Howard women were in the room. The other one—was it Magoffin's wife? . . . he must be getting old to forget a charming woman—was upstairs, suffering some female complaint, he had heard.

"You have heads like *los niños*," he went on, savoring the attention. "Little children, you Americans. Filled with—how do you say it?—daydreams, which have as much chance as *la violeta* to bloom in the desert. It is so much easier, is it not, to contemplate lost treasure than all those nasty hours of work?"

"You must admit, it's a diverting thought." Manuel Harmony grinned good-naturedly. He was American only technically, having been naturalized some years before. "It does help to pass the time, especially since some of us have been stuck in this hole for more than two weeks while our soldiers try to figure out how to settle things with yours. And since when have you been so devoted to 'nasty work,' *amigo?*"

Samuel Magoffin snorted contemptuously. His brother, James, had lived among the Mexicans and was believed to be paving the way for a peaceful entry into Santa Fe, but he himself had little patience with some of their ways. "You're as lazy as any American—more so! Don't tell me *your* head is filled with dreams of harnessing oxen and fording streams!"

"You're an old fraud, Ollie," Cornelius Davy agreed with a chuckle. "You'd be lusting after the silver yourself if you thought it existed."

"Ah, but you see, that's where I have the advantage." Satisfied that all eyes were on him, he took the time to readjust his plump body. "I know it does not."

"You seem very sure, sir." Lieutenant Paul Thomas pushed lean shoulders away from the wall and came to sit cross-legged in front of him. "You really believe there isn't any silver? The whole story's a fabrication, then?"

Olivares squinted slightly against the dusty light streaming through the door. Ordinarily he didn't like American soldiers, with their blue coats and brash manners. But this one had the softness of the south in his speech, and he seemed pleasant and polite.

"I didn't say I don't *believe* it exists. I said I know. Oh, it existed once—and it was indeed a fortune to bring the saliva to men's mouths. But it has been gone for some time now. There is nothing left to hope for. Or dream of."

"Dreams die hard, friend Ollie," Davy put in. He was rewarded with a soft murmur of laughter from the others. "It is, after all, entertaining to speculate. And while it's unlikely, it is not *impossible.*"

"No, no, there you are wrong." Olivares paused with an instinctive sense of the dramatic. "For the silver still to exist, you see, it would mean that Antonio Vargas was a thief. If it had been removed from his keeping by force, it would have been melted down and scattered. Only if he secreted it someplace for his own motives—if for some reason he never managed to get back—could the treasure remain intact. And that, *señor,* is impossible. I knew Antonio Vargas well. He was a fine, honorable, decent man."

"But fine, decent men *have* been tempted by money," Paul Thomas interjected thoughtfully. Olivares shot him a sharp look, but there was no disrespect in the soldier's expression.

"Perhaps . . . but this man had no need of money. He had to get up from a sickbed to answer his compatriots' call. His health had not been good for some time, and he had just suffered a death in the family. The worst death a father can endure, the death of his only child . . . his only heir. So you see, even if Vargas did not already have a fortune of his own, he had no reason to risk what was left of his health—and damn his soul forever—for treasure he could not use."

The room was silent for a moment, an uncomfortable, contemplative silence. Then a voice cut through the stillness.

"A pretty story, but aren't you forgetting one thing?" Ryder's eyes glittered with amusement, backlighted by something that seemed to come from within, a naked hunger he made no effort to conceal. "That fine, honorable, decent man was seen heading north a week *after* he was supposed to have handed over the silver. In San Antonio, wasn't it?"

"So they say." Olivares' voice was calm as he fixed the other man with a curious look. Like a cat, he thought, playing cat-and-mouse games. As if he knew something—though, of course, there was nothing to know. "Men are frequently seen in places they haven't been. Mistakes, perhaps, a similarity in appearance. And, of course, rumors *are* started. It was a trader who started this one, I heard, though no one remembers who. . . . Or perhaps that was a rumor too."

He let his eyes scan the room again, taking special note of the Howard party. If it weren't for that faintly sinister quality, Ryder could almost be considered handsome; perhaps women would think so anyway. He was dressed, as usual, in black, not a jacket like the other traders, but tight trousers and a tailored shirt. Garland Howard, seated on cushions against the far wall, was as stout as his partner was slim, aging and showing it. He was dabbing with a dirty handkerchief at his brow, pretending to be bored, pretending he wasn't listening. But he was.

Such a contrast between the two men, and between the women who had come with them. Olivares was vaguely surprised that he wasn't particularly interested in the wife. Flame-bright tresses usually captivated him. A flashy, obvious type. Even now the young officer was inching closer, thinking the gesture unobtrusive. Ah, well, perhaps he *was* getting old. The other one, now, the little daughter . . .

He sighed as he indulged in a long, open gaze. There was a beauty. Every line, every feature, perfectly chiseled, but with spirit behind them. A subtle sensuality, but infinitely intriguing. And those eyes! A man could lose himself in eyes like that.

Funny, the way they had married her to the wagon master. Even funnier that it should be Cord Montgomery. But funny things happened all the time. And the girl *was* attractive.

He leaned forward impulsively.

"And you, *señora,* what do you think? All this talk of treasure has your cheeks glowing. Do you believe, in spite of everything I say, that it might possibly exist?"

"I? Well . . . yes . . ." Diana looked down, caught off-guard for a second. She had never been privy to masculine conversation before—ladies always retired from the dining table when the talk turned serious—and she had not expected her opinion to be solicited. But when she raised her eyes again, they sparkled with boldness. "Yes, I suppose I do. It might have been stolen long ago—it *could* have happened the way you said—but I think I prefer the other version."

"Even if that makes a thief and scoundrel of my friend? How cruel you are, *señora.* But then, the young are always cruel."

"Not necessarily." Diana frowned unconsciously. She had nearly forgotten the Mexican silver and the silly suspicions that had come to mind when she first heard about it. It was jolting to have them come back. "You did tell us that your friend—this Antonio Vargas—was seriously ill. Couldn't he have died before he had time to deliver the silver, and it was hidden so well no one found it?"

"He could, but that does not fit with the circumstances. Vargas was no fool. He knew how sick he was. He would never have taken such a chance. He dismissed most of the drivers, yes, but one was kept on—the one he trusted most. That man was attacked, *señora.* By Comanche. In an area where Comanche had not been known to raid for some considerable time."

"Are you saying . . . ?" Diana faltered, horrified as she

grasped what he was getting at. "You believe the Indian attack was . . . provoked?"

Olivares shrugged. "Such things can be arranged. A few horses, a brace of mules, ammunition perhaps, and Comanche can be persuaded to do almost anything. Do you not think, *señora*, it is a very strange coincidence for Indians to kill one of the two men who knew where the treasure was at the exact moment the other was dying?"

"Yesss . . . but coincidences do happen."

"And the sighting a week later? Another coincidence that such a 'mistake' should be made? No, *señora*, there are only two possibilities. Either Antonio Vargas *was* in San Antonio and he was a thief. Or someone was trying to make—how do you Americans say it?—the frame."

A shadow fell across the doorway. Glancing up, Olivares saw Cord Montgomery looking in.

"We were just speaking of the lost silver," he said, raising his voice jovially. "It is a favorite subject, it seems, these idle days."

"Were you?"

The words were a slow drawl, no hint of expression. Olivares felt a prickle of curiosity. He liked not only to talk but also to observe, and he would have given a great deal to know what was going on in the other man's mind. He had been extremely surprised when he heard that young Montgomery had taken up the job of wagon master. Even more surprised to hear he had signed on with Garland Howard.

"Yes, yes—we were trying to make up our minds if it exists or not."

"And what did you decide?"

"*We* decided nothing. I know, of course—as any sensible man would—that it was plundered long ago. These poor *sonadores* are still harboring foolish hopes."

He watched the other man closely, but still nothing showed. Joseph Montgomery had looked like that sometimes—one of the few *gringos* on Mexican soil for whom there had been respect—and it struck him now how like the father the son was. The same features, the same intense gray eyes, the same way of closing his face when he didn't want his feelings to show. Only the raven-dark hair of his beautiful mother, Margie, set him apart.

It seemed impossible that the son of two such sensible

people could think the silver was out there waiting for the one with wit to find it. And yet . . .

There *was* something in his manner as he turned with a curt nod and went back into the courtyard. Wary and controlled. Could it be that he did believe it?

Olivares willed the thought away, swatting at it mentally, as one might drive off a fly. The silver did *not* exist. He would be as foolish as the others to let himself consider it, even for the briefest of moments.

The gathering broke up a short time later, most of the men strolling across the court to the dining room, where the noon meal was about to be served. Olivares took out a pouch of tobacco and one of the excellent papers he had picked up in St. Louis and began to roll a *cigarito*.

Snatches of conversation drifted back with the dust: "They say Kearny's pulling out in the morning. About time, if you ask me." "We'll be in Santa Fe before the month is out. That scoundrel Armijo's too cowardly to fight." "I'm following the troops myself—won't be more than a day or two on the fringes before we get in." "Damn right. We've been cooling our heels long enough as it is."

Olivares cast a look of amusement at Diana, who had remained behind, looking thoughtful, as the others emptied the room.

"They are still children, I see."

She looked up, startled. "What?"

"The traders. They play at being angry because they must 'cool their heels,' but all the time, they know they are better off behind the army. When the territory was Mexican, they paid heavy tariffs to bring in their goods, while I, a citizen, parted with the smallest fraction of my profits. Now, it seems, the boot is on the other foot. . . . But you do not hear a word I say, *señora*. You are still lost in dreams of silver?"

"I was just wondering . . ." Diana stared at a cloud of blue-gray smoke undulating over his features. "Can it really be worth that much? One shipment of silver? I heard there were eight or ten wagons."

"Actually eleven. One broke down and had to be left along the way. The rest, ten wagons, were last seen crossing the Rio Grande, heading toward the Nueces, an indirect route, but one which would not attract attention—or so it was thought. How much were they worth? As much as a hundred and fifty thousand dollars a wagon. Perhaps two hundred at today's prices.''

"But . . . Why, that's two million dollars!''

Cord Montgomery paused in the doorway again, briefly, glancing in, as if to see that the woman was there. Olivares watched with extreme curiosity. Such hunger on his face when he knew she couldn't see.

"Enough to dream of, yes,'' he said as the younger man drifted off again. "But do not let yourself hope, *señora*. The treasure, it is gone, one way or the other, whether Vargas was the thief or the victim. It matters little now, except perhaps to his family, which still suffers the shame. But the silver will not be seen again.''

Wouldn't it? Diana sat alone in the room after he was gone, trying to sort things out. Everything Olivares had said made sense. A dying man with no heirs wasn't likely to jeopardize the few months he had left. And if someone else had stolen the silver, surely it had been disposed of by now. But . . .

The seeds of suspicion that had been planted before began to grow in her mind, like wildflowers on a rain-watered hillside. The look on Ryder's face, right after they started talking about the silver. Odd and greedy . . . and strangely gloating. And the way her father made such a show of not listening . . .

It could have been bravado, of course. All wishful thinking. Men had been looking for the silver for years, smarter men than Garland Howard.

She looked around, just in time to see her father framed in the doorway, the expression on his face eerily reminiscent of Ryder's a moment before. He was just standing there, in the center of the sun-baked yard, staring into space as people drifted past. That same speculation was in his eye, that same look of dark amusement—almost as if whatever he was thinking had taken him by surprise—that same raw greed.

The silver of Antonio Vargas? What else could make a man look like that but the lust for wealth? *Did* he know something that had evaded the others all these years?

But if he was searching for the silver, Cord had to know about it. He was too good a wagon master not to realize what was going on.

And Cord *couldn't* know.

Diana pulled her knees up to her chin, wrapping her arms around her legs. Cord was the man she loved. He might not love her yet—he might never love her—but she loved him, and she could not allow herself to think such disloyal thoughts.

Cord would never steal anything that belonged to someone else. Cord was strong and honorable, and, God help her, totally honest, as she had already learned to her regret. With that fetish for honesty, how could he be involved in something so despicably underhanded?

Outside, in the nearly empty courtyard, Garland Howard was staring, not into space, as his daughter had imagined, but at something just out of the range of her vision—his beautiful young wife, who had paused in the shadows of the gate to exchange a few whispered words with Lieutenant Thomas.

But Diana had been right about the look on his face. It was a look of lust, tinged with surprise as a new and provocative thought slithered like a snake into his brain.

Perhaps he had given up too easily. Perhaps he wasn't going to have to settle for *half* a dream, after all. Perhaps he could have everything . . . and Rosalie would help him get it.

A dry tongue ran over his lips as he contemplated the ways in which he would express his gratitude—and pleasure—later that evening.

His gaze was so intense, it bored into Rosalie's back, a tangible physical sensation, drawing her around with a shudder.

The color washed out of her face, leaving unnatural patches in the center of each cheek as she saw the way her husband was looking at her. He hadn't heard what they were saying—he couldn't hear from that distance!—but she had the terrible feeling that he knew anyway. And he was already planning her punishment.

"I have to go," she murmured hastily. "I *have* to go."

She didn't look back as she scurried across the courtyard, trying desperately to look casual, but those last bittersweet words echoed in her ears.

Oh, God, he *couldn't* have heard. He couldn't!

"I love you," Paul had been telling her. "And you love me. You can't deny it."

She hadn't tried. "I *do* love you. With all my heart. I always will . . . but what good does that do us?"

"All the good in the world—if we just have courage."

"Courage?"

Her mouth had gone dry all of a sudden. She had told Paul everything, all the terrible, self-indulgent things she had done—she had even told him about that brief affair with Cord Montgomery—and he still loved her. But she hadn't told him that Garland was coming to her bed again. Or the awful, shameful way her body responded.

"I want you to run away with me, Rosalie. I'll take care of you. And the baby."

"Oh, God." Her heart had contracted, a terrible pain, she wanted it so much. But it was impossible. "You would be a deserter, Paul . . . and so would I. If the army didn't find us, Garland would."

"He might not mind so much."

"About me?" She had laughed, a short, brittle sound. "Probably not, as long as it didn't cause a scandal. But his vanity would never let him give up the child. Maybe if it were a girl . . . I don't think he'd care about a girl . . . but don't you see? He has money . . . connections. We'd never get away."

She stopped at the edge of the yard, catching her breath by the steps that led upstairs. Her heart was thumping so wildly she couldn't go on. *Courage,* Paul had said. But courage was a thing she did not have. Even if it were possible, even if she believed they could escape, she wouldn't dare attempt it.

Rosalie and Diana were not the only ones who had noticed the feverish brightness in Garland Howard's eyes. Cord, standing in a shadowy doorway, had seen it too. Unlike either of the women, he read those flickering changes objectively. Speculation first, then surprise, then sheer evil pleasure.

What the devil . . . ?

He waved aside an acquaintance who had started across the yard and continued to watch the man. Howard did not move, even after his wife vanished from view. It was not mere physical passion in the gaze that had lingered insinuatingly on every swollen curve of her body, though that was part of it. Cord had not failed to note the change in their relationship—or Rosalie's reaction to it—and while he pitied her, he knew it would not last. Bullies tired of their prey soon enough and moved on. In the meantime . . .

His jaw tightened as the man threw a glance at the parlor, where his daughter now sat alone. *Diana.* . . . This had something to do with Diana. But . . . Rosalie and Diana?

He took a step forward just as Howard turned and started toward the dining room. A pretty serving girl, passing with a tray on her head, glanced in Cord's direction, then sighed and went on when it became clear he was not going to take his eyes off that odious *cochino* with the hands that never failed to find a *señorita's* behind.

Swaggering, Cord thought, his brows knitting speculatively. The man was swaggering, with a spring in his step that had never been there before.

"Now, what are you up to, I wonder."

The troops left at ten the next morning. The quiet of the sabbath had been shattered since dawn by traders and officers thronging the courtyard. Whinnying horses scattered chickens this way and that; enlisted men and valets scurried through the melee, tending to last-minute purchases at the store, and black-eyed *señoritas* called out bawdy farewells to their favorites. A jangle of spurs and harnesses mingled with clattering swords, blaring trumpets, and the metallic ring of the blacksmith's hammer as company after company took shape. Then suddenly they were moving, a thin blue ribbon, stretching out onto the plains, farther and farther, until they disappeared in a whirl of dust.

Three days later, most of the traders had followed, and the fort was as silent as a country churchyard. Diana stood in the stable and listened, fascinated by the almost eerie change that had come over the place. The doors were open, but the only sound was a low wailing in the distance, a Spanish lullaby slightly off-key. Inside, it was so still she could hear the flies buzzing.

Effie was standing beside one of the stalls, an indignant expression on her plain brown features.

"That ain' no kine o' horse fer a lady ter ride. I doan know what come over Mist' Mont'gomy, I surely doan. That bag o' bones ain' good fer nothin'."

Diana suppressed an almost irresistible urge to giggle. "He doesn't look like much, does he?"

"Less'n much! A *mule* is better-lookin'. Look there, missus! See how his eyes rolls in his head. If his ears was bigger, I'd think mebbe he *was* a mule."

Diana could hold her laughter no longer. Poor thing, he did look like a mule, only maybe a little less graceful. Scars from the whip were apparent on his emaciated flanks, so maybe he acted like one too, though he had given no trouble earlier when she went into the stall of see if any of his wounds needed salving.

"He must have hidden talents or Cord wouldn't have bought him. You can take pity on a scrawny dog, but a horse has to earn his keep. Maybe he's got a good gait."

"The only gait that animal's got is an uncomf'terble one. Doan 'spect nothin', an' that's what you'll git. He's as no-'count as he looks, that—"

"What, you don't approve of my gift?" Cord's voice boomed from the doorway. "You disappoint me, Ephronia. Here I thought you were loyal as well as pretty, and I catch you complaining behind my back."

Effie eyed him warily, not certain whether to bristle at the scolding or be flattered because he had called her pretty and remembered that she once told him her name was really Ephronia.

"I ain' never complain 'bout you, Mist' Mont'gomy, an' you knows it. Ain' no husband in the world better'n you. But husbands is s'posed ter give their ladies beautiful things. Jewels 'n such. An', Mist' Mont'gomy . . ." Her lower lip jutted out. "They ain' nothin' beautiful 'bout *that* animal!"

Cord gave up and broke into a grin. "There's an old saying, Effie. Beauty is in the eye of the beholder. You would do well to commit it to heart. And what about you, madam?" Twinkling gray eyes settled on Diana. "Are you preparing to look a gift horse in the mouth? If so, I think it only fair to warn you, he has all his teeth, and they're in remarkable condition, considering the ill treatment he has received."

Diana's heart caught in her throat as she felt the teasing caress in his gaze. Sunlight filtered through the doorway, emphasizing the darkness of his hair, the deep bronzed tones of his skin, reminding her again how strong and masculine he was. He was dressed, not as a wagon master, but in dark trousers that covered the tops of his boots, with a black string tie and fitted pearl-gray shirt.

He was so handsome it hurt to look at him. In the darkness he turned maddeningly aloof. He hadn't shared her bed since that first night with the strangely dreamy sensations that still made her feel funny inside to think about them. But in daylight, and the tallow-scented evenings, he was hers again, tender and thoughtful, always within call, almost the husband of her dreams.

She caught him looking at her and realized he was waiting for an answer.

"I grant you the teeth," she said. "I'll take your word for that. But his other parts are anything but promising. I suppose he has a name."

"I call him Brutus . . . because he looks like a brute. You can change it if you like. I don't know what it was before."

" 'Brutus' will do fine. He does look rather coarse."

"And I grant *you* his lack of looks, but he's solid and steady. I traded him for a healthy mule, and at that, I don't think I was cheated too badly. I'll hire a more elegant mount in Santa Fe, but Brutus will be better on the trail. And safer." He turned to Effie. "I made the mistake of giving your mistress a beautiful horse before, and she paid for it dearly. It is because I care that I'm giving her an ugly one now."

A slow smile lit up the girl's face. "Yassir, I know. An' it's 'cause I know, I doan git angry—though you're more sometimes'n a body kin bear."

Cord held back a chuckle as her tiny form floated, spine-rigid and almost queenly, through the door. It had been a stroke of genius, setting Aaron to watch over her—even the slave overtones were easing from her speech. She was going to be a beautiful woman someday. Not outside, like her impetuous young mistress, but inside, where it counted.

Diana, watching the softness that came into his face, felt her heart leap again. As he strolled over and ran his hand down the horse's nose, his arm brushed her sleeve, and she remembered suddenly the strange, disturbing dream that had come over her that one night they spent together.

She had awakened once. She remembered that clearly, and he had almost taken her into his arms. Then he turned away, and after that everything was hazy.

She stared at his hand on the horse's muzzle. His fingers, so strong, yet gentle too. She could almost feel the calluses

. . . the way he had touched her . . . the way she *thought* he had touched her.

Cord saw the flush that painted her cheeks, and he sensed she was thinking much the same thing he was at that moment, though he would have been shocked at how graphic the images were in her mind. He was embarrassed to feel himself growing hard, though bodily functions had never discomfited him before.

He gave the horse one last pat, with a broader gesture than necessary, to make sure her eyes were where they belonged.

"I think you'll find Brutus here somewhat better than a mule. His gait may not be smooth, but he's fast and doesn't tire easily. He's also gentler than he looks, and loyal, I suspect—especially if you bribe him with an occasional sugar lump."

"What, and deprive myself again?" Her voice was low and surprisingly throaty, almost as if she were challenging him. "You're so mean with rations, I had to give up my own sweets to have anything left for Pal. I suppose I'll have to drink my coffee black and bitter all the way to Santa Fe."

"I'll see if I can't find a little extra," he said gruffly. Then, because he could not bear those devastating eyes any longer—and because he couldn't get away from them—he pointed to a gaudily embellished saddle that had been flung over one of the stalls and began to tell her about it.

Diana listened as he warmed to his subject, describing the elaborate Mexican equipage, *sillas* and ornate silver trappings frequently weighing a hundred pounds or more, that was so different from the simple, utilitarian saddle of a western American cowhand. It was truly fascinating—at least it would have been at any other time—but right now she was finding it hard to concentrate. He did not look at her, making a point instead of indicating each piece as he discussed it, but she sensed that he was as aware of her as she was of him.

"I admire your boundless energy," she said, dropping her voice again. "I would have thought you'd be so tired you couldn't stand."

"Tired?"

"You can't have had more than three or four hours' sleep a night. Unless, of course, you sleep sitting up . . . with your eyes open and the lantern shining into them."

The minx. Admiration drew him closer, a mistake. His erection was so insistent he was afraid it was going to pop the buttons on his trousers. She *was* challenging him.

"And you think . . . What? That I should turn down the light and rest my head on the table?"

"I think you would be much more comfortable in bed."

Damn. When had her voice gotten husky like that? His arms seemed to move of their own accord, and he was drawing her into them, slowly, deliberately, kissing her. A long, hungry, achingly passionate kiss, rough, like that first kiss on the servants' porch, but tender too, because now his lips knew her, his tongue was familiar with the sweet warm regions it was exploring, and somehow his heart had gotten involved. He was aware of a tremor in his own body as he released her.

"You're playing with fire, you know."

There was no fear in the incredible turquoise eyes that gazed up at him.

"Perhaps I am a moth and cannot help myself."

"Perhaps we are both fools," he said dryly. There was no denying his body now, and no assuaging it, unless he wanted to seek out some brazen-eyed *señorita,* which for the first time he could remember was not appealing. "Luckily for both of us, your health is still precarious and I can't throw you on the hay in one of those conveniently empty stalls and show you what men do to little girls who look at them like that. But I warn you, don't play this game too often. I might not always be so considerate."

And I might not want you to be, she thought, surprised at the sudden, almost overwhelming urge to tell him why he didn't have to be considerate, *why* her health was not in jeopardy. The lie was starting to suffocate her. It just went on and on—and *on*—and she never seemed to get out from under it.

But before she could say anything, before she even knew if she would have said anything, Cord's gaze shifted, and she realized someone was standing in the doorway.

Turning, she saw Samuel Magoffin, the last of the traders still at the fort. His wife had suffered a miscarriage too—a real one—and he had held his wagons back a few days so she could recover her strength. Diana noticed that he wasn't at *her* bedside with a cup of broth.

"Ah, there you are, Montgomery. I've been looking for

you.'' If he noticed the flush on Diana's cheeks and realized
he had come at an awkward time, it didn't seem to bother
him. ''We're leaving tomorrow, Friday at the latest. Thought
you might like to join us. There've been enough bluecoats
around to keep the Indians at bay, but with the army so far
ahead, it wouldn't hurt to double our forces. I've spoken
with Howard, and he thinks it's a good idea. I assume his
partner, Ryder, will agree.''

''I assume he will,'' Cord replied coolly. ''But I don't.
And in a situation like this, the wagon master's vote is the
one that counts. Sorry, Magoffin, but my wife has been ill,
as you know. The Indian risk is slim—at most—and we're
fully manned and armed. I don't see any reason to risk her
health.''

''There's still safety in numbers. Think about it. My
wife's had problems too, much more recently, and I'm not
worried. The pace is so blasted slow over the Raton, the
ladies won't suffer any hardship.''

''There we disagree,'' Cord said curtly, taking the man's
arm and drawing him into the courtyard to finish the conversation.

Their voices drifted back, but Diana barely heard as they
continued to argue, neither man giving ground. All she
could think was how close she had come to telling Cord,
and how much she minded the lie that was holding them
apart.

She *loved* Cord. It was not just a word anymore, not the
pretty fancy it had been before, but a deep emotional commitment. She loved him, and, God help her, she wanted
him. She wanted him to draw her, not into one of the horse
stalls, with hay strewn over a hard dirt floor, but back to
the room they shared, the bed where they once had lain side
by side. She wanted him to take her in his arms and kiss
her, as he had kissed her before, and teach her what it was
to be a woman.

She wanted to be his wife . . . in every way. But could
they really have a marriage, could *anyone* have a marriage,
with such a lie between them?

The lie was still on her mind three days later. Curled up
miserably at the end of the bed, she gritted her teeth against
the pain of cramps that came and went with rhythmic per-
sistence. Why did her period have to be so irregular? Other

women could look at the calendar and know, every twenty-
eight days exactly. She had gone ages on the trail without
anything—ages!—and now, barely three weeks later, here it
was again!

She had almost told Cord the truth a dozen times. She had
tried and tried, but something always seemed to get in the way.
The time never seemed to be quite right. And she wasn't sure,
absolutely sure, that that was what she wanted to do.

She got up and started toward the window, but the cramps
set in again and she dropped back down on the bed. It was
Sunday evening, a little quieter than usual perhaps, because
it was the sabbath, but it would have been quiet anyway. The
Magoffin party had gotten off as anticipated, and only a couple of trappers remained, their voices raised in garrulous con-
tention drifting through the open window. The few soldiers
who had stayed behind were nursing dysentery and broken
bones. Two had already died and been buried on a desolate
slope outside the fort; a third was not expected to make it
through the night.

She was still curled up on the bed an hour later when Cord
came in. One look at her, and his face paled.

"My God, Diana, what is it?" Sitting beside her, he took
one hand. "Are you in pain? Damn, why didn't I make it
worth Masure's while to stay? Midwives are fine for Indian
women—they have their babies and are bathing in the stream
an hour later—but they can't handle something like this.
Where does it hurt? Try to describe it."

Diana stared at him blankly for a minute.

"I . . . I'm all right. Really." She managed a weak smile
as she realized what he was getting at. "It just hurts like . . .
as usual. It doesn't have anything to do with . . . *that!*" She
crossed her fingers superstitiously. "It's just my regular . . .
well, you know . . ."

"Ah . . ." Cord's face relaxed; the tension eased out of his
body. "This is your monthly bleeding? It's started again?"

Diana nodded mutely.

"You mustn't feel self-conscious, love, talking about such
things." He tried not to laugh, but it was hard when he saw
the embarrassment flooding her features. "I'm your husband . . . at least on paper. It's permissible for a lady to
speak frankly with her husband. I'm not unacquainted, you
know, with the vagaries of the feminine physique."

He paused with a wry grimace. In fact, he was *well* acquainted with them. The ladies he had known had never shown the least shyness when it came to their bodies, though that was hardly something he could discuss with Diana.

"This is a good sign, sweet," he said gently. "It means your body is getting back to normal. You're not going to suffer any lasting effects. And it means"—he threw his head back, letting the laughter come out freely for the first time in months—"I'm not going to spend the rest of my life feeling guilty because I didn't find a good solid Brutus the first time round."

Diana felt a twinge of her own guilt as a fresh cramp seized her.

"It wasn't your fault, Cord. Truly—"

"It doesn't matter . . . anymore. What matters is that you're all right." He gave her hand an awkward little pat, as if he had just realized he was still holding it, then let go. "Do you have everything you need? All the, uh . . . supplies?"

"No. I . . ." Diana hesitated, still embarrassed. Except for one small trunk of dresses, everything was in the wagon. She had torn an old petticoat into the rags that now held her flow, but she was bleeding heavily, and she didn't have another to spare. "I didn't think . . . that is, I . . . I didn't expect . . ."

"No, of course not. It *is* soon, but that's good. Very good. You stay here, and I'm sure I can find what you need. That little hussy who makes up the rooms doesn't seem bashful—or maybe one of the *señoras*. Yes, a nice motherly *señora* might be best. I'll be back in a minute."

Diana stared after his lean hard back as he disappeared through the doorway and hated herself all over again for the things that were still unsaid. She *would* tell him, she decided impulsively, putting her doubts to rest once and for all. She was sick to death of the lie. He had been kind, and caring, and his concern for her was genuine. He had a right to honesty in return. Only . . .

Only . . . not just yet.

She moved over to the table, feeling better somehow now that she had resolved things in her mind. When they knew each other a little better, when they were just a little closer, then she would find the words, and he would understand.

He had to.

15

MOONLIGHT PLAYED on Diana's hair, turning
it nearly to gold as she stared at her reflection in a small
chipped mirror propped on the low branches of a spreading
pine. The air was almost deathly still. The cattle had settled
down after a long day; mules and horses and men were all
resting, and only a faint breeze rustled the needles overhead.

She traced her finger along the glass, surprised somehow
at how cold it felt. The moon was nearly full, and she could
see a faint flush on her cheeks. Her skin was not milky
tonight, but almost amber, absorbing the colors of the light
and the rich apricot *mousseline de soie* of her gown.

Apricot *mousseline de soie?*

Something caught in Diana's chest, making her heart jump
as she remembered the only other time she had worn it. She
had been so frightened then, yet daring too, standing in a
livery stable, staring at a slit of light under the door in the
back, wondering what was going to happen when *he* threw
it open.

What on earth had possessed her to put it on tonight?
Thirteen days out of Bent's Fort and the road was unbelievably rugged. When she changed at all in the evenings, it
was to a simple cotton frock. Yet some compulsion had sent
her rummaging through her trunk, hands digging to the bottom, not resting until her fingers recognized the faintly
rough feel of the silk.

Almost without thinking, she pulled the shoulders down,
creating a décolleté effect. Another mirror, another dress
. . . she had done this before. Only Cord had been there
that morning, watching, anticipating, like a cat ready to
pounce. He wouldn't even see her tonight. Unless . . .

She stood absolutely still. The girl in the mirror looked

back, pretty, appealing, the color in her face not all a reflection of the gown.

Unless . . .

It came to her suddenly. What her hands had known when they rifled through the trunk. What her body understood instinctively at the first cool caress of silk. She was going to do something no decent girl could even *think* about. She was going to be totally, absolutely, utterly shameless.

She was going to seduce her own husband.

Cord spread out his bedroll and leaned back, propping himself on one elbow as he stretched the kinks out of his legs. A whisper of water hinted at the stream beside him, lost in blue-black shadow. Every muscle in his body ached, but it was the good, clean ache of work well done.

The worst was behind them. The notorious Raton Pass, five days and fifteen miles of precipitous pitches and wheel-crushing beds of rock. Up was hard, half a mile an hour at best, oxen straining, the veins standing out on their massive necks, double and triple teams required at times, but down was excruciating. The weight of the wagons was staggering, even the lighter carriages too much for mules to handle on the steep grades, and grunting, sweating, cursing men had to haul them down on ropes.

It was a rare vehicle that came through the Raton intact. If a rock didn't get one of the wheels, a stony hillock did, or a deep crack, half-hidden in clouds of dust, and wagon tongues were constantly snapping like brittle autumn twigs. Delays were many, tempers short, as they stopped again and again for repairs.

But it was also the most glorious scenery a man could ever see, and Cord's heart, which thrilled to beauty, as his body responded to physical challenge, never failed to soar when they paused for the evening and he looked out on purple mountains and long, deep valleys mysteriously turning to blue in the dusk. The sky was crystalline sometimes, so bright it almost hurt; other times, a froth of clouds veiled the earth below, lone peaks rising out of the mist. Even the trees were different, scrubby piñon giving way to stately pines, and wild cherries half-hid gurgling brooks, their waters icy clear and tasting of sulfur.

He had just started to lie back when his ear caught a faint sound. Instinct drew him up, hand reaching automatically for the gun at his side. Seeing nothing, he let himself relax again.

A turkey probably, or a hare. He had set his bedroll apart from the others because he liked the solitude and the murmur of the stream, and because he knew there was little danger here. The Comanche were farther south, the Plains Indians north and east, and the pueblo dwellers in the areas they were approaching rarely attacked without provocation.

Had he turned again, he would have seen a slim figure in apricot silk slip out of the shadows of a small grove of pine.

Cord might have been unaware of Diana, but she was very much aware of him. His face was strong in profile, and strikingly virile—the natural sensuality of a man whose body was in tune with the earth and the wind—and for an instant she panicked. What had she been thinking? He was so much more worldly than she. So much more experienced. What if he found her schoolgirl fantasies tedious? What if he were angry? What if he told her to go away and leave him alone?

Oh, dear heaven—what if he *laughed?*

She hesitated, acutely conscious that there was time to change her mind. He hadn't seen her. She could turn around and go back, and he would never know she had been there.

But if she went back, she wouldn't have the courage to come again. And what if he never came to her?

Steeling herself against the hard, arrogant, scornful expression she half-expected, Diana took a step forward, forcing her foot down firmly, so he had to hear. If he looks angry, I'm going to cry, she thought helplessly. And if he laughs, I'll just curl up right here on the ground and die!

But there was no laughter in the deep-set gray eyes that widened as he turned and saw her. Or anger. Just surprise, and for one brief, miraculous instant, before he pulled the mask over his features again, a flicker of pleasure.

Why, he's glad I came! she thought, and suddenly it was she who was laughing, but inside, where male pride couldn't see. All those fine speeches about how he wasn't right for me, how he wouldn't make me happy—and what he really meant was: *he wasn't sure I wanted him!*

What a fool she had been. She should have made up her mind long ago, and let him see how much she cared. They did belong together, and they would be together. Even the silly lies she had told couldn't keep them apart.

"Hello, Cord," she said softly.

"Hello, Irish." One brow went up, an amused look, the first hint that perhaps things weren't going to be quite so easy. "Aren't you afraid you'll catch cold in that dress? There doesn't seem to be as much of it in front as before."

Diana had the uncomfortable feeling she was turning crimson. Her body *had* changed on the trail, leaner and firmer in some places, considerably rounder in others, especially where his eyes were settling now.

"You're trying to embarrass me, but you're not going to succeed. And I like it when you call me 'Irish.' It reminds me of . . . of what happened when we met."

"Are you sure you want to be reminded? You were quite indignant at the time, as I recall." Laughter vibrated in deep masculine tones as he lounged back with maddening composure, stretching his legs out again. Diana clung to the brief look she had caught before, and willed herself not to be intimidated.

"I *was* indignant. You were a disgusting boor. You stuck your tongue in my mouth!" She sat beside him, feeling at the same time the cold that came through the blanket, the warmth of his thigh, almost touching. "But that doesn't mean I didn't like it. I did—and you knew it, as you hatefully pointed out! Are you going to be hateful now . . . if I like it when you kiss me again?"

"But I'm not going to kiss you again. I'm going to put my hands on your shoulders, like so, and I'm going to pick you up bodily if I have to and escort you back to your tent. And I'm going to stake Buddy by the door so you can't slip past again."

There was enough firmness in his voice to let Diana know he meant it. She felt her heart sink. He *had* been glad to see her! She hadn't been wrong about the joy in his eyes. How could everything have been so right and now suddenly be so wrong?

"And if . . . if I don't want to go back?" To her humiliation, her lip started to tremble. Oh, please, God, she prayed, don't let me cry. If she cried, he was sure to laugh.

But he only released the pressure on her shoulders, not removing his hands, but softening them as he gazed at her in the moonlight. Her youth, her tears, the naked feelings so close to the surface, had she but known it, were the one thing that could touch him.

Only, if she had known, then they would have been calculated—and they wouldn't have succeeded.

"I don't want you to want to go, Irish . . . and, God knows, it isn't what *I* want. But you have to. We've discussed this before—"

"You said we had to be careful. Because of my . . . my accident. You said I needed time to get better." Now that she dared hope again, now that his hands were gentle on her shoulders, holding, not pushing her away, she was suddenly, perversely, frightened. "But I *am* better. You said so yourself. That night in Bent's Fort when . . . well, you know . . . before we left. You don't have to be afraid of hurting me."

"Not physically, perhaps, but there's more than one kind of hurt. I am not the man you want, love, though you may think so now. I can't give you what you really need."

"You're my husband."

Cord's mouth twisted wryly. "On paper, yes."

"But isn't that all most people have . . . in the beginning? Half the girls at school already had matches arranged for them. Sometimes a woman doesn't meet her bridegroom until the betrothal, and the first time they're alone is in the marriage bed." She was talking much too fast, trying to convince herself as much as him. This was what she wanted. She knew it was. *He* was what she wanted. "You offered me a wedding night once . . . in the carriage, on the way back from the minister's cottage. You told me I was going to learn about love—soon—and who better to teach me than my own husband?" She gulped. "I want to learn tonight, Cord . . . and I want to learn from you."

Cord felt his resistance ebbing. Blast the minx. She had moved somehow; she was almost on his lap, firm young buttocks rubbing his thigh, and he was responding, inevitably and excruciatingly. She was still innocent in so many ways—she *would* be learning about love tonight. Her body had been touched, but not her heart, the virginal purity of her spirit.

"I don't think you know what you're saying."

"I know that I am a woman. You think I'm a child, but I'm not. And you are a man."

"A very dangerous combination."

"Perhaps . . . but don't you find danger appealing?" She had almost stopped breathing now. How could she be so calm and terrified all at the same time? Was it really, finally, going to happen? "I want you to hold me again, Cord. The way you did that . . . that night we slept in the same bed. I want you to kiss me . . . touch me . . ."

Every muscle in Cord's body stiffened. Without even being aware of it, his hands were sliding down her back, easing her off his lap, onto the blanket beside him. "Touch you . . . how, love?"

Her eyes were deep mountain pools filled with moonlight.

"It wasn't a dream, was it? I thought it was, but it wasn't. My head was so fuzzy—did you give me all that beer on purpose?—and I don't remember very clearly. But I know you were touching me in the strangest ways. You were making me . . . feel things. I want to feel the same way again, Cord. I want you to show me how to make *you* feel things too."

"Oh, God." If she had said anything else, if she had simpered and played coy . . . But she was so direct, so giving. He felt the heat of her against his chest, the quivering softness, and all he could think of was the soft, hot moisture waiting inside her. "This isn't a game anymore, Irish. Don't let it go any further if you don't mean to see it through. Another minute, and I'm not going to be able to stop."

"I don't want you to stop." She startled him by taking his hand, placing it on her breast. "I want to belong to you. Now."

Cord groaned. The silk of her bodice was so thin; he could feel the exact shape of one gently rounded breast as his fingers surrendered, cupping and fondling. Small yet . . . she was still so young . . . The nipple was already rigid, from cold or longing or both, and his mouth ached to suck it in.

What kind of a fool was he? Denying himself—and her? The doctor hadn't told him to leash in his lust forever. It wasn't as if he'd be deflowering a virgin; she might not have experienced the full sweetness of lovemaking, but the physical technicalities had been taken care of.

And if she had known the mechanics . . . shouldn't she know the beauty as well?

"I'm going to make love to you, Diana," he said, his voice, like his body, throbbing with desire. "You know that, don't you? I'll try to be gentle, but I want you very much. I'm going to take off that pretty gown . . . this little button . . . and this one . . . and this . . . and then I'm going to lie beside you, and you know what I'm going to do.''

Diana nodded, but her face was buried in his shirt, and he couldn't see. She did know what he was going to do. Many a long night at school had been filled with whispers that would have singed the headmistress's ears. But she didn't know how it was going to feel. Or what she was expected to do in return.

''I . . . I'm not sure. I know about that part of you . . . that you're going to put it in me. And I know a good wife is supposed to be dutiful and submit. Only . . . I don't think you're looking for submission from me. I think you want something more . . . but I don't know what it is.''

Cord laughed. Ingenuousness, with a touch of humor—he hadn't expected that.

''I'm looking for a great deal more—fortunately. I don't think you have a submissive bone in that luscious little body.''

His teeth touched her neck, biting lightly, nipping her earlobe. Diana shivered as she felt him kiss her cheek, her throat, one slim white shoulder, sliding the sensuous silk aside. Every place he touched seemed to burn, as if he were searing his brand into her skin.

Then he was drawing back, only his eyes ravishing her now, and the dress was falling to her waist. Bare breasts heaved in a gasp of shock, little pink-nippled peaks bright in the moonlight. Oh, God . . . the way he was looking at her. The air was cold, jolting against the feverish flush of her skin, and she wrapped her arms across her chest. Was it right to let him look at her like that?

He laughed again, softly, deep in his throat.

''You offered me your body, Irish . . . and I am very greedy.'' His hands were on her arms, coaxing them back, fingers grazing her bosom. ''I want all of it. Every beautiful, soft, warm, very female part. Don't shield yourself from me.''

''I . . . I didn't mean to . . .'' She felt a sudden stab of fear, bitter as the night air and terrifyingly unexpected. Now that it was happening, now that she was half-naked and his eyes were raking her with undisguised desire, all she could think about was that hard bulge at the front of his trousers.

"Then don't pull away from me. I warned you, love, that if you let this go too far, I wouldn't be able to stop."

"I don't expect you to. It's . . . it's just . . ."

"I know, darling. You want me to be very tender . . . and very patient. And just this time, I will."

He stretched out full length, drawing her down beside him, every muscle in his clothed body taut with desire. Hands tangling in long, loose tresses, he pulled her into his arms and began to tease her with little kisses again.

Her forehead first, damp from body heat that had already begun to rise—soon tendrils of hair would be plastered to her skin. Then her cheeks, the side of her mouth, the pulse at the base of her throat. She sighed as his lips dared to find and challenge hers. Gently at first, a slow, leisurely kiss, his tongue tempting, playful, coaxing her to explore him too.

His mouth still glued to hers, intense now, aching with restrained passion, Cord let his hands run down her body, fondling her first through the thin silk, easing it off until she lay beside him totally naked. One hand was under her buttocks, curving around them; the other had found her breast again and was doing things that made her feel strange and suddenly wanton.

Sensing the change in the tremors that quivered through her, Cord allowed himself to pull away briefly. Eagerness made him clumsy, and he cursed under his breath as he ripped at his shirt, taking twice as long in his haste.

His hands hesitated as they reached his belt. The moon was so bright—he didn't want to frighten her. But dammit, she wasn't a virgin! She had seen "that part" of a man before.

Diana watched, fascinated in spite of herself, as the last of his clothing fell away and a bronzed body gleamed in the moonlight. Just for an instant, she *was* frightened. It was so much bigger than she remembered. But he was caressing her breasts again, expertly, enticingly, and it was hard to concentrate on anything else.

He must have seen her confusion, for he smiled.

"Yes, love . . . that is the part of me I'm going to put in you. But you needn't look so apprehensive. It won't hurt this time, I promise."

But it would hurt. Diana knew that it would hurt terribly,

and she didn't dare let him see. He couldn't know—not yet—that she'd never done this before.

"I'm not apprehensive. I . . . I've seen it before."

A flash of jealousy caught Cord off-guard as he thought of Jordan Crofte and "that part" of him which she had probably gazed at with even more awe. Damn the bastard! But then, she was probably damning every woman he'd been with too.

"Not too many times, I hope," he quipped, regretting it when he saw her blush.

"I didn't mean that. I . . . I meant . . . I saw *you*." She raised her hand, almost reaching out, as if she wanted to touch him. "That night . . . when you undressed. You thought I was asleep, but I wasn't. And you turned around . . ."

"And you didn't close your eyes?"

"I did—later. But I kept them open for a second."

The little hussy. His blood simmered as he thought of that evening, when he had released his aching, uncooperative member from its denim cage. His arms moved unconsciously, drawing her close again, his hands finding the sweet, soft places that were already familiar. He had ached all night, and she had felt him pressing into her back. And then . . .

"I am going to touch you again, Diana . . . like I did then. Here, on the inside of your thigh—what a smooth thigh it is, love—and *here*. See how wet you are. That means you want me."

Diana cried out, a soft, involuntary sound as his hand slid intimately between her legs. Like last time, she thought—only *not* like last time, because then everything had been hazy and dreamlike, and she hadn't known what he was doing.

"I . . . I remember now. What happened before." She remembered *vividly,* every detail, including her own surprisingly brazen reactions. "But it was dark then . . . the light had gone out. And I had my eyes closed."

"You mustn't be embarrassed, sweet." He was holding her gently, but his hand had not stopped its provocative movements. "You can close your eyes again if you want, but I'd prefer you didn't. Nothing is wrong between a man and a woman if it gives them both pleasure. And I am getting a great deal of pleasure from this."

"It's giving me pleasure too," she said recklessly.

And oh, God, it was. She knew she shouldn't be behaving like this, no matter what he said, even if they were technically married—decent women weren't supposed to show their eagerness so openly—but how could she help it when he was touching her like that? Sensing her response, Cord let his fingers grow bolder, finding and separating those moist little lips, claiming them with the familiarity of a man who already knew what she liked.

Diana did close her eyes, but instinctively, not from shame. She seemed to be reaching again, as she had before, only this time she knew what she wanted. And this time it seemed to come quickly, bright and tantalizing, almost within grasp.

Then, just as she nearly had it, he drew his hand back.

"No, don't stop . . . *please* . . ."

His laughter was soft in her ear.

"I will do that for you later, if you like—we have all night to indulge ourselves—and I will teach you to do it for me. But now, the first time, I want us to find our release together."

He was moving as he spoke, rolling on top of her. How fragile she seemed beneath the pressure of his weight. He had never been so conscious of his body before, the hard, hot, pulsating rod he longed to plunge into her, and it was all he could do to hold back. He wanted her so much, he had never wanted any woman like this. He had never waited so long.

God, it was hard to be patient. Getting a hold on his uncooperative member, he rubbed it against her, as he had caressed with his fingers before. He wanted her to be ready too.

But he was too eager—the tension was too much, the urgent rushing of blood to his swollen manhood. With a grunt of defeat he let himself go.

He was conscious of an instant of surprise as he penetrated her. A resistance that shouldn't have been there. His mind caught at it, half-wondering for a second. But the warmth was too tantalizing, the tightness, the moisture surrounding and enveloping him, and he forgot everything else as he began the deep, rhythmic thrusts he had craved with every fiber of his being from that moment he had stepped onto a servants' porch and seen a silver-haired seductress preening in the mirror.

Diana bit her lip to keep from crying as pain cut through her like a flame-hot blade. It hurt so much! She hadn't known it would feel like *this*. She felt a sudden irrational sense of betrayal, as if he were hurting her on purpose.

She had expected him to be gentle, to ease himself inside her, not tear her apart with searing pain. But how could he be gentle when he didn't even *know* she had a hymen to penetrate?

Her jaw clenched, body rigid with the shock of intrusion, Diana lay beneath him, praying it would be over soon. Her female relatives had been right after all: this was one more cross a woman had to bear. Everything had been so good before; she had thrilled to the way he touched her, the sweet ecstasy he evoked in her body. Was this how she was expected to repay him?

He seemed to sense her stiffness, for he slowed suddenly, each downward motion shallower, gentler, easing the pain. Diana curled against him, instinctively finding the places where feminine curves fitted into the hard, muscular hollows of his body. After a moment, it hardly hurt anymore. The soreness was still there, but another pain had taken its place, a sweet excruciating agony that seemed to fill her until there was room for nothing else.

Her lips searched for his—or was it he who found her?—and he was sucking her into his mouth, and she was sucking back, hungry to taste every part of him, know everything, feel everything a woman could feel with a man. Her hips had a will of their own, taking over where inexperience failed her, moving in ways that were only partly aided by the skillful manipulation of his hands, and she was following the rhythm he had set, faster, deeper, throbbing with mutual urgency.

This was the way he had made her feel before—only so much more intense. The sweet, devastating yearning between her thighs seemed to grow and expand until it was everywhere at once, and she had the frightening, exhilarating feeling that she could not endure it a second longer. That her body would explode in a thousand fragments and she would die in his arms.

And then she *was* dying, the sweet death that comes to a woman each time she surrenders to a man; and the cry that escaped her lips was a cry of pain and pleasure, and infinite surprise that it should be so.

She was barely aware of the long, heaving shudder that racked his body as he collapsed on her with a hoarse moan. She knew only that he was clinging, as she was clinging.

"Oh, Cord. Oh, my darling . . . I do love you . . . I love you so . . ."

Even in the groggy aftermath of their coupling, she knew she shouldn't have said it—*love* was something he had not promised—but he didn't seem to mind, and how could she help herself? All she wanted was to lie like this forever, feeling the strength of him, the spent passion, the sheer heaven of lying in his arms.

When at last he withdrew, it was slowly, reluctantly, only because nature forced the parting. Even then, he took care to be attentive, knowing that the sweetness after lovemaking was as important to a woman as what had come before. His lips offered one last adoring kiss; his eyes were still devouring her as he pulled back to sit beside her on the blanket. Somewhere in the distance, a lone wolf was howling; otherwise only the soft murmur of the brook broke the stillness.

It was a perfect moment, the sweetest Diana had ever known—until his expression changed abruptly, his breath coming out in a sharp hiss.

"Damn!" He rocked back on his heels, face darkening with anger and disgust. "Damn, damn, *damn!*"

"Cord . . . ?" Diana sat up, alarmed. "What is it?"

She started to shiver, and he held out a hand, as much to steady his own nerves as hers. "I've hurt you, sweet. I didn't mean to. God, why wasn't I gentler? I knew it was too soon, but all I could think about . . . Why couldn't I *wait?* I don't want you to be alarmed, but you're bleeding slightly. It might not be serious . . ."

"Oh." Diana stared at him. So that was what was upsetting him. She added up the days in her head, hoping she could persuade him it was her monthly flow. But it was barely two weeks, and he seemed extremely knowledgeable about such things. "It's all right . . . truly. I'm the one who came to you. Remember?"

"Yes, but I'm the one who should have known better. You're a child yet, Diana. You have a woman's body, and, God knows, a woman's way of responding, but you don't know anything about life. I'm the one who should have shown some restraint. Damn!'' He got up and strode naked to the edge of the clearing. Moonlight and shadow played on tanned male muscles as he stared broodingly into the darkness. ''What kind of man can't even control the urges of his body?''

Diana watched helplessly from her place on the rumpled bedroll. There was pain in the way his head snapped back, the taut set of his shoulders. He was feeling guilty because he thought he had hurt her with his lust. Feeling somehow less of a man.

She should have told him the truth. She slid forward, half-rising to her knees. Long ago, when it would have been easier. But no, she had kept putting it off, telling herself the time wasn't right. How could she claim to love this man and let him go on blaming himself for something he hadn't done?

He had called her a child before—and he was right. It was time to grow up and face the consequences of her folly.

''It's not what you think, Cord.'' She felt strangely gawky as she stepped up behind him, not sure what to do with her hands, not knowing whether she should touch him or not. ''I'm sorry . . . I should have told you before. You didn't hurt me tonight . . . or, if you did, it wasn't in any way that is unnatural. I was bleeding because . . . because this is my first time. I've never been with a man before.''

He turned slowly, his expression wary.

''You were pregnant.''

''No, I . . .'' She took a deep breath. ''I lied!''

''You . . . *what?*''

''I didn't mean to. It just happened. He was so awful—my father—when he told me Jordan was dead. I just wanted to hurt him. I . . . I said the first thing that came into my head!'' She tried desperately to explain, to tell him that she had completely forgotten by the time she got to Independence—she hadn't meant to lie to him, not really—she just hadn't wanted to be sent back east! But everything she said only seemed to make things worse, and her voice trailed off in stammered half-words.

Cord just stood and looked at her for a minute after she finished. If he had burst into a torrent of curses, Diana could have handled it somehow. If he had berated her, railed at her, called her horrid names, his face black with scorn. But she was totally unprepared for the thing that he did.

He threw back his head and laughed.

"By God, madam, you give new meaning to the word 'deceitful.' Do you mean to tell me, all this time I've been so concerned about you—*everyone* has been so concerned— you were playing childish pranks?"

"Not everyone," she said miserably. "My father was just annoyed, and Ryder, because they thought they had been cheated out of a male—"

"You know what I mean. Did you ever once stop to think about the inconvenience you were causing? We pulled out of Independence a week late, towing a blasted cow—and half a wagon light so there'd be room for tinned vegetables! And not a peep out of you every time I held the caravan back, though you knew I wanted to get ahead of the army. You let me carve a cross for your 'baby,' for God's sake! I cared about that child, I *grieved* for him, and you didn't have the decency to tell me."

"I . . . I was afraid."

"*Afraid?* That makes it all right? Because you were afraid for yourself? You *are* a user—and I'm a fool! Any man can get burned by wistful looks and a seductive smile once. It takes a special sort to jump into the fire again."

He started away, then turned back, eyes brittle as glass.

"You have my admiration, madam. I thought I was hard-hearted, but I have met my match. I salute you . . . but don't expect me to come to your bed again. And don't come to mine. You won't be welcome." He turned on his heel and stalked off, still naked, into the night.

Diana sank back down on the bedroll, too heartsick even to weep. Heaven help her, everything he said was true, but she hadn't meant it to happen this way! She loved him so much, and he had come so close to loving her. It had not been just passion between them tonight; there had been tenderness too. He had held her in his arms, even afterward . . . he had let her whisper that sweet, forbidden word—and she had ruined everything!

The irony of the situation did not escape her. She had lied and lied, and somehow always managed to get away with it. Now she had finally told the truth, and her world was falling apart.

A chill wind made her draw the blanket tighter. She *had* inconvenienced him, but he might have forgiven that. Even when he was angry, he admired her spirit, and a thirst for adventure was something he could understand. He might have forgiven all those long days and nights, pacing back and forth in front of her tent, worrying about whether she was going to bleed to death from the miscarriage.

He might even have forgiven the child that never was. He cared for her—she *knew* he cared—and when he cooled down, he would have realized how frightened she had been, trapped by the lie that kept growing and growing.

But he would never forgive her for tonight. She had come to him, made love to him, knowing there was deceit between them. She had not come as a user this time—she had wanted to give as much as take—but how could she make him believe that now?

The moon was cold and cruel, casting long deep-blue shadows. She had not meant to use him, but she had. He had given pleasure and she had given . . . What? Remorse? Shame? He had hated himself for losing control; he had thought he hurt her; he had felt angry, bitter, diminished somehow. For the first time, she understood, truly understood, the awful thing she had done, and it was time to pay the piper.

She had wanted to grow up. She closed her eyes, shutting in the darkness and despair. She had thought all her problems would be solved, everything would magically come out all right if she could just find the maturity to face her folly.

Well, she had grown up in a hurry. And it wasn't at all the way she had imagined.

IV

Santa Fe,
early September 1846

16

SANTA FE in 1846 was a sleepy mountain town. Any other year, the large central plaza would have been lazy at noon, even dusty cottonwoods dozing in the midday heat. The siesta was a time-honored tradition, and peasants took a break from hawking their produce to sprawl around rough plank tables and satisfy their bellies with a bowl of *atole*—thin cornmeal gruel—or stewed goat's meat and tortillas, while children played at their feet and chickens scratched in the straw.

But since the coming of the Americans, everything had changed. Harnesses jangled now, even in the hottest part of the day, spurs clicked as heels echoed on the covered walks around the square, and raucous bursts of laughter could be heard at any hour through the open doors of bars and gambling houses.

A boy paused at the edge of the plaza. He appeared to be eight or nine—he could not himself have said his exact age—and was dressed in ragged trousers held in place with a rope.

He did not take any particular note of the buildings surrounding the square. To him, they were neither beautiful nor ugly, graceful nor squalid. They were simply there, and he accepted them, as he accepted the wind and the dust and the mountains. He did not notice the *palacio*, the Governor's Palace, a long shedlike structure filling most of one side. He did not notice the customhouse, the barracks, the *calabozo*, the chapel of the *soldados;* he did not notice the roofed *corredores* in front, which offered some shelter from sudden deluges that came and went with unpredictable frequency. He did not even notice the *parroquia*, the cathedral, the one distinctive building in the plaza, constructed of sand-colored stone.

What he did notice was the flagpole in the center. A red-white-and-blue banner hung limp in the windless air, no longer bright, as it had been that afternoon three weeks ago when the Army of the West marched unopposed into silent, empty streets. That coward Armijo, the governor, had turned tail and run! The boy spat in the dust. Even for Mexico, his regime had been notoriously corrupt. If the Americans hadn't gotten him, a bullet from his own countrymen would have found his well-clothed back!

The boy liked the *yanquis*. There was nothing political in his feelings; they were the practical considerations of a businessman. Americans were brash, open, jovial, especially the traders, whose shops could be found around the square. They had a way of slinging their jackets over hitching posts or bending down to look at something, leaving their back pockets exposed. Since his business had to do with slipping his hands into those same pockets, such trusting manners were extremely agreeable.

Their women promised to be even better. The first of the wives had already appeared, a fawn-eyed *señora* who bargained like a tigress in the market—as if the few *reales* she saved could mean anything to her—and left the little bag with her money sitting on the side while she sniffed and pinched the peaches! And there were said to be two more in the group that was arriving this afternoon, the Howard caravan.

He frowned as he passed a man, half-lying in the dust, propped against a cottonwood, the remains of a bottle of tequila neatly corked beside him. Drunkards irritated the boy. He saw them as a useless aberration of nature, though he had to admit this one rarely begged, and then only half-heartedly.

Pausing, he glowered down. Juan José had simply appeared two years ago—from where, the boy had no idea. He seemed to have a slight accent—on the rare occasions his voice wasn't slurred—but there were many ways of speaking in the lands to the south. He usually stayed a few weeks, just long enough to go through the coins in his pockets, then headed out again.

"You are a disgrace, old man." The boy nudged the drunk with a bare, dirty toe. "If you must lie in a stupor all the day, at least have the decency to do it on a side street."

Juan José looked up with lazy eyes, enormous black pupils surrounded by rings of surprising paleness. He did not consider himself old, but comfortably middle-aged. Coffee-colored hair showed streaks of dust, not gray.

"You are right. A terrible disgrace. It should not be allowed."

"You ought to be ashamed of yourself!"

"*Ay de mí!* I am. Most horribly ashamed. So ashamed I feel the need of solace." He popped the cork out of the bottle and held it to his lips with an exaggerated wink. The boy's tongue made an appropriate noise against the roof of his mouth, and he turned and wandered off again.

It did not occur to him as he headed toward the outskirts of town that he might be considered disgraceful himself. Pickpocketing was, to him, merely a profession. He never stole from anyone poor—poor people had nothing to steal— and he never took more than a few coins, having learned from experience that the beating was less likely to be severe. He had a mother to support, and younger siblings; if he had qualms, they dealt not with morality but with the fact that existence was often precarious.

With so many Americans, however, it looked like he wouldn't have to worry for a while.

He paid no more attention to the streets he was passing through than he had to the broad open plaza. Buildings closed in on either side, blocking out the sun. There was no room for walkways, and the boy darted back and forth, dodging army mules and burros with long, hanging baskets and ox-drawn *carretas* wobbling past on wheels that were never quite round. The drabness of mud-spattered adobe and flat, sagging roofs was broken occasionally by a braid of chilies or dried corn dangling from posts at the top of the walls.

Sounds became audible, somewhere in the distance. The caravan? The boy started toward them, wondering about this new group of traders. Howard he did not know, or his partner, but he remembered the wagon master, Montgomery. Their first encounter had been the embarrassing discovery of his hand in the man's pocket. He had been greedy that time; he had expected a harsh beating, but the American had taken one look at him and given him the cash instead.

They were like that sometimes, these *yanquis*—you never knew what they were going to do. But he noticed that the man didn't leave his pockets vulnerable again.

He could make out words now. *Los carros! Los americanos! La entrada de la caravana!* So they were here. No matter how many trains appeared, the entrance of a new one always occasioned excitement. The Americans might be conquerors, but they brought goods to supplement the rough blankets and homespun fabrics in local shops, and a fiesta atmosphere prevailed as everyone rushed out to greet them.

The boy's steps quickened. When he was home, or working the crowded plaza, he was strictly a man of business. But when his ear caught the sound of a caravan, he became a child again, and his heart beat with an anticipation that would have been recognized by any youth the day the circus came to town.

Diana, seated beside Slim on the high seat of the second carriage, was almost as excited as a child herself. The heart of the city was still indistinct, barely a splotch of brown against snow-dusted peaks in the distance, but here on the outskirts, small plazas had begun to appear, squat adobe houses and storage sheds with an occasional shabby church plopped down in the middle of cornfields and vegetable plots.

Right now, the fields were empty. Tools had been hastily scattered, hoes and machetes, sharp-pronged forks, as everyone flocked to the roadsides to gape at the passing caravan.

Diana gaped back, fascinated. Men were grinning, coarse trousers rolled halfway to their knees, waists bound by sashes that echoed the colors in the *sarapes* over their shoulders; dirt-encrusted children, their clothing barely more than filthy strings, shouted boisterously; and women in scoop-necked white *camisas* and ankle-long skirts, with here and there an embroidered shawl or flash of golden earring, waved and tossed flowers.

Diana was surprised to see a pretty girl jump onto one of the front wheels, agilely treading the spokes as she thrust a blood-red rose in Slim's face. Diana was even more surprised when he took it and, blushing all the way down his thick neck into his collar, tucked it behind his ear.

The caravan swung around a corner, and Diana laughed as the wagons behind came into view. Deadeye already had a flower at each ear and was tucking another into his buttonhole. One more, and he'd have to hold it between his teeth!

The traders and their crew were almost as exotic as the crowd. Their clothing might not have been as colorful, but it was fresh and unfaded, and it looked like every man had set aside a clean shirt or red bandanna. Cord came first, as wagon master, alone at the head of the train. Behind, Ryder in his usual faintly sinister black shared second place with Randy Blake, who was concentrating manfully on the cheering throng and trying not to imagine what it would have been like to enter the city as a young lieutenant with the fabulously successful Army of the West.

Even Garland rose to the occasion. Diana caught glimpses of him in the lead carriage, his little rockaway, grinning and actually waving. Rosalie was leaning out as far as she dared, the pallor gone from her face for the first time in weeks.

But it was Cord who caught and held Diana's eyes. He looked tall and slim on his favorite, Lance, and dashing in black trousers and a flowing white shirt, with a gracefully curved black hat. Even the powerful bay had been caught up in the excitement. Silver ornaments jingled from his reins as he tossed his head and pranced spiritedly, almost side-stepping while Cord struggled, laughing, to rein him in.

He's so handsome, she thought with a pang—and just for a moment, he was mine.

Giggling black-eyed *señoritas* ran alongside, smiling up at him, and he was smiling back. He had not said a word to Diana this last week and a half. He had not raged or mocked, cursed or scolded. He had simply ignored her, looking the other way—or worse yet, right through her. She had pretended not to care, wrapping herself in pride. She had pretended not even to notice.

But she had noticed, and she did care. She missed him desperately, missed the friendship as much as the passion, and it didn't help in the least to realize it was all her own fault.

A girl with luxuriant black tresses and an exceptionally low neckline placed her foot on his and swung up beside him. Laughing good-naturedly, Cord caught her by the waist and pulled her onto his lap, where she snuggled impudently, whispering something in his ear that Diana could just imagine!

How little Diana knew about this man. The girl jumped

down, calling something in Spanish—probably coarse, for the crowd howled its approval. All Diana knew was that he was extremely virile, and he had been in Santa Fe before. How many of these brazen *señoritas* with their long, loose hair and gaudy jewelry did he already know?

And how intimately?

All the sunshine seemed to go out of the afternoon as they threaded their way into the narrow lanes leading to the plaza. Diana had no claims on him, as he had never tried to make any claims on her. She would not have had the right to demand fidelity even if she hadn't angered him with her lies. But, oh, it hurt to think of him tonight in someone else's arms.

Diana had little time to brood over her shattered dreams in the days that followed. The duties of a young matron, as she was quickly learning, left little time for self-indulgence.

The house Cord found for them was far from uncomfortable. High adobe walls, drab and mud-spattered, gave an illusion of shabbiness from outside, but when the massive double gates swung open—more than wide enough to accommodate the coach he had hired—an unpaved court of surprising breadth and grace was revealed. Brightly painted clay pots overflowed with fruit trees and flowers, and arcades led to shadowy doorways in the rear and along the sides. A double-tiered fountain murmured musically, setting off the trill of songbirds in intricately wrought cages, and pigeons cooed on the roof.

Inside, the house was even more luxurious. The living quarters centered around a large *sala*, a parlor and dining area combined, with thick walls, deep-set isinglass windows, and a massive corner fireplace. The floor was polished stone, over which Mexican carpets had been laid, black and white or rainbow-vivid like the famous Saltillo blankets. Sand hues set off an odd but pleasing combination of woven wall hangings and formally framed European-style landscapes; and the furnishings blended sofas and armchairs, imported no doubt at considerable expense, with carved pine tables and rough cabinets in Indian motifs.

Whoever had lived there must have had stunning taste. Diana paused to study one of the paintings, an impression of mountains in the distance. Now that she was closer, it didn't look European at all. The form perhaps, and the brushstrokes, but the colors were uniquely Mexican, the purple of the slopes deeper than anything she had ever seen on canvas, the snowy summits almost impossibly bright.

"That was painted by the lady of the house." A masculine voice came from behind. "Margarita Cordero. Quite a remarkable woman."

Diana turned to find her husband watching from the open patio door. "She's certainly a remarkable painter. Where is she now?"

"She died. Many years ago."

"Oh." She was aware of a sense of disappointment as she looked back at the picture. "I would have liked to meet her. She was exceptionally talented."

"She came from an exceptional family. Her father believed in encouraging daughters. The older sister, Luisa, was a musician. They could have gone to Europe to study, but they met the 'men of their dreams' and married instead. Ah, well . . . I suppose that's the way with women."

Diana sighed as he turned back out to the sunlit court. Brief exchanges were all that passed as conversation between them these days. He did not seem angry anymore—in fact, he went out of his way to be scrupulously polite—but anger would at least have some feeling in it!

The rest of the house was smaller than the *sala,* but no less charming. The bedroom that had been allotted to Diana—the one she and Cord would have shared if she hadn't been so stupid!—could be reached only through a narrow corridor, unlike most of the other rooms, which opened onto the central patio.

Clearly, it was a woman's chamber. The woman who had painted the landscape? Everything was fragile and feminine, whitewashed walls draped in a dainty rosebud fabric, matching the spread on the golden-pine four-poster. Windows frothed with crisply laundered white lace, and a border of painted flowers, chipped and fading, paraded whimsically around the ceiling.

But the pleasantest aspect of the room was just outside—a small enclosed garden with its own tiled fountain and climbing crimson roses. So it *had* belonged to her. Diana could almost see the soul of that imaginative artist in the beauty, the perfumed serenity, the utter originality of this place that was like nowhere else she had ever been in her life.

The only incongruous touch was the appearance of a face now and then—most frequently Slim's—peering down from above. Diana had been surprised to learn that Cord had stationed men on the flat roof, even pitching tents so it would be guarded at all hours. Just for a moment, her heart beat faster, and she dared to hope he was worried about her. But Ryder would hardly scale the walls and search a labyrinth of rooms to attack her again. And with the possibility of a male heir eliminated, her father was no longer a threat.

No, it was just a routine precaution—to keep them from being robbed! Cord hadn't been thinking of her at all.

If Diana did not see much of Cord during those early weeks in Santa Fe, she was hardly unoccupied. Though their stay would be brief—they were only waiting for the army to clear the route to Chihuahua—she had a full staff to supervise. Buddy yapping at her heels, she spent a good part of her mornings trying to communicate with cooks and kitchen maids, laundresses, stableboys and yardmen, and thanking heaven that a thorough grounding in French and Italian had enabled her to pick up a little Spanish. All she lacked was a personal maid, and Effie—who, to Diana's secret amusement, now insisted on being called Ephronia—was actually beginning to fit into the role.

After that, there was marketing to be done. Meat, primarily mutton and pork, came from local farms, and chickens squawked and pecked in the kitchen yard, but fruits and vegetables, other than corn, which was stored in the *granero*, involved a daily game of wits with vendors in the plaza. Dusting had to be constantly checked, and gardening and laundry, and provisions inventoried to prevent pilferage, and everything entered in the household accounts. No wonder those female cousins with the keys dangling from their belts had looked so exhausted at the end of the day!

Only the evenings were lonely. Garland appeared occasionally, belatedly and rather surprisingly interested in her welfare, and Randy stopped by sometimes, accompanied by one or another of the young officers, Lieutenant Warner or Gilmer or Hammond, but no one stayed long, and she dined by herself at the pine table in the *sala*. Afterward she retired with a book from the surprisingly varied English collection in the library and tried to read, but thoughts of Cord kept intruding, and all she could do was wonder where he was

. . . and whether the brazen black-eyed *señorita* with the plunging neckline was on his lap again.

It was the marketing Diana enjoyed most. She loved the color and bustle and smell of the *mercado*, which sprawled out from under the covered arcades at one corner of the plaza. Everything seemed sharper in the mountain air. Piles of pink-cheeked *duraznos*, peaches, and slightly darker apricots set off the greenish redness of *manzanas*, small, tough apples with a tart flavor. The exotic mingled with the familiar—sweet-scented melons and pungent wild cherries, bunches of purple grapes hauled by pack mule from El Paso to the south, and little piñon nuts, thin-shelled and oily, about the size of kidney beans.

The competition was aggressive, the bargaining fierce. Men called out or caught her sleeve, trying to interest her in bushels of rice or corn, dried beef jerky, red and green peppers, squash and tomatoes and goat's-milk cheese. A little girl might unfold a dirty napkin to reveal sweet young peas while a boy held out a squawking chicken by the legs; a peasant woman in a short skirt and revealing blouse—no longer quite so scandalous now that Diana was used to them—would elbow them both aside to present fresh *tortas*, little cakes, at a wildly exorbitant price.

It was, Diana soon learned, a game in which she was expected to participate. A melon would be offered at *"tres reales, señora—muy barato,"* very cheap, and she was supposed to look pained, as if it would be a great favor to take such inferior merchandise off their hands for half a *real*. The haggling continued, with considerable allusions to the quality of the wares, the generosity of the seller, and the beauty of *la señora*, which was, of course, the only reason the price was being dropped from *tres reales* to *dos y media* to *dos*, and onward toward the market price.

It was not a game with which Diana was totally comfortable. A few coins made such a difference to these people! Yet to accept the first price was to lose face and somehow, inexplicably, spoil the fun. In the end she compromised, allowing herself to be cheated, but not too much, as if the difference was due, not to her naiveté, but to their shrewd skill at bargaining.

It was in the market that she was to form two unusual friendships, both in unusual ways.

The first occurred one morning as she tucked a squash

into her basket and paused to look over some especially tempting melons. She had been in Santa Fe barely a week, but she was already beginning to see the advantages of local dress. The *camisas,* the loose blouses with their high puffed sleeves, still seemed scandalous, but skimpy skirts made sense on muddy streets, and she had taken to wearing one herself, a deep, vibrant blue with a ruffled hem.

She also had a *rebozo,* a long woven cotton scarf like the ones peasant women wrapped around their heads and bodies, using them to carry everything from produce to laundry to sleeping babies. She loved the way it made her feel, almost anonymous in the crowded plaza, though it had fallen to her shoulders now, exposing pale blond curls.

Something brushed her side, and she glanced down, surprised to see a small clenched fist emerging from the drawstring bag at her belt. Black eyes widened as she reached out and grabbed.

"Dispénseme, señora. You pardon me," a boy's voice whined in the mixture of languages that was not uncommon in the market. "I have bumped myself against you. *Por casualidad, naturalmente.* By the most misfortunate accident."

"I think not." Diana put her other hand under that little fist and squeezed. A pair of coins dropped onto her palm.

The eyes grew even wider, as if in great surprise.

"How can such a thing happen? I know not, *señora*—I swear to you. *Santo Dios!* It is that I stumble and—"

The torrent of protests broke off as fingers tightened around his wrist. A thin layer of sweat glistened on the boy's upper lip, and he began to wonder if it had not been a mistake after all, taking on this woman. She looked so sweet and delicate. But that was not sweetness in her expression now.

"How old are you?" she said unexpectedly.

He eyed her carefully, trying to see what she wanted. "Eight," he ventured.

"Only eight." The faintest smile showed at the corners of her lips. "I would have thought ten, at least. You look such a big boy."

The flattery worked. "I am big for my age," he lied. In fact, he was undernourished and quite unusually small. "And there is much responsibility on my shoulders. *Mucha responsabilidad.* " Pinched brown features turned sly again as he began his usual story, exaggerating only slightly, as if he were the sole support of his family and *Mama* did not sit up half the night when they could afford candles and embroider designs on *camisas*. It occurred to him that this was the wife of the man Montgomery. Perhaps if fortune was with him . . .

"So you see, *señora*, those two coins"—he eyed them greedily—"those two very *small* coins, were for my brothers and sisters. So they would not go to bed hungry again."

But she only opened the bag with the little strings and dropped them inside, one at a time.

"What I see is that you would rather steal money than earn it."

"Earn money? *Señora!*" The indignation in his voice was genuine. "How am I to earn money? I am only nine years old. The men in the shops, they hire boys sometimes, to run errands, but older boys, and—"

"Nine? My, how you are growing. You were eight a minute ago."

He gulped. "Eight . . . nine . . . how is one to know? Even *mi madrecita* does not remember. *Y que importa, señora?* There is no work for a boy of *ten*."

"And if *I* were to offer . . . What is your name?"

"Panchito."

"If I were to offer you a job, Panchito, would you prefer that to picking pockets in the plaza? . . . Tell me, how much do you steal in a day?"

The boy studied her warily. This could be a trick. If he named too high a figure, she might say he was greedy and have him beaten. But if there really was a job . . .

"Five *reales*," he said cautiously. "Sometimes six."

"What would you say to eight? I could use a strong boy to help with the marketing. These baskets are heavy. And of course, it would be good if he knows how to bargain. So I don't pay too much."

"Ten *reales*."

Diana laughed. "Nine. I think you have the idea, Panchito. Is it a deal?"

"A . . . deal?" He looked puzzled until she held out her hand. "Ah, *sí, señora*. It is, as you say, the deal."

After that, Panchito was waiting each morning when Diana left the house. She had deliberately offered more than he could possibly steal, but even then she had been afraid the novelty would wear off and he would slip back into old habits. But he seemed to enjoy the work—rather too much for all those peasants she'd been allowing to cheat her!—and a touching swagger came into his step.

She could only hope it would last after she was gone. And that she hadn't overpaid him so much it would be beneath his dignity to accept whatever job she managed to find for him.

The second friendship was even more unconventional. The man was known as Juan José—she supposed he was what might be called the "town drunk"—and they met one morning when she stumbled across him in the square. Literally.

It had been raining off and on for several days. The sky was clear now, but the ground was damp, and he was sprawled on an Indian blanket under one of the arcades. Diana noticed him out of the corner of her eye as she approached, but she didn't notice the boot that seemed to come from nowhere.

Suddenly he was there, half on his knees, half-squatting, hands reaching out before she could fall. Just for an instant she almost had the feeling he had tripped her on purpose, but the eyes that gazed back at her were guileless and full of concern.

They were the most extraordinary eyes, large dark pupils with irises that might have been any color, though just at that moment they were reflecting the brown of his shirt. She noticed, rather to her surprise, that he was clean-shaven, and recently, too, for not a trace of stubble showed on his cheeks.

"A thousand pardons, *señora*. I am a fool, a dolt, a bumbling oaf. I beg your gracious forgiveness."

"It's all right." Diana smiled shakily. It was hard not to respond, his accent was so broad and comical, though he seemed to have a surprising, almost flowery grasp of English. A faint aroma drifted up. Tequila? "Really, I wasn't hurt. Just startled. I . . . I should have watched where I was going."

"No, *señora*, it is I who should have watched. I am devastated to think I dozed off. Juan José is not the man to lose sight of a beautiful woman. Especially when her hair is the color of silver in the mines at Chihuahua and her eyes are as bright as turquoise. That is what I shall call you—

turquesa. And I shall not take my eyes off you, I promise, ever again.''

Diana could not keep from laughing. She knew the man was wildly unsavory—Cord would be furious if he found out she had been talking with him in the square . . .

But Cord didn't care about her. He had let her know that, in no uncertain terms. She didn't take orders from him! Besides, she liked Juan José and what she quickly discovered was his refreshingly candid way of looking at things.

''Don't you ever get tired of lounging around drinking in the plaza?'' she asked him one day. She had just finished her morning shopping—Panchito had been sent back to the *casa* with a load of supplies—and had stopped for a cup of sweet, strong coffee when Juan José appeared at her side. Taking a small coin from his pocket, he insisted on buying her a *torta*.

''But where *should* I lounge around drinking?'' he asked reasonably. ''The leaves are on the trees, people come and go—much of interest happens here. Later, of course, when the weather turns bad . . . But for now, what could be more pleasant?''

''You might try working and save your money.'' Diana bit into the cake, rich and spicy, with tender little raisins that surprised her teeth.

''For what? So I can have a book that says how many American dollars I have in the bank and boast of it like other men? But I am not other men, *turquesa.* They drink too, but they drink in secret. I am honest. It is sad, of course . . .''

''Sad?'' Diana sensed he was teasing.

''If I had more money, I would not be forced to drink this cheap Mexican tequila. *Por Dios!* it is a trial. Even here, in humble Santa Fe, one is acquainted with the bourbon of Kentucky. But we all have our sorrows.'' He tapped the bottle of colorless liquid beside him on the table. ''This is mine.''

''You are incorrigible.'' Diana tried to look disapproving.

''So I have heard. It has been said more than once—but me, I do not care. A man has only one life to pass on this earth. He must live it as he chooses—do you not think so, *turquesa?*—and not worry what others say.''

It was the kind of reasoning that appealed to Diana. She

had followed more than a few unconventional instincts herself, and while most of them had brought nothing but grief, she clung to the right to make her own mistakes. She did not, of course, approve of excessive drinking. She hated the way Juan José was living his life, but it was, as he pointed out, *his* life, and so she found herself raiding Cord's well-stocked supply room: if Juan José was going to drink anyway, he might as well have what he preferred.

"Ah, *turquesa,* you have not only the face of an angel but also the pure sweet heart." Those strange, luminous eyes lit up as he uncorked the bourbon and took a deep whiff. "You have a friend for life. A willing slave. Anything you want—*anything*—you have but to ask. Juan José is at your service."

"I'll remember that." Diana laughed. She could not for the life of her imagine any "service" she might require from a drunkard, but he sounded sincere and she didn't want to hurt his feelings. "Maybe I can forget my scruples long enough to see if there isn't something else where that came from."

As it turned out, both friendships were to stand her in good stead a few days later.

It was well into the morning. The rain had continued intermittently, pelting down with particular force just after dawn, and swampy-smelling puddles spilled across the plaza. The sky was still overcast, only an occasional sliver of blue showing through billowing thunderheads, and most of the vendors had not bothered to set up their wares.

Diana took advantage of the empty square to dismiss Panchito and wander off on her own. With no work, there was no reason to keep him, and she'd been so busy these past weeks, she had hardly had a chance to see anything.

The town proved disappointing. The streets that had seemed so colorful with crowds thronging both sides and waving from the funny flat-topped roofs now looked drab and blandly uniform. Exotic, yes—where, in Richmond or St. Louis, could one see a peasant wading barefoot through the heart of town, driving goats ahead of him with a long stick, or hear pungent strings of Spanish as the irregular wheels of a *carreta* bogged down in the mud?—but exotic did not mean intriguing. The same dirty brown buildings seemed to line every narrow street, opening onto the same squalid plazas, and the same sounds of pigs and chickens and crying children came from the same filthy hovels.

After wandering aimlessly for an hour or so, she turned back toward the central square. The blue patches in the sky were bigger—it looked like it wasn't going to rain anymore—but moisture was already soaking through the seams of her boots, and she was tired and cold and ready to go home.

She had just started into a street that led to the plaza when she stopped, dismayed. People were coming out; she could see soldiers on horseback cutting across the square, and farmers with baskets of produce on their heads and shoulders. But between her and them was an enormous puddle, running from one side of the street to the other.

Just for an instant, Diana was tempted to take off her boots, hike her skirt up, *and slosh* through. But she had no way of knowing what—or *who*—lay beneath that mirror-glassy surface, and the thought of strange things slithering around her ankles and oozing between her toes was enough to make her shudder. Hadn't she passed a cross street a few yards back?

She had. Less a street than an alleyway, cramped and unpleasant, but a wider road showed at the end, and the few water-filled indentations were small and easy to get around. It wasn't until she was well into it that she noticed with a faint prickle on the back of her neck that no one was in sight.

Not that the city had been crowded in the aftermath of the storm. But always before, there had been someone. A horseman in the distance . . . a beggar huddled in a doorway . . . a woman sweeping water off a flooded roof. Now the stillness was so eerie it was almost sinister.

Diana paused. Should she go back? But that meant finding another way around or wading through the puddle. The street was short, after all, with busier streets on both ends. It was just the strangeness of the place that gave her the jitters. The smell of mud and manure that never seemed to go away.

Footsteps came from behind as she started down the narrow lane. She felt her heart jump.

Silly. She was being silly again . . . but the footsteps seemed to speed up when she did, slowing as she slowed down.

Was it her imagination?

Turning her head, she darted a cautious glance over her shoulder. A man was there, poorly dressed—but who in that shabby town wasn't in tatters? Nothing about his dark hair set him apart, the droopy mustache covering his mouth, the dirty-looking stubble on his cheeks.

She clutched her skirt instinctively, eyes scanning the street ahead. Not far to the corner. She had always been swift on her feet. She could be there before he had a chance to react.

She might be making a fool of herself—she probably *was*—but right at the moment, all she wanted was to be back in the plaza, surrounded by people.

But before she could do anything, a pair of men appeared at the far end of the street. Diana saw them scurry around the corner, then slow down abruptly, easing to an ominous shuffle, their breath coming in audible pants.

Nerves tensing, she looked back, just in time to see the man behind give a slight nod. They were together! They must have seen her turn into the street. Two had dashed around to approach from the far side while the third cut off her escape in the rear!

A cold sweat broke out on her skin. Diana could feel it coating her palms as the most unspeakable images flashed through her mind. All those lectures from old-maid schoolmistresses had not been in vain! Lovemaking had never been discussed in that prim setting—marital "duties" were referred to only in the vaguest terms—but the consequences of wandering unescorted in strange places had been spelled out in vivid terms.

The *fate worse than death*. How quaint—and empty—those words had seemed. Now, remembering the hideous pressure of Ryder's body in the wagon and the fear and disgust that had swept over her then, Diana knew they were anything but empty. She *would* rather die than let these men use her like that.

Her eyes searched the street again, desperately this time. The humid stench was almost unbearable. There were doors, but they were few and far between, and she sensed she would find them bolted if she gave in to her panic.

There was a ladder, too, braced against a wall on the other side, a few yards ahead, leading to the roof, where a second layer of dwellings had been constructed pueblo-fashion over the first. She could reach it if she dared. The men were still some distance away.

But what if she didn't find anyone up there? She would be even more isolated then. Or what if—God help her—she found *more* men, like the brutes closing in on her now?

Terror grew like a lump in her throat, making it hard to swallow. Thirty yards to the end of the street? . . . Forty? . . . No matter how fast she ran, they'd be ready by the time she got there. And there were two of them.

If she went back instead, if she surprised the man behind her, threw him off-guard . . .

She picked up her pace, trying to trick him into walking faster. A chance in a hundred, but she had to take it. Just a little faster . . . *now!*

She stopped abruptly, looking down, as if something had caught her boot. Please, God, she thought, let him be careless.

A quick backward glance told her it had worked. The man had not adjusted his speed in time. He was almost there, only a few feet away, skidding to a stop. If she could just whirl around before he caught his balance . . .

But the mud was too slippery. No sooner had she turned than she felt her feet sliding out from under her.

Her arms flailed frantically, but there was nothing to catch onto. Then suddenly she was on her knees, mud-drenched and terrified, and men were coming at her from both directions.

The one behind got to her first. Diana felt a sickening rush of fear as hands lurched out, clawing at her waist.

He's going to tear my skirt off, she thought helplessly. Oh, God, he's going to force himself on me, right here in the mud!

But the hands only grabbed the drawstring bag at her belt, wrenching it free with a sickening jolt. Before Diana could catch her breath, he had tossed it to one of the other men and, whirling on his heel, raced back down the street.

Thieves! They were *thieves!* They had scared her half to death, and all they wanted was the few small coins in her purse! Fear exploded suddenly in a wild, illogical burst of anger, and scooping up a handful of mud, Diana hurled it furiously at that tattered, retreating back.

The missile hit the man squarely in the head, spattering onto his hair and down the loose neck of his shirt. Not until he turned, black eyes even blacker with rage, did Diana realize what a mistake she had made.

She had been safe! He had been running, and she had been safe! Now, God knew what he was going to do to her.

She would never find out, for just at that instant a figure came hurtling around the corner, moving so fast it was only a blur. As Diana watched, gasping, a hand came out, grabbing the man by the back of his shirt, spinning him around, sending him with a loud splat into the mud.

The thief had barely managed to raise himself when that same fist smashed into his startled features and he was back in the mud again.

Diana, almost as startled as the thief, found herself staring at a surprisingly sober-looking Juan José. His body loomed solid and muscular over that crumpled heap; his face was as dark as the thunderclouds in the sky.

Almost simultaneously a commotion sounded at the other end of the street, and Diana turned shakily to see Panchito, one arm out, finger pointing dramatically at the two men still standing. A stream of Spanish poured out of his mouth, sounding like remarkably proficient curses. Then Cord was there and one of the men was sailing through the air, crashing into the wall, followed almost immediately by the other. A last feeble stirring and they collapsed, defeated, in a pool of muddy water.

It was all over in less than a minute.

"Señora!" Panchito's voice, cutting through the sudden silence, quivered with reproach. "Are you crazy? You hire me, Panchito, to take care of you, and then you go off by yourself. Of what can you be thinking?"

Diana did not have a chance to answer, for suddenly the street was mobbed with people, all talking, all moving at once. The three men were dragged groaning and protesting to their feet and hustled off toward the far end of the street.

Spanish words were flying all around, much too fast for Diana to understand, but the word *calabozo* came through loud and clear, and she sensed that the men were going to be very sorry they had messed with her. Panchito, puffing importantly, scurried after them, not wanting to be left out of the excitement.

The street emptied as quickly as it had filled. Only Juan José was still left at one end, Cord Montgomery at the other.

Diana was struck, as she looked from one to the other,

by the similarity between these two men who came from such different backgrounds. Not so much in appearance, though there were certain facial resemblances, but in the lean, hard style she supposed was characteristic of the west. Except Cord's eyes were flashing, while the other man had slipped into lazy nonchalance, as if the alcohol had oozed back into his system and he was comfortably drunk again.

"Did I not tell you, *turquesa*"—he winked—"that I was at your service?"

"So you did." Diana managed a weak smile. Now that she was all right, she was surprised to find herself trembling. "And I didn't believe you. I think I owe you an apology—and another bottle of Kentucky bourbon."

"I think *I* owe you a case, Juan José." Cord's voice was dry and controlled. "If that little urchin hadn't found me when he did, you would have had to take on those men by yourself. Two you might have managed, but three? . . . Besides, that bottle my wife gave you is looking kind of lonely."

"Ah, but it was nothing, *señor.*" Juan José's accent turned broader, his speech slurred, as the last of the tension flowed from his body. "It is my pleasure to help a lovely lady. You owe nothing in return. As for those three *cabrones*—they were never any threat. But, of course . . ." He raised one brow ingenuously. "A gift, freely offered, among friends, is always welcome."

Sweeping a low, almost courtly bow to Diana, he sauntered back down the street, as if nothing had happened.

Diana watched curiously as he swung around the corner. That Cord was acquainted with Juan José was not surprising. Everyone in Santa Fe probably knew the town drunk. Nor was it odd that Cord liked him. Juan José was extremely likable. But apparently Cord also knew that she had pilfered a bottle of bourbon for him.

And he hadn't minded.

She did not have time to ponder that, however, for another, more startling—and considerably more intriguing— thought popped into her mind.

Cord still had feelings for her! He tried to pretend he didn't—he had been trying ever since that wonderful, terrible night on the trail—but he had been frantic when he thought she was in danger!

"I'm sorry," she said, trying to look contrite. "I didn't mean to cause any trouble. Truly . . . I *am* sorry."

"You damn well should be," he replied gruffly. "Apparently you've forgotten why I brought you along in the first place. Just because there's no male heir doesn't mean you're out of danger. I wouldn't put it past your father or his henchman, Ryder, to pull something fancy. Like maybe kidnapping."

Kidnapping? Her father? Diana stared at him, puzzled.

"But those weren't my father's men. Or Ryder's. They were just thieves, after my money."

"I had no way of knowing that. Do you have any idea . . . ?" He broke off, checking the urgency in his tone. "Nor did you, madam. Those three could have been anyone. After *anything*. I'll thank you to be more careful in the future. I prize my neck too much to stick it out every time you get in trouble."

But that wasn't what he meant, Diana thought exultantly. It wasn't his neck he was worried about, but his heart. And his fierce male pride.

Her spirits soared as she walked beside him to the plaza, struggling to keep up with his long, brusque strides.

He *cared!* He could pretend all he wanted, but it wouldn't do any good. She knew the truth, and so did he!

He had been furious with her, and rightly so. Her childish prank had gotten wildly out of hand. He hadn't wanted to care—maybe he'd even convinced himself that he didn't—but thinking she was in danger had shocked his feelings into the open.

He couldn't fool himself anymore. And he couldn't fool her.

He cared. And if he cared, surely, somehow, she could find a way to win him back.

17

PERFECTAMENTE!''

Doña Gertrudes Barcelo stepped back to admire her handiwork in the lamplight. No longer young, she had been in Santa Fe so long no one even remembered what she looked like with her own teeth and hair. ''La Tules'' still ran her popular establishment, with the lively faro game in the *sala* and the even livelier amusements upstairs, but most of her profits nowadays came from bankrolling legitimate businesses, and it was her powerful network of spies which enabled the Americans to keep their hold on the city.

Now, at an age that was beginning to show, even beneath layers of paint, she was hungry for new challenges. And the young woman who had appeared, half shyly, half boldly on her doorstep that afternoon offered the challenge of a career.

''*Bella,*'' she said, smacking her lips with an unnaturally pearly grin. ''*Bella, bella . . . bella.*''

''*Bellísima,*'' one of the girls agreed, waving a kohl-darkened eyelash brush for emphasis. ''Even in daylight, no one would guess. Under the *candelas* at the *fandango* this evening, she will indeed look perfect.''

The others crowded around, giggling their approval. ''And very mysterious,'' a sloe-eyed *señorita* put in. ''Every man is going to be wild with excitement to know who she is.''

Diana tried not to blush as La Tules' ''ladies'' ran their eyes up and down her body. She could just picture the men at the ball doing the same thing. She had not been looking for modesty, heaven knew, when she rapped on the door of the most notorious woman in town and asked to be turned into a sultry Spanish beauty. But she hadn't expected to feel *quite* so naked beneath the scoop-necked silk *camisa*. Even without looking down, she was distinctly aware of the outline of peaked young nipples against the flimsy fabric.

La Tules saw her reaction and laughed.

"The *señores*, they will find her *simpática*, yes. All will fly into her web. But it is, I think, only *one* man our little spider is hoping to snare."

She snapped her fingers, and the youngest of the girls, the pretty one with the slanting eyes, held up a glass.

"Here . . . look in the mirror. You will see. The *espejismo*—the illusion—it is *consumado*."

The illusion was indeed complete. Diana's eyes were clouded with belladonna, but she could make out enough to see that she had been completely transformed. The image in the glass might have been another of the laughing *señoritas* who crowded the small upstairs room of La Tules' house of pleasure. Her hair, colored with strong coffee, was a stunning chestnut brown, elaborately dressed to set off etched-silver combs, over which floated a black-lace *mantilla*. Her eyes, dilated by the drug, showed only the faintest edging of blue, deepened by shadow almost to sapphire. Her skin was bronzed and bare all the way down her slender cleavage. No gaudy earrings or flashy jeweled necklaces to scratch the makeup or detract from her natural loveliness.

La Tules was right. Every man would be drawn to her, as surely as helpless winged creatures were drawn to the spider's web. And there *was* only one she wanted.

Cord was certain to be there. People had been talking of nothing else for days. It was the *fiesta* of the season. There would be dancing and drinking and great hearty bursts of laughter. No man with blood in his veins would stay away.

And the mysterious *señorita* in the black *mantilla* was going to catch his eye. Catch and hold it. And she would never be fool enough to let him go again.

The *fandango* had begun. Diana left the conspicuous black coach with its curtained windows around the corner and approached on foot. Latecomers were still arriving, dashing *caballeros* leaping out of the saddle to assist young ladies as they spilled from light carriages in a jumble of satin and velvet and lace. Every man seemed to have a lantern, which he hooked on a peg or post, and blazing torches were jammed at jaunty angles into the soil.

Diana hesitated a moment, her pulse quickening. She could almost picture herself inside, floating with the music that drifted through the open doors, caught up in an exotic rhythm of fiddles and marimbas and Indian drums.

That was where Cord would see her. He would look up and be captivated—as he had been once before when he caught a glimpse of a pretty stranger in the mirror. And suddenly she would be in his arms and they would be spinning round and round in the center of the room.

He wouldn't be able to resist her. How could he, when they had never resisted each other before? It would all be over then. The torment and anger and terrible heartrending misunderstandings. He would recognize her and his own deep feelings at exactly the same instant.

In her fantasies, that was where he swept her up in his arms, oblivious of watching eyes as he carried her, ruffled petticoats billowing in a froth of color, to the waiting carriage.

Diana smiled suddenly, realizing that people were watching. Well, let them! Tonight was her night. She was going to follow the music into the hall, feeling wonderfully, scandalously naked beneath her skimpy costume, and dance as she had never even imagined she would dance.

Inside, the light was almost dazzling. Hundreds of candles sputtered and sparkled from massive chandeliers and hammered-metal sconces on the walls.

The glow was warm and deceptively pretty, creating a romantic atmosphere in what was essentially an ugly room. The floor, typical of even elegant homes in the area, was hard-tamped dirt, wetted and smoothed so many times it had the dull sheen of fired clay. The walls had been whitewashed once, but they were badly chipped and gray with fire soot and candle smoke. Even patterned chintz, tacked shoulder-high along the walls to protect the men's jackets, was faded and dirty, its once sprightly colors now barely distinguishable.

But there was no lack of color in the swirling center of the hall. Masculine heels clicked in the formal pattern of a *contradanza,* blue military uniforms contrasting dramatically with waist-length black *chaquetas* and flowing white silk shirts, sashed in jewel tones. The women were as vibrant—and bold—as a tropical garden. Their *camisas,* which came in every conceivable pastel shade, left even less than Diana's to the imagination. Skirts in slightly darker hues, sometimes blending, sometimes wildly clashing, flared as they danced, showing shocking amounts of leg. And every one of them seemed to have a slender black *cigarito* dangling from her lips.

Just for a moment, Diana felt a twinge of doubt. Every time she had gotten in trouble with Cord—every time he had been angry—it was because she had deceived him. Would he look on this new escapade as a lark? A bit of harmless fun? Or would he think she was being devious again?

And how had she imagined she could ever fit in with these bold, brassy, cigarette-puffing *señoritas?*

"Well . . . hello." The voice that cut into her thoughts was distinctly American. Diana whirled with a thump of her heart to see a young officer beside her. "You look like you're waiting for someone to ask you to dance. I'd be happy to oblige."

"Señor?" Diana dropped her lashes self-consciously. Now that she was actually here, she wasn't at all sure she didn't want to turn and run away!

"Pay no attention to him, ma'am." A second man appeared next to the first, nudging him aside. "You're an impudent puppy, Gilmer—and totally out of line. The lady is looking for a *gentleman* to escort her onto the floor."

"And I outrank you both." The good-natured banter was joined by yet another officer, to whom the first two grudgingly deferred. "Ah, yes, I see you understand . . . Captain Moore, *señorita.* Ben Moore. It would be my pleasure to rescue you from these overeager youngsters."

Diana barely remembered to keep her eyes lowered so they wouldn't notice the faint rim of blue around her pupils. It was all she could do to keep from laughing. Lieutenants Gilmer and Warner had been visitors in her home. And she had seen Captain Moore several times at Bent's Fort.

If they didn't recognize her, maybe this wasn't going to be so hard after all.

"I must beg you to forgive me, *señor,*" she said, her accent so broad, she sounded as comical as Juan José. "I have just arrived. You must allow me time to dispose of my *capote,* my—how do you say it?—cape and refresh myself. Later it will be a pleasure to be 'rescued' by so gallant a *caballero.*"

Slipping away in what she fervently hoped was the direction of the cloakroom, Diana thanked whatever fates arranged such things that Santa Fe evenings were cool enough to require a wrap. She needed time to orient herself and get used to the local style of dancing.

Five minutes later, the velvet-lined *capote* safely stowed in a small room that reeked of perfume and tobacco, she positioned herself in the shadows of one of the doorways and stared in frank fascination at soldiers and traders and local ladies cavorting enthusiastically around the floor. As far as she could see, Cord had not put in an appearance, or her father—though that was hardly surprising. Garland Howard was not a graceful man. A *fiesta* setting would not show him to advantage.

Nor was Ryder there. Diana breathed a sigh of relief. She had the decidedly unpleasant feeling that those sly, scornful eyes would have seen through her disguise—and she had no idea what she would have done if he'd had the effrontery to ask her to dance. Slapped him in the face probably, and given the whole thing away! Just the thought of being touched, however casually, by that man made her skin crawl.

Another five minutes, and she was feeling considerably more at ease. If Cord just stayed away a little longer, she'd have the dance steps figured out. The band switched to a waltz, which, if somewhat livelier, at least resembled the waltzes she was used to. A hauntingly lovely Mexican dance followed, quite similar except the partners placed both hands on each other's waists and leaned back as they spun around.

She could do it! She knew she could, especially if she drew a nimble partner. All she had to do was watch the others.

Suddenly she was glad she had had the courage to dye her hair and dress in costume. Even if Cord never showed up, at least she'd have an evening of fun. She didn't think she could have borne dressing as a proper American matron and sitting on the sidelines.

"Ah, there you are, *señorita.*" The young captain's teasing tones drew her out of her sheltered alcove. "All refreshed . . . and most charmingly. You did promise me a dance, I believe."

Diana hadn't exactly promised, but she wasn't averse to the idea. After all, she had to start somewhere, and Captain Moore seemed like the sort who would be generous if she trod on his toes.

"It would be my pleasure, *señor.*"

She need not have worried. The music had a tinny twang, the beat was raw and primitive, but all she had to do was let go and follow her instincts. In fact, it was her partner whose feet dragged as the band struck up another waltz and he tried manfully to accommodate those raucous strains to his own staid American style. To her amusement, Diana caught herself coaxing him along, daring him to be a little less inhibited.

After that, she danced every dance, blithely switching from one partner to the next, always taking care through lowered lashes to search out the blue jackets of the military. Her accent might fool the soldiers, but she very much doubted it would pass muster with a Mexican.

Diana had always loved dancing—it was the one social grace she had excelled at in school, singing and sketching and, heaven forbid, needlepoint having defied her—and she let the music flow through her, carrying her along like driftwood on an ocean wave. Every new dance was an exciting challenge, every old one a welcome respite to be savored and indulged. The atmosphere was so spirited, the mood and sound and rhythm so engrossing, she didn't have time to think of anything else—even the fact that Cord was still not there, and might not be coming at all.

Her eyes darted along the sidelines, picking out faces. She almost laughed aloud when she caught sight of the only other *americana* in Santa Fe, besides Rosalie of course, whose condition did not allow her to attend. Magoffin's wife. Diana had glimpsed her at Bent's Fort, though she doubted the other woman even knew she was there. She looked amused now, and slightly disdainful, as she sat with her hands primly folded in her lap.

"It seems you *yanquis* do not permit your wives any enjoyment," she said impulsively. She was dancing with a young lieutenant whose name she did not know or had forgotten, and who seemed to come with two left feet.

"Our wives are ladies, ma'am." Blushing, he missed a step, almost causing Diana to stumble. "I mean, uh . . . we expect different things of our ladies. Our customs are . . . well, they're . . . different. Naturally, an American woman wouldn't feel comfortable dancing like this . . . but I'm sure she's enjoying herself."

"Yes, I'm sure she is." Diana let him off the hook. In truth, the young matron did seem to be having fun. She smiled at the man beside her and even appeared to be joking as he pretended to offer her tobacco and papers to roll a cigarette.

But it wasn't Diana's kind of fun, and she had a vague sense of pity for this woman who didn't even seem to know she was missing anything. And for the lead-footed young lieutenant.

One day he was going to go home—if he was lucky in California or Chihuahua or wherever the battles were fought—and marry the "lady" he thought he wanted. And wonder why his dreams kept drifting back to Santa Fe.

Was that why Cord had expressed a decided disinclination to wed? Because he'd be bored to tears with someone like that?

She was so caught up in thought, she didn't even notice that the dance had ended and the man who approached, prompting younger men to step aside, was a distinguished-looking Mexican. Not until she glanced up did she see Esteban Olivares.

All she could do was look down again and pray he hadn't noticed her eyes.

"*Señorita?*" Taking her arm, he guided her onto the floor with an unsettling stream of Spanish. Diana could only follow helplessly, unable to protest without giving herself away. Mercifully, for all his age and bulk, Olivares was a skillful dancer, and she dared hope it might somehow work out.

But when he continued speaking—he barely seemed to pause—she realized she had to do something. She could hardly go through the entire dance pretending to be deaf and mute.

Taking a deep breath, she forced herself to interrupt.

"I must protest, *señor*. I come here not merely to dance, but to practice my English. Surely you will not deprive me of that little pleasure."

His answer was a disconcerting chuckle.

"English it is, then—if such is your desire. I would never deprive so lovely a lady of anything in my power to give. Your English is charming, and your wit. But I think you do not need the practice . . . Señora Montgomery."

"Señora *Montgomery?*" Diana completely forgot her accent as she looked up to see that he was laughing. Not just his mouth, but his eyes, his plump cheeks, his entire face. "How . . . how did you recognize me?"

"How could I not recognize you, *señora?* I am an observer of life and people, especially beautiful female people. I see a lithe young body, I remember it. I remember the way a woman walks, the way she holds her head . . . the very special way she smiles. Most of all, I remember her eyes. The belladonna, it does most remarkable things, does it not? But it cannot completely turn *la turquesa* to black.''

"But . . ." Diana faltered, feeling suddenly awkward and foolish. "Has everyone recognized me, then? Are they making fun when they ask me to dance?''

Olivares shook his head gently. She looked so young, the little *señora*, he was reminded suddenly that he had a girl of his own this age. He *must* be getting old, to look at a sensuous woman the way he looked at his daughter.

"I think not. It would be cruel, making fun of a pretty lady. Whatever else they are, these young American officers, they are not cruel. Besides"—he chuckled again, kindness suffusing the amusement in his voice—"I think they would be too shocked. They are bold enough with the *señoritas* in their pretty silk *camisas*. But to dance with a countrywoman and feel that she is not wearing a corset? I do not believe they could keep up the pretense.''

He hesitated, touched by the faint flush that rose to her cheeks. Understanding more, perhaps, than she thought.

"I have told you, I am an observer. I see many things. I see, for instance, that you have an admirer. In the doorway—there. I think it is the admirer you seek.''

Diana turned in spite of herself, drawn almost hypnotically toward the shadowy recess that led to the street.

Cord. She had no idea when he had arrived, but it must have been recently, for he was standing just inside the entry, a Spanish-style cloak dangling carelessly over one shoulder as he stared at her with eyes so dark they looked almost black.

Anger? Diana lost the beat and would have stopped altogether if her partner's deft guidance had not kept her moving. Had he seen through her disguise so quickly?

Just for a second, her heart stopped beating. Whatever had possessed her to think she could get away with this? . . . But no, that wasn't anger she saw in his strong, chiseled features. It was some other dark passion. Darker than anything she had ever seen. Strange and intense . . . and somehow compelling.

Her knees felt weak. It was all she could do to keep from swooning. The arrogance she had sensed that first time seemed even more blatant now as he lounged against the chintz-draped wall, openly, insolently raking her with his gaze, sending out invitations it was impossible to misunderstand. Sheer physical sensation, the animal magnetism she had never been able to deny, seemed to flare out, hot and terrifying and utterly tantalizing. Never before had she been so achingly conscious of how desperately she loved this man.

And how devastated she would be if she lost him.

"Yes, *señora.*" Olivares' voice was soft in her ear. "It is he. And that *is* the look you wanted to see. But have you thought, I wonder, what it means?"

"What it . . . means?" Diana looked back at him, confused.

"If it works, this game you are playing, this very dangerous game, he will come to you with desire in his eyes. But he will not be coming to his *wife.* He will be coming to a black-eyed seductress. And he will be thinking of adultery. Have you considered how you will feel then?"

No, she had *not* considered. Diana clung to the music, trying to ignore the churning feeling in her stomach. She hadn't considered anything, except how much she wanted her husband back—and what fun it would be to parade in front of him like one of the scantily clad *señoritas* who had thrown roses when they came to town.

It hadn't occurred to her that the very attraction she sought might weaken the already fragile underpinnings of her marriage.

She would never know how she managed to get through the next minutes. She did not look back, staring instead at the toes of her slippers, but she was aware every second of insolent gray eyes boring through her skimpy blouse. Finally, after what seemed forever, the music stopped. Diana broke away abruptly, not even pausing for a perfunctory thank-you as she slipped through one of the doors to a deserted plaza in back.

She had to be alone. She had to find a way to collect herself and think.

How could she have been such a fool? The air was cold, but Diana barely noticed as she leaned against an empty hitching post and stared into the darkness. The moon was barely a sliver, the mountains in the distance lost in inky black. The stars were so clear, it looked as if someone had strewn a handful of diamonds across the sky.

Everything had been so much fun only a few minutes ago. Her dreams had seemed so pretty then. Cord would see her and be dazzled, not because he lusted after bare bosoms and flashing ankles, but because there was something between them, some instinct too powerful to resist. He would come to her, draw her into his arms, and suddenly, miraculously, everything would be all right.

Well, he had seen her. And he had been dazzled. But it wasn't *her* he was thinking about. And it wasn't all right.

She leaned forward, resting her forearms on the post. The music started up again, another waltz, slower this time. The smell of Santa Fe at night was like nowhere she had ever been, the coldness in her nostrils, the sand, the pungent pine, and she knew she would remember it all her life.

She was not even aware of the exact moment she realized she was not alone. She sensed rather than heard the footfall behind her, knew a second before it happened that she was going to feel hands on her shoulders.

And she knew without looking down whose hands they were.

For an instant all reason abandoned her. She should have been angry, hurt, resentful; she should have remembered what he was doing and hated him for it. She should have pulled away, longing to protect her identity and berate him for his treachery all at the same time.

But everything got confused somehow. All she could feel were rough, startlingly bold hands, impudently toying with the edge of her blouse. Her body arched back, seeking and finding the strength of his chest, all thoughts of resistance lost in a swirling kaleidoscope of overpowering emotion.

Emboldened, Cord began to caress her neck, hands slipping down, arrogantly, surely, cupping her breasts. Did he always approach strange women like this? But then, he had been bold that morning on the servants' porch. Diana's knees gave out, and she felt herself sway against him, unable to think of anything, feel anything but the physical longing that swelled her body. His laugher—that deep, husky sound she knew so well—was muffled as his lips sank to the curve of her neck.

Then her blouse was coming off, falling to her waist. With a gasp of shock, Diana felt the cold air on her breasts, and what little sanity she had left came rushing back.

This was not her he was caressing in the moonlight. This was some trollop he hadn't even met! She didn't know how ladies of easy virtue were usually treated, but she had the feeling he was perfectly capable of dragging her into the bushes and finishing what he had started!

"*Señor!* You are much too bold." She barely remembered to disguise her voice. What was there about this man that made her yearn to respond, even when he was betraying her?

"Not bold at all." He was still laughing, his hands still on her breasts. "And not unwelcome. You were not surprised when I touched you, *querida*. You knew I was watching. You knew I would follow when you slipped outside . . . and you were ready."

His voice dropped somewhere deep in his throat; his lips were on her neck again and she could not bear the things his hands were doing.

"You want me," he whispered provocatively. "As much as I want you. Why do you pretend?"

Oh, God, he *was* going to drag her into the shrubbery.

"I was not pretending." She didn't dare turn, didn't dare let herself look at those strong, scornful features. "I was just . . . shocked. I'm not accustomed to having men come up from behind and place their hands on me."

"Ah, I see." The mocking remained in his voice, but he drew back. "You were too surprised to move. That's why you wriggled against me and that little groan came out of your lips."

"I didn't groan. That's disgusting!"

"Didn't you?"

"No!" She spun around, facing him at last. "You *yanquis* are all alike. Bah—I despise you!" She spat on the ground. "You think all you have to do is present yourself to a woman and she'll fall into your bed. No pretty words first, no dancing, no flirtation. Just, 'Here I am and you'll love it!' "

She waited for the flash of anger, the wounded ego that might save her. But he only threw back his head and laughed.

"Is that what you want? A dance and some pretty coaxing? Well, then, you shall have it. Madam . . ." He pulled himself to attention, extending his arm in formal invitation. "May I have the honor of escorting you into the hall?"

Diana hesitated. Olivares had been right: this was an extremely dangerous game she was playing. If she had any sense, she'd refuse and stomp off with her nose in the air.

But to refuse him meant denying herself.

"Very well, *señor*. I will dance with you . . . in the public *sala*. But only if you behave."

Disdaining his arm, she started toward the hall, as if she didn't care whether he followed or not. She had gone only a few steps when he called her back.

"Haven't you forgotten something?"

"Forgotten?" Diana turned warily.

"Surely you're not going in like that." His hands were impudent as they caught her blouse again, pulling it up this time instead of down, rearranging it with extremely intimate gestures across her front. "Your breasts are lovely . . . and I enjoy looking at them. But don't you think you'd cause a bit of a stir?"

Diana blushed, as much with fury as embarrassment, but there was nothing she could do, for he was steering her into the *sala*. The music was just beginning, the waltzlike dance she had glimpsed before. Cord put his hands on her waist, and she did the same—she could hardly make a scene here—and suddenly they were out on the floor.

As in her dreams, she thought helplessly . . . only not her dreams at all. Because in her dreams, somehow, Cord had been dancing with *her*.

Too late she saw the trap she had laid herself. If this went on any longer, if the lewd insinuations got out of hand—if she had proof he was unfaithful—their relationship would be damaged beyond repair. But if he figured out who she was now, he'd be so furious he'd never speak to her again.

"Is this what you expected, *señor*," she murmured huskily, "when you came here tonight?"

"I have learned never to expect such unexpected pleasures." He spun her around deftly, tempting her to lean back, as the others were, farther and farther and farther, until she would have fallen if he weren't holding her. "In fact, I came tonight hoping to find a business associate."

"But your eyes are not searching for him now?"

"My eyes are not occupied with anything but you . . . and you know it."

Diana let herself go, bending deeply, trusting him as she had never trusted anyone. It was as if they were all alone, not just in the hall, but in the world, and this sweet, haunting, achingly lovely music would go on forever. It was not he who had fallen into the trap, but she, and by the time the dance ended, no matter what happened, she would be lost.

"But you, *querida* . . . this *was* what you expected."

His voice lured her eyes up, and she saw that he was smiling. A strange smile that had more than seduction in it.

"I? I don't know what you mean."

"Why else would you rinse your hair with coffee—you make a fetching brunette, though I like you better as a blond—except to capture the attention of your husband? Or do I flatter myself?"

Diana's eyes opened wider. "You *knew?*"

"Of course I knew. Did you honestly think I wouldn't spot my own wife? After all these months? There's a certain intimacy on the trail—to say nothing of a very, uh, memorable evening when I saw you in even less than you are wearing now." He caught her confusion and grinned almost boyishly. "As a matter of fact, I came forewarned. I happened to notice the coach around the corner and came in expecting to see you . . . though I didn't expect to see you looking quite like this."

"You're not angry?"

He shook his head. "Why should I be? I've always admired your spirit. The truth is, love, if I were a woman I'd want to join in the fun myself instead of sitting like a lump on the sidelines. And if I were married to a stubborn, self-righteous bastard like me . . . well, I'm not sure I'd consider him worth the bother."

Diana caught her breath, trying to think but finding it impossible. The whole room seemed to be reeling.

"What . . . what are you saying?"

"I'm saying that you win. I want you, Diana . . . I wanted you the minute I walked in that door. Hell, I wanted you when I saw the coach and knew I'd find you dancing. And that I couldn't bear to see you dancing in someone else's arms. Is that what you wanted to hear?"

"I've dreamed of nothing else for weeks. But there were times I didn't think it was going to happen."

"You should have more faith in dreams, *querida*. Sometimes they do come true." Cord paused, forgetting the music for a moment as he drew her subtly closer. The mist in her eyes touched him, the tremor on her lips, and he knew he had surrendered more completely than he intended. "And you should have more faith in your own very enticing charms."

Other couples spun past, a dizzying montage of color and laughter, the last burst of exhilaration before curfew closed in and it was time to empty the hall. The music stopped. Still he did not move, holding her instead, lightly, until it began again, the waltz that marked the finale of the evening.

"Tell me, love, these dreams of yours . . . did you picture us dancing like this?"

Diana looked up, her face glowing. "Exactly like this."

"And how did it end . . . your dream?" He was holding her close. Much too close. Scandalous even in Santa Fe.

"Shall I really tell you?"

A hint of teasing caught his ear, intriguing him. No woman had ever been able to play games like this and make him like them so much. "By all means . . . I am dying to hear."

"I dreamed you wouldn't be able to resist me, that you'd sweep me up and whisk me off to the carriage. I pictured my skirt floating out, like banners in the breeze . . . and everyone standing aside as we passed."

"With their mouths hanging open? You surprise me, love. I had not known you were such a hussy. Well, why not?" The idea took hold suddenly, her fantasy becoming his. "This town is too damned sleepy. Let's wake everyone up and give them something to talk about!"

He was moving as he spoke, lifting her in one swift, fluid motion, strong arms warm and supporting as he headed with long strides across the room.

This time it really *was* her dream. Her cheek rubbed against the slightly rough texture of his jacket; her skirt flared out, not quite billowing the way she had imagined, but dramatic enough to catch everyone's eye. The music faltered, fiddlers and drummers as startled as the dancers, then faded altogether. Not a sound could be heard except the echo of Cord's boots.

Diana could not see a thing—her face was buried in his chest—but she knew everyone was watching.

And no doubt their mouths *were* hanging open!

"I warn you, love . . ." Cord paused just inside the doorway. "You're going to have to endure looks of great pity tomorrow."

"Pity? Why?"

"Because every man here is going to think he saw your husband indulging himself shamelessly with another woman!"

18

"I DON'T CARE." Diana giggled as the night air swirled around them, black and golden where light and shadow mingled. "I don't care what anyone says or thinks. I don't care about anything! As long as you're taking me home . . . to my bedroom."

"Your bedroom, love?" He strode into the darkness, around the corner where the coach was waiting. "What would I do there?"

"Lay me on the bed, I hope, and take off all my clothes . . ." Diana drew in a deep breath, bolder than she had ever felt in her life. "And make wild, passionate love to me."

The coachman jumped down to open the door, then climbed back, ruddy features suddenly redder. Cord relinquished Diana slowly, settling her on the cushions.

"What makes you think I'm planning on doing that, sweet?"

"But . . ." Diana felt her courage falter. His voice was caressing as he slipped in beside her, but there was something not quite right in the words. Had he just been teasing after all? "I thought . . . I thought you wanted me . . ."

"I do want you. Very much. And the idea of pillows and a feather bed is extremely appealing . . . but I'm not sure I can wait that long."

As he pulled the door closed behind him, shutting out the light, Diana discovered that he meant what he said. He couldn't wait . . . and rather to her surprise, she couldn't either.

It had been so long. She leaned forward instinctively, searching for him in the darkness. She had thought about this so often. She had ached to feel his lips, as she was feeling them now, hot, hungry, assaulting her own. She had longed for impudent fingers, making her breasts ache, her body burn everywhere he touched.

"The curtains," she murmured as the carriage jolted forward, but it was too late. His arms were around her, iron hard, no escaping that arrogant pressure. Her hands flailed against his chest, not protesting, but grasping, clutching, as eager for him as he was for her. Suddenly they were tearing at each other's clothes, Cord expertly as her blouse came down, her skirt up almost at the same instant, Diana clumsily trying to work the fastenings that held a man's costume together.

Light flickered through the windows, giving her one brief glimpse of him, then disappeared, and they were drowning in velvety blackness. No sight to guide her now, nothing but sensation, the feel and smell of him, the male taste of his mouth as he drove into her, deeply, abruptly, filling her with hardness and urgency and sudden swift satisfaction.

She was surprised, afterward, to hear the soft sound of her own laughter. Satiation mingled with the wonder and contentment that poured over her. They were only half-undressed, their bodies twisted in the most improbable positions, but there was an incredible sweetness that had not been there the first time they made love.

And an even sweeter sense of security, because now there was no secret to rip them apart.

"I hope no one happened to ride by," she said demurely. "I did try to warn you about the curtains."

"No one was there," he replied gruffly, surprised at the intensity of his need to protect this fragile creature in his arms. "I would have heard if there were." At least he thought he would. God, when had he lost control of himself like that? She'd be the death of him, this little minx he had been so arrogantly sure he could handle.

"Well, let's hope you're right. We had put on enough of a spectacle already. One show an evening is sufficient, thank you. I don't mind providing a little gossip, but I wasn't planning on going down in the folk history of Sante Fe."

Cord drew her into his arms, laughing as he had not laughed for years. Comfortably, easily, surrendering the last part of himself that he had been holding back. If she had said anything else, if she had been shy, angry, embarrassed, if she had reproached or wept . . . But a woman who could love with such abandon and then laugh was a woman he could not resist.

They were still nestled together when the gates opened and the carriage pulled into the yard. Cord had removed his jacket and it was draped loosely over Diana's shoulders. Now he wrapped it closer, regretting the cloaks that had been left behind.

His trousers were done up, his shirt buttoned, but Diana's bare legs stuck out of a tumble of ruffles and black broadcloth as he carried her across the tiled patio.

"Do you suppose the servants are watching?" he whispered wickedly.

"I suppose they are," she whispered back. "What do you think will shock them most? The sight of their mistress in wild disarray? Or the thought that her husband is bringing a black-haired *puta* to her bedroom?"

Cord stopped with a look of mock horror.

"Where did you learn a word like that?"

Diana snuggled her head into the side of his neck. "Oh . . . I'm very good at languages."

"That's not all you're good at," he conceded.

A single lamp was burning on a low side table as Cord kicked open the door to the bedroom and carried her inside. Diana was dimly aware of the things that had become so familiar, the carved pine four-poster with its quilted spread, the whitewashed walls, the gay little pattern of flowers on the ceiling. It was funny how different things looked now that she was not alone anymore.

Cord laid her on the bed very gently and went over to the lamp. He started to turn it up, then glanced back.

"I'll put it out if you prefer, but I don't like to make love in the dark."

Diana shook her head. Somehow it had not even occurred to her that he would.

"Good." He raised the wick until the lamp was glowing. "We made love once in moonlight, once in a darkened carriage. I want to see you this time, and I want you to see me. I want us to experience tonight with all our senses."

He sat beside her on the edge of the bed, making no attempt to disguise the longing in his smoldering gray eyes.

"I am going to undress you now, Diana . . . and you are going to undress me. Then I'm going to lie beside you on the bed, and we are going to enjoy each other. Thoroughly.''

His hands were almost trembling as he reached for the jacket, parting the dark wool that had fallen closed in front. A spurt of agony surged through his groin. Incredible . . . he had forgotten how breathtaking she was. Young, yet womanly too, her breasts small but perfectly formed. Little rounded hills peaked with nipples that made him hard just to look at them.

Stifling a moan, he slid the jacket from her shoulders. Every muscle, every nerve in his body, ached to possess her again. It was all he could do to hold back.

''That is a very pretty *camisa,*'' he muttered hoarsely, ''but it's all crumpled around your waist. It's time to take it off. And this charming ruffled skirt.'' His hands were tender, tantalizing her with a subtle patience that was not shared by his urgent, throbbing member. Her unclad body was exquisite torment, raking him with conflicting responses. He wanted this moment to last forever—and he wanted to rip off his own clothes and bury himself inside her.

When he did not move, but sat there looking down, eyes half-teasing, half-expectant, Diana realized, embarrassed, that he was waiting for her.

''I . . . I don't know what I'm supposed to do.''

He took her hand and laid it on his chest. ''These are buttons, *querida.* You know what to do with buttons.''

''Yesss . . .'' She laughed, self-conscious, but curious too, liking what he was making her do. Feeling warm and suddenly tingly all over. ''I think I can manage buttons.''

Indeed, she managed them well. The shirt was silk, sleek beneath her fingers, an oddly sensuous affectation, more Mexican than American. The little buttons seemed to pop out almost without being coaxed.

She was surprised and vaguely amused to see that it was torn from the haste of their previous passion.

Cord shrugged his shoulders, easing the shirt off, but otherwise made no move. Diana was aware of a strange sense of power, the same power he must have felt when he undressed her.

The partial nudity of his body, his nearness on the bed beside her, was compelling, and she almost felt as if she were seeing that powerful masculine chest for the first time.

A faint layer of moisture glistened on dark tangles of hair. Daring herself to reach out, she traced the hardness of his muscles, felt the bristling stubble beneath her fingertips, but tentatively, not yet sure.

He seemed to approve of what she was doing. She grew bolder, following the line of black curls that ran down his belly, disappearing into his trousers. Only when she reached the bulge in front did she stop with a gasp.

"Don't be frightened, love." His voice was muffled as his hand closed over hers. "There is no reason to feel awkward when two people desire each other."

Guiding her fingers over the unfamiliar fastenings, he taught her to undo them. Then suddenly his trousers were open, coming down, and Diana was aware of something hard and extremely male.

How huge it looked . . . like before. But not quite as intimidating.

"So soon?" she said, only half-coyly.

He smiled back. "So soon."

"Is this going to go on all night?"

"Oh, God." Cord groaned. She *was* going to be the death of him. "Probably, *querida* . . . probably. I'll be an old man by morning, sapped of all my strength."

"Then I'd better take advantage of you now . . . while I can."

Lamplight played on their bodies as they stretched out next to each other, limbs intertwined, but gently . . . touching, fondling, not yet demanding. Shadows were muted, colors enriched, the jet-darkness of Cord's hair, the bronzed angularity of hardened muscles contrasting with the softness of Diana's femininity, her skin pale now where the makeup had worn away. They did not hurry, but took time with each other, he knowing, she sensing, that the final moment would be sweeter for having waited.

This new intimacy with a man's body both frightened and fascinated Diana as her fingers explored, hesitated, ventured forth again. She had not known he would feel like this, warm, mysterious, tantalizingly forbidden. Sinewy ripples glided, one into the other, not just on his chest and broad shoulders, but on his back, his buttocks, all the way down the rock-hardness of his thighs. The man-smell of him, tobacco and leather, the faint scent of horses, the sweat of their recent lovemaking, was pungent in her nostrils.

Her hands grew freer, her lips finding the boldness to follow, sampling the textures of his skin, the distinctive taste of him, conscious every second of the things his hands and lips were doing to her. His reactions told her she was right—her instincts merged with his—and she longed to know every inch of him, every dimple, every hair, as he longed to know, intimately, every secret part of her.

Or *almost* every inch. She faltered, turning timid as her hand reached that one sweet spot still unexplored.

"There, too, love," he prompted gently. "You must touch me everywhere . . . and I will touch you. Pleasure is meant to be shared."

His fingers tightened over her hand, wrapping her around him, teaching her how he liked to be caressed.

Then he was caressing her too . . . so much the same, yet different . . . the way he made her feel . . . and the dizzying eddy of sensation that had already been roused rose and swirled around her until she was sucked like an autumn leaf into the terrifying, exhilarating vortex of her own emotions.

At last passion became too much, the yearnings could no longer be contained, and Cord slipped between the legs that opened to receive him. He entered her slowly this time, savoring the warmth, the tantalizing moistness, the way she seemed to close around him, clinging as he retreated, then plunged, retreated, and plunged deep inside her again.

There had never been anything like this for him before. No passion had consumed him so completely, and he was dimly aware for the first time in his life that he had lost control of his body. It was master now, not he. He could no more have denied his desire for her than he could have denied the air that gushed into his lungs. Somehow in these last weeks, when he had been unaware, this beautiful, devious, treacherously seductive enchantress had woven silken cords around his soul.

Desperately, one last moment, he tried to reclaim the direction of his destiny, tried to defy the feelings, the passions, this thing he could not yet bring himself to call love. But it was too much for him. *She* was too much, and with a shudder of defeat he felt the warmth of his manhood spilling into her.

Almost at the same second, Diana quivered violently, fluttering like a little trapped bird, and he knew that she, too, had surrendered. Only hers was a willing surrender, while his had been torn with excruciating agony from his heart and loins.

It was a moment before he became aware of anything but the harsh gasps coming from his throat, the warring emotions lined up like opposing armies in his breast. When he did, he saw that she had raised herself on one elbow and was looking down at him.

"Does this mean you aren't angry anymore?"

Not angry? The unbearable swell of emotions seemed to break, as if a floodgate had opened and everything had come spilling out. God, where did she come up with things like that?

"I am wildly furious," he said, trying not to laugh as silver-golden tresses tickled his chest. "As well I should be. My hair stands on end every time I think about what you did. But fury is a passion too, and passions have a way of getting mixed up together. A very sweet way, sometimes."

"Then you've forgiven me?"

"If 'forgiveness' is the word for what just went on between us, yes . . . I suppose I have. What you did was more than wrong, Diana. It was inexcusable. I hate dishonesty, and you piled lie onto lie. But you were very young . . . and foolish. I can understand that. I have been young myself, you know."

"And foolish?"

He grinned. Blast the minx. She took away all his weapons. "I wouldn't go that far. Let's just say I have a soft spot in my heart for clever pranks, and that trick you played on your father would probably have amused me if I hadn't gotten caught in it myself. I just wish you had felt you could trust me. Though I suppose my temper *might* make you hesitate."

"That wasn't it." Diana shook her head slowly. He did have a temper, but . . . How could she explain? She had come to love him so much; she had just wanted the time to be right. She had kept putting it off and putting it off—and then she had seen that painstakingly whittled cross on a desolate stretch of plain. "I had no idea you would grieve for the child, Cord. If anything, I thought you'd hate it. It never occurred to me you might actually care."

"It didn't occur to me either," he admitted wryly. "I

was taken as much by surprise as you. Hell, more by surprise . . . but I think, sweet, we are on dangerous ground. There are wrongs on both sides . . . old angers that need time to heal. It might be best for a while not to dwell on the past.''

''What is there, then?'' She stared at him with troubled turquoise eyes. ''The future?''

Cord sat up on the bed, deliberately looking away. What she wanted now, womanlike, was promises, commitments. A passionate declaration of love. But ''love'' was a word he had vowed never to use again.

''I cannot offer you a future, Diana. I never pretended I could. No tomorrows . . . and no yesterday.'' He turned back. ''Only today. You must learn to believe in the present.''

He caught a flicker of sorrow, but she managed gamely to hide it. ''I've never been too sure of the present,'' she said. ''It hasn't always been kind.''

''Not even tonight?''

''Well . . . perhaps tonight.''

''Thank God. My pride was in serious danger. But we're becoming much too solemn. What we need is a distraction, and I have just the thing. Don't go away. I'll be back.''

He scrambled out of bed before she could say anything and started down the hall. Diana's irrepressible sense of the outrageous returned as she watched his extremely bare buttocks disappear. If any of the servants were around, they'd be in for a surprise!

He was back a minute later, a bottle of Madeira in one hand, a pair of etched-crystal goblets in the other.

''I believe we have cause to celebrate,'' he said with a rakish twinkle in his eye.

Diana watched as he set the bottle on the table and popped the cork. ''You'd better be careful. You remember what happened last time I had too much to drink.''

''I do indeed . . . and it was delicious.''

He poured the wine, expertly twisting the bottle so not a drop was lost. Diana accepted a glass and stared into it. Tiny beads of lamplight danced like elfin spirits in a darkened amber pond. She was remembering herself, as she took a sip and felt the warmth spread out from her belly, how wanton she had been that night at Bent's Fort. She had a feeling she was about to be even more wanton now.

But when she looked up, she saw that Cord was watching her curiously.

"Do you ever think of *him?*" he asked unexpectedly.

The question caught her off-guard. "Him?"

"The man you were so wild about before you met me. The one you would have married if death had not claimed him first."

"Oh . . . Jordan." Diana felt a twinge of guilt as she realized how little she had thought of her former suitor in the months since she had left Missouri. "I . . . I was fond of him, of course . . . it tore me apart when he died. But I don't think I was really surprised. A man like Jordan courts death. I suppose I'd always known, instinctively, he would end up like that."

"Like . . . *that?*" Cord threw her a quizzical look.

"Father implied that he was caught with an ace up his sleeve." She half-smiled, sad and bemused at the same time. "He was probably right. Jordan liked winning, and he wasn't too particular how he went about it."

"Even if it meant risking his life?"

"Especially if it meant risking his life. Jordan was a gambler. And he liked cheating. I rather suspect he preferred cheating and winning to winning fair and square."

Cord raised one brow. "Strong words coming from the lady who was hell-bent to defy her father and marry him at any cost."

"That's just it. I *was* hell-bent to defy my father." Diana stared into her glass again, forcing herself to confront the realities she had been avoiding. "I think that was most of Jordan's appeal, though he did have a certain disreputable charm. But there was no love, on my part or his." She took a slow sip, surprised at the thoughts that were running through her mind. Even more surprised that they didn't hurt.

Jordan had known all along about her great-grandfather's will. She wondered why she hadn't figured it out before. It had to be a matter of public record, somewhere, and Jordan was just the sort to ferret it out. Oh, he had liked her all right—as she had liked him—but he hadn't loved her. He had loved the money she was going to come into.

"It was over long ago. Even before he died, though I didn't realize it at the time. It was a very brief, very fragile infatuation."

"And you have no regrets?"

She smiled as she raised her glass. "I'm here tonight with the only man I want. The only man I've ever wanted . . . like this."

Cord took the glass and set it with his own on the table.

"I don't think I need to get you intoxicated this time, *querida*. Here, put this aside, and let me show you how I feel about the woman *I'm* with tonight."

Cord stood alone in the enclosed garden. Somewhere the wind had started to howl; he could hear its wail over the rooftops, but here he was sheltered. Behind, in the lamplit room, Diana was tucked into the quilts, sound asleep, unaware that he had slipped away.

You have forgiven me, then?

The words came back, haunting, disturbing. The mingling of hope and doubt in her voice. If she only knew, he had forgiven her long ago. That same night, when the first heat of anger had cooled. His temper flared quickly, but it died quickly too, and with the return of reason had come the somewhat clearer realization that her sin was less intent than accident.

She *had* lied, but the lie had never been directed at him. She had been lying to her father—a fact that Cord could appreciate. That son of a bitch deserved what he got. She couldn't have known that her little deception about being pregnant was playing into his hands.

That she hadn't seen fit to enlighten *him* later was despicable, of course. Cord stepped around the fountain toward the far wall, the nip of autumn frost exhilarating against his naked skin. But "despicable" was probably the exact word she would have used to describe some of his actions. Like the way he had introduced himself to her on the servants' veranda. Or his roguish behavior later.

Dammit, she had had no reason to feel any loyalty toward him! He had done nothing to earn it. She had no reason to trust him, no reason even for gratitude, since she had offered half her fortune for his help. And what had she done, really? If it weren't for the way he felt about the child . . .

But that wasn't *her* fault. He reached out automatically, snapping a rose from one of the vines that trailed up the wall. He hadn't let her see what was happening. Hell, he hadn't let *himself* see the hunger for home and family that had festered in his heart, transferring somehow, insidiously, to the child he had come to accept as his own.

He hadn't pushed her away because he was angry. He knew that now, as he had known it then, in the stillness of another night. His coolness these many weeks had come not from disgust or disillusionment, or even disapproval. It had come, God help him, because he approved too much. Because he admired her spirit and feisty independence. Because he had already begun to sense in himself the feelings that finally had betrayed his body tonight.

Feelings. . . . He held the blossom to his nose, breathing in the perfume, reminded with an aching in his groin of the sweet scent of hair sprawled across his pillow.

Not love. He still could not bring himself to call it love. But feelings . . . truer, deeper, more consuming than he had ever known, even for the beautiful dark-haired cousin whose tragic death spelled an end to his youth.

A faint noise came from above. Cord glanced up, hoping that the sentries hadn't chosen that moment to check the garden. What a picture he would make. Bare skin bluish in the moonlight, body at parade attention, the stiff rod of his manhood a smart salute in front.

But no one was there, and he turned again to the glass-paned doors that led to the room where Diana lay sleeping. *I hate dishonesty,* he had said. God, what hypocrisy! It was not Diana who had been dishonest. She had never set out to lie to him.

It was he who had been brutally dishonest with her.

He reached for the knob, then hesitated. He hadn't told her what he had really been doing, strolling around her father's estate an hour early for his appointment. He hadn't told her why he had agreed to accept the job as wagon master for a second-rate trader he despised. He hadn't told her what was going to happen in a few weeks when they branched off the Turquoise Trail.

He hadn't even told her, truly, why he had married her.

And he accused *her* of being deceitful!

Cord lingered for a moment, his hand on the latch, surprised somehow at how cold it felt. There would be many perils in the days ahead. There was a chance he wasn't going to come out of this alive.

And if he did . . . would she want him when she found out what he had done?

The warmth inside beckoned, a contrast to the chill of the night. If he were fair, he'd follow the same instinct that had prompted him to stay away before. He would tiptoe through the room and out the door on the other side and leave her to wake alone and wonder if it had all been a dream.

But he did not have it in him to be fair, any more than he had it in him to be sane or rational. His passion for her was a kind of madness, and he could not stay away.

Diana stirred sleepily, her eyes opening as he slid into bed and laid the rose on the pillow beside her. Misty turquoise, all the belladonna gone now, but lashes still sooty with kohl.

Cord felt one last moment of guilt. She needed so much from him, this girl-woman cuddling instinctively into his embrace. Commitment, security, a future together, children perhaps. Love.

And he could give so little.

"I cannot promise to love you tomorrow," he said huskily as his arms twined around her. "I make no promises for tomorrow. But I can promise to love you tonight."

Diana looked up in the lamplight. His hair had fallen over his brow, dark and disarmingly boyish. There was something in his face she had never seen before. And that word she had never heard, save as a casual endearment, on his lips.

Perhaps, after all, she *could* believe in the present.

"Love me tonight, then, and let tomorrow take care of itself. Unless, of course, the love you have in mind is something pure and innocent."

Cord laughed, feeling the pliant, yielding softness of her body molding against his.

"It is not."

19

SANTA FE in the brittle autumn air took on a shimmering new beauty. To Diana it almost seemed as if the sweet perfection that had begun the night of the *fandango* were reflected in the city itself. The rains let up, the mud that clogged the streets and spattered the adobe walls began to dry, and every leaf, every pine needle, every late-blooming rose glittered in the sunlight. The mountains turned the most incredible colors, from lavender-blue in the morning to a deep mystical violet at dusk.

She was aware, when she thought about it, that this happiness could not last. They would be leaving soon, and Cord had promised nothing for the days ahead. But it did seem silly, fretting about what *might* happen, when there were other, considerably pleasanter distractions at hand.

In the mornings, Cord would saddle the horses while the air was still cool. Breakfast might be peasant cheese and tortillas, taken by the waters of an icy stream; then they were off across the fields again. Diana, who had seen the fringes of town only briefly, then with the distraction of mobs thronging the roadsides, was fascinated as Cord explained the agriculture and history, the racial mix of the people, the surprisingly complex social structure that existed in the *pueblos* and *villitas*.

"You seem to know a great deal about Santa Fe," she said as they paused at the base of a steep slope. It seemed surprising somehow that a wagon master would be so well-informed. "In fact, you know a great deal about everything Mexican."

"Do I?" He flicked the reins nonchalantly. "Perhaps, after all, you have not attached yourself to an *ignorante*." The stallion, needing no spurring, fairly flew up the hill, leaving Diana to follow as best she could.

The wind was brisk, setting shirtsleeves flapping, as they

stopped at the crest. The air was almost unbelievably clear; the vista seemed to stretch on forever.

Diana thought she had never seen anything so lovely. Clusters of buildings settled like little hamlets in green-and-brown valleys, sheep and cattle lolled under spreading boughs, and gaudily dyed hides, laid out to cure, added whimsical patches of color. Here and there, the hillsides were dotted with freshly washed wool, cloud-fluffy and white, echoing the brightness of an early dusting of snow on the mountains.

Only the intrusion of Fort Marcy, looking new and raw on an adjacent hill, shattered the illusion of serenity.

Diana had been a little surprised at the speed with which the military had erected the fort. Surprised in fact that they felt a need to build it at all. Two acres of structures, double-walled adobe, filled between with mortar and rock, seemed somehow excessive—especially when there wasn't an enemy in sight. According to Cord, though, the fort, which had been designed by Lieutenant Gilmer and named for the Secretary of War, was not just for show. The army would be pulling out soon, for both California *and* Chihuahua it appeared, and only a token force would remain behind. If an uprising occurred, a sturdy stockade might be the difference between life and death.

"Peaceful though it may look," Cord reminded her, "Santa Fe is a frontier. And frontiers are lands of fear. The Americans, knowing they are conquerors, live in constant fear that the Mexican soldiers will return. And the Mexicans, remembering they were not the first to occupy the territory, fear that the original inhabitants will slaughter them in their beds."

Diana looked down at the slopes and valleys below. Except for a faint rustling of leaves, the only motion was a peasant guiding his goats along a rough dirt path. A silvery tinkle of bells floated on the wind.

"It seems so sad," she said. "These aren't warlike people. All they want is to till the soil and eke out a living."

"Life is sad sometimes, *querida*. Men do sad, and terrible, things. But it can be happy too. And very sweet. You must cling to the beauty of the moment and let the rest go."

"I know." Diana smiled. "I must learn to believe in today."

They were still laughing as they wound their way down

the slope, Cord on his spirited stallion, Diana falling behind on her own considerably less elegant mount.

True to his word, Cord had offered to buy a more fashionable horse, or at least to rent one, when they reached Santa Fe. But Diana, by that time accustomed to Brutus' quirks and foibles, had surprised herself by refusing. He might not be as showy as the pintos and palominos she passed on the street, but he was sturdy and remarkably swift.

Cord had been quick to approve.

"I hoped you'd see it that way," he had told her. "Beauty is only important in a parade. All the style in the world can't take the place of reliability. Or loyalty. And Brutus is strictly *your* horse."

Diana laughed again as she pulled the reins and felt the animal respond. Brutus was indeed hers, perhaps because she was light in the saddle, perhaps because she had a gentle hand, but more likely because she never showed up at the stable without a sugar lump. He allowed Cord to saddle him, and even tolerated him on his back, but he was ornery as a mule when anyone else approached.

Cord spurred ahead, unable to resist the impulse to gallop across an open stretch of plain, and Diana tactfully refrained from pointing out that his own magnificent Lance was beautiful enough for any parade, and so spirited only the strongest rider could handle him.

Her breath caught in her throat as he wheeled suddenly, the horse half-rearing, mane blowing dark against a crisp blue sky. But Lance was loyal too, and so in tune with Cord's own will and spirit, it almost seemed as if man and mount were one, bone and sinew flowing together until it was hard to tell where one left off and the other began.

Afternoons were a lazy contrast. Long, languid hours spent in bed, listening to the wind rattling the windows, the fire hissing and crackling on the hearth. Or riding in the same black coach that had brought them home the night of the *fandango*.

Sometimes the curtains were open, and Diana would peer out at cornfields merging into cramped rows of pueblo-style buildings, opening onto fields again. What had seemed strange and somehow menacing when she wandered the streets by herself was intriguing now, and she drank it in with her eyes.

Other times, Cord would reach out and close the curtains,

and she was vividly reminded of that first night in the carriage, though now at least he had the delicacy to postpone the final pleasure for the privacy of their bedroom.

Cord, as she was rapidly discovering, knew nothing remotely approaching shame. The fact that it was broad daylight didn't even give him pause. "Anything that can be done by the glow of a candle," as he pointed out, "can be done as well in the sun." And if the curtains weren't drawn, that simply meant his hands were confined to a somewhat more restricted space.

The things he could do within that space, however, were not restricted at all. She was likely to be looking out the window, smiling and waving at an acquaintance, when a hand slid under her skirt, up to the knee and beyond, daring her to go on smiling and waving and keep her features composed.

She was also discovering that he expected the same abandon from her. In the beginning, it had been he who initiated their lovemaking, he who fondled her first, guided her hands in timid exploration. Now he expected her to touch without being asked, to make the first move sometimes, to surprise him if she could.

And she was finding, rather to her astonishment, that she *liked* being a hussy.

"I wonder what the mistresses at school would do if they could see me now," she said as their carriage rolled along a narrow street behind the plaza. Cord had been studying something outside, and she tucked her hand between his legs, feeling from his instant reaction that he was not displeased.

"Cane you within an inch of your life, I suspect."

"Girls aren't caned." She laughed. "Girls are expelled and sent home in disgrace. With sighs of bitter disappointment. . . . They did so try to make me a lady."

"It seems they didn't succeed."

He was reaching for her breast with one hand, the curtain with the other, and Diana had the distinct feeling he was not regretting the failure. Cord Montgomery had little interest in ladies.

Which was just as well, because it looked like she wasn't turning into one!

Late in the afternoon, they would stop in the plaza for a cup of sweet cinnamon coffee. The square was quiet at that hour. Burros and chickens and peasants were gone, produce and children packed and carted off, and only a few of the tables were occupied.

Diana missed the bustle of mornings in the market corner. She missed the cries of the vendors, the fierce haggling, the cajoling whines. But most of all she missed the energy and braggadocio of young Panchito. Now that the boy was no longer needed, Cord had found him a place with Esteban Olivares, in whose shop on the far side of the plaza Panchito now worked twenty times as hard for less than half the money, a situation to which he had adjusted quite well, as Diana soon discovered.

"If an *hombre* is offered nine *reales* for the work of three," Panchito explained to her ingenuously, "he is a fool not to take them." He had paused by the table on his way back from an errand. "Panchito is no fool. But if all that is available is three *reales* . . . well . . ." He shrugged elaborately. "Señor Esteban, he is hard, but he is fair. And there is Mamacita, you know . . . and the small brothers and sisters . . ."

"And you're still getting more than you would by dipping into someone's pocket," Diana said.

His eyes widened. "Perhaps. Some days. But the work, it is steady. We may not get rich 'quick,' as you *yanquis* say, but I do not worry that we will starve."

"Or that you'll end up in the *calabozo*," Diana murmured under her breath, laughing as the boy headed toward the store, shoulders swaggering, heels clicking importantly.

Juan José sauntered over to join in the laughter.

"A *diablillo*, that one. But engaging . . . and very clever. It would not surprise me if he managed the shop one day."

"It wouldn't surprise me if he ended up *owning* it," Cord said, pulling a paper-wrapped parcel from under his jacket. Another installment on the debt he owed, Diana thought, though it came with a camaraderie that seemed unusual in men of such dissimilar backgrounds. "Olivares has no sons to take over the business, and no one else to buy him out. They say the husbands of his daughters have no interest."

"Except when it comes to spending the profits. . . . Ah, *señor*, you have long since repaid your obligation, if ever there was one. But a little gift, and such excellent quality—you have superb taste in the fruits of Kentucky—cannot be refused. Of course you will share."

He had uncorked the bottle and was pouring a portion into Cord's coffee. Cord could be a hard drinker when the occasion demanded—he was known for holding his liquor—but for the most part he imbibed lightly, and Diana noticed that he raised his hand almost immediately with a quiet *"Bastante."*

Juan José did not press, but poured his own bourbon into a glass, diluting it, rather surprisingly, with water. "Your health, *señor.*"

"And yours." Cord glanced back, obviously still thinking of the boy. "He's going to be a terror, Juan. One day you and I won't recognize this plaza. There'll be shops all around, and God knows what other businesses, and industrious youngsters like that making money hand over fist. I wonder if it will be as charming then."

Diana smiled as she glanced around. Except for blue-coated soldiers scurrying off to wherever soldiers went before supper, no one was moving. "I can't imagine this square ever being busy . . . or industrious. I think if we come back in twenty years, it will look exactly the same. Or a hundred."

"Nothing is for a hundred years, *turquesa,*" Juan José said in his funny accent. "Or twenty. Or, very often, one. But I am forgetting my manners. You must enjoy a taste too." Tilting the bottle over her cup, he tipped in about a thimbleful of bourbon.

"You are incorrigible, Juan," Diana said, laughing, but not objecting too strenuously. "And a very bad influence."

"But incorrigibility—it is the spice that adds savor to life, is this not so? And impropriety. Where would we be without those delightful qualities?"

Diana, recalling several extremely improper incidents in the past few days, felt her cheeks warm.

"Propriety does have its place," she insisted.

"To be proper is to be dull, *señora.* To be tiresome. To be tedious. Life is too short for tedium."

"Hear, hear." Cord raised his cup. "Here's to impropriety . . . especially in beautiful women." Then, seeing the blush deepen all the way down Diana's neck, he relented and, with a gentle smile, took her hand across the table. "And to the men who adore them just the way they are."

Diana smiled back, relaxing enough to enjoy the sunlight

splashing across the square. Even risqué comments somehow didn't seem quite so ribald in that colorful setting.

The day was unusually hot, exceptional for September, and Diana was surprised to notice a darkened trail of perspiration running down one side of Juan José's face, just in front of the ear. Why, he dyes his hair, she thought, surprised and strangely touched. It seemed an odd vanity.

She also noticed that his pupils were dilated, almost the way hers had looked with the belladonna. But then, alcohol was a drug too. She could just imagine the amount in his system to take such an awful toll.

"I don't think I've ever seen you without a bottle," she said impulsively. "Don't you worry about what that stuff is doing to you?"

"Ah, and here I thought we were friends. Friends do not try to change each other, *turquesa*. They accept . . . and understand. I do worry, about many things. But a drop or two of bourbon when I am on holiday is not among them. Soon enough, it will end, and I will be back at work—so 'corrigible' you will not recognize me."

Diana laughed in spite of herself, and the conversation eased into lighter channels. It was not until they were riding back in the carriage that she remembered his eyes again. And that funny streak on his face.

"Did you know Juan José dyes his hair?" she asked Cord. "Probably with coffee, like I did when I went to the *fandango*. It's a good sign, I think."

"A good sign, *querida?*"

"He's too proud to let the gray show. He really dresses quite well—have you noticed? And shaves every day. If a man still has some pride, that means there's hope for him."

"*Some* pride?" To her surprise, he started to laugh. "I think perhaps you do not understand a man like Juan José. Pride is as much a part of him as his fondness for bourbon. More. And incidentally, he's not always a drunkard. He has quite an excellent reputation on trail drives between his sojourns in Santa Fe. I'm thinking of signing him on when we head south."

"But . . . ." Diana stared at him. "Surely we have plenty of men. And, Cord . . . Juan José is Mexican!"

He looked amused. "I'm aware of that, sweet."

"My father hates Mexicans! He'd rather take on a . . . a cripple. Or a blind man. He'd never permit it."

''Your father may not have a choice. And no, we don't have plenty of men. Or won't in a few days. Rumor has it that Kearny is heading for California tomorrow with four hundred of his best troops. The rest will follow as soon as reinforcements arrive—or join Colonel Doniphan's volunteers when they mount the assault on Chihuahua. Every man anywhere near the right age is itching to go with them.''

''You mean my father really *is* going to have to hire men here?''

''I mean precisely that.''

''But . . . he's going to be very annoyed!''

Cord leaned back, laughing. ''He's going to be extremely annoyed. But there isn't a damned thing he can do about it.''

Garland Howard was *more* than annoyed. His face was purple with rage as he sat in his sporty rockaway on the edge of the plaza and glowered at the man standing in front of him.

''You're going to . . . What the *hell?*''

Randall Blake returned the gaze calmly. ''I'm going to ride out with the army tomorrow. As a lieutenant. General Kearny has very generously restored my commission.''

''The devil you are. You signed on to Chihuahua, and you're damned well going to keep your word! A bargain is a bargain. I'm paying top wages and I expect—''

''You're paying bottom-of-the-barrel and you know it. If it hadn't been so late in the season . . .'' Randy caught himself. Brushing back a lock of hair, he plunked the floppy-brimmed hat on his head again. ''But that's not the point. I did sign on . . . and I'm signing off. My country needs me.''

''Like hell!'' Garland reared up in the seat, the anger in his face so dark, the younger man feared he was going to have a stroke. ''You walk out on me now, you'll never work on a wagon train again. Shit, you'll never work anywhere! I'll blacklist you so bad, you'll be lucky to get a job sweeping floors.''

''No, you will not, sir,'' Randy said quietly. He was still wearing the dusty Levi's that had seen considerable service on the trail, and a patched and faded shirt, but his posture had turned military, chin up, feet slightly apart, shoulders unconsciously squared. ''You haven't heard a word I've said.

I'm going back to the army. I should never have left in the first place. And the army isn't the least bit interested in what you think.''

He turned on his heel and began to walk slowly toward the center of the square, where the Stars and Stripes was rustling in a light breeze. Garland flung the door open and would have started after him had not a chuckle sounded in his ear.

"He's right. All the bluster in the world won't keep the army from taking him on. Or the others.''

Garland swung around to find his partner leering down from the saddle of a powerfully built black gelding.

"What others?'' he said warily.

Ryder's teeth flashed. "The other young men who've had a sudden rush of patriotism. I've talked to two personally, and there are rumors of three more. My guess is we'll be eight men short tomorrow night. And we'll probably lose as many again in three or four weeks when Doniphan and his raiders turn south.''

"But . . . my God, man! That's *sixteen*. Half the crew!''

Ryder nodded as he leaned forward. "We can manage without three or four. I expected some attrition. And I've been flooding the market with merchandise, so eyebrows won't go up if we leave a few wagons behind. But at least six of the men are going to have to be replaced. That sets up an interesting situation . . . don't you think?''

"You find this funny?'' The older man glowered. "Dammit, Ryder, you have as much at stake as I do. The only men for hire are natives. I'm not getting stuck with a passel of Mexicans!''

"You are if you want to go on.'' Ryder eased his spine straight, not bothering to point out that he didn't, in fact, have anywhere near as much at stake. Garland Howard had offered ten percent, and he'd probably try to get that back if he had any gumption at the end. "What's *really* funny is that they're Mexicans of your wagon master's choice. Ah, well, it was to be expected, I suppose, considering the average age of the crew.''

His eyes drifted back to Randall Blake, who had changed direction and was heading toward a black coach that had just entered the square. An extremely expensive coach, for all its lack of ornamentation.

The expression that twisted his lips made the hair on Garland's neck bristle.

"Who is that, anyway?"

"You don't know?" Ryder whistled through his teeth. "That's your son-in-law. Quite a fancy rig, isn't it, for a wagon master? But then, he has a very rich wife. Did it occur to him, I wonder, how many young men he was taking on?"

"You think he planned . . . ?" Garland gaped in horror as an extremely unpleasant thought popped into his mind. "No! He couldn't have. He expected to be *ahead* of the army. There's no way he could have foreseen this. Dammit! I had everything all worked out. Down to the last detail. It was going so well."

"It was going well as long as it was going the way you expected. What you didn't make arrangements for was the *un*expected. That's the trouble with you, old man. You put all your eggs in one basket. Now you don't know what to do."

"And I suppose you do?"

Ryder grinned maliciously. "Of course not. Only a fool sets himself on a rigid course. Fast and loose, that's the way to play it. Roll with the punches and see what happens. I have ideas, of course. A man always has ideas . . ."

He broke off, his voice trailing away as a cloud of dust followed a second, smaller carriage into the square. This was a cabriolet, two-wheeled, with the top down. A mustachioed driver was perched on the seat in front; alone in the rear sat a woman with flame-colored hair and an extremely expanded waistline.

"Well, well . . . well." He began to chuckle. "It seems the lady has spunk after all."

Garland's face, which had gone back to its normal color, turned florid again.

"She's not supposed to be out!" Blast it, everything was going wrong all of a sudden. "I gave very strict orders. She is not, under any circumstances, to show herself in public!"

"My, my, such touching concern. What did you expect? Now that her 'delicate condition' is so advanced she doesn't even get attention at night, she's dying of boredom."

Garland started to bluster again, but Ryder held up a hand.

"There's probably no harm done. That's Olivares' carriage—I recognize the driver. Ever the thoughtful neighbor, isn't he? Fortunately, you're too cheap to rent a house next to one of the American traders, who might be expected to spend time in St. Louis in the near future. . . . Of course, it won't do to let her sit there like that. Anyone might come along and see her. If I were you, I'd put her in my own carriage and send the cabriolet back with heartfelt thanks.''

He laughed aloud as Garland stuck his head out the window, bellowing for his man to pull across the square. There he was, putting all his eggs in one basket again. Counting on Rosalie and her baby—as if such a thing could ever be sure.

''Fast and loose, old man,'' he muttered under his breath. ''Fast and loose.'' But if Garland Howard were flexible enough to play it that way, he might be a danger.

And there was going to be plenty of danger as it was.

By the time Ryder turned back, Randall Blake had nearly reached the coach. Ryder recognized in those long military strides what Garland had only sensed, the authority and cool confidence of a professional soldier. It occurred to him it was just as well Blake was leaving.

''One for our side,'' he said softly. ''One for our side. Or, more exactly, one for *my* side.'' Because in the end, there was going to be no one in this but him.

Diana, watching from her seat in the carriage, saw the same subtle changes that had struck Ryder, and something tugged at her heart. A second before Randy reached them and Cord leapt down to greet him, she knew what he was going to say.

''Where is your uniform?'' she called out.

Randy looked surprised, then sheepish. ''The tailor is rushing to finish it. It was a last-minute order. I'm afraid I'm not going to make a very elegant officer. . . . You knew, then? Here I've been dreading telling you.''

Diana shook her head. ''I didn't realize until just now. When I saw you walking across the plaza. You may not have your blue coat with the red and orange or whatever-color facing, but you look like a lieutenant.'' She made an effort to smile as he stopped by the carriage. ''If this makes you happy, then I'm happy for you . . . though I am going to miss you. Terribly. I think I'm just the tiniest bit jealous.''

''Jealous? Surely you don't pine for the glamour and adventure of a soldier's life?''

''Hardly.'' Diana laughed. ''A trail drive is adventurous

enough, thank you! I didn't mean I was jealous that way. I was thinking of all those beautiful *señoritas* in California . . . and how soon you're going to forget me."

She regretted the words the instant they were out. Casual flirtation wasn't casual to someone who cared.

"I will never forget you, lovely Diana," he said, eyes turning solemn just for a second. "And I would never leave if I didn't know you were happy."

Then, conscious of Diana's husband a few steps away, he turned awkwardly.

"And you, sir? I take it you did know."

Cord nodded. "Unlike my wife, I didn't just figure it out. I've been expecting it for some time."

"And you're not going to make it hard for me?"

"What for? To vent my spleen like my choleric father-in-law? Or play on your loyalty? I did consider it, as a matter of fact—a man of your abilities might come in handy— but . . ." He reached out abruptly, as if making up his mind. "I can't ask you to trade in your dreams for my convenience." Or my wife's, he added mentally as he gave the other's hand a firm shake. "You have your life. You must live it. *Vaya con Dios*, Blake. Take care—and try to dodge the bullets."

He was aware, as he moved away to give them a moment's farewell, of a stab of totally illogical jealousy. For all that had happened in the past days—and nights—for all that he and Diana now were to each other, he still couldn't bear the look of puppy love in another man's eyes.

Was that why he was letting Blake go so easily? He hesitated briefly, unsure for the first time. Because he wanted to keep him away from his wife? But no—no matter what his personal feelings, he had done the only thing he could. Every man had a right to his dreams. The glory of California and the Army of the West would not come again.

Cord was just about to turn back when he caught sight of a pair of carriages on the far side of the plaza. Garland Howard in the rockaway, Rosalie in the other—though she was being hastily removed, a flurry of taffeta and half-audible protests as her husband hustled her off.

Cord frowned distractedly. Furtiveness oozed out of the man's pores, the sly way his eyes darted across the plaza to where Diana was leaning out of the carriage, the expression on his face smug, almost evil, as he glanced back at the high expanse of his wife's waist.

Rosalie and Diana. . . . Something nagged at the back of Cord's mind. Rosalie and Diana. Where had he seen that look before? . . . Bent's Fort. Of course—in the courtyard! He had looked from one to the other then too. Rosalie and Diana. But there wasn't any connection between them.

Or was there?

Damn! Cord's blood ran cold as he realized suddenly what the one—the *only*—connection between the women could possibly be. It was so clear now, so obvious.

Damn!

He knew what the bastard was up to.

"You might say, *amigo*, that things are a little more complicated than I expected." Cord lounged back, body lean and taut as he peered through a haze of smoke at the man on the other side of the table. "It looks like I'll be taking on some hands. Six, probably. I'd like to make it eight or ten, but under the circumstances, that doesn't seem feasible."

"No." Juan José's eyelids drooped subtly. "It is rumored your employer is not overfond of *los mexicanos.*"

Cord allowed himself a wry smile. "One wonders why."

It was approaching curfew, and the small, seedy cantina was nearly deserted. Only one of the other four tables was occupied, by a tousle-haired *ranchero*, sloppily snoring into a puddle of beer. The last soldiers had long since departed, and the harried barman was too busy with a raucous trio of locals to be interested in what was happening across the room.

"Since you are telling me this, *señor,*" Juan José said, glancing with distaste at his glass, "I assume you wish me to be one of those six. *Ay!* this tequila, it is disgusting. Pedro in the square, or even Juanito, is cleaner. Or you are asking perhaps that I choose the men for you?"

"Both." Cord's eyes drifted toward the group at the bar. One of the men had fallen silent. Listening? "It is said you are a good man—sober. It is said you know horses and cattle, and because you are stubborn yourself, the mules do not try to resist you. It is also said you are an excellent judge of men."

"Sober *or* drunk," the Mexican admitted with no undue

modesty, "Juan José is the best. You will not find him wanting. Ah, Miguel . . ." He looked up as the last drinkers ambled toward the door, the silent one supported between the others. *"Que hace Usted? No desea vivir para ver la mañana?* His wife, she is a *tarasca*. A terror of a woman. She will beat him with a *tortilla* stone if he comes home like that. But she will beat him even harder if he stays out all night."

He watched until the men were gone, then turned. The barman had disappeared, probably to a room in back with a bottle for company. The air was sour with whiskey and stale beer.

"And yes, I am a good judge of men. I have already in mind the five that you want. You will be pleased, I think."

"They are young?" Cord asked sharply. "And tough? We'll be moving fast. I want to get ahead of the other traders—and stay there. I don't want anyone following in my dust."

"Young enough." One brow went up slightly. "But what about your own men, *señor?* The ones who stay. They are as 'tough' as you would hope?"

Cord shook his head. Easing closer, he propped his elbows on the table. "All I've got are some of the old-timers. Good workers, and feisty, but I'm not sure of their strength."

"Ah? I would have thought the assistant might stay. What is his name? Blake? Or the young mulatto."

"Blake is trained in the military. The call of the bugles is in his blood. He might stay if I pressed . . ." Cord hesitated briefly, recalling the scene that afternoon in the plaza. "But I can't. As for Aaron, there's a girl. Ephronia. A man in love is not quite as enamored of the, uh . . . risks of the trail. Or eager to leave his *novia* behind."

Something in his voice caught the other man's ear. A candle sputtered at the next table, then went out, leaving only the light of a pair of foul-smelling tapers pressed into whiskey bottles on either end of the bar.

"This is not what we are talking about, is it?" he said slowly. "This certain, perhaps not altogether inconvenient shortage of men? There is something else."

Cord's mouth twisted faintly. "Is that instinct, Juan . . . or am I so transparent?" Without moving his head, he took in the room again, as if reassuring himself that the bartender was still gone, the drunk still passed out on his table.

Then, leaning forward, he lowered his voice.

"I'm worried about my wife."

"Diana?" The name slipped out, the voice too startled to be hushed.

Cord nodded. "You have your finger on the pulse of this town. Gossip festers in that little square. Is it common knowledge? About her great-grandfather's will?"

"No." Juan José's eyes narrowed speculatively. "It is known, of course that she is an heiress, but I have heard nothing about a will. It is important?"

"More than important—it's diabolical. That woman-hating old misogynist couldn't have set things up more cruelly if he spent years agonizing over it."

"Woman-hating misogynist? I think, *amigo*, that might be redundant."

"Consider it emphasis." Cord laughed shortly. "If Diana had been a man, she'd have gotten her inheritance outright. Instead, everything was placed in trust, with the power vested in attorneys—and entailed everlastingly. Until she produces a boy heir."

He paused dramatically.

"When we left Missouri, it was believed that Diana was pregnant." He held up a hand, forestalling the obvious question. "She wasn't—but the matter was aired in an extremely public way. It could not have failed to receive attention. Rosalie, on the other hand, was uncharacteristically modest about her own impending motherhood. And she hadn't begun to show."

"So . . ." Juan José drew in a deep breath. The implications were obvious. "You believe, then, if his wife's baby is a boy, Garland Howard is going to try to pass it off as his daughter's?"

"I'd stake everything I have on it. Hell, I probably *am* staking everything. That child is the key to a fortune. Howard will do whatever he has to to make the switch work. Think about it. It's so simple, it's brilliant. Two women set out from Independence, one pregnant—apparently—the other not. When a baby turns up nine months later . . ."

Juan José twirled his glass, watching the way the smudges caught the light. "You think she will agree?" he said after a moment. "The young mother with the fiery hair?"

"I doubt it. Rosalie is a silly creature—God knows, she's not very bright—but she has her limits. No, something would have to be done about Rosalie . . . but that isn't the real problem."

"No. I daresay it isn't." The man's voice was quiet, his features thoughtful as he set the glass on the table. "You don't believe Garland Howard would *kill* his own daughter?"

"I don't believe he'd kill anyone—except maybe with a bullet in the back. He hasn't got the gumption. And, no, I don't believe he'd hire someone to do it for him. But there are other ways. He could, for instance, have her locked up in an asylum for the rest of her life. What court wouldn't grant him custody of her child? Assuming, that is, the husband was out of the way."

"All the more reason, then, to persuade young Blake to stay. If not for your sake, for hers."

Cord leaned back, the shadows catching and lengthening his face. "But he'd only do it because of his feelings for *her*. One can't ask a man to risk his life for another man's wife. Especially when that wife is one's own."

Juan José did not try to argue. For a proud man, some things were beyond compromise.

"There is," he said slowly, "another alternative."

"Go back, you mean?"

Cord was startled by the sharpness of his own laughter. God, hadn't he thought about that, and thought and thought! Give it up. Pack a couple of saddlebags and take her away, someplace where she'd be safe—and he'd be safe—and the whole damned nightmare would be over!

Only it would never be over until that bastard was in the dust. With a bullet in his gut.

"I can't, *amigo*. I wish I could, God help me, but I can't. I've come this far. I'll see it through. Now, about those men you mentioned." He slid his chair forward, all business again. "Who are they? Can I trust them?"

Juan José smiled. A slow, lazy smile.

"You will trust them, *señor* . . . with your life."

20

AS IT TURNED OUT, they did not stay ahead of the others for long.

They left on schedule, while October was still warm, well in advance of Doniphan and his troops, while the other traders were still packing and making hasty plans. But three weeks out of Santa Fe, twenty-two wagons and thirty men came to a halt in a squalid little village on the banks of the Rio Grande as Rosalie went into premature labor.

As long as she lived, Diana would never forget that night. A sandstorm had started; the wind was howling savagely outside, and she was terrified when she realized she was expected to go into a stifling back room in the dingy *casita* that had been placed at their disposal and help with the delivery. I'm too young! she longed to cry out. I've never had anything to do with illness or pain. Why, the only blood I've ever seen was from cuts and scrapes.

But the only person to listen was a swarthy-skinned midwife, and she had other things on her mind.

Choking back her fear, Diana forced herself to the threshold, almost retching as she stared in at Rosalie, white-faced and clinging to a knotted length of fabric tied to the bedpost. The stench was foul—the midwife's greasy hair, her fetid breath, the rancid odor of wicks sputtering in shallow saucers of lard—and sweat poured off Rosalie's body, saturating the coarse sheets and straw-filled mattress.

Filthy . . . it was so filthy.

Diana hesitated in the doorway. This was no way to have a baby. Then Rosalie held out a hand, eyes pleading, and somehow she found the strength to bend over that painfully cramped bed for the next several hours, wringing out rag after rag in a bucket of water and whispering words of encouragement. Mercifully, it was an easy birth, and Rosalie, unexpectedly, bore it with courage. She cried out only once, then more a gasp than a scream, at the moment her body surrendered its burden.

Diana's heart stopped as the midwife held up an alarmingly still mass of blood and flesh and examined it in the dim light. Noting with a toothless grin the equipment that proclaimed a boy, she gave him a sound whack on the backside, and suddenly he started yowling. A loud, blustering, indignant yowl, and Diana dared to breathe again.

He was making his presence known. She laughed with relief as sweat poured down her brow into her eyes. The little tyrant! He was going to have the whole house dancing attendance on him!

It was Diana's arms that first received the child. Rosalie was so exhausted she didn't seem to know, or care, that she had a son. But Diana, all her own tiredness suddenly gone, was filled with the most incredible wonder as she cuddled him against her breast. He felt so warm beneath the scrap of wool flannel that served as a swaddling cloth—his breath was a soft quiver on her cheek—and she was aware for the first time of what a miracle it was, this thing called life she had always taken for granted.

How tiny he was. Born too soon, but he seemed sturdy, and she sensed the strength and will that would see him through. A little hand peeked out from the blanket, and Diana touched it, marveling, as if she were the first ever to notice such a thing, at how wonderfully, amazingly perfect each baby finger was.

Her little brother. This was her *brother*. She felt a rush of joy and sorrow both as she realized how much she loved him and how sad it was that she wouldn't be there to see him growing up.

Rosalie continued to ignore her son in the days that followed. They remained in the village on the riverbank for several weeks, Cord and his men chafing at the delay as train after train pulled in front of them. But the notorious Jornada del Muerto, eighty grueling miles without water, lay just ahead, and even Garland Howard did not suggest that his wife was strong enough to be subjected to that.

In fact, Garland seemed quite complacent about being left behind. If Diana had not been so concerned about the baby, she might have noticed his behavior and wondered. He had always been in such a hurry before. But Rosalie was still rejecting the child, and a wet nurse had to be found, a local woman with a babe already suckling at one breast.

Not that the little scamp wasn't thriving. He grew bigger day by day . . . but it didn't seem right that he wasn't with his mother. Diana tried once to bring them together. Rosalie had been languishing on the pillows, staring as always now at cracks in the raw adobe ceiling, and Diana had thought somehow it might help.

At first it almost seemed to work. Rosalie didn't object when Diana laid the baby in her arms. In fact, there was a flicker of response for a second. But she didn't move either. She just lay there, not speaking, not even looking at him.

Then, to Diana's horror, tears formed in her eyes and began to roll down her cheeks.

"But . . . he's beautiful, Rosalie!" she assured her, alarmed. She had no idea how women were supposed to behave after childbirth, but surely this was wrong. Was it her fault for pressing the baby on her too soon? But if Rosalie didn't hold him, how was he supposed to know who his mother was? "He's little, but he's healthy, and absolutely perfect. He's going to be very clever. Look, he tries to take hold of your finger if you touch his hand. He just doesn't know how yet."

"It doesn't matter . . ." Rosalie's voice seemed to come from far away. Diana had to strain to hear. "I'm glad he's healthy. Truly. But it doesn't matter."

"Rosalie!" Diana was genuinely shocked. "What a thing to say. He's your son!"

"No." The woman on the bed shook her head. The tears were no longer flowing, but her eyes were bright with despair. "He is not mine. He never can be. He is Garland's . . . and Garland will never let me forget it."

She turned her face to the wall, and Diana took the child and tiptoed wordlessly out of the room. She could not for the life of her imagine what had gotten into Rosalie. She had been so brave when she went into labor—she had suffered all that pain with such dignity. Now she was behaving in the most incomprehensible way.

If Rosalie was not pleased with the birth of her son, Garland was beside himself. He turned almost jovial as he passed out cigars, the one extravagance he had allowed himself in Santa Fe, and even shared some of his private stock of brandy.

To anyone watching, it might have seemed that the birth of his son had mellowed him. But Cord, who knew better, felt himself growing warier by the day. Blast the bastard, he thought as he paused one evening in the doorway of the front *sala* and stared at him. His face was flushed and smug, as if he had created the child all by himself and the woman suffering in a room on the far side of the house had had nothing to do with it.

"It doesn't bother you," he remarked dryly, "that your wife is not recovering as she should?" He had, as usual, refused an offer of brandy but the other was too pleased with himself to be insulted.

"No. Why should it? Women have these whims all the time. They're often depressed after the birth of a child—I heard that somewhere. She'll snap out of it."

"And if she doesn't?" Cord's voice was casual, but his eyes narrowed.

Garland shrugged. "If she doesn't . . . well, I have my son. That's what matters. *My* son! Who wouldn't be proud to say that? Every man's dream . . . a boy to carry on his name. Naturally, that's all I can think about."

Your son. Cord felt his blood run cold. The red spots had grown brighter in the other man's cheeks. Not just drink, but something else. . . . You think you're putting something over on me, you son of a bitch. You think I don't see through your evil, lying soul!

If there had been any doubt in his mind, it vanished at that moment. When Garland Howard got back to St. Louis—when he and his henchman, Ryder, got back—the boy was no longer going to be *his* child. It was going to be the child of his daughter and son-in-law.

And that son-in-law wasn't expected to be around.

Watch your step, Montgomery. Cord turned on his heel and headed out into the yard. Watch your step—and don't let anyone behind you. The man was stupid, but he was cunning. And cunning men could be deadly.

There was still Rosalie, of course. Nothing could be done with Rosalie in the way, but her health was extremely precarious. Rosalie was a problem that might take care of itself.

And with Rosalie gone, only two people stood between Garland Howard and the fortune he craved.

* * *

The problem of Rosalie did indeed take care of itself, though not quite in the way her husband might have imagined. In fact, Garland would have been surprised—and amused—if he could have seen his wife a few nights later in the moon-deepened shadows of a scrubby piñon overlooking the river.

"I'm sorry," Rosalie was saying. "Truly I am . . . but we don't have a choice."

Diana, facing her in a thin silk wrapper which did nothing to keep out the biting wind, could only gape in shock and dismay.

"You can't mean that, Rosalie! You aren't thinking. I know you're unhappy, and I don't blame you. It must be dreadful being married to my father. But to run off—"

"She does mean it," the young man at her side cut in. Paul Thomas looked tall and extremely slender in a dark-dyed homespun shirt and denim pants. "We've been talking about this for a long time. Since Bent's Fort. It took me weeks to persuade her. This is not a whim."

"I love Paul," Rosalie told her passionately. "I've never loved anyone else. I never even knew what love was! And Paul loves me. I can't give him up!"

"No . . ." Diana faltered. "Of course not, but . . . the baby. Oh, Rosalie, he's such a sweet little thing. And he needs you. How can you even *think* about leaving him behind?"

"I don't want to." Tears gathered on her dark-red lashes, glittering like beads of crystal in the moonlight. "With God as my witness, I don't! That's why I couldn't take him in my arms . . . or nurse him. I knew Paul would be coming soon. I thought it would be easier that way . . . but it isn't. It isn't easy at all."

Diana heard the pain in her voice, and her heart contracted. "Then don't do it," she urged. "There must be another way. At least wait a few days. Maybe if we all think about it, we can come up with something. He's your child!"

"No." The wind picked up, blowing long, loose hair back from features that suddenly looked gaunt and twenty years older. "I told you before. He isn't mine. He's Garland's. And Garland would never let him go. Not a boy-child. His only son. He'd track us to the ends of the earth if he had to."

"He won't worry about us," Paul Thomas added quietly.

"As long as we don't cause gossip. When he gets back to St. Louis, he can put out word that Rosalie died in childbirth. All the talk will be sympathetic."

"There won't be a breath of scandal to ruin his precious career," Rosalie agreed bitterly. "He can go on to be governor or senator or whatever he wants, and no one will be the wiser."

"All he cares about is his son," Paul said. "If we give him that, we should be safe."

Diana pulled the wrapper tighter, wishing she had thought to grab something warmer when Rosalie scratched at the window and beckoned her out. She had the awful feeling that they were right. Garland didn't care about his wife. He was bored with being married. He might even look on this as a convenience.

"I do understand," she said impulsively. "I know how much you want to feel safe—how much you *need* to feel safe. But at the cost of giving up your son? Security isn't everything, Rosalie. Go, if you must. I wish you Godspeed. But take the baby!"

"Oh, Lord . . ." A sound slipped out of Rosalie's lips, halfway between sob and a wail, and her face turned ashen. "I would if I could. I've thought about it . . . I've longed for it! But I'm not brave like you, Diana. I've never been brave."

"No." Even that night she gave birth was only stoic acceptance—because she knew she could not keep the child. "No, I know you're not brave—"

"But I am," her young lieutenant put in. "I have courage enough for both of us. And I'm not so mean-spirited I'd turn my back on a child because he isn't mine. If I thought we could handle it, I would encourage Rosalie to bring him. I would insist on it!"

"But it wouldn't be fair! Don't you see, Diana? We'll be fugitives, running from place to place. God knows where we might have to go."

"I've left the army," Paul explained. "Not just without permission, but on the eve of battle. That makes me the worst kind of deserter. They'll be looking for me. Hard. I won't even be able to get to my bank account. We're going to have to live on what I can scrape up . . . and I can't work openly. It will be a hand-to-mouth existence. Shabby rooms at best—an open field sometimes, with maybe a cave for shelter. A newborn wouldn't survive.''

"I do love my baby," Rosalie said urgently. "That's why I couldn't bear to hold him in my arms. It's *because* I love him I have to give him up.''

Diana stared at them in the wispy light, feeling her resolve weaken. If she were Rosalie, if this were Cord standing beside her, could anything, even the child of her body, keep her from him?

"Why are you telling me all this," she said dully, "if you don't expect me to stop you? Why didn't you just sneak away and leave me out of it?''

"I wish I could have. Truly . . . but I need your help. Oh, Diana, I'm so frightened for him! I tried not to care. I *tried!* But I can't go without knowing he'll be all right.''

"That's what you're after?'' Diana felt something cold and prickly creep up her spine. "You're going to run off and you want *me* to take your place?''

"You're already more of a mother to him than I. You're the one who fusses over him all the time. The one who dangles her finger in front of his hand to see if he can catch it. You're the one he recognizes. He didn't even know me when you put him in my arms.''

"Maybe not . . .'' The prickles were growing. Rosalie was going to leave—she knew that suddenly; there was nothing she could do to talk her out of it. "But it doesn't make sense! What you're asking. You said it yourself, Rosalie: this baby is my father's. He's *thrilled* to have a son. He's even generous with his brandy! Dear heaven, if he wouldn't let you take him, what makes you think he'd hand him over to me?''

Rosalie laughed harshly. "Garland gets tired of things. Who should know that better than I? He thought he wanted a son before. He was excited when I told him I was carrying his child, but then he tired of the idea. He'll tire again soon enough. Promise me, Diana—*promise*—there'll always be someone to love and take care of my boy. I don't want him growing up in boarding schools, the way you did.''

The barb struck home, as Rosalie had known it would. "I can't promise," Diana protested, wavering. It *had* been lonely, all those years without love. "I'm not sure I'll be able—''

"You have to be sure." Paul Thomas' quiet voice carried

above the eerie whistling of the wind. "She can't leave if you don't promise. And she has to. It will destroy her if she tries to stay."

Diana looked from one to the other, hating the position they had put her in, but knowing there was nothing they could do about it. If this were me, she thought again. *If this were me . . .* And she had her answer.

"All right," she said. "I'm a fool . . . but all right. I promise. I'll see that he's loved and happy. I don't know how, but if I can't take care of him myself, I'll make sure there's someone."

"Rosalie ran away? Last night? She didn't take the baby?" Cord's face was drawn; gray eyes snapped and flashed against the sun-bronzed darkness of his skin. "And you just *let her go?*"

Diana stared at him, stunned. It hadn't occurred to her he would be angry. She hadn't even bothered to tell him until he'd come back from tending the wagons and seeing that the livestock was watered and fed.

"I had to, Cord. You should have seen her. She was desperate. I couldn't have stopped her if I wanted to."

"You could have gotten help," he reminded her sharply. "You should have come to me—I'm your husband! My God, Diana, this isn't the sort of thing a woman handles on her own."

"But there wasn't anything you could have done," she protested. "There wasn't anything *anyone* could have done. They'd made up their minds. They only told me because Rosalie was worried. She wanted me to promise to look after the baby."

Cord groaned. "And I suppose you did."

Diana nodded unhappily. She had also gone back and gathered what little cash she had to help the fugitives on their way, but it didn't seem quite the moment to mention that.

"Dammit, I wish you'd trusted me—or at least mentioned this a little sooner!"

"What would you have done? Sent men after them? Dragged them back by force?"

"If I had to." Cord's face was grim as he stepped over to the only window in the small, dingy front room. Outside, Garland had just returned from a stroll, no doubt down to the wagons for another bottle of brandy, and was dozing in a low-slung chair, chin bobbing on his chest.

The devil take him! One problem down—and he hadn't had to lift a finger. There he was, lolling in the sun, dreaming of Rosalie's early demise, and all the time, she'd exited his life in a much simpler manner. Things couldn't have gone more neatly if he'd planned them.

Take care of the baby, Rosalie had said . . . and Diana had promised. And nobody but the natives in one obscure little village even knew that Rosalie had a baby.

But everyone who crowded the roadsides when they rode into El Paso del Norte in a few weeks would see him cradled in Diana's arms!

"I couldn't tell you, Cord." Diana's voice cut into his thoughts. "I just couldn't. She loves him. I kept thinking what it would be like if I lost . . . if I had to give up someone *I* loved, and I knew I couldn't bear it. And I couldn't bear spending the rest of my life with a man like my father!"

Cord turned slowly, seeing her as if for the first time. The sun came in a dusty shaft through the window, catching her hair and setting it aglow around incredibly delicate features. He had never felt anything more fiercely than the protectiveness that came over him now.

"Be careful, Diana," he said thickly.

"Careful?" She looked at him curiously. "Of what?"

He drew in a deep breath. Should he tell her? If she knew she was in danger, she'd be in a better position to take care of herself. But she might be *too* cautious. She might arouse suspicion. So far her father and Ryder didn't know he was onto them.

No . . . better to leave her in ignorance. He held out his hand, coaxing her closer, dazzled by the tentative half-smile that lit up her face. There would be people to look after her in El Paso. He had already picked them out in his mind. People he could trust with the one thing that had become more precious than anything on earth. They would tell her, if it came to that. If they felt she needed to know. Until then, why frighten her unnecessarily?

"Be careful of *me,* love. I might ask too much of you."

"Oh?" The smile was coy now, her lips pursed in a little pink circle. It delighted him when she was so sure of herself, when she turned more woman than girl. "Do you really think you can?"

"I can . . . and I might."

"Try." Her voice dropped, low and sultry. "I dare you."

Cord felt a lump rise to his throat. He should have taken her back east while he could. He knew that suddenly, just as he also knew it was now too late. If they tried to flee, Howard would be after them. And Ryder. She'd be safer in El Paso.

Especially if he wasn't there. They would concentrate on him first.

"I have many regrets, sweet," he said quietly. "Perhaps someday you will know . . . and understand. But the one thing I will never regret are the days, and nights, I have spent with you."

Blue-green eyes clouded faintly, but her chin was up. "I hope not," she said tartly.

Cord laughed as he took her into his arms. The saving humor was there, the little touch of whimsy in her tone at what must have seemed an outrageous statement. He did not deserve her, and he knew it.

"I told you once I could promise nothing for the future. That I could love tonight . . . and not beyond. I might amend that somewhat. I *can* love you tonight. But I think I can promise tomorrow morning too."

"I am very greedy." She did not resist as he drew her gently toward the small back bedroom they shared. "I might ask for the afternoon as well."

His mouth was on her neck, nuzzling, teasing. "I might give it."

"And the evening?"

"You *are* greedy." He swept her up in his arms, the way he had at the *fandango*, unable to bear the slowness of their progress any longer. "Well . . . I might be persuaded. We can talk about it . . . later."

V

El Paso del Norte
mid-February 1847

21

DIANA SEETHED as she stood in the center of a small, crowded plaza and watched the caravan, only twenty dust-brown wagons now, and another man short, pull out of town.

Cord's words were still ringing in her ears, no more convincing than they had been early that morning when he first uttered them. Yes, the road ahead *would* be rugged and grueling. Yes, there would be fighting if the rumors were right and thousands of dragoons were swarming up from Chihuahua to challenge Doniphan and his volunteers. Yes, the Apache had been emboldened by the white man's quarrels, bandits were a constant menace, and frightened *rancheros* were moving into town.

But she had faced hardships before! Diana's jaw squared unconsciously. She had faced storms and stampedes and the threat of Indian raids, and she had acquitted herself with courage. She had earned the right to take her place beside the others. Not be left behind like so much baggage!

I can promise nothing for the future. How often had Cord told her that? And how often had she convinced herself he didn't mean it?

A brisk wind blew across the plaza. Diana shivered as she glanced over at Cord, looking tall and defiantly proud on his magnificent bay. The sun could be relentless, blazing when the air was still, but a thin layer of ice appeared on water basins in the morning, and the shadows were cold.

Cord. Her heart ached. He had never seemed handsomer, his hat dangling on a thong down his back, the wind ruffling his black-black hair. What was it, this power he had to make even her fingertips tingle as she longed to reach out and touch him? He had dressed differently today, not for the road, but almost elegantly, in dark moleskin trousers that hugged his thighs and a burgundy shirt with silver-and-turquoise buttons.

Almost as if he knew this was the last time they would see each other and wanted to create a memory picture in her mind.

Damn him! It was the strongest word she knew, and Diana clung to it, using anger to drive away the hurt and rejection.

He was tired of her. Like her father with Rosalie—and no doubt her mother too! Were men always so beastly self-centered? He had played at being the gallant husband, and he had enjoyed it for a while, but now he was ready to move on.

He didn't intend to come back. The thought stabbed like a knife in her chest. This was too final, too definite a parting. But his pride wanted her to remember him looking debonair!

A dark-skinned *señorita* flashed a brazen smile as she sashayed past the skittish stallion. Lance started to rear, and Cord reined him in, but not before he smiled back with a rakish intimacy that hinted at previous acquaintance. Apparently he had not just "ridden through" El Paso before.

Was that why he was leaving her now? Because the pleasures they had shared, no matter how tantalizing, had begun to pall? Because he was longing for the company of more experienced women?

Well, there would be plenty of *señoritas* like that in Chihuahua. It was rumored to be a lively town.

Tears stung her eyes, and she turned away, not wanting Cord to see. The train had nearly passed. She had to squint through the dust to see the leaders, just turning a corner onto the path that followed the river out of town. Ryder, assistant wagon master now, was at the head, his familiar black-clad form arrogant and faintly sinister. Cord would not take his place until they were on the open road and he had assured himself everything was running smoothly. The men followed, some driving, others on mules, Juan José and his Mexicans interspersed among the wagons, almost inconspicuous in somber browns and blacks.

Then the caravan was gone. The street was empty except for a rough *carreta* angling across the square with the languor of a Mexican morning. Sensing a movement beside her, Diana turned to see the reddish-brown of the stallion's coat. At least Cord had had the decency to linger for a semi-private farewell!

All the anger came back as she looked up and saw the expression on his face. He expects me to make a scene, she thought. He expects me to cry and carry on and *beg* to be taken along!

And because he expected it, she did the opposite. Smiling sweetly, she pitched her voice low.

"This is good-bye, then?"

A funny look came over his face.

"This is good-bye," he said stiffly.

Diana dropped her eyes, lashes fluttering coyly. "Are you going to miss me? . . . Even a little?"

The effect was more vulnerable than she realized. Cord leaned forward, tucking a finger under her chin. The tears she was trying so hard to hide were there. The anger too, and he was grateful. She had spirit—it would see her through.

"I will miss you, *querida.*"

"But not enough to take me with you?" A faint tremor came through the bravado, plainly annoying her.

"You are needed here—to look after your brother. The trail to Chihuahua is difficult under the best of circumstances. It would be too strenuous. You did promise Rosalie you'd take care of him," he reminded her dryly.

"I promised *someone* would take care of him. These acquaintances you arranged for me to stay with, the Garcías—they seem like good people. They could care for—"

"No," he cut in sharply. "Dammit, Diana, we've gone all over this. I want you *here*. I'm your husband. I expect obedience!"

God, how arbitrary, he thought. And how pompous. He was acutely conscious of the irony of that moment. He, who always insisted on honesty, was lying through his teeth. But to tell the truth would place her in unthinkable jeopardy.

The Garcías were more than acquaintances. They were old and valued friends. But she had been right about one thing. They were good. And loyal. And he was leaving one of his own men behind—the only one he was sure of, Slim—with the flimsy excuse of a bad case of dysentery, which was partly true.

If things worked out, if he got through this alive, he could come back for her . . . if she still wanted him.

He didn't mind gambling his own life. Cord drank in her face in the sunlight, this wife he had never thought he would have, bitterly aware that one way or the other this might be the last time he would ever gaze into those enchanting turquoise eyes. He had always known his life would be at stake. He had not known he would be gambling his heart as well.

"Good-bye, *querida*. God be with you." He drew her closer, kissing her, not lightly as he had intended, but hard and hungry, with all the pent-up longing in his heart. Every muscle in his body ached at the separation as he reluctantly released her. "*Vaya con Dios.*"

Diana, reeling from the unexpected fervor of his kiss, could only watch helplessly as he flicked the reins and rode away.

"*Vaya con Dios,* Cord," she whispered—but he was too far away to hear.

Heaven help her, no matter what he did, she loved this man. No matter how furious he made her, how insulting he was—and he could be extremely insulting—she had never been able to resist his kisses, and she never would. He was her man, born for her, as she had been born for him. If she let him ride out of her life, she would regret it forever.

Her eyes flashed suddenly with rebellion. What was she, some spineless ninny, settling for regrets and sighing over lost love? Cord turned, and she put on her meekest smile and waved.

Who said she had to let him go? He thought he wanted freedom. He thought he was looking for the excitement and independence he had left behind, but he did care for her. She had sensed it in the passion of that parting kiss, the way his lips had clung to hers—to the sweetness of their love.

Not just a love for tonight, but for tomorrow . . . and all tomorrows to come. That was the real reason he was running away. Because he was afraid of his feelings!

How far could the wagons go in a day? She composed her features as the Garcías came to collect her, but her mind was whirling, sorting out everything she could remember about the road to Chihuahua. Seven or eight miles, ten at most. A sturdy horse could treble that.

And Brutus was nothing if not sturdy!

They would be following the river for some time. Diana wished now she had listened more carefully when the men discussed the route. There were several *jornadas*—long waterless passages—but they came later . . . and the trail was supposedly well-marked. She could pump Slim for information.

How risky could it be, after all? The army had secured the area around the Rio Grande. The Mexicans and Apache would all be farther south.

She would give Cord a week's start, then go after him! It was all she could do to keep her exhilaration from showing as she followed the Garcías toward their surprisingly luxurious *hacienda*. Cord was already shorthanded as it was. He couldn't spare a man to escort her back.

And he could hardly send her alone.

She was not going to let him walk out of her life without a fight!

Three weeks later, Diana was nowhere near so confident. The sun was scorching; there was no wind, and her lips were chapped and cracking. She stood on a drab brown plain half a mile from where the Chihuahua road left the river and gaped with dismay at the old mule skinner, Nate. His beard was caked with dust, his arm in a makeshift sling fashioned out of an old shirt.

"But that's crazy!" she said. "Cord would never split up the train. Twenty wagons are barely enough for safety, and they're well behind the others. They have to be together!"

"Yeah . . . well, they ain't." Nate winced as he shrugged a pack from his good shoulder, dropping it with a stirring of dust. "Six wagons broke off, 'bout a mile short o' here. Headin' east. Your husband an' your father. An' that Ryder nobody likes."

"You're . . . sure?"

"Sure I'm sure. I was with 'em when they started. Be with 'em still if that danged mule hadn't caught me lookin' th' other way." The old skinner took a last chaw and shot a wad of tobacco into the brush. "Ain't no mule ever got th' best o' Nate Nathan b'fore. Knocked my shoulder clean outta joint. Weren't no good for nothin' after that. Had t' send me back."

Diana could have wept with frustration. It had taken two weeks to get out of El Paso. The people Cord had left her with had proved unexpectedly solicitous—kind, but so clinging she never had a minute to herself. And Slim had been even worse. Not only had he insisted on acting as her personal escort—as if every stranger in that frontier outpost were a coyote ready to pounce—he had positively refused to be drawn into conversation about routes to the south.

Even Buddy had turned skittish, barking if she so much as went for a stroll.

If the Garcías hadn't been exceptionally sound sleepers and Slim's dysentery hadn't kicked up, keeping him for hours at a time in the outhouse, she would probably be there still. Thank heaven Buddy was bribable with a bone! She had managed to avoid the first *jornada*, taking the long way round by the river, but another lay ahead, and she'd been stuck four days at the last watering hole, waiting for a party to join.

Now, after all that, this man was telling her Cord wasn't even *on* the Chihuahua road.

"I don't believe you," she cried irrationally. Nate had no reason to lie. But she couldn't bear to think that it had all been for nothing. That Cord had eluded her, and she might never see him again! "You're saying fourteen wagons went on alone? Without the wagon master or his assistant? Or the owner?"

"You believe it, missy," a new voice chimed in with an unpleasant chuckle. "Fourteen wagons—I counted 'em myself—an' nothin' like a leader anywhere." The man who shuffled over had introduced himself half an hour earlier as Millie Dawson. Milton, Diana supposed, though she didn't much care. He had said he was a prospector, but "leech" would be more like it.

"I thought you told me you hadn't seen—"

"I didn't know them was the folks you was askin' about. The name Howard wasn't mentioned. Or Montgomery. An old coot called Deadeye was in charge . . . and was he mad! They didn't have enough men to begin with, he says. Then right in the middle of the *jornada*—when they weren't nothin' nobody could do about it—his Mexicans walked out on him."

"His Mexicans?" Diana felt something knot in her stomach.

"They'd took 'em on in Santa Fe, he says. Damned fools. I guess he found out what they was good for. I coulda told 'im. You don't count on Mexicans. Soon as there's work to be done, you find 'em sprawled out with *sombreros* over their faces, hankerin' for a *siesta.*" Rubbing his palms on his trousers, he sauntered over to a scummy pool, still chuckling as he scooped up a handful of brackish water and splashed it on his face.

Diana was scowling faintly as she turned back to Nate.

"Now I really don't believe this. Juan José wouldn't run off. I'm not sure about the others. I don't know them, but Juan—"

"Juan José wasn't there." Nate hesitated, not liking the scared look that had come into her face. He was as crusty with men as mules, but a pretty woman's tears did something to his innards. "The boss took 'im an' one o' the other Mexes. An' five drivers an' me for the mules. Eleven men in all. Ain't but ten now."

"But . . . why?" Diana felt her throat go as dry as her mouth. "Those wagons are loaded with merchandise. There's nothing to the east . . . no one to buy anything."

"The fourteen goin' south are loaded. Though not as heavy as they might be. Your daddy's been greedy. Real greedy. Sold more'n he should of, in Santer Fe an' El Paso. Th' other wagons—the six—ain't got nothin' but crates o' rocks."

"Rocks?" Diana made no effort to conceal her astonishment. "Why would anyone fill shipping crates with rocks?"

"So no one'd notice how light they was."

"So no one . . ." Diana broke off as the truth dawned suddenly and brutally. All the time, she thought. It was there all the time. She should have guessed. She *had* guessed, but she had been too stubborn to admit it.

The Mexican silver.

Anger mingled with frustration and disgust. God help her, there had been plenty of clues. Again and again. Pauses in the conversation when the subject came up. The way her father pretended not to notice. Ryder's reaction. No wonder Garland hadn't minded lagging behind. And Cord . . .

That was why he had left her. Not for women, but because he was a thief! Diana choked on the bitterness and betrayal. She had loved him so desperately. Hungered for him until it hurt her heart. And all the time he had been unworthy!

She could not go after him now, even if it were possible. She was going to have to swallow her pride and slink back to El Paso, like Buddy after a scolding, belly to the ground, tail between his legs. There was no way she could let herself chase after a thief.

"You knew all the time, didn't you?" she said. "About the silver? You knew where the wagons were heading. And why."

Nate had enough shame to look sheepish. "Not all the time. The last little bit mebbe. A real powerful lure, silver. A man lives poor all his life, he reckons he wouldn't mind dyin' rich. Well, never mind. I'm jist as well outta it."

"I expect you are, bub." Millie had finished dousing his face and ambled back in time to hear the last sentence. "If what you was sayin' before is true."

Nate shot him a warning look, but it was too late.

"What do you mean?" Diana's eyes darted from one to the other, the knot in her stomach coming back. "I didn't know you two were acquainted."

"Shoot, yes." Millie either didn't notice the frantic signals Nate was sending or didn't care. "He wandered in a couple hours ago. Been off lookin' for better water for his mule. The old fool treats animals better'n some people. Can't spare a bit of kindness for someone down on his luck. He says he seen signs o' Injuns out there. Near ran into 'em, he says. Looks like they's trackin' the wagons."

"Indians . . . You mean Apache?"

"No, ma'am." Millie shook his head, a malicious grin spreading over his spare features. "Comanche."

"Comanche?" Diana tried not to feel the way her heart was pounding. "But I thought this was Apache territory. I didn't know Comanche came this far."

"They don't. Usually. Somethin' must be real interestin' to draw 'em out like this."

"Oh, dear heaven . . ." All the anger, all the self-righteous indignation vanished as Diana struggled, horrified, to take in what he was saying.

Cord was out there! She felt as if someone had dropped an enormous weight on her. With nine other men. And they were being systematically tracked by the one tribe even the other Indians feared!

"Can they find him?" She turned to Nate, ignoring the prospector. "If they really *are* there? Will they succeed?"

Nate hesitated. He liked this feisty woman who had proved herself almost as good with the mules as he. Liked

the husband too, if it came to that, but there wasn't a lot he
could do about it.

"Yep." He nodded. "There's a road most o' the way.
Hard as a rock. Won't nothin' show, even wagon tracks.
But it's real easy to see where someone leaves, if they ain't
takin' the time to cover their trail."

"Then someone has to warn them!" Diana felt giddy,
and pounds lighter, as she impulsively realized there was
something she could do. It might be dangerous, it might be
futile, but anything was better than sitting around wringing
her hands. "If they're on guard, they have a chance. Otherwise they're as good as dead!"

She had already reached her horse when Nate's voice came
after her.

"Don't do it, missus. Don't be a fool! Ain't no way you
kin reach 'em."

"Who's going to stop me?" She swung into the saddle,
laughing suddenly, recklessly, as she stared across that
parched stretch of oasis. "You, Nate, with your shoulder? On
a mule? Or your fearless friend there . . . I thought not!"

She wheeled around, galloping off in a cloud of bravado,
as much to raise her own spirits as to impress the men who
gawked after her. She knew only too well who was likely
to stop her—and she knew from Cord's story about his
mother's tortured death that they wouldn't be gentle. Or
merciful.

But she had to try.

She reined in the horse out of sight, conscious that it was
important to conserve his strength. The road was hard, Nate
had said . . . and it was easy to tell when someone went
off. That meant she would be able to follow. If she kept her
eyes on the horizon, if she watched for signs of movement
. . . surely the Comanche would be too busy tracking to
look back.

She *had* to try! Fear came over her suddenly, nauseating,
as the enormity of what she was about to do sank in. But
she couldn't let herself go back now. She couldn't give up!

All that mattered was Cord. Nothing else counted. Not
the past, not the rage she had felt before, not any of the
silly things she had thought were so important. He could be
a thief, he could be a scoundrel, he could be the most despicable thing on earth! But he was still the husband of her
heart, and she would die if anything happened to him.

Oh, please, she prayed silently—*please*, let me reach him. Let me be in time.

The stallion raised his head, nostrils flaring as he sniffed the air. Cord, a few feet away, stiffened instinctively.

Too quiet, he thought. It's too quiet. But everything looked all right. The wagons were arranged in a tight circle, as always now when they stopped for the noon break. A hand stuck out from under one of them, a fitfully twitching leg from another as the men dozed in the shade. Only a lazy buzzing of flies broke the stillness.

Should he have let so many of them wander off?

Cord strode over to where the horse was staked and ran a hand down his neck. It was unusually hot for early March. The air was prickly when the wind settled down, the dust so thick it coated his lashes.

Ryder's going to search for water was not unusual. He was assistant wagon master, and they'd been dry since noon the day before. But Garland had gone with him—for the ride, he said. And Garland never did anything that required exertion.

Cord's head tilted unconsciously, like Lance's, his own nostrils testing the air. The hills were low and close, but there was nothing to see or hear. Nothing to smell but the sand and the heat, the faint salt odor of land without water.

Was that what was making him nervous? Him and the stallion both? They had been together so long they were almost a single being sometimes, the mood of one becoming the mood of the other.

Damn, he was getting careless. He shouldn't have let the boy go off too. The young Mexican, Roberto. But the rolling dunes reminded him of the hills of his boyhood around El Paso. He had wanted to try his skill at hunting, and Juan had offered to go with him. Juan José.

Cord's mouth twisted wryly as he took off his hat and mopped a rumpled bandanna across his brow. Two names. Like a moneyed aristocrat. An odd affectation for a man who spent most of his time drunk in the town square. Like the hair dye Diana had noticed and attributed to vanity.

Diana. . . . His heart hurt at the thought of her. The anger and pain in those beautiful eyes the last time he saw her. So much. Damn, he was giving up so much. And for what?

His eyes scanned the hills in the distance. Brown, like

everything in that blasted country. Even the sky. Browner
than usual this time of year. They hadn't seen a cloud in
days. Was it a sign?

How much longer now?

Cord slid the hat back on his head. Two weeks if they
picked up the pace. He had been lightening the load every
night, sending the men off to water the mules or gather
firewood while he relieved the crates of some of their weight.
Tedious work, all alone, but he couldn't afford to show his
hand.

Two weeks, and it would be over . . . one way or the
other. He would have everything he'd come for. Or he would
have nothing.

Sixteen years, ten months, and twenty-two days. . . .
Cord ran a dry tongue over dry lips, hating the taste of the
dust, but water was strictly rationed. Garland Howard had
followed this same road with another Ryder. Sixteen years,
ten months, and twenty-two days—was he counting too? It
must have killed him, leaving so much of the silver behind.
Not enough wagons or manpower. And he'd never had the
guts to come back. Not with the area a hotbed of *bandidos*
and revolutionaries, and Comanche continually on the war-
path.

But he had remembered. Cord felt something hot rise
from his gut, mingling with the blaze of the sun. He had
remembered and schemed . . . and longed for the day he
would return. It had become a compulsion. For him, for the
son of the partner he had cheated, for every man who knew
that Antonio Vargas had not soiled his hands with his country's treasure—and that the real thief couldn't have made off
with it all.

Compulsion. The word amused him, grim and accurate.
Sixteen years was a long time to live with a single goal. To
be consumed by one thing to the exclusion of everything
else. A long time for Garland Howard. A long time for
Ryder the younger.

A long time for *him*.

Cord glanced back at the wagons. Even the flies were
silent now. The air was so still, it felt heavy. Too quiet, he
thought again. Too quiet.

Maybe he ought to wake up a couple of the hands. Have
them stand guard in shifts. Send one up on the nearest hill

to have a look around. See what Ryder and Howard were up to.

But which one? He grimaced. Ryder hadn't liked the five drivers he had chosen. A good sign—if he wasn't bluffing. Or the Mexicans. In fact, Ryder had put up quite a fight for some of the older hands.

"Experience counts," he had argued the morning they broke off from the others. "I want men who know what they're doing."

"Strength counts too," Cord had reminded him. The teamsters he had picked were not exactly young—except for one he'd persuaded a little too easily to give up the army—but they weren't old-timers either. "And endurance. This isn't a Sunday canter across the meadow."

Ryder had continued to argue briefly. Especially when it came to Deadeye, who was as wiry and tough as they came. But there was no denying he was the logical choice to lead the rest of the caravan to Chihuahua.

So Deadeye had been one of Ryder's. Too bad, Cord thought. He'd liked the feisty old driver with his independent ways and salty speech. Nate, too, probably. Ryder had been a little too smug about Nate. But he was the only one besides Juan José who could handle the mules, and Cord had had to give in.

Well, Nate was gone now. Cord leaned back against one of the wagons, mulling things over in his mind. He was safe enough there, but what about the others? Maybe he *should* send a man up the hill. But, God, which one?

The horse whinnied suddenly, breaking into his thoughts. Shrill and alarmed.

A snake maybe. It *could* be a snake . . .

Hair rising on the back of his neck, Cord whirled to face the hills in the rear. Too late, he thought as his eyes took in the crest of the closest one. Too late to send a man now. Why hadn't he paid more attention to his instincts?

He let out a shout as he grabbed his rifle.

Diana noticed it first as a faint hint of gray. Like wisps of storm clouds clinging to the summit of the hill just ahead.

"Rain," she said softly, though in truth it didn't look like rain. Brutus, grazing nearby on a patch of spiny brownish scrub, paused to look at her curiously. "Wouldn't it be heavenly if it *pelted* from the sky?"

She leaned back, closing her eyes for a second. She had dozed off once or twice in the brief time they'd been stopped, but it was a restless sleep, disturbed by troubling dreams, and she had been glad enough to wake up.

Not that a downpour wouldn't be her undoing, wiping out the trail she'd been following for a day and a half. Nate had been right. The road was hard. Even wheel ruts didn't show. Only occasional circles in the sand hinted at nights and nooning, with hoofprints nearby where the stock had apparently been herded to water, though so far off that even Brutus couldn't scent it.

At least they were moving slowly. Diana sighed in the dusty heat. She ought to catch up soon at this rate.

So far, she'd made good time. Plodding on for an hour or two, day or night, pausing to rest a bit, then pushing on again. Never quite long enough to renew her strength, but never exhausting her either—or Brutus, which was more important. She could lash herself to the saddle if she had to, but if anything happened to him, she'd be lost.

She opened her eyes, blinking in the sun. She was never quite comfortable sleeping in the daylight. The moon was bright at night—no danger of missing anything in the softer soil beside the road—but somehow she felt less exposed.

It wasn't that she had exactly seen signs of Indians. But then, she hadn't expected to. Comanche moved stealthily, covering their tracks. They might be there; they might not. It might all be a false alarm. There was no way of knowing.

The gray seemed to deepen on the horizon. Odd, Diana thought, studying it intently for the first time. It was rising from just behind the hill, all clumped together in one place. Not like clouds at all, but . . . What?

It was a second before she realized. Like a fire. Her heart leapt as she dared to hope, just for an instant, she had reached Cord.

But Cord would never light a campfire in the daytime. Disappointment rose like bile in her mouth. He might not know about the Comanche, but his was Apache country. And she had heard it was rife with *bandidos*. At night maybe, when the sun went down and the desert turned cold, when he was sure the smoke would not be noticed . . .

No, it was just a peculiar formation of clouds. She was getting edgy, seeing things where they didn't exist.

She pulled a canteen, the last one, out of her saddlebag

and twisted the cap. She was so thirsty, but all she could do was wet her lips. It was the purest luck that she had just finished filling them when she took off in such a hurry. But she had to share with Brutus, pouring his portion into a tin plate, and it wasn't enough. Maybe next time the tracks branched off, she'd follow and see where they led. She could ill afford the time, but she had to get water.

Funny, the way the clouds seemed to have gotten darker. She untied the scarf she had knotted around her neck like a cowboy's bandanna. She had taken it off so many times to cover her mouth and nose, it was caked with filth and cracked like old parchment.

She reached in the bag again, searching for something to replace it. She had packed so foolishly. She'd been so sure she would catch up with Cord, and she had wanted to look pretty. All she could find was a square of sky-colored silk, edged with blue lace, that he had had made for her in Santa Fe. "To match your eyes," he had said.

It didn't, but it didn't matter. Diana loved it because he had given it to her. She had wanted him to see she remembered.

She had no doubt now that they were headed for the place where the silver of the disgraced patriot Vargas had last been seen. Her knowledge of Mexican geography was sketchy at best, but she had seen maps spread out sometimes in Cord's study. And she had learned to tell direction by the sun and stars.

She had no doubt—but she no longer cared. Now that she had had time to think it over, she had rationalized things in her mind. Cord wasn't a thief. Every instinct told her that. If he was going after the silver, he believed he had a right to it.

And perhaps he did. She had no idea what laws governed lost treasure, if, indeed, there were any. Perhaps it was just the spoils to the finder. Whoever got there first could have it.

Cord Montgomery was a proud man. Diana had learned that over and over, often to her regret. He didn't want *her* money, he said. He wanted his own. If he felt this treasure was his, she loved him enough not to question it.

She buckled the bag shut and was about to tie the scarf around her neck when she glanced back and saw that the gray had turned into great puffs of black, billowing over the hill.

It *was* smoke! She stood where she was for a moment, petrified, feet rooted to the spot. Not the smoke of a camp-fire, but something bigger, fiercer, raging out of control.

"Oh, God . . ."

An awful surge of terror heaved through her. Racing over to Brutus, she barely touched the stirrup as she leapt onto his back. The silk still clutched in her hand, she urged him wildly up the slope. She was galloping now, no longer even thinking of caution. No longer caring if anyone saw.

She reached the top, but it wasn't there. Oh, God, she thought again. Oh, God! There was another hill beyond—distance was so deceptive—and another beyond that.

It couldn't be what she feared, she told herself frantically. She was like a madwoman now, spurring the horse on, desperate to get to the end of that terrible, nightmarish ride. It couldn't!

But even before she reached the last rise and reined in to look down, she knew what she was going to see.

22

ON THE nearby hillside where Garland lay in the jagged shade of a stunted mesquite, everything was quiet and swelteringly stagnant.

Half-awake, half-asleep, he had been drifting in and out of dreams for the last hour. Vivid, erotic dreams. Black hair brushed his shoulder, unexpectedly titillating . . . hot breath quivered on his cheek . . . long limbs writhed and twined, bringing him to an abrupt and rather embarrassing culmination.

"Uhhh!" Grunting gutturally, he pulled himself to a sitting position. The sticky moisture between his legs was echoed in sweat that poured from thinning hair and saturated his collar.

God, he thought he had forgotten her . . . What was her name? Cristina, Carlota, something like that. So long ago, he couldn't remember her face. But she was the only woman he had ever known whose skin felt like silk when he touched it.

Where the devil was Ryder? He glowered restlessly at the unrelenting aridity that seemed to go on forever. How long did it take a man to find water?

Desolate. That was the trouble with this place. So damned desolate. He loosened his collar; he was having trouble breathing in the heat. Sixteen years, almost seventeen, since he had first laid eyes on it.

He had been younger then, and down on his luck. The lowest point in his life. Stuck with a wife he didn't want, cut off from the fortune he'd been so sure she would bring—cheated again when the only child she'd been able to carry to term was a girl. Even the expedition to Santa Fe hadn't worked out the way they'd expected, he and Bill Ryder. They were going to be lucky to break even. Six months of his life, and nothing to show for it.

They had had only two wagons left. He remembered it clearly. Every detail. Bill had fallen behind with one of them and with that no-good guide who kept demanding more cash or he'd leave them in the desert! Garland had gone on alone, looking for help.

And how had they treated him—the Vargases and Corderos and Valerosos, the great *hacendados* who ruled like kings from San Antonio to Chihuahua to Santa Fe?

Like shit, that was how!

Garland could still taste the dregs of humiliation. They might be renowned for their hospitality, but they were hospitable only to their own kind. Him they had treated to a cot in the stable!

Well, he had gotten even with them. Damn, he had gotten even. The only way those *macho* Spanish bastards understood. Through one of their women.

He eased back slightly, the strain leaving his body. She had been a pretty thing, the Vargas daughter, Cristina or Carlota or whoever. Her features came back briefly, a fleeting glimpse. Tall and dark, with the arrogance of her people in her nose and brow. And a woman's fire beneath.

Pious. That was a good word for her. Almost smugly pious, always talking about God and her saints. But she had been curious, too, especially about men—and she had been sheltered. It could be dangerous, sheltering a daughter too much.

She hadn't even realized what he was up to. Garland felt a faint contempt, thinking back on it. He had suggested that she meet him for walks by the river, out of sight of the house, and she had been flattered enough to agree. She hadn't even balked at taking refuge from the sun and wind in a little-used storage shed.

But he had cut a finer figure then, slimmer and handsome, with fairish hair and light skin that must have seemed exotic.

It had been the easiest thing in the world, playing on her gullibility. Telling her he was really a man of substance, even wealthier than her father, and couldn't risk using his real name because he was on a dangerous "secret mission." Hinting that life could get lonely in far-off St. Louis, and men had a hard time finding suitable women to share their lives.

Not happening to mention, of course, that he already had

had a wife, pregnant again, despite the doctor's dire predictions, because he was determined to get a son, no matter what.

She had lapped it all up. She had believed because she wanted to believe. And there, in that rustic building, with the current of the river in the background, he had become the first man to drive his shaft between her legs.

He was startled to feel his body respond, rising to the memory, though it had been depleted rather ignominiously only moments before. The act had been less seduction than rape, but such subtle distinctions had never bothered him overmuch. She had whimpered and begged him to stop, she had wept when he hurt her, but she had been too frightened and ashamed to cry out for help.

He had reminded her of that afterward, when she tried to protest. She had asked for it, he told her bluntly. She had come with him to an isolated spot, she had teased with her eyes, she had flirted and giggled. And she hadn't even *tried* to scream.

What fools women were. He got up and wandered out of the shade, feeling the heat like the blast from a coal stove in his face. She had accepted everything meekly. No blame for him after those first pained tears. She had convinced herself she was wildly in love with him. She had to, for he was possessing her regularly by that time, and he was skillful enough when he chose to touch the core of passion deep within her.

She had even convinced herself *he* was in love with her.

That was how he had learned about the silver. By accident. She had taken to prattling, almost feverishly, when they were together, though normally she was quite reticent. She had needed to brag about her father. To prove that he, too, was important enough to be entrusted with mysterious missions. That she came from a proud line, which no man need be ashamed to marry into.

She had been a little too obvious, and Garland had been bored, listening with only half an ear—until she started to drop hints about some of the more extraordinary details of Antonio Vargas' "sacred trust." Like the amount of bullion he would be carrying. And the clever route he had worked out to avoid attention.

Nothing substantial, of course. She was too loyal for that. Just bits and pieces, a little here, a little there. He doubted she even realized he was storing it up and putting it all together. She was pretty, but she wasn't very bright. And she hadn't been thinking too clearly lately.

But he *was* putting it together. An idea was taking shape in his mind. The plan that would never quite come off, but bore fruit enough to make him rich for a while. A few days later, he had slipped away to find Bill Ryder and get rid of the guide.

He had tried to be decent about the girl. He shrugged his shoulders, feeling the weight that had come with the years. He hadn't wanted to hurt her. He rather liked her, as it was, and after all, she had given him what he wanted. He had left a note in the storage shed where she would be sure to find it. A brutally frank admission of everything, including that fact that his wife was due to deliver in a couple of months.

It was better that way. She wouldn't waste time fantasizing about his coming back. She could get on with her life. Marry someone else. A little detail like a missing hymen wouldn't matter with her father's money.

That was the thing with women. They always bounced back when another man came along.

"Exercisin' your treaders, pard?" Ryder's voice had an unpleasant twang as he slipped up from behind, on horseback, but so quietly Garland hadn't heard. "I wouldn't hang around in the sun too long if I were you. Especially since it looks like we aren't going to be getting a lot of cover from now on."

"What . . ." Garland started, then broke off as he turned and saw an enormous swirl of black filling the sky. "What on earth . . . ? Oh, my Lord! The wagons! What happened? A brushfire? We've got to do something!"

"Save your energy." Ryder eased his mount into the path between Garland and the stunted shrub where he had tethered his horse. "It isn't a brushfire . . . and you wouldn't get there soon enough anyway."

He seemed to relax, slouching forward in the saddle, a faintly amused look crossing his features.

"Looks like the Comanche got a little riled up when they didn't find what they were expecting."

"Comanche?" Garland's face turned ashen beneath a leathery tan. "You mean they *attacked*? You saw them—"

''I didn't have to see. I didn't want to. Only a fool would let curiosity draw him out in the open at a time like this.''

''Then you can't be sure—''

''I heard the shots, while you were off in dreamland. Funny thing about sounds in the desert. You can hardly hear them sometimes. Little *pop-pop-pops*, off in the distance. Right on schedule.''

''On . . . schedule?'' Garland felt the first hints of apprehension. ''Speak plain, man. You're not making sense.''

''I told that old skinner, Nate, to spread word when he got back that Indians were stalking the train. In case anyone got curious later. But they were never following us. They didn't have to. Why do you think I was so anxious to bring you along on this little ride today?''

Garland's mouth fell open. ''You set them up?''

''You always have been a little dense, old man.'' Ryder stared down at him with distaste. The front of his pants had a spreading stain, as if he'd wet himself in his sleep. ''Have you forgotten what my father's job was? Last time? He was in charge of the Indian attack that took care of Vargas' buddy.''

''But he . . . he didn't handle it himself,'' Garland stammered. ''He got someone to do it for him.''

''Yeah, an unsavory character just east of El Paso. Fortunately I had the foresight to look him up when we were in town. We made plans to run into each other at the last watering hole. You might have seen him. Called himself a prospector.''

''Yesss . . .'' He had seen someone, but he hadn't taken him seriously.

''It was real easy to persuade him—*real* easy—to reactivate some old acquaintances. I didn't even have to give him anything to pick up 'presents' for the Comanche. I told him there was enough ammo packed in the wagons to satisfy a dozen tribes. He believed me.''

''But . . .'' Garland's mouth was hanging open again. ''Surely you knew what they'd do to the men when they split open the crates and found they'd been duped.''

''They'd have done it in any case.'' Ryder chuckled nastily. ''That was the deal. Mules and ammunition for the lives of the men. . . . By now every last one of them is dead.''

* * *

Fear rose from deep in her stomach, strangling and choking her as Diana urged her mount down the steep slope. The smoke was so thick she could hardly see. She had no idea what she was riding into, but she had to press on.

Oh, God, what if she was too late?

Brutus lost his footing, whinnying in terror as he slid several yards through the sand. It was all Diana could do to keep a grip on the reins. But he was game—he'd always had courage, and he had learned to trust her—and somehow she managed to keep going.

She had ridden so hard. She had risked so much to reach them. She couldn't have come so close only to lose at the last minute!

Maybe things weren't as bad as they looked. She squinted desperately into the haze. Those might not even be her father's wagons. She might be working herself into a frenzy for nothing.

The smoke was even denser when she reached the base of the hill. She hadn't known it would be so hot. Her mouth was burning; her lungs scorched with every breath she took. Brutus balked at last, whinnying again and rearing, and she lost her seat, half-falling, half-leaping to the ground.

Her ankle twisted, sending a jolt of pain up one leg. But it was not the pain that was consuming her now. It was terrible, agonizing fear as every last vestige of hope disappeared.

The wagons were theirs.

Tears smarted her eyes. A cloud of smoke hung over the smoldering wagons, suffocating and concealing. But here and there something showed through—a painted scene on the side of one of the massive Conestogas, blistering and blackening in the heat . . . a rent in the cover of another, which she had helped to mend herself.

Frantic, ignoring the danger, Diana plunged into the heart of the conflagration. The wagons were blazing now, open flames shooting into the air, so near they threatened her sleeves and hair. Too fast, she thought helplessly. Everything is catching too fast. Wagons shouldn't burn like this!

Then her eyes fell on the first of the crates that had been pulled out and smashed open. Nate had been exaggerating when he said they were full of rocks. There were some stones and a sprinkling of sand. But for the most part, it was pine needles and brush.

No wonder the fire was so hot. They had been like boxes of tinder waiting for the spark!

That this was the work of Indians, she had no doubt. The wagons plundered, the camp set afire . . . the animals gone. *Bandidos* might have broken open the crates, they might even have been enraged enough to start the blaze when they discovered nothing of value, but what use would they have for all those mule teams!

Nate had said that Comanche were tracking the train. Obviously they had caught up.

Anger swept over her, and self-disgust. A terrible sense of her own uselessness. If she had only ridden faster, if she'd pressed her mount a little harder . . .

She thought she was prepared for the first body she found. She had steeled herself for it as she pushed into the still-flaming ruins of the train. Comanche didn't take male captives, Cord had told her once, grimly. And she had heard often enough how they treated the men who fell into their hands.

But nothing could have prepared her for the sight that met her eyes.

She recognized the clothes first. That was all that was identifiable. Scuffed boots worn down at the heels, patched denim pants, a dark blue shirt drenched with blood. The youngest of the remaining crew, a surly hothead who had been talked out of joining the army at the last moment.

Diana stared down at him, rigid with shock. He had been scalped, savagely, brutally, hair and flesh hacked away, probably while he was still alive, judging from the amount of blood that caked his face and oozed into the sand.

Cord? . . . Was this what had happened to Cord?

Sick with horror, Diana forced herself to search the rest of the wagons, braving the fire to peer inside, underneath, cringing every time she found another body. Hating that heart-stopping, stomach-churning moment when she looked down and, just for a second, couldn't be sure.

But this one was too tall, that one too wiry, that one too thick in the waist, and she dared to breathe again as she came full circle and still hadn't found him.

Could it be that Cord hadn't been there? That he had been off somewhere when the attack occurred? The heat finally drove her back, coughing and choking. Part of her wanted to believe—*longed* to believe—he had somehow escaped.

But another part, the thinking, rational part, was more frightened than ever.

At least if she had found him, she would know. It was not knowing that was the worst. She couldn't grieve; she couldn't let herself give in to the anguish and despair. But oh, dear heaven, she couldn't let herself hope either!

The brush alongside the wagons was burning now, turning the area into a raging inferno, and Diana took refuge on a gentle slope opposite the steeper one she had charged down before. Her brain felt numb as she sank down and stared dully at leaping tongues of red and orange.

Five bodies . . . She had been too desperately frightened to count, but all she could remember now were five bodies. Half the men with the train.

Slowly, things started to come into focus. Five grisly remains. Who besides Cord was missing? Her father?

It startled her to realize that she hadn't even thought about him. She hadn't been looking specifically, but surely she would have recognized that portly figure. Or Ryder. No one had been dressed all in black.

Or the Mexicans. She felt a little guilty as it occurred to her that she was more relieved about them than about her father. But Juan José was her friend, and young Roberto had seemed an amiable sort. The clothing of the Mexicans was uniquely their own, the boots, the belts, the shirts, the high-crowned broad-brimmed hats.

Or had she missed them?

Brutus, still skittish, nuzzled her shoulder, but she was too preoccupied to respond. Had the smoke blinded her at the wrong moment? One body she might have overlooked. Or two. . . . But five?

The fire was agonizing now, roaring in its savage culmination. Diana had the awful feeling that she ought to be doing something for the bodies she had found, ought to drag them out somehow and take care of them.

But the ground was so hard, she had no tools—she couldn't have given them a decent burial anyway. At least flames would be a cleaner end than the carrion birds circling overhead.

Had she missed them? Had she missed *him?* Weariness overcame her, and she dropped her head in her hands. Her father perhaps. Ryder, the Mexicans—one of them might have gone for a ride; another could have been hunting. But

Cord was the wagon master. Cord would never have left while they were in camp.

Had she lost him? Not to quarrels or misunderstandings or other women. But to the terrible finality of death?

The area was deserted by the time Ryder finally returned with his uncharacteristically silent senior partner. The fire was still smoldering as they rode down the slope; an occasional ember burst into flame, and trails of smoke rose from the charred remains of crates and wooden wagon frames.

The smell was stifling, soot and ashes undercut by a vaguely disturbing odor Ryder couldn't identify at first.

Burning flesh.

Saliva rose to his mouth, making him retch, and he turned his head so Garland wouldn't see. The other man had dismounted at the base of the hill, a dazed, almost dim-witted expression on his face as he gaped at the blackened devastation.

Not for the first time, Ryder was glad his partner was so slow at picking things up. He had always had a weak stomach. He could kill a man if he had to—he *had* killed once—but he couldn't look at him afterward. It would have been humiliating as hell, throwing up in front of Garland Howard.

At least the bodies were no longer recognizable. He kicked at the skeleton of a wagon wheel, which dissolved under his boot. All he had to do was smell them. Forcing himself into the wreckage, he covered everything with a few quick glances, enough to tell him there was no point digging further.

Too bad, in a way. He'd have rested easier if he could have tallied up the corpses. Made sure they were all there. But at least his stomach was grateful.

And, shit, where would they be, if not in that heap of cinders? The Comanche earned their reputation. Any man who'd been in camp when they showed up was cremated by now.

He was startled to turn and find Garland Howard behind him. The older man's eyes were not dull anymore, but bright with anger.

"They're gone!" he blurted. Then, in a torrent of words: "The wagons . . . the men . . . all of them, gone! Even the mules. Blast it, man, weren't you thinking?"

Ryder regarded him with amusement. So the little worm had a backbone after all.

"Yes," he drawled coolly. "As a matter of fact, I was. I was thinking very clearly."

"But we needed them! We agreed on this, dammit. The rest of the silver is still in that cave where Vargas hid it. I could never get to it—the area was crawling with rebels and outlaws—but neither could anyone else. Now that the Americans are moving in, we've got to get it fast. We needed five wagons, minimum. And five drivers!"

"We didn't *have* five drivers," Ryder reminded him. He turned back to the carnage, checking it one last time. "We had two. You. Me. *Two.* Three if you count that kid I bribed to stay out of the army, though I was never too sure about him. We lost old Nate to a bad shoulder, and Montgomery outfoxed me when it came to Deadeye. Or maybe he got lucky. What the hell—you can't win all the time."

"Maybe not . . . but at least we could have used two of the wagons." Garland started to follow, then stopped as the ground crunched under his feet. "We do have two drivers."

"Yeah, well . . ." Ryder set his features in a noncommittal grin. He hadn't counted on losing the wagons—that little possibility had slipped through his web of planning—but he wasn't about to say so. "Fast and loose, old man. How many times do I have to tell you? Things don't work out one way, try 'em another. The wagons were never a good idea anyhow."

He had the satisfaction of seeing Garland's eyes pop wider. "What do you mean?"

"I mean they'd be too conspicuous. As you said yourself, settlers are going to be pouring in any day. Some of the boldest may already be there. A wagon train, way off course—don't you think that'd catch their eye? To say nothing of the *bandidos,* who are still working the territory. Better to stash the silver someplace unobtrusive. Say, a dirt-poor *rancho,* which we could pick up for a song, with maybe a dilapidated storage barn or root cellar. And who would look twice at an old buckboard passing back and forth, heavy with hay?"

Garland nodded, rather to Ryder's surprise. He wasn't always as slow as he seemed.

"And Montgomery?" he said thoughtfully. "He was here? When the Comanche attacked? You're sure?"

"Of course he was here." Ryder's brows went up, an impudent exclamation point. "A good master never leaves his wagons. He's still here . . . in somewhat different form."

"Yes . . . I suppose so." To his discomfort, Garland found himself picturing Cord Montgomery. Dark, arrogant, always looking down his nose, like those damned aristocratic Vargases and Valerosos! He would have thought he'd be glad to hear he was dead. Why was he feeling queasy? "You're sure it was wise? Getting rid of him so soon?"

"Montgomery was expendable. We don't need a guide anymore. We're close enough to where we're going, and what use is a wagon master when they are no more wagons to master?"

He was laughing as he sauntered over to his horse and swung lithely into the saddle. Garland, watching, was impressed with the pantherlike darkness of the man. The sheer arrogance. Like the rival he had just eliminated.

Everything felt cold suddenly. Even the perspiration on his brow. Dark and arrogant . . . and dangerous?

"You kill so easily."

"Why not? Montgomery had to be dealt with sooner or later. You didn't think he was going to take his pittance of silver and say *'Hasta la vista, señores*—nice knowing you.' Only then he would have been on his guard. Much easier to take care of him now. I don't know about you, old man, but I've had enough of this place. The stench is disgusting. I'm going back to that spring we found and wash off the smell."

"Aren't you going to go through the, uh . . . remains? Just to make sure."

"Go through them yourself. If you want to. I *am* sure. Comanche never miss anything. No one got out of this alive." Spurring his mount, he galloped up the hillside.

In fact, Garland did not want to. His own stomach was starting to churn, and he had no desire to put it to the test. Besides, Ryder was right. He went over to where he had left his horse and followed the trail of dust that was already disappearing over the hill. Comanche were renowned for their savage thoroughness. They would not have let anyone escape.

Ryder had already removed his shirt and was bending over a shallow pool by the time Garland reached him. He had taken off his gunbelt and placed it on the ground. His pants, open at the waist, hung loose as he splashed water over his head and chest.

Garland was struck again by how alike the two men were, Ryder and the wagon master who had just perished in the Comanche raid. The same strong shoulders, the same lean torso, the same deep tan and general coloring. Ryder was a little smoother—there was less hair on his body and somewhat burly arms—but otherwise the resemblance from certain angles was uncanny.

So alike, he and Cord Montgomery . . . who was expendable.

The thought came swiftly, as thoughts always did to Garland Howard. He had no gift for methodical planning. But he could be shrewd, and instinct sometimes served him well.

He looked from the man to the gunbelt, a few feet away. He had brought Ryder along to help with the crew. Ryder had a meanness the others would respect. But there was no crew anymore. He had brought Ryder along to handle Cord Montgomery when the time came.

Only Cord Montgomery had already been handled.

Howard reached for the gun slowly, stealthily, sliding it out of the holster. It came easily, no resistance, smooth as a gunfighter's rig. It was amazing how quietly even a bulky man could move when he had to. He sat for a long time, patiently, listening to the sound of splashing water.

The look on Ryder's face when he turned and saw himself staring down the barrel of a Colt was worth everything Garland had endured on that hellish journey.

" 'Expendable' is such an interesting word," he said.

23

DIANA SANK to her knees, too tired and defeated to go on. A trail of hoofprints rose out of the parched streambed beside her—dry for years, it looked like—and cut across the sand. Just about enough for six mule teams and a number of spares. Apparently the Comanche who had attacked the wagons were making no attempt to cover their tracks.

But then, they hadn't expected to be followed. And they would hardly be afraid of a lone woman armed with a small camp knife.

She let her head drop heavily into her hands. Perspiration poured like tears through her fingers. It had been a foolish impulse, coming after the Comanche. As if somehow she could do something, *learn* something, if only she caught up with them.

She hadn't been thinking clearly; she realized that now. The tracks had simply been there, and she had started after them automatically. Maybe, she had hoped, Cord will see them too. Maybe he'll head in the same direction.

Brutus made a soft snorting sound and she looked up wearily. The sun was almost touching the hills to the west; her eyes were dry and red, and everything had a shimmery glow. Even if Cord was alive—if, somehow, miraculously, he had escaped that brutal slaughter—he wouldn't pursue a pack of Indians for some mules and a few captive horses.

If he was alive . . .

She tried to get up, but her legs wouldn't move. The smoke had been so intense, the heat of the flames so unremitting . . . Wouldn't it have been easy to miss a body? Not all of them—but one? The Mexicans might have been hunting, Ryder perhaps, even her father, though that seemed unlikely.

But Cord was too conscientious. He would never have

left. He *must* have been there when those savages came whooping down from the hills.

She stood up slowly, every motion excruciating as strained muscles cried out from the exertion of the day. There was no point trying to go on. The likelihood that Cord was alive was growing slimmer every minute. And how could she ever hope to find him in that vast, sweeping wasteland?

All that was left was to retrace her steps. She started over to where Brutus was quietly waiting. Cord's acquaintances in El Paso might understand when she told them why she'd sneaked away, or they might think she was flighty and disapprove. But they were kindly people. They would take her in.

She had just flipped the reins over the horse's head and was preparing to mount when she caught sight of something small and glittery on an open stretch of sand a few yards away. Curious, she started closer, then stopped.

It was a round silver object, ornately wrought, with a piece of turquoise in the center.

A button. Cord's button? Diana's heart did flip-flops as she recognized the distinctive craftsmanship. Surely it couldn't be a common piece.

She was there in a flash, bending to clasp the little circlet of silver in her palm. Now that she saw it closer, she was even more certain. This was one of the buttons on the shirt Cord had been wearing the day he left El Paso.

Had he been wearing it again this afternoon?

Energy infused her step now, tapped from some deep inner strength she did not even know she had, as she hurried along the trail again, sometimes leading Brutus, sometimes trusting him to follow. The hoofprints carried her across a shrubless plain and into a rocky ravine. The sides were steeper than they looked, and her hands were scraped and bleeding as she slid down, but she willed herself not to notice.

The stones formed an awkward path, obliterating the trail she had been following and making it hard to walk. Her feet slid constantly, an ever-painful reminder that she had twisted her ankle before, but she didn't dare ride. She had to stay close to the ground, scouring every inch with her eyes, searching for something—anything—to give her hope again.

It might mean nothing; she knew that. The shirt was a

rich wine color, the buttons bright and striking. Just the thing that would appeal to Indians. They might have found it when they split open one of the crates. They might have torn it from Cord's body after they killed and maimed him.

Comanche don't take male captives. Fear mingled with the hope, swelling until Diana thought she would choke on it. Cord's words; he had told her that . . . but he had been speaking in generalities.

Comanche didn't usually range this far into Apache territory either. If they had broken one rule, might they not break another?

She found the second button about a mile beyond. On a flat stretch of sand again, like the first—away from stones and crevices, where it might slip unseen into a crack.

This time she was sure. Once could have been an accident. The savages might have dropped a bit of plunder and not noticed. But twice, in a conspicuous place, was beyond coincidence.

Cord was carefully, systematically leaving a trail.

Why or for whom, Diana had no idea. Obviously not for Ryder or her father. And Juan José and Roberto were virtual strangers. Strangers didn't risk their necks for people they barely knew.

More likely an act of defiance, better than not doing anything. A wild gamble that someone might happen along and guess what had happened.

But it didn't matter, she realized with a sudden thrill of pure elation. Any more than it mattered *why* the Indians had broken their rule and taken a white man. It only mattered that they had.

Cord was alive!

" 'Expendable'?"

Ryder's usual drawl had a sharp edge that Garland Howard found extremely gratifying. Where is your cockiness now, bastard? he thought. You aren't calling me "old man" anymore, are you?

"Wasn't that your description of Cord Montgomery? Only, you see, it fits you too. I really don't need your services now. That was quite an interesting idea, taking over a *rancho* and moving the silver bit by bit in a hay wagon. But one man can do it alone."

"So you're going to kill me. Just because you don't *need* me?"

"As you said yourself—why not?" Howard tipped the pistol slightly, the silvery barrel glinting in the sun. "I can't think you'd be any more satisfied than my son-in-law with a 'pittance' of silver. Are you going to tell me, if we'd gotten to that cave, you wouldn't have been the least bit tempted? You might call this self-defense . . . a little in advance." He started to chuckle under his breath.

Ryder's jaw tightened. "You find it funny?"

"Ironic, anyway. You did say this was the time to get rid of Montgomery. While he wasn't on guard. It seems he wasn't the only one who forgot to look over his shoulder."

Ryder eased back slowly, his lean, catlike body tensing and relaxing at the same time. Whatever fear he was feeling didn't show as his gray eyes caught Garland's and held them.

"I don't think you have it in you to shoot a man. In the back maybe. Hell, yes, in the back . . . but not while he's looking at you."

"Don't I?" Garland raised the gun, aiming at the bridge of Ryder's nose. Just for a second he imagined that arrogant face exploding, blood spattering everywhere, all over the ground . . . and just for a second, he wanted to do it. But the urge passed. "Well, perhaps you're right . . . but it's all irrelevant. I don't have to shoot, you see. I just have to take your gun . . . and your horse . . . and leave. And your water canteen, in case you're foolish enough to try to follow on foot. How long do you think you'll last?"

To his annoyance, the other man began to laugh quietly, almost coolly. As if that first flicker of doubt was over, and he was beginning to be amused by the game.

"You think you can carry water enough for two horses, old man?" The swagger was back in his shoulders, the disdain vibrating insolently in his voice. "Yours and mine both? Even with an extra canteen, you'll never make it. You'll spread the supply too thin, and they'll both perish. Then you'll be in the same position I am."

Garland hesitated a fraction of a second. There was just enough truth in the taunt to set him thinking. "I won't be needing two horses," he said slowly. "I'll take yours a few miles down the road and set him loose. A pity. He'll die, like you, in the desert, but it can't be helped."

"Well, I have to give it to you . . ." Ryder let his lips

curl slyly, calculating the effect. Not too docile; that wouldn't be in character. But not bold enough to arouse suspicion. It was easy to underestimate the Garland Howards of this world. "I didn't realize you were so clever."

"Fast and loose . . . isn't that what you told me? Take your opportunities where you can. Unfortunately for you, I learned the lesson too well. I'm afraid this is good-bye, partner. You really should have shown a little more interest in that ten percent I offered. And Diana's fortune." He started toward the horses, then looked back unable to resist a last childish thrust. "You're a lot like your father, you know. Greedy. And stupid."

Ryder watched with expressionless eyes as Garland scrambled up onto one of the horses, juggling awkwardly with the second set of reins, and disappeared into the dusky shadows of the northern hills. A fat little man, smugly pleased with himself.

Fast and loose . . . but not very bright. Garland Howard didn't know much about horses. He could take the animal five miles away or ten—or twenty. The minute he turned him loose, instinct was going to bring him straight back to the last place he'd had water. And one would get you ten that that second canteen would still be in the saddle bag.

He didn't know much about men either. At least not men like Ryder.

Sweat was forming on his forehead, not hot, but chilling, as he recalled the danger of the last few minutes . . . and how cleverly he had averted it.

He didn't know, for instance, that Ryder always carried the mate to that neat little Colt in his boot.

And that he could track like a Comanche.

Diana finally gave up as the sun sank into the horizon.

The air was still hot, the dust suffocating as she sat on a flat-topped boulder and willed her fingers to work the knot on the blue silk scarf around her neck. She hadn't seen another button for miles. There had been several at first, a regular succession guiding her through the maze of ravines and dry gullies the Comanche were now following exclusively. She had had to strain constantly, going back occasionally, making sure she hadn't missed one, for there was no more straying onto the sand, no more hoofmarks to tell her which way to go.

Then, suddenly, they had stopped. Mopping at the caked-on dirt that prickled her face and neck, Diana tried desperately not to think what that meant. Seven buttons. She had found seven buttons. But surely a man's shirt had more.

She closed her eyes, trying to visualize it. Two buttons had decorated the collar—she was positive of that. Hadn't there been two more on the cuffs? And at least eight or nine down the front? Why only seven, then?

Of course, he might have discarded some before she spotted the first one. Or they might be watching him more closely now as they approached wherever they were going. Or . . .

Diana gulped. Her throat was so dry it hurt. The buttons might have stopped because Cord was dead. Because for whatever cruel reason, the Comanche had finally taken his life. Perhaps they had caught him leaving a trail.

Dear heaven, she was right back where she'd started! She would have wept, but she was so dehydrated, there wasn't even enough moisture for tears. She had been so excited when she found the first button, sure somehow that everything would work out. But she had been following the Comanche for miles, and all she had succeeded in doing was losing the trail.

And she still didn't know if Cord was dead or alive.

No, she thought bitterly, not *exactly* back where she started. She scanned the skyline, realizing for the first time that she had no idea where she was. She had been following the buttons for some time, going from one dry ravine into another, backtracking and trying yet another until a flash of silver told her she was on the right track.

Now the buttons were in her pocket. There was nothing left to follow!

She started to tie the scarf back around her neck, then impulsively tucked it into a crevice in the rocks, leaving one end to dangle out and flutter in the wind. Futile perhaps, like Cord and his buttons. But he had left a trail for her. If by some chance he managed to get free, this would be a sign for him.

She rose slowly, feeling suddenly helpless and alone in that endless expanse of red-glittering sand. The sun was disappearing; the first chill of evening could be felt, but she shivered not just from the cold. She couldn't go on—she had no idea what lay ahead. But she couldn't go back either, for the ravines were a hopeless labyrinth, all branching from each other, all looking exactly alike.

All she could do was pick a direction from the sun and go that way. And pray to heaven it led somewhere.

24

A MIRAGE. Diana longed to double her hands into fists and beat on the ground in frustration. Another mirage! She had been so sure this time. The trees had looked so real, thick groves of cottonwoods, the undersides of dusty leaves glittering like mirrors as the wind caught and turned them.

She had even heard voices. Masculine murmurs, half-whispers mingling with the rustling of the leaves. As if she had stumbled on some inhabited place and people were coming to help her.

And all the time, it was a mirage!

She curled her knees up, coiling into a ball. Every time they were different, these eerie images that had first appeared as the caravan neared Santa Fe. Sometimes she could swear she was looking at an oasis, exotically shaped trees swaying above the waters of a placid lake. Other times, whole medieval cities seemed to sprawl, miles and miles of crenellated towers soaring out of the sand.

Then, as they approached, everything melted away. Like a candle held too close to the fire, until all that was left was a puddle on the ground, and then even that was gone.

It was caused by something called refraction, Cord had told her. A trick on the eyes. Rays of light, changing direction as they passed through the atmosphere, created distortions that took on the illusion of reality. As visible as the patterns of light and shadow that formed on a sunny day . . . and as insubstantial if you tried to reach out and touch them.

Cord. . . . She sat up slowly, sensing that something was wrong, that she oughtn't to be lying on the sand. Cord, who had looked so dashing when he rode out of El Paso—and made her so furious! How her heart had soared when she saw that first button.

But a long night had passed since then, and an even longer morning, and there had been no further sign. Whatever
they wanted, the savages who had taken him, surely they
had it by now. Would they continue to hold him? Or would
they kill him and leave him to rot in the desert?

She brushed a lock of hair back from her brow, her mind
still fuzzy, but beginning to clear. She *had* been lying on
the sand, not leading her horse toward an inviting pool of
water. A dream, then. Not a mirage . . . but a dream.

It was a moment before she became aware of gently rolling dunes, sparsely covered with stunted vegetation. It had
been flat when she lay down. She remembered now. Distinctly. The last of the water had gone to Brutus, and she
had been too thirsty and exhausted to go on.

Almost completely flat. And it had been noon!

Diana stared with dismay at the western horizon. A ball
of fiery orange was just settling on the hilltops. Had she
been delirious and wandered off without realizing it? From
the difference in the terrain, she must have trudged for miles!

Brutus?

She tensed her ears, listening.

Nothing. Not a whinny, not a snort. Nothing! Diana felt
a sudden stab of terror. Could she have left him behind,
hobbled someplace, helpless to follow while she meandered
half-crazed with delirium over the sand?

Forcing herself to stay calm, not to give in to her mounting panic, she turned around. Surely she was wrong. Surely
she would find him just behind her.

Only it wasn't Brutus that met her eye.

A small group of men was standing a short distance away.
Three of them. Not speaking, not moving, just staring at
her. Their clothes must have been colorful once, typically
Mexican, but everything was brown now and stiff with
grime. Bandannas had been tied around their mouths and
noses; one was still struggling with the knot, and thumbs
looped through gunbelts at their hips.

No, not three. Four. Another man was approaching with
Brutus on a lead. Apparently he didn't know she was awake
for his face was still unmasked.

Bandidos! They must have stumbled across her while she
was sleeping. *Those* were the voices she had heard in her
dream.

Why hadn't she been more careful? Regret stung like a

slap in the face. She had known the area was riddled with outlaws—she should have stayed under cover! She had been so preoccupied with the Comanche, she hadn't stopped to worry about anything else.

The young man leading the horse made a slight noise, drawing Diana's gaze, almost hypnotically. The beginnings of a scraggly beard covered his face, and his hair was long and unkempt, but there was something about those dark eyes with their dust-smudged lashes . . . something in the way he moved, the way he looked at her . . .

Her mouth fell open as a soft chuckle came from behind. Whirling, she saw two more men outlined against the blazing pink and orange of the sky. One was also bearded, a substantial bush, yellow-brown on top, salt-and-pepper beneath. The other was clean-shaven—and instantly familiar!

"Yes, *turquesa.*" The voice, only subtly accented now, was tinged with laughter. "That is young Roberto. Not quite as handsome with the beard, and his hair wants trimming . . . But do not look so alarmed. He is taking excellent care of your *caballo.* Roberto has a way with animals. Have you ever seen Brutus so amiable?"

"Juan José?" Diana gaped at him, too stunned to take in everything at once. She ought to be glad to see him, she ought to be dancing jigs with relief, but she couldn't shake the feeling that something was wrong. "What . . . what are you doing here? And why do those men have masks over their faces like common bandits?"

He ignored the second question. "I could ask the same about you. Your husband left you in El Paso. In the care of friends, who had instructions to watch over you. Why did you leave?"

"I . . . I was following Cord." Diana felt strangely groggy, as if she had just woken up and couldn't quite focus. This was Juan José, yet it wasn't. He even looked different. The lazy mien of the drunk was gone, in its place a lean ruggedness that reminded her somehow of Cord. His eyes were clear, no longer dilated with the effects of whiskey—not black at all, but hazel. "I thought I could catch up with the train, but I got stuck at one of the watering holes. Then, when I learned some of the wagons had broken away from the others, and Comanche had been seen follow-

ing them . . . well, I had to warn Cord. I had to! But I was
too late . . .''

Her voice trailed off miserably as she recalled that grim
scene she had stumbled onto at the remains of the wagon
camp.

Juan José studied her for a minute, then nodded. "I know,
turquesa. I saw when I came back. We were lucky, Roberto
and I. We happened to be hunting when the Indians struck.''

"And you just happened to run across the others, I suppose—at exactly that time.'' A note of bitterness crept into
her tone. Things were finally coming clear. The men had
their faces covered like bandits because they *were* bandits.
And Juan José, always so friendly, so agreeable . . . "You
all just happened to be riding in the same direction, and you
just happened to meet up!''

"No, of course not. We did not *happen* to meet. It was
planned, naturally. But it was a coincidence that we happened to meet at that time.''

"Naturally,'' she echoed sarcastically. How could she
have been such a fool? She had thought there was something
funny about Juan José—the way he dressed, much too neatly
. . . the way he slipped from drunk to sober, and back to
drunk again. "Those are the Mexicans we took on in Santa
Fe! The ones who deserted Deadeye in the *jornada*. They
thought if they hid their faces, I wouldn't recognize them.
Dear heaven! They were your men all along. *You* picked
them out—and somehow you got Cord to go along with it.
You found out he was looking for the silver Antonio Vargas
had stolen, and you wanted it for yourself!''

The look of vague surprise that spread across his features
did nothing to calm her. Did he think she was too stupid to
figure it out?

"You're wrong about one thing. Vargas did not steal the
silver. He wasn't a thief. As for the rest . . . well, that's as
good an explanation as any for why I am here.''

As good as *any?* Diana felt something snap inside. So
nonchalant, as if betrayal and masked outlaws were things
one encountered every day. All the pieces were tumbling
into place. His eyes—hadn't they looked like hers when she
darkened them with belladonna? And the hair dye wasn't
covering gray but some lighter shade—like the stubble on
his cheeks, which caused him to shave regularly!

"You were just pretending to be Mexican! That's why you

made such an effort to fit in. You were afraid someone would catch on. What are you—pure-blooded Spanish? The arrogance fits! From some impoverished *hacienda* family, I suppose, like the Vargases and Valerosos, only down on your luck. Longing to be wealthy again and not too fussy how you go about it.

"That explains why you know so much about the silver," she went on. "Maybe you even know who the real thief is. Don't deny it! Even your accent is less comical now. Or are you going to tell me that's another coincidence? You just 'happened' to polish up your English on the trail. You must be very pleased with yourself, taking us all in!"

Throughout this tirade, Juan José had made no attempt to interrupt. He simply stood there shaking his head.

"It is the most amazing thing," he said when she finally finished, "the female mind. I had not realized a pretty lady could be so clever. Or so devious."

"You call *me* devious?" Whatever little control Diana had left deserted her in a torrent of fury. "You *used* me. And Cord! You tripped me on purpose that day in the plaza—then pretended to be concerned! You wanted me to think you were my friend so you could get to know my husband. Get him to trust you. And I was gullible enough to fall for it!"

"Gullibility is not such a terrible thing . . . even if it does make you feel foolish. And friends sometimes have to do things they don't like. But that doesn't mean they aren't friends." He turned his head, speaking in Spanish to the man beside him. Too quick for Diana to follow, but he seemed to be asking for something, for the man went over to a pile of supplies she had not noticed before.

"I think, *turquesa,* this is not the time to quarrel. Here, let me make you a peace offering." He was holding out a leather canteen the man had placed in his hand. "Drink all you want—there is a spring nearby—but drink slowly. Water gulped too quickly in the desert has a way of unsettling the stomach."

Diana would gladly have taken the canteen and flung it in his face, but she knew she needed the moisture, though, strangely, she was not thirsty. Probably because she was too edgy. Removing the stopper, she held it to her lips and sipped slowly, not taking her eyes off him.

He was a thief. He hadn't denied it. He had planted his

men in the caravan—and ''happened'' to meet them just as the Comanche attacked! A coincidence, as he claimed?

Such things can be arranged. . . . A few horses, a brace of mules, ammunition perhaps, and Comanche can be persuaded to do almost anything.

Esteban Olivares. In Bent's Fort. He had been talking about another death. Another time. But Comanche were Comanche.

''My God, you planned it!'' she cried, horrified. The doubts crystallized suddenly, overwhelming her, and she realized she was in terrible danger. A man who could do that would stop at nothing. ''You knew exactly when the Indians were going to show up. And you made sure you were nowhere around!''

Her eyes were moving as she spoke, raking the area surreptitiously. Roberto had stepped away from her horse; the reins were draped loosely over the saddlehorn. Could she get there in time?

''Turquesa—'' Juan José began, but she did not let him finish.

''What did it cost you?'' she asked bitterly. ''A couple of hunting rifles . . . a thoroughbred horse? . . .''

She wandered over to a flat ledge of rock, moving dazedly, as if too stunned to think. But her mind was working every second as she set the canteen down and pushed it slowly back. There was a small stone nearby, not heavy, but sharp-edged, the only thing that remotely resembled a weapon.

These men were killers, as treacherous in their own way as the Comanche. More, because they pretended to be civilized. She had to get to Brutus quickly, before they saw what she was up to. She had to get away!

Diana took a deep breath, hesitating one last second. Only Roberto was close to the horse. If she could disable him . . .

It was a chance in a hundred. She might be making things worse, she might anger them into even more brutal reprisals, but it was her *only* chance, and she had to take it.

She grabbed the rock, spinning around at the same time and racing for the horse. Roberto reacted an instant too late; she was already hurling it with deadly aim. He stopped abruptly, dark eyes widening as a trickle of blood started down the side of his face.

"*Señora*," he murmured, shocked. "Why did you do that?"

Why? Diana was laughing and crying at the same time. He looked so comical, for all the world as if he couldn't figure out what was going on. Because she wanted to live, that was why! Because she hated what was happening in this bleak, desolate place, and she was terrified out of her wits. Why did he think?

She nearly reached the horse. Another split second and she would have made it. But one of the men was there before her, the mask slipping from his face, fingers huge and callused as he reached out and grasped the reins. Then another man was coming up behind, and Diana realized with the horrible finality of despair that it was over.

All she could do was stand there, her breath coming in painful gasps, as Juan José strolled over and, raising both hands, gestured the men back. Damn him, she thought. Damn him, damn him, *damn* him!

But instead of leading Brutus away, as she had expected, he swept off his hat with a mock-courtly bow and stepped aside.

"Your steed, madam . . . if such be your desire. But I warn you"—he pulled himself erect with what she could have sworn was a twinkle in his eye—"you will be making a mistake."

Diana had the idiotic feeling her mouth was hanging open, and her brains were turning to mush again. "Are you telling me I'm free to . . . *go?*"

"Of course. You were never a prisoner. It was not necessary for you to resort to such extreme behavior. You had but to ask." He threw an amused glance at Roberto, who had recovered somewhat, but still looked surprised. "Ah, well . . . the wound doesn't seem deep. It will heal, and that handsome face should be smooth again. If not . . . scars add a certain romantic appeal, eh?"

Roberto smiled wanly, and one of the men pulled out a clean bandanna and shoved it at him. Every muscle in Diana's body tensed as Juan José turned back to her.

"Where did you think you were going, *turquesa?* You don't know the desert. You'd be as helpless as a coyote pup without a mother. You don't even know how to find water. Your canteen was dry. You might make it through the night, but you'd last only a few hours in the heat of midday."

"Better that than dying here." Diana's chin went up, the defiance more instinct than reasoned reaction. She had always been a fighter, as long as she could remember. She wasn't going to give up now. "At least there I would have a chance—no matter how slim."

"What do you think? That we have designs on your life?" To her consternation, he started to laugh. "If we were planning on killing you, we'd have done so already. We wouldn't have *had* to kill you. We could simply have left you to die where you were. How do you think you got here?"

He laughed again at the look on her face.

"Roberto found tracks yesterday afternoon—one horse, shod, and small boots, belonging to a woman or a young boy. He followed them for some distance. He had to give up at night—the moon is waning—but he and one of the other men started out again in the morning. You were delirious with heat and dehydration when they found you. They gave you water, and you fell asleep. You didn't even wake when he picked you up in his arms and brought you here."

"It could be . . ." Diana admitted warily. It all fitted in. There had been voices in her dream, male voices . . . and her thirst had been slaked. "But why? You're after the silver. You didn't even try to pretend you weren't! You want to get to it before anyone else. Why would you take all that time to search for someone who just *might* be in trouble?"

"Because we're not animals, no matter what you think." He stepped closer, between her and the horse, and Diana had a moment's panic as she realized her escape was cut off, though she had to concede there was nothing menacing in his manner. "I did not plan that attack on the wagons. I give you my word. I would not do such a thing to my worst enemy, much less a man I have called my friend."

"But you were away from the camp . . ." Diana hesitated. She wanted desperately to believe him, but how could she?

"Coincidence, as I have said. Or luck. You may accuse me of being a thief, and I will permit it. You may call me a liar. I permit that too. But I will let no man or woman accuse me of cowardice. And it is a coward who arranges for others to do his killing."

His face was solemn for a moment. Then, replacing his hat at a jaunty angle, he let his eyes drift back to Roberto, who was seated on the ground, dabbing at his forehead.

"I think I'd better check on that wound, though it doesn't look serious. You are free, of course, to do as you choose. But before you go flying off into the sand, you might consider that it's a big empty desert out there. Even the unpleasant necessity of casting your lot with thieves is better than certain death. And the desert *is* death for those who do not know it."

Yes, the desert was death, Diana admitted to herself as she watched him amble over to where the others were gathered around Roberto. At least it would be for her. She had been at the end of her resources before; it would all be over now if these men hadn't found her. Like it or not, survival depended on them.

But casting her lot with thieves could be more than "unpleasant." It could be extremely dangerous, and she would be a fool to forget it.

They remained where they were for the night, risking only a small fire, and that under an overhanging ledge, for coffee to go with the crackers and dried beef that almost tasted good, Diana was so hungry. She lay awake for hours, ears straining for the slightest sound, shivering at the spine-tingling howls of coyotes in the distance. But when nothing happened, she began to relax, and was surprised to open her eyes and see that the soft gray of dawn was seeping over the horizon.

She was still in danger—she did not for a minute doubt that—but apparently the *bandidos* meant her no immediate harm.

They pressed on throughout the morning, not even pausing for brief rests as the sun splashed hot and yellow over bleak stretches of sand. Making up, Diana assumed, for the time they had lost tracking her down. Kindness was kindness, but it wouldn't do to lose sight of what really counted. The silver of Antonio Vargas, stolen or not, was still out there. And it was still worth a fortune.

The landscape changed, taking on patterns Diana began to recognize. One moment everything would be desolate beyond belief. Bone-dry sand flats, not a sprig of vegetation for miles; shallow mesas so barren they looked as if they had been carved out of granite; dust-browned shrubs picking themselves up and blowing, great eerie balls buffeted on the wind. A noxious stench rose from salt marshes as unpalatable water oozed out of the ground, drying into a grayish crust that crunched under their hooves as they rode across it.

Then they would reach the top of a rise, and she would be surprised to find herself looking down at a cluster of buildings. Webs of *acequias*, laboriously carved ditches, carried water from a muddy stream to fields that looked as if they could barely support a crop of beans or corn. There was nothing like a town—the area was too sparsely settled— but dirt-poor *ranchos* huddled together, as if in this inhospitable land men were hungry for the company of others.

Obviously, Diana thought uncomfortably, there was water if you knew where to find it. And just as obviously, she didn't.

They stopped for the long noon break at a deserted hovel. Not even a farmhouse, just a shack in the middle of nowhere. It didn't look as if anyone had been here for some time, though the men seemed familiar with it. At least they knew where everything was as they tended the horses and saw to the midday meal. But then, one adobe hut was probably much like another.

The men sprawled out afterward in the shade of a dilapidated shelter, rather like a barn or stable, but open along one side, with the others half-rotted away. The one-room *casita* was left to Diana. For modesty, she supposed, though it seemed unlikely that outlaws would be concerned with a lady's feelings.

Little air was stirring. It was stuffy in the small room, and foul-smelling, but the walls were thick and there was at least a hint of coolness.

Diana had just decided to take a chance on a rickety cot jammed against the wall when she heard a noise behind her. Startled, she spun around.

Juan José was standing in the doorway.

"I brought your canteen, *turquesa.*" He shook his head with a mildly reproachful look. "You left it outside, which was extremely careless. You might wake and be thirsty. It is always good to know where one's canteen is in the desert."

"Uh . . . thank you." Diana could not keep a faint tremor out of her voice as he set it on the table and glanced back.

"You are still afraid? Even after the assurances I have given you? You think we plan to harm you? But look . . ." He stretched out his hand, taking in the shadowed, empty room. "There is no one here. No one within miles. Where better to dispose of a pretty woman, if that is what we have in mind? . . . And you are still alive."

"There are other ways to harm a woman," Diana reminded him, "besides killing."

"Ah, yes." He grinned unexpectedly as he headed for the door. "The 'fate worse than death.' Isn't that the American-schoolgirl way of putting it? But you have been with us nearly twenty-four hours now. Unconscious by the spring . . . all night in the middle of the desert . . . hours in an isolated shack. What do you suppose we are waiting for?"

Diana bit her lip. Put like that, it did sound silly. But she didn't reply.

"I told you before," he said from the threshold. "My men are not animals. Nor am I. I know it is not easy, but you are going to have to take us on trust."

Not *easy*? If she hadn't been so exhausted, Diana would have hurled something at the door as it swung shut behind him. It was *impossible*—and yet, what choice did she have? She couldn't run away; this morning's ride had made that painfully clear. There was water all around, and she hadn't even known it was there!

But if she stayed, she would be completely at their mercy. They could do anything they wanted to her. Anytime.

She managed to sleep a little, but fitfully, and she was tired when they set out again late in the afternoon. She didn't even try to protest as they wound their way from one steep-sided ravine into another. The desert had a way of sapping even her fiery spirit. If this went on much longer, she thought, she wouldn't care what they did. Or what happened to her.

There was almost no moonlight—the earth turned from dusk to black in minutes—and they stopped shortly after nightfall at another adobe structure. This one was inhabited by a man, a woman, and two small boys, who gaped at her frankly in the faint light of a crude oil lamp.

Diana was too weary to be insulted as the woman fingered her shirt and hair, uttering comments in some guttural accent she couldn't make out. She didn't even care about eating. All she wanted was to lie down somewhere and lose her fears in the merciful oblivion of sleep.

But sleep did not come that easily. No sooner had the

door closed behind her in the small back room, from which she sensed the entire family had been evicted to accommodate her, than the one fear she had been suppressing all day came back.

The Comanche. The images came with a vengeance, every detail vivid. That awful scene in the camp, flames everywhere, smoke, the first body she had found . . . the terrible anguishing thought that that must have been Cord's fate too. The brief hope later when she found the buttons.

A false, cruel hope. She knew that now as she huddled in a corner of the bed, too frightened even to lie down and shut her eyes. Death in the raid would have been painful and ugly, but at least it would have been swift. God knew what they had done to him later. What they might be doing now.

"You didn't even try to find him!" she said accusingly as Juan José came into the room with a bowl of *frijoles* and warm corn *tortillas* in a surprisingly clean napkin. "Cord. He survived that attack. I'm sure of it! But I think the Indians have him captive."

"He did survive." There was no table and Juan José placed the simple dinner in the middle of the bed, settling himself on the far end. "The ashes were still smoldering when I returned, but I managed to search them. Thoroughly." He did not mention how it had felt, the tightness that had closed around his chest as he probed the charred remains of men he had known. "There were only five bodies. Your husband was not among them."

"Only . . . five?" Diana was too relieved for a moment to think of anything else. "But . . . that's all I saw too. Just enough for the crew. My father, then? And Ryder?" she added shuddering.

"Ryder had gone to look for water. He left before Roberto and I went hunting. Your father was with him." His brow puckered almost imperceptibly. "Hardly usual, but . . . he was. You might call it luck again. At any rate, they both escaped."

"And Cord," Diana reminded him, barely daring to breathe. "You said you didn't find him. I'm almost positive the Indians took him. I don't know why, but—"

"I don't either," Juan José agreed, "but I believe you're right. He would never have left of his own accord. Especially with Ryder and your father still gone." He hesitated, as if making up his mind, then reached in his pocket and pulled out two circles of silver, which he set beside the *frijoles* on the bed. "I found these, one a short distance from the wagons, the other a quarter of a mile on. It looks as if he was trying to leave a trail, though it didn't go far."

Diana gaped at the buttons, bright against the darkness of the blanket. They looked so innocuous—just pretty pieces of silver and turquoise.

"I have the others," she whispered hoarsely. "In my saddlebag. I'm surprised you didn't see them when you took the canteen to fill it. I picked them up. I didn't think about it, I just kept taking them . . . until I didn't find any more." She looked up slowly, a new thought dawning. "He was leaving them for *you.* I wondered . . . but it didn't make sense. You're barely a stranger. Why would he think you'd come after him?"

"Men take measure of each other in the desert, *turquesa.* Perhaps he took mine . . . and he was not wrong. How many times must I tell you? We are not animals. I would not leave my most hated enemy in the hands of Comanche."

"Then . . . Oh, my God. It's my fault!" Diana gaped in horror. "He left those buttons for you—and I picked them up! I ruined the trail. If it weren't for me, you'd have found him!"

"No, no, no." He shook his head quickly. "You must not even think such things. Did you not tell me yourself that the trail ended? I would have gotten as far as you. No farther. They are cunning, these savages. There was no attempt at stealth when they started, but later, as they approached their camp, they stuck to stony ravines where tracks do not show. I doubt I would have found him. And if I had, what could I have done?"

"You could have tried—"

"Six men against an entire band of Comanche? No. I said we are not animals . . . and we are not fools either. It was a distant hope at best."

"But now there's no hope at all."

"There is always hope, *turquesa.* You are still young enough to believe in hope. Your husband is a resourceful man, and he understands the ways of Indians. If it is possible to escape, he is the one to do it. You must have faith in him."

Diana sat on the bed a long time after he was gone, staring at the cooling beans and unable to bring herself to touch them.

Have faith, he had said. She did have faith in Cord. She had always had faith in Cord. She loved him dearly, believed in him absolutely. Nothing would ever persuade her to doubt him again. But oh, dear heaven, it was hard to keep on hoping when the odds were long and getting longer.

She didn't even know if he was still alive. Here she was, thinking of him, dreaming of him, longing to feel his arms around her—and she didn't even know if he was still a part of the world that would seem so empty without him.

25

"YOU ARE ASKING YOURSELF, *señor*, why you are here."

The voice seemed to float out of the shadows, disembodied, Spanish in the words, but not the harsh, guttural accent. Cord crouched back on his heels, Indian-style, trying not to squint as a face come through the smoke and firelight. The smell of grease coated his nostrils, cooking fat and rawhide robes and hair that fell in matted clumps; and he was a boy again, thirteen years old, afraid with the fear he knew he had to conceal.

"You will tell me when you are ready," he said evenly.

The mouth on the face twitched slightly, as if amused, though amusement was not a Comanche emotion. The face was strangely ageless. The skin, leathery from years of exposure, was stretched over high cheekbones, unlined except at the corners of dark, cruel eyes; the long braids were barely flecked with gray.

It was also a face that was somehow familiar, though Cord couldn't place it. As if he knew this man. Thirteen years old. The same smells then. The same awful, stomach-knotting sense that things were about to happen.

Figures flitted around the edge of the firelight, women and old men, like bats in the shadows. No dogs—times were hard and meat scarce—but there were plenty of children, curious, giggling, whispering.

So . . . this was a family camp. Cord didn't know why that surprised him, but it did. He had expected to encounter warriors, to be dealt with man-to-man. Hoped for it. Anything was better than being turned over to the squaws, who had perfected the most exquisite methods of torturing their victims to death.

"You speak excellent Spanish," he said, breaking the silence that was setting his teeth on edge.

The face allowed itself a half-smile. It had won the battle of nerves. "One of my wives is of the *ranchos*. She is old now, but she has given me many things, including a knowledge of the white man's tongue. But maybe you like better we speak English," he added, switching to that language.

"Spanish is fine." Cord stared at the face, still unsettlingly familiar. Why? No doubt there's an American wife too, he thought, steeling himself to keep from cringing. "I am equally comfortable with both languages . . . and you do better in Spanish."

The eyes flashed briefly. It had been a calculated risk, that implied criticism of the man's English—Comanche warriors didn't like having their pride pricked—but Cord sensed he had scored a point. They didn't like enemies who groveled either.

"You said I would tell you why you are here. It is not, as you know, the custom among us to take captives. If I had you brought here, it is because I want something. Perhaps I am curious."

"Curious?" Cord uttered the word guardedly. Curiosity was no more a brave's emotion than lighthearted amusement. Women were curious. Children were curious. Not a warrior chief.

"Curious to see what you have become, Señor Montgomery." The corners of the mouth moved again—laughing?—at the reaction Cord could not conceal. "Did you think we had forgotten you? You were with us only a brief time before the ransom came. A cousin, was it not? But you showed mettle, even as a child. You absorbed our spirit. I was interested to see if a part of you remained Comanche."

"The devil it did!"

"Do not speak so quickly. These things happen—even when we do not will them." He seemed to be watching, waiting for something. "You do not remember me?"

Yes, Cord thought suddenly. He did remember this man. He was older now, leaner, jaw and brow more angular, but the force of his presence was the same. The intense savagery. One of the women had crept closer, yellow firelight lapping a grotesquely deformed face with a gaping hole in the center. They had terrified him as a child, these mutilated women; now he knew that braves routinely chopped off the noses and ears of wives who had been unfaithful.

"You are the man they call Lone Coyote." Cord spoke

the name in the dialect of the tribe. "You were arrogant even then . . . and particularly vicious. I knew you would be a chief one day."

The face did not change. "You are not afraid of me?"

"I am afraid," Cord admitted. "But a man does not let fear dictate his actions."

These seemed to be the words the Indian expected.

"We were promised six wagonloads of rifles," he said. "With bullets and powder. We were told where these wagons would be and what day—by a man we can usually trust. But in the wagons were only boxes. And in the boxes stones and branches of dead trees. I do not think this man lied to us. I think someone lied to him."

"What do you expect *me* to do? Make good on the promise myself? Those were my wagons you burned, my stock you stole, *my* men you slaughtered!"

"They were killed in a fair fight."

Fair, like hell! Cord thought. They were ambushed without warning, greatly outnumbered. If he hadn't been stunned by debris from a burning wagon, he'd be dead himself.

"You were cheated," he said bluntly. "My enemies wanted to get rid of me, and they used you to do it. They outsmarted you, *amigo*—as simple as that. And I don't think you like it."

Lone Coyote didn't. Anger flared, the first crack in that unfathomable facade. Was that what had prompted him to have Cord tied across the back of his horse—leaving his hands free because he seemed to be unconscious? If only he had been able to reach more of the buttons . . .

"There was a reason you were leading your men into the desert where no towns lie," the Comanche was saying. "You were seeking the lost silver of the Mexican legend. Others have looked, for many years. They have all come back with empty wagons. But I think you know where it is."

"I don't, but I know the men who do. The same men who duped you and tried to get me killed. I have a score to settle with them myself."

"But for that, you must live." Cord was extremely conscious of dark eyes burning into his face. "What would you be willing to give for your life?"

Now we're getting somewhere, he thought, every nerve

starting to tingle. This was something he could deal with. Greed, pure and simple. But a greed for silver?

"Indians have never been interested in cash. Or bullion. They look for guns, horses, women. Things they can possess and use."

"In the days that are past, yes. Paper and gold do not warm the body or fill the belly or protect a warrior's tepee in times of danger. But I have learned more than my enemy's language. I have learned that his pieces of paper and little coins can be traded for things that do."

"You want the silver?"

"I want it, white man. You can get it for me?"

Cord hesitated. Like the animal for which he had been named, this Comanche was cunning. To try to deceive him might prove fatal. But to tell too much could have the same effect.

"I can get it . . . if it is still where it was placed," he said warily. "But it may be gone. You know yourself how many men have searched. And for how long. All the wagons that went back may not have been empty."

"I know this," Lone Coyote agreed, almost too quickly. Had it been a trap? "I have not been to the white man's schools, but my brain understands how to think. I know the bars of silver may not be there. But if they are . . . ?"

"Then I will lead you to them. And you can have them. I have no interest in the treasure for myself . . . but I think you know that too. My aims are personal. Once they're satisfied, I don't give a damn what happens to the silver."

"How do I know I can trust you?"

Cord dared a sudden grin. "It is not a matter of trust. You will have many braves following me. The men in my camp will be few, and at least two will not be my friends. You don't have to take my word for anything. But I will have to take yours."

"Mine is the word of a Comanche. It will be kept . . . if I give it."

He turned toward a group of men squatting in a semicircle just beyond the reflection of the fire. Silent shadows, listening intently, as if somehow they could understand. Now they leaned forward, faces catching the glow as Lone Coyote spoke in Comanche, translating, no doubt, giving and taking opinions.

Every muscle in Cord's body tensed. This was the mo-

nent that would decide his fate. He had spoken his piece.
All he could do now was crouch in the stench and soot and
try not to sweat.

Comanche were like wolves. They could smell fear in a
man's sweat—

The thought broke abruptly as one of the braves moved,
easing half-naked into the firelight. His chest was bare and
smooth; a pair of white man's trousers hugged his hips, one
of the legs torn up the side to reveal a rock-hard thigh.

Tied to his belt was a piece of sky-colored silk!

"Where the hell did you get that?"

Every sound ceased abruptly. Even the children were
quiet. Cord could have bitten off his tongue. Lone Coyote
caught the scarf and tugged until it came loose. His eyes
glittered with speculation as he looked back at Cord.

"Among your people, this would belong to a woman.
You have recognized it, I think. She is your woman, Montgomery? You care for her?"

"For the woman . . . yes." Cord willed his hand not to
tremble as he reached out to take the scarf. The last thing
he needed now was for this chief to figure out there was a
better way to get at him than threats of torture or death.
"But this little whimsy? No. It's quite common. Very much
in fashion at the moment. There are probably a thousand
like it."

"You were surprised to see it. It made you feel something."

"For a second, perhaps. It reminded me of someone—
but as I said, it is extremely common." Keeping his voice
light, trying to seem casual, Cord flipped the lace-edged
silk over in his hand. "It doesn't even look the same now
that I see it closer. But I am curious. Where did you find
it? Not in the boxes you split open. All salable goods went
to Chihuahua."

The ploy seemed to work. Lone Coyote relaxed, leaning
back, but his gaze was still intent.

"It was caught in a crevice, about the place where we
began to retrace our tracks. When you regained consciousness, I think, but you were not letting us see. It looked as
if it had been placed there on purpose. But perhaps it was
dropped some distance away and blown by the wind."

Or perhaps it *had* been placed on purpose. It was all Cord
could do to control the muscles in his face. He tucked the

scarf half in, half out of his pocket, letting it dangle care
lessly. He had been so sure when he left Diana in El Paso
He had turned for one last look and thought how meek and
demurely innocent she seemed.

But when had Diana ever been meek and demure? He
should have known she wouldn't stay behind, the dutifu
little wife, just because he told her to. It was much more in
character for her to bide her time, wait until she could slip
away, and follow him.

The men were talking among themselves again, some
voices low, others hotly urgent, but Cord barely heard. His
mind was too busy working things out, not liking what he
was coming up with. She had followed, all right. Maybe
she had even found those blasted buttons. Why else would
she have gone so far in that direction?

Only, instead of leading somewhere, the trail of buttons
had dropped her abruptly in the middle of the desert. All
alone, lost probably, and he couldn't even pinpoint the spot
without arousing suspicion!

A shadow fell across the ground in front of him. Looking
up, Cord saw the brave who had had the scarf before, a
youngish man with a nasty-looking scar running from one
eye down the side of his cheek. For an instant Cord thought
he wanted the trinket back, and was debating whether to
surrender it nonchalantly or feign annoyance.

Then he saw that Scarface had something else on his
mind. So that was what that hasty conversation had been
about! Every muscle coiled, like a forest animal scenting
danger, he eased slowly to his feet. Lone Coyote might be
willing to take a chance on him, but the younger braves
were not. They wanted him to prove himself.

And to do that, he was going to have to fight this man
who would neither ask nor give quarter.

Cord's hands slid up to his waist, finding the knot that
secured his buttonless shirt, working it loose. The smell of
ashes and grease was stronger now, the memories more in
tense. The braves were right. They remembered the Co
manche ways better than Lone Coyote with his smattering
of enemy ideas. Quick and clean, man-to-man, the strongest
to walk away.

Taking his time, showing neither fear nor undue eager
ness, Cord removed the shirt and let it drop, kicking it to
the side. Now they were even, except for his boots, which

put him at a slight disadvantage, for a barefoot man could move like a cat on the balls of his feet.

The scarf was still in his pocket. Pulling it out, he tossed it in the air.

"The prize," he said with a harsh laugh. Every eye watched as the square of silk fluttered like a wounded bird to the ground. "Yours . . . or mine. Whoever's alive at the end."

He took a step forward, cautiously, then stopped; Scarface mimicked the gesture, arms rising in a menacing pose. The scarf lay between them, a flash of color on the ground.

Out of the corner of his eye Cord saw something move. One of the men was coming up from the side and slipping a knife into the warrior's hand. The blade caught the fire- light, sparkling like a mirror in the night.

Cord waited for a similar movement in the shadows be- hind him, but all was deathly still. So, he thought, it's not going to be a fair fight.

But if it were fair, then they would *both* be bound by the rules.

They began circling, slowly, each man taking measure of the other, the Comanche with the knife thrust outward, Cord with his hands up, fingers extended, as if to form a shield.

The blade flashed suddenly, and Cord leapt to the side, exhilaration and fear surging through him at the same time. A rush of adrenaline sharpened every sense.

The man fought like an Indian. That was good. He would be a ferocious adversary, but he would be predictable. Anyone who knew the Comanche would know what to expect. But a Comanche had no idea of the wiles of the white man.

Impossible to beat the Indian with sheer brute strength. Cord realized that as the knife flashed again, catching his arm, drawing blood with the razor-sharp tip. A man un- armed was no match for one who was. But he could beat him with guile.

Favoring his right leg, he set it down gingerly, eyes brightening warily like a wounded wildcat's. As if he had been injured in the raid and couldn't make it bear its weight. Scarface saw, and reacted, as Cord had known he would. The attacks were aimed at the other leg now—the good one, he believed—fierce and viciously intent.

All right, Cord thought grimly, let him concentrate on that. And see where it gets him!

The fight continued for some minutes, going first one way, as Cord managed to get a lock on his opponent's arm and nearly brought him down—then the other as the warrior broke loose and with deadly accuracy drew blood again. Sweat was pouring freely from both bodies, powerful shoulders and backs and bronzed, muscular chests gleaming as if they had been oiled.

Then came the moment Cord had been waiting for. He stumbled on a small stone—the boots made his feet unresponsive to the changes in the earth—and grunted as he landed on his right leg.

Scarface let out a sharp hiss. Victory was his. He could feel it, taste it. He wanted the life of this arrogant white man as he had never wanted anything before. He renewed his assault on the uninjured leg, allowing himself to become careless, sure that all he had to do was find a sinewy thigh with his knife.

But Cord was already shifting his weight, in mid-motion, coming down on the right leg unexpectedly. At the same time his left knee went up, catching the man in the groin, then down again with the sickening crunch of leather on a bare instep.

It was all over in a second. The man had been flipped on the ground, and Cord was on top, one knee on his chest, the other wedged against his shoulder. The knife, which had come out of the Indian's grasp, was in Cord's hand now, the blade crosswise against the Comanche's throat.

Black eyes blazed with anger and surprise . . . and one brief flicker of fear. It would be so easy, Cord thought, throbbing with a sudden savage thrill he had never felt before. All he had to do was pull the blade swiftly to the side.

The man expected it. They all expected it, those faces in the firelight, mouths agape, not a breath audible. A Comanche would kill now—it was the code of the tribe—but a white man? They were looking, listening, watching for a sign of weakness.

Was it a test?

Cord did not look around, but he knew Lone Coyote was watching with the others. A test of courage—to see if he was worthy of being given his life? If he had the stomach to finish what he had begun?

Only that *would* make him a Comanche.

Cord was aware of the quickened pulse in the neck beneath his fingers; the man was disarmed, no threat to him now. To kill him would mean that they had won, that they had finally captured the spirit—and soul—of the boy who had escaped all those years ago. They would have turned him into something as low and debased and barbaric as themselves.

God help him, even for his freedom, even for his life, he could not let anyone do that to him.

"Bah, this 'brave' is beneath contempt!" He spat disgustedly, flicking the knife aside and rising to his feet. "I would not soil my hands with such a puny adversary. Send him back to the women and see if they can teach him how to fight."

There was a snicker of laughter, guttural but feminine. Nothing was crueler than the derision of a Comanche squaw. Cord was surprised, as he turned, to see an expression of quiet exhilaration on Lone Coyote's face.

It *had* been a test. Not a test of his courage, which had never been in doubt, but of his honor and determination. Lone Coyote knew his braves well; he had known that this swaggering bully didn't stand a chance, even with a knife against bare hands. What he hadn't known was whether Cord could be intimidated.

And a man who could be frightened into killing when he didn't want to was a man who wouldn't balk at lying to save his skin.

"The silver is yours . . . if it is still there," Cord said, his breath coming in gasps. "I have given my word and I will keep it. I make no claim for myself."

Lone Coyote inclined his head slightly.

"You are most unusual . . . for a white man. I have learned from you. You may take your horse and your water canteen and any one gun you choose. It will be interesting to learn if you find what you are looking for."

. . . if you find what you are looking for . . .

Cord hunkered naked in the dawn-brightened current of a shallow stream and sloshed water over the cuts on his arms and legs. They were not deep; only one, on his thigh, was going to leave a scar, but the flesh around the wounds was beginning to pucker, and they stung like hell. What *was* he looking for? He didn't even know anymore.

It had been so clear when he started out from St. Louis.

He had thought he knew; everything was precisely spelled
out in his mind. He strode over to the saddlebags, water
dripping on the sand as he tore a shirt into rags and began
to bind his wounds. But that had been before he had taken
a little slip of a woman into his arms, felt her heart beating
against his, and fallen asleep with silver-pale hair spilling
across his face.

He loved her. Now that it might be too late, he could
finally accept his feelings. Diana. The sweetness he had
denied himself, the passion, the rage, the sheer delight . . .
the maddening frustration. And, yes, the love. Diana. She
had driven every other emotion from his heart.

He had loved her all along. Realization came incredibly—
it was so obvious now that he was no longer putting up
barriers to protect himself. Not deeply in the beginning perhaps, but the first stirrings had been there when he pulled
her away from that mirror on the servants' porch and forced
her to kiss him.

And she had been furious—not because of his boldness,
but because she had responded!

Now that it might be too late . . .

His throat constricted as he pulled out his last clean shirt,
ripping the sleeves just above the elbows so the friction
wouldn't irritate his wounds. Why had he let this stupid,
arrogant, selfish obsession go on so long? Why had he been
so determined to take chances with her life as well as his
own? Why hadn't he had the guts to tell her the truth and
take her home where she would be safe?

He turned his head, staring into the emptiness behind
him. Somewhere . . . she was out there somewhere, and he
couldn't even go after her. He had a vague idea where the
Comanche had found the scarf, but they were going to be
on his tail for some time now, and he couldn't risk leading
them to her. He had to find the silver first, had to find some
way to satisfy them, if that was possible, before he dared
do anything else.

By that time . . .

He finished dressing, replaced the bags, and swung slowly
into the saddle. By that time, she could be anywhere . . .
or nowhere.

26

MAÑANA . . .

The word drifted through the window, catching Diana's
ear as she lay, fully dressed, on a narrow rope cot and tried
to sleep. It was the first warm night, and she had left the
shutters ajar to get some air.

Mañana . . . por la mañana? Tomorrow, or tomorrow
morning. Diana sat up, more restless than curious as the
voices outside dropped to a murmur. What was going to
happen tomorrow or in the morning?

Dangling her legs over the edge, she reached for her
boots. The floor was strewn with bits of garbage and chicken
bones, and she could hear the slithery sound of lizards scurrying through the darkness. The only light came from a
jagged-edged ray that filtered through the space between the
shutters. It was hard to believe she had been with the outlaws almost two weeks. The moon, which had been dark
before, was on the rise again, nearly full.

The voices were clearer when she got to the window.
Diana held her breath, afraid they would pause suddenly
and catch her listening. Her Spanish was improving dramatically, though she had been careful not to let them see.
Some of the accents were difficult to pick up. But some of
the men, like young Roberto, spoke almost pure Castilian,
which, with her tutoring in Italian, was becoming more un-
derstandable every day.

"They found tracks," one of the voices was saying. Roberto? "Down by that *arroyo* we passed this afternoon. He
seems to be heading north."

"Alone? It is he?" The second voice was rougher,
slightly muffled. "The one we are looking for? They are
positive?"

"They just got back. They went with the lanterns to make
sure. There is a pattern in the horseshoes. Juan José chipped

one of them, just in case, so it could be identified. And the boot prints, when he is walking, are right.''

"One set of boots?"

"One man alone. They must have split up. Perhaps there was a confrontation between them."

"This is the one man we want?" Diana strained to hear. Why did people always whisper in the dark? Had he said the man we *want* or the man we *think?*

"It is he," the voice that sounded like Roberto said. "The condition of the boots was noted too. There is no question. The tracks are fresh. We will have him tomorrow morning. Tomorrow afternoon at the latest."

A faint hiss floated on the wind. Like someone whistling through clenched teeth.

"Fifteen years, *amigo*. That is a very long time to wait."

"A *very* long time," the younger man agreed, as if he could remember that far back. "This time tomorrow, Señor Garland Howard will be in our hands."

"This time tomorrow," the other replied, "Señor Garland Howard will be dead."

Diana stood stock-still as the men drifted away, the sound of their boot heels echoing on the stone-hard sand.

Dead? It was a minute before the word registered, with all its horrifying implications. Dead! Not just thieves and treasure hunters, but cold-blooded killers—and hideously efficient. No witnesses were going to be left behind to point the finger at them.

Only . . . the silver had been stolen in the first place. Surely one man's claim was as good as another's. It was almost as if they hated her father. As if they wanted his death as much as they wanted the booty they were fighting over.

Or maybe they just liked the idea of killing.

Diana shivered as a breath of wind blew through the crack in the shutters. It was cold now; the desert night had settled in with a howling that promised a sandstorm by dawn. Even now she could feel the dust in her nostrils.

This time tomorrow, Señor Garland Howard will be dead.

She turned back into the room, trying to remember where everything was in the darkness. A table over by the door, a chair beside it—no, a stool. Two beds along the wall, one larger, covered with lumpy straw that smelled of decay and sweating bodies. The other a rope cot on which she had spread her blankets.

She had never really known her father, never particularly wanted to. He had never been there for her. He hadn't picked her up when she fell; it was always some servant who washed the scraped knees and elbows and sent her out to play again, with admonitions to be more careful this time. He hadn't held her in his arms when she woke from a nightmare. Or teased her when she grew older and started blushing at the most awkward times. Or expressed even a moment's pride when she finally, just once, did something right at one of the many boarding schools to which she had been banished.

He had not acted like a father. A real father. But he was the only father she had, and if she let Juan José and his outlaws track him down, without even *trying* to warn him, she would be as guilty as they of his death.

She was fumbling for her things in the darkness. The leather water pouch—she had left it on the table. "It is always good to know where your canteen is in the desert," Juan José had told her. Well, she did, though she had an idea this wasn't what he meant! She reached for her jacket where she had thrown it across the stool. It was getting chilly. She would need it.

Laying them on the floor beside the window, she went back to roll up her blankets, clumsily, for it was hard to tell what she was doing in the dark. Striking off on her own wouldn't be nearly as dangerous now. She had figured out some of the tricks of the desert, the kind of terrain that went with water, the sort of vegetation to look for.

And she would be following her father's tracks. Presumably he knew where he was going. They could help each other.

Besides . . .

The thought held her motionless one last second next to the window. Besides, it was not only Garland Howard who was going to be in danger tomorrow when these men caught up with him. If they didn't want to leave any witnesses to their search for the silver, what would they do with a witness to murder?

She pushed the shutters open, cringing as they creaked audibly. No matter how careful she tried to be, there was still the dull thud of wood striking adobe walls. Had some-one heard? Would they investigate?

Her heart thumping wildly, pounding against the wall of her chest, she stuck her head out and peered into the yard. Blue-black shadows everywhere, impossible to fathom. If anyone was there and happened to look in that direction . . .

Diana picked up the bedroll, trying not to think as she raised it over the high sill and dropped it with a faint plop on the ground. Someone would look . . . or wouldn't; there was nothing she could do about it. A second later the jacket followed, then the canteen. Risky, but she had to take the chance.

If she didn't get away, she was as good as dead. She had been a fool not to realize that before. They had lulled her into complacency, Juan José and his men, treating her al-most kindly, almost with courtesy—though it was absurd to apply that word to a pack of *bandidos!*

She didn't know why they had spared her so far. She could only suppose they expected something, thought they could use her in some way when they caught up with her father. But she wasn't going to let them get away with it!

Her shoulders went back, chin up, jaw tightening grimly. She had been a fool once. She was not going to be a fool again.

The shadows were even more ominous as she dropped out of the window and, head down, arms loaded with the few meager possessions she could carry, darted across the yard. Miraculously, nothing happened. No one moved, no startled shouts came from the darkness, and she almost dared to breathe as she reached the small semiopen struc-ture where the horses were stabled.

"Shhh, boy. Shhh, shhh," she whispered. Brutus' head had jerked up, lips pulling back from yellowed teeth as if to greet her. "It's going to be all right. We're going to be fine . . . but we have to be quiet. Shhh, quiet . . . quiet. . . . ''

Her hands were shaking as she saddled him, tying the canteen and blanket in back. Dust was blowing up from the ground; the night air was heavy and somehow threatening. Diana eyed the other horses nervously, afraid one would get skittish and whinny, but aside from an occasional faint stir-ring, they were still.

They had been watered and grazed. Their bellies were

full, the storm still hours away, and this was no stranger in their midst, but a woman whose voice and scent they recognized.

The wind was picking up. She led the horse across the yard, through the shadows and out into the moonlight again. Grit stung her face as she mounted and, slapping Brutus sharply across the rump, dared a desperate gallop onto the plain.

Still no shouts behind her. No sounds of pursuit, no gunshots echoing in the night!

"We made it, Brutus," she cried, exhilarated. "We made it!" She didn't know how. She didn't care. All that mattered was that, somehow, luck had been with them.

They had gotten away. They were safe!

Damn the nag! Garland Howard jammed the toe of his boot into a boulder—just as he had kicked the inert body of his horse a short time before. Damn, damn, damn, damn the nag!

He dropped to the ground, exhausted. The dust was getting so thick he could taste it in his mouth. A sandstorm brewing, but strange, unlike anything he had ever seen. Currents of air seemed to cling to the earth, bringing not coolness but intensified heat as the dust gathered into balls, like giant tumbleweeds rolling across the sand.

He had almost been there! It couldn't have been ten miles more when the nag had fallen. Garland had ridden him hard; he supposed it was his fault, but he had been so blasted close!

He had just been coming out of the last ravine—open desert from then on—and the horse had slipped. Nothing on the ground, no stones or holes, just a careless misstep, and the horse had gone down. Garland had barely managed to roll out of the way, and was still on his knees, shouting incoherent curses, when one last convulsive shudder had run through that gaunt body and then it lay still.

"Damn the nag!"

Garland mopped his brow with a filthy bandanna. Disgusting, the way it smelled. He hated this, living like an animal, hiding in gullies at night, afraid all the time. Not knowing what was going to happen.

He had managed a mile or so on foot. Maybe more. It was hard to tell in that godforsaken wasteland where everything looked alike. Nine miles left, then. Eight and a half. But even three miles without water would be a superhuman feat.

Maybe if he rested. A fly landed on his eyelashes, an annoying, buzzing thing, but he was too tired to swat it away. Half a mile at a time—a quarter—then rest again before he collapsed. A slow pace, agonizing, but it was all he could do.

He wasn't going to die here like some desert creature that crawled out from under a rock at night! He had suffered too much, risked too much, to lose it all within nine miles of the treasure that had consumed his thoughts for the last fifteen years.

Was it still there?

For the first time he felt a pang of doubt. Something tightened in his chest, sending a dull pain down one arm. It was a question he had asked himself before. He thought he had considered all the angles, but he understood now, dimly, that he hadn't.

His mind had accepted the possibility of failure. But his heart, his soul, every breath in his body had continued to believe that the silver was where he had left it.

And, dammit, of course it was!

He closed his eyes, calling back a picture of the place. A cave, shallow, but cool, cut into the steep bank of what passed for a river in that part of the world. No doubt it had been next to the water once, but years of erosion had left it stranded perhaps fifteen feet up. Vargas must have stumbled on it by luck. The only access was down a natural path from the plain above, virtually undetectable unless you knew it was there.

Garland grunted his satisfaction. The tightness in his chest was easing. Scrubby bushes grew partway up the slope, nurtured, he supposed, by the river beneath. It had been Bill Ryder's idea to transplant a couple of them to cover the low, horizontal mouth of the cave.

He hadn't thought it would work. It had seemed to him a harebrained idea, but he had done it anyway, and to his surprise, they seemed to take. If they were still there, if they had grown, multiplied, the cave and its contents would be hidden.

And if they hadn't, what the hell? Comanche might follow the stream, but they'd stick to the water. Besides, Comanche weren't interested in silver. And any *bandidos* passing through wouldn't be likely to explore an anonymous cave. Until U.S. law moved in, *bandidos* could camp in the open.

The heat . . . Garland shifted his weight, trying to find something to lean against, but there was only a pile of rocks that kept digging into his back. It was so blasted hot. Not a scrap of shade anyplace.

It had been hot that afternoon too, but the air coming from the cave had had hints of coolness that had beckoned him closer.

Vargas had been alone. He remembered it distinctly, with the same tingle of apprehension that had tensed every nerve then. Garland had been alone too; Bill had been off tending to the other man. He had just stood there for a moment, staring, as the outline of a slender brown-clad back showed in the narrow slit of an opening.

I don't think you have it in you to shoot anyone, old man. . . . Not while he's looking at you.

Well, maybe he didn't. Maybe Ryder was right. Maybe all of them were right, the men who jeered and snickered behind his back. But he had never had to put it to the test. Vargas had never turned around. Garland had just raised his gun—and fired.

Garland watched, fascinated, as Antonio Vargas fell again, as clear in memory as he had been that day fifteen years ago. His body had jerked abruptly—back, not forward, as if resisting the bullet—then, like a doll with all the stuffing torn out, he had crumpled in a heap to the ground.

Bill had shown up a short time later. With bad news— dammit, couldn't he ever do anything right? The Comanche had taken care of the other man all right, but he'd had the wagons with him and they hadn't fared well in the fight. Most were badly smashed, and what oxen hadn't been driven off by the savages had scattered in terror every which way over the sand.

They'd had a devil of a time getting even some of the treasure back. One of the wagons was salvageable, and enough cattle straggled down to the river to hitch them up, making three with their own rigs. But they'd overloaded badly, cramming in nearly half the silver, and two had broken down along the way. They'd had to move in relays, stealthily, at night, until they were far enough north of San Antonio to risk picking up more wagons and teams.

But they *had* gotten it back, and found someone to melt it down—for a price. Bill, of course, had balked at his cut, but Garland had stood firm.

It was he who had learned about the treasure in the first place. He who got the information out of Vargas' daughter and laid the plans. He who had fired the shot that made it theirs. All Bill Ryder had done was see to the second man—and he hadn't even done that himself!—and he had the nerve to whine.

Well, Garland had taken care of him. Just like he'd taken care of Bill's son!

Garland squirmed uncomfortably. The rocks were sharp; his back ached, but he was too weary to move. It probably hadn't been necessary, leaving Ryder behind like that. He still had the goods on Ryder. He knew how his father had been murdered, and why—and the information was in a nice sealed package in the hands of Garland's lawyer. Ryder wouldn't dare double-cross him, but it was better to be safe than sorry.

Anyway, he really was expendable.

The silver had made Garland rich for a while. It might have lasted a lifetime if he had been thrifty. But thrift was not in Garland Howard's nature, even before he married an extravagant young wife. God, how it had galled, not being able to get back to the silver. But there had been the revolution—it would have been all his life was worth—and later he had heard the most alarming tales of *bandidos*.

And it hadn't been urgent . . . not then. Not until he started running out of cash and rumor had it that Texas was about to join the Union.

Settlers would be swarming all over the place. They would be farming the land, exploring the riverbanks . . .

It had to be there! The tightness was back in his chest. The dust had died down momentarily, but he was finding it hard to breathe. If it was gone, he was ruined. He had spent all his cash, run his credit up to the limit. There was nothing else . . . except Diana's fortune. And he didn't know if he had the strength to make it all the way back to El Paso, to take care of her somehow, to steal away with the baby.

It had to be there. It had to! He would be all right then. Everyone would be all right. He would have his money, and

Diana would have hers, and they could all live happily ever after.

The flies were crawling over his face. He brushed them off, but they came back settling like glue on his eyelids. Just like in the fairy tales. The prince and the princess . . . and the wicked wizard and the frog . . . and they all lived happily ever after. . . .

The heat was making him sleepy. The wind was howling again, off in the distance, but here the air was almost deathly still. He didn't even hear the sound of approaching hoofbeats. His first warning was a slight uneasiness, a sense somehow that he wasn't alone.

His eyes opened with a jerk.

At first he couldn't see anything. The sun was too bright, the figure in the foreground a shimmery-edged block of shadow.

Then slowly he made out the horse, a slim rider poised on top, and he began to laugh. A dry sound that began in his belly and rose until he was laughing so hard he couldn't stop.

"Father?"

Diana stared in amazement. She could barely recognize this apparition rolling on the ground in front of her. He must have sweated off twenty pounds, and the dust was caked so thick it was hard to make out his features. Everything was the same sickly yellow-brown: skin, clothes, boots—even the week's growth of stubble on his sunken cheeks.

"Father?" she said again. Leaping down, she hurried over in alarm. "It's me. Diana. What's wrong? Are you all right?"

"Wrong?" The laughter turned into little hiccups, even more comical somehow, setting him off again. He had worried about how he was going to get back to El Paso to find his daughter if things didn't work out—and here she was, finding him instead! "Water," he gasped when he finally managed to speak. "Do you have any water? I'm parched."

"Yes, of course." Diana ran back to the horse and jerked the canteen loose. Garland grabbed greedily, making a smacking sound as he gulped. A little trickle of water dribbled out of the corner of his mouth and down his neck.

"Be careful." Diana reached out to steady the canteen. "That's all I have, and I don't—"

"There's plenty more ahead. They call it a river, but it's more like a damn stream. You can get all the water you want there. I hope that nag can carry double. Mine gave out a mile ago."

"Closer to two miles," Diana said. She had been holding on to the canteen, but now she released it. Garland took another swig, though she noticed he was careful not to spill any more. "I saw the carcass. And yes, Brutus can carry two, but we're going to have to take it slow. I'm not going to risk losing him the same way."

Garland capped the canteen and handed it back. Little tendrils of silver-brightness peeked out from under Diana's hat—even the dust couldn't dull them—and he was almost surprised at how pretty she was. He had never cared much for the mother; she had brought nothing but disappointment. He hadn't thought he cared for the daughter either.

But every once in a while there was a spark of something. A pride in her spirit, in the feisty way she held her own, even when she was wrong. A sense of wonder that anything so beautiful and unique should have sprung from his loins.

Not love exactly. Garland was not a man to feel love. But months on the trail had brought a kind of admiration that made him suddenly sad.

"You shouldn't have come," he said abruptly. "I don't know how you got here or why, but you shouldn't have come!"

Diana looked at him in surprise. "Why?"

"Because I'm going to hate like hell to have to shoot you."

27

"SHOOT ME?" Diana could only stand there, too stunned even to be frightened as she stared at her father. His face was grim, his eyes troubled, but . . . "Surely you don't mean that. You can't know what you're saying!"

"I can . . . and I do." Garland ran his tongue over his lips. They were dry again; he could feel every brittle crack. "There's a possibility, a very nasty possibility, that things aren't going to go the way I planned. If they don't . . . well, I'm afraid I won't have a choice. You'll have to die." His voice was even, almost matter-of-fact, as if he were contemplating some business arrangement.

"You must be mad." Diana's breath caught in her throat. "Why would you want to kill me?"

At last the fear was coming, a jolt of terror that showed in the quavering of that stubborn little chin. Garland saw it and responded as he always did when he sensed weakness in a woman. He liked being the master, liked to feel them quaking inside. If only he could hold on to that . . .

But it wouldn't do to let her know what he was thinking. He pulled himself cagily to his feet, trying not to stumble, though his legs were wobbling. If she realized what he had in mind, she would be wary. And a wary Diana might be hard to handle.

"I didn't say I would *want* to kill you. I said you would have to die . . . which you will if we don't find a way out of this place. Naturally, in that case, I would shoot you. I couldn't leave you to perish of exposure—or, worse yet, be taken by Indians or *bandidos.*"

"Oh." Diana could feel her hands trembling as she looped the strings of the canteen around the saddle horn and prepared to mount. It was idiotic, she knew, being frightened like this. Why on earth would her father wish her harm? But there had been something so intense in his gaze, she still couldn't throw off the feeling that somehow she was in danger. "But that's ridiculous, Father. Of course we're going to get out of here. There's a stream just ahead. A river. You said so yourself. We can follow it until we reach some sort of settlement—''

"We won't find any settlements," Garland broke in sharply. "There are no *ranchos* this far north. And we're only going five or six miles after we reach the river."

"Yes . . . how silly of me." Diana paused, one foot in the stirrup, and looked back. Garland Howard's greed had nearly cost him his life. She had found him in the middle of the desert, his horse dead, his canteen empty—and still he couldn't give it up! "The lost silver of Antonio Vargas. You're looking for it . . . even now. You're still determined to get your hands on it."

"Silver?" Garland made a great show of dusting himself off, slapping at his shirt and trousers. "What are you talking about? Oh . . . you mean that old story . . . ?"

"Spare me the pretense, Father. I know perfectly well you've been after the silver from the start. That's why you organized this expedition in the first place. Not because you expected to make your fortune trading in Santa Fe. I'm not a fool, and I've had my suspicions confirmed. What I don't understand is why you think you're clever enough to find it when everyone else has failed."

Garland glowered. She didn't like being called a fool herself, but she didn't mind implying *he* was.

"Maybe I'm clever enough to have known where it was all along. You didn't ask how I came to be so well-acquainted with this area. Didn't I tell you there's a river just ahead? I know because I've been here before. When I picked up the first half of the silver. . . . And yes, I'm still determined to 'get my hands' on the rest."

He paused, watching her face, wanting to say something to impress her. To see the flicker of fear in her eyes again.

"I killed once for half of that silver. I can kill again if I have to."

It did not quite work. Diana did feel fear again—she realized now what it was that had aroused her instincts before—but she was too spirited to let it show.

"Is that a threat, Father?" She swung into the saddle and looked down at him. "If it is, I don't like threats."

"No, no, no, of course not," Garland hastened to say.

He was aware of an odd sense of disappointment. She was not like the other women, not like her mother, who'd been so easily cowed. "I only meant I wouldn't let anyone *else* get in the way. I would never hurt you. You know that. But we ought to get going—"

"All right," Diana said impulsively. She could hardly leave him stranded. "Climb up behind. But I told you before, we're going to have to go slowly . . . and we can't take the direct route. I didn't have a chance to tell you, but we're being followed by outlaws. I barely got away myself . . ."

She was already heading back toward the rocky arroyo where he had lost his horse as she explained tersely what had happened. She left out a few details—like what she had been doing in the desert, and the awful anguish she had felt when she realized Cord had been captured by Comanche— but her father didn't seem to notice the gaps. At least he didn't ask any questions as she described the course the *bandidos* were taking and what she had overheard just before she escaped.

She felt him suck in his breath when she mentioned that they were the same Mexicans Cord had taken on in Santa Fe.

"Dammit, I knew they were up to no good," he muttered behind her. "That blasted Montgomery was too arrogant to listen. He had to have everything his way! You can't trust a Mexican out of your sight. Hell, you can't trust 'em *in* sight! It would have been better to leave half the wagons behind."

"Well, never mind. There's nothing we can do about it now. They're here, and that's all there is to it. They're probably about three hours behind us." Diana cast a tentative glance at the sky. The wind, which had been whistling some distance away, was closer again; she had a feeling they were in for an even rougher time when it swung back. The dust was thicker, but solid now, shimmery and drifting. "I'm going to double back and leave a false trail. It'll buy us a little time. And the storm may work to our advantage."

Garland grumbled but offered no real resistance as she steered Brutus past the place where the dead horse lay, lightly covered with a layer of yellow dust. She had noticed another ravine a short distance away. If she cut over boldly, across the sand—if she left a few distinct prints in sheltered places where the wind wouldn't disturb them—Juan José and his men would jump to the logical conclusion.

It was far from foolproof, but it was the best plan she could come up with. If they caught on, they'd find the real trail easily enough, a mile or two down. But why should they? They wouldn't expect any more tracks once they got to the ravine. And they wouldn't see any coming back, because she'd brush everything clean behind them. Or clean enough, the way the sand was drifting.

It took longer than Diana expected, but the arroyo was still empty as they returned and she pushed Brutus into a fast trot along the stony bottom. At least she thought it was empty, but it was hard to tell. The dust was howling all around now. Sometimes it died down briefly and everything was almost clear. Other times it was so thick she couldn't see twenty feet in front.

"Here we are!" she cried as that heavy veil lifted momentarily and she caught a glimpse of their tracks leading out of the gully. Or what was left of their tracks, for they showed only faintly in a couple of crevices. If the storm kept up like this, she needn't have worried about covering their trail!

"Straight ahead," her father shouted over the wind. "Three miles . . . four at the most. Aim for that butte over there, if you can see it."

"They aren't going to stop following us, even with the storm," Diana warned. "Sooner or later they'll figure out where we went. We'd be better off making a run for it. Forget the silver for now—"

"I won't forget. I can't. I told you, I killed for that silver. And I mean to have it."

Garland's voice was cold on the surface, but Diana sensed the pulsating heat beneath, and she knew there was no point arguing. She remembered that moment of terror when he had looked her right in the eye and told her he would shoot her, and she had the awful feeling he meant it. He *would* shoot anyone who came between him and the silver.

Even if that someone was his own daughter.

It must have been noon when they reached the river. The sun, no more than a scarcely brighter patch in a soupy dust-brown sky, was directly overhead. The storm had reached its height—it raged with a wild, almost eerie intensity—but the banks protected the river somewhat and Diana could see her father clearly as he slid to the ground.

Unbuckling his gunbelt, tossing it impatiently on the shore, he waded into the shallow current and ducked, head and all, underneath.

Diana watched with a kind of fascinated horror as the dark waters parted and his grinning features reemerged. His hair seemed to melt into his eyes, and streaks of dirt were running down his cheeks.

Is this a man who can kill? she thought with a sudden uncontrollable shiver.

He said he had—to get the silver—but that might have been bluster. Garland Howard was the sort of man who liked to boast. He said he could kill again, if he had to . . . but that might be bluster too.

Her eyes drifted toward the gun. Still in its holster, a few feet from the water. Should she make a grab for it? But that might only precipitate the violence she wanted to avoid. He was so much closer. He was almost certain to get there first.

And besides, she was probably being foolish.

Diana slid out of the saddle, but stayed where she was, half-leaning against the horse. Her father was many things she didn't like—a thief, and maybe a murderer—but he was still her father, and she couldn't bring herself to believe she was in danger.

The water was shallow, not even coming to Garland's waist as he stood and shook off the excess. His shirt clung to a torso that was almost trim again; his face, half-turned away, held echoes of something Diana had never seen in it before, and just for an instant she caught a glimpse of the dapper young swain who had stolen her mother's heart.

It seemed to be a family failing—falling for the wrong man. Hadn't she done the same herself? First Jordan Crofte, a gambler and scoundrel who had found it all too easy to charm her. Then Cord Montgomery, whose interest in her was strictly one-dimensional.

He hadn't even cared enough to tell her the truth, for all his hypocritical insistence on honesty. If he hadn't been captured by Comanche and probably tortured to death, she would hate him thoroughly and forever!

Pain stabbed her heart at the thought, swift and agonizing, and Diana grasped at the first thing that came to mind to drive it away.

"You must have hated her very much," she said abruptly
"My mother."

"Alice?" Garland frowned as he turned to face her
Muddy water streamed from his hair into his eyes. Hate wa
something he thought no more about than love; intensitie
of emotion made him uncomfortable. "Yes, I guess I did
I might not have minded so much if she'd had some back
bone."

"Or if I'd been a boy. You did want a son from her?"

"Of course I did. Why the hell wouldn't I? All that mone
sitting there in trust and no way to get our hands on it. Bu
Alice couldn't even manage that. First you, then the mis
carriages. They were probably girls too. Even the one tha
finally killed her was a girl."

"But . . ." Diana hesitated. She could feel the hair
standing up on the back of her neck. "I thought she die
when I was born. That's what I was always told."

"Your mother's relatives," he said contemptuously
"That pack of Virginia lily-livers. They couldn't bear to tel
you what a beast your daddy was, still trying for babie
when he knew what they would do to his wife. She wa
pregnant when I left for Santa Fe the first time, fifteen year
ago. The baby was born shortly after I got back. Prema
turely. It didn't even live to whimper. Neither did she."

Diana stared at him. Was he really so callous? Had he
mother's suffering meant *nothing?*

"You must have hated me too."

"Did I? Well, I suppose so." Only that was the funny
thing, Garland thought. He hadn't. Not really. He just hadn'
known what to do with a lively, active child. It had bee
awkward, having her around. "You weren't exactly what I'c
been hoping for. Not that there was a lot I could do abou
it."

"Except wait. You must have been wildly upset when you
found out I was involved with Jordan. It didn't matter in the
least whether he was 'suitable' or not—you weren't eve
worried about your precious reputation! You were just afrai
he'd talk me into running off and getting married."

"He would have, too. Clever bastard, Crofte. You aren'
under any illusions that he loved you for yourself?" He
didn't wait for an answer, but went on. "Jordan was you
cousin, after all. Families talk—especially yours. He woule
have known about your great-grandfather's will for years.

All he had to do was wait until you were old enough to court.''

Diana nodded. "I know. I figured that out a while ago."
She watched as he strode back onto the shore, the dust caking again in his hair. Too late to go for the gun now. He was standing next to it, letting the heat and wind dry him off. "You must have been relieved when you heard he was dead. What a lucky coincidence that Jordan liked to cheat at cards.''

"You really think I *am* stupid, don't you?" He was looking at her strangely, sending shivers up and down her spine. "You think I just sat around and waited for luck and an extra ace to take care of things for me. Jordan didn't just happen to die . . . and he didn't die in a gambling hall. He died in a doorway outside his lodging house. In a sleazy part of town.''

"You . . . killed him?''

"I had him killed, which is the same thing. Then I arranged a nice convenient marriage for you before the shock wore off. It would have worked, too, if you hadn't gotten mixed up with that son of a bitch Montgomery." He was picking up the gun, buckling it on again. His trousers were still wet, but not dripping, and Diana sensed the leather holster would protect the gun.

"I see." She squatted down, not even feeling the water as she splashed it on her face, then went back for the canteen and began to refill it. Not empty boasting his time—she was sure of that. He *had* arranged to have Jordan killed. "But tell me, why did you want me to marry Ryder?" she said, stalling for time. He had murdered Jordan, and probably Antonio Vargas, and if she didn't keep her wits about her and figure out what was going on, she could be in a lot of trouble. "He's as slimy as a snake, and twice as venomous. I wouldn't have thought you'd trust him.''

"He wasn't my first choice," Garland admitted. "I had someone else picked out. An old friend, who would have been prefect—if he hadn't already had a wife. She was extremely ill. He would have been available soon . . . but not quite soon enough, as it turned out. Fortunately, a piece of information came into my hands that made the snake a little less, uh . . . venomous.''

Diana didn't look up as she continued to fill the canteen. She was amazed at how steady her hand was. Inside, she felt like a plate of quivering jelly. The silver her father was risking his life for was only a fraction of the fortune he had lost when she married someone else. If he thought Cord had been killed in that raid . . .

But no. She finished with the canteen and started back toward her horse. Even if Cord were dead, there was no body, no proof. It would take years to straighten out in the courts. And surely he'd learned by now he couldn't bully her into marrying a man she didn't want.

No—she was safe there. But if he thought she'd get in his way when it came to the silver, God knew what he might do.

They continued along the riverbank on foot, Garland pushing her out ahead where he could keep an eye on her. Brutus would tolerate no one else's hands on the reins, and Diana soon realized that her father had no intention of letting her regain control. He had told her too much . . . and he was afraid.

As afraid in his own way as she?

Diana was constantly aware, as they plodded along the water's edge, of the shuffling sound of footsteps behind her, slipping occasionally, as she did, on the rocks. His boots must be wet too. Squishy inside.

How had they gotten to this place? she wondered. The wind seemed to rise in waves, whipping blasts of fine sand down the steep banks, and her eyes were smarting. A father afraid that his daughter might somehow try to harm him. A daughter terrified every second she would feel his bullet in her back.

"You really *must* have hated me," she said, turning once to glance back at him.

"You looked like your mother," he replied enigmatically. "It wouldn't have been so bad if you hadn't looked like her."

Only she *had* looked like Alice. Garland focused on the back ahead of him as the wind kicked up. Damned storm, sometimes it seemed to let up—then it was spitting grit in his face again. A miniature of Alice . . . yet not Alice at all. The same silver-blond hair, but tousled, unruly . . . the same slender figure without the fragility . . . the same haunting turquoise eyes, alive with excitement . . .

He found himself wondering what would have happened if the mother had been more like the daughter. If Alice had

ad some of the fire, the tartness, he had seen in Diana
ᵒday. Would he have loved her then?

It wouldn't have made any difference, of course. He would
ave wanted a male heir no matter what. But he might have
een sorry when she died.

They made better time than Garland had expected, or per-
aps he had miscalculated. He had never been good with
istances. They couldn't have been following the river for
ᵃore than an hour, maybe an hour and a half, when he
ᵗarted to pick out landmarks.

An odd rock formation on the side of the cliff. Higher
ow—the river had cut deeper in the last fifteen years—but
ᵃnmistakable. A snaking back and forth in the otherwise
ᵗraight course. He remembered that distinctly.

It couldn't be more than a quarter of a mile now.

He picked up his pace, overtaking Diana, gripping her
ᵃrm and making her hurry with him. Damn, why was his
ᵃouth so dry all of a sudden? It was going to be there. It
ᵃad to be there!

The air cleared slightly. He could see all the way down
ᵒ the turn in the river . . . the last turn . . .

Faster. He had to go faster. Diana stumbled beside him,
ᵃnd he tightened his grip, jerking her up. He had to get
ᵃere before the dust closed in again and he couldn't see.

The banks were higher here. Wider. Garland could make
ᵃut places where the cliffs had nearly eroded away. An
ᵃmen? But the vegetation was denser too, growing almost
ᵒ the top.

Maybe those silly shrubs Bill had insisted on planting
ᵛere still there. If the roots were deep enough, they might
ᵃave held the soil. The area around the cave could still be
ᵃtact.

The dust was shimmering, gold-red from the sun above,
ᵃs they rounded the last bend. If the calm just held another
ᵃinute . . .

He saw instantly what had happened. The river must have
ᵒoded, swelled to a torrent in one of the blinding down-
ᵒurs that frequently inundated the desert. Trapped by the
ᵃnyon's curve, the water had risen, finding fissures in the
ᵒorous stone, weakening, until everything had come tum-
ling down. All that was left of that sheer cliff was a sloping
ᵃscade of rocks.

And what had once been a cave was a gaping hole.

Garland felt as if someone had twisted a knife in hi
stomach. Most of the cavern floor had washed away. H
could almost see the silver spilling out, caught at odd angle
in various spots down the slope. Glittering in the sun—wha
a surprise for some horseman rounding the corner!

"No!"

The word tore out of his throat, the anguished cry of a
animal in pain. His fingers gouged into Diana's arm, an
he was dragging her with him up the bank.

It might not be as bad as it looked. He clung to th
thought desperately, as if willing could make it so. Th
silver might still be there. The collapse of the cliff migh
only have buried it deeper.

But he knew even before he scrambled up the last fev
feet and stood gasping for air on a wind-whipped ledge tha
he was not going to find anything. No telltale crevices, n
promising heaps of soil. Just the slightly rounded back o
the cavern and a shallow stretch of dust and sand and sharp
edged stones.

Gone! He would have wept if he had known how. Th
silver was gone. Fifteen years of dreaming and planning an
hoping—and some scavenger or desperado had made off wit
it long ago!

Only one section of the cave was still intact, a deep hol
low that had been just to the right of the entrance. Garlan
laughed hoarsely as his eyes picked up something brow
and crumpled on the ground. Antonio Vargas. They ha
thrown a blanket over him—Bill's doing again. He hadn'
wanted to look at him while they hauled out the silver.

Damn him! Anger rose, a burning inferno exploding in
side him. Damn his haughty, sneering, supercilious soul
He was still there, bones and hair and whatever was left o
his clothes, under that pathetic blanket, and the silver wa
gone!

Dropping to his knees, Garland began to claw at the earth
Frantic now, irrational, driven by the dream that would no
let go. It couldn't be gone, he kept telling himself. H
wouldn't let it be gone! If he just dug deep enough, mayb
he could make everything all right.

Diana pressed back into the hollow, mercifully unawar
of what lay beneath the blanket a few feet away. Her arr
ached—her father's grip had been cruelly bruising—but sh
barely noticed as she watched him crawl closer to the bac

wall, scooping into the soil, as if he actually thought he was going to find something.

Just for a second she felt a sad sense of pity. But with the pity came a sudden, even stronger sense of her own peril. Her father was going to be half-crazed when he turned around, full of fury and frustration—and looking for someone to take it out on.

She did not believe he actually meant to shoot her. She had never believed that. But she couldn't help thinking it would be a good idea to put some distance between them.

She inched slowly toward the front of the hollow. The dust was so thick outside, it almost formed a wall. Brutus was just at the base of the slope. She had left him untethered—they could be lost in the storm in a minute. She would come back later, when her father had cooled down . . .

Something whizzed by her head. Diana felt it, a faint breeze, a split second before the shot registered. Then dirt was spattering all around.

Horrified, she whirled back. Her father had drawn his gun and was pointing it at her.

"I'm sorry," he said. "I had hoped it wouldn't come to this."

Diana felt her whole body go numb with shock. This can't be happening, she thought. It can't be real.

"I'm sorry too," she said. She didn't move—she didn't dare—but her brain was working desperately, trying to find the right thing to say. "I know you're discouraged, I know how much you were counting on this . . . but killing me won't bring back the silver."

"No, but there's *your* fortune. That's all that's left, you see. I can't live as a pauper." He was almost whining now. "I don't like being poor."

"My fortune?" Diana was too dazed for a moment to catch on. "I'll share it with you, of course. You're my father. I wouldn't let you starve, but . . . Oh, my God . . . you think if I'm out of the way, you can have it all!"

Garland nodded silently. His eyes were bright, almost feverish, but his hand never wavered.

"Are you crazy, Father? That money's in trust. I don't know the first thing about the will. I don't know who gets it if anything happens to me. But I'm sure it doesn't go to you."

"Of course not. It goes to your son."

"But I don't *have* a son." Diana could feel the fear mounting—her palms were tacky with sweat—and she knew she had to control it. She had to keep her mind clear. "Don't you remember? I . . . I had a miscarriage. On the prairie . . . before we got to Bent's Fort. I never had a baby."

"No, but Rosalie did."

"Rosalie?" Diana held her breath one last minute, unable to believe what she was hearing. He really was crazy! "But you'd never get away with that! You can't bring back a baby—any baby—and convince people it's mine."

"Why not? No one will associate it with Rosalie. No one even knew she was pregnant. She was too prissy to talk about it. And I was careful not to let any of the St. Louis traders see her after she began to show." He was laughing softly. An ugly sound with no mirth in it. "She probably thought she was annoying the hell out of me when she ran off with that lieutenant. Actually, she was playing into my hands."

His voice faded into the wind, which had risen suddenly, a shrill, screaming wail. This is it, Diana thought. It's now or never. He's going to fire if I don't do something.

"You're cleverer than I thought, Father . . . but not quite clever enough. How do you think you're going to get out of here? The only horse is Brutus, and he's not tied up. Go anywhere near him, he's going to bolt. I meant what I said—about sharing my inheritance. You might reconsider the offer. It's a long way through the desert on foot. Especially since there aren't any settlements around."

"Oh, there are settlements, all right. Plenty of them. I just said that so you wouldn't get any ideas."

He *was* clever, Diana thought, shivering. In a devious way. But she was clever too. There had to be something she could say to get through to him.

"I don't believe you really want to shoot me, Father." She kept her voice low, even, trying not to let him see how frightened she was. "I know I was a disappointment to you. You were a disappointment to me too, but there's still a bond of blood between us. I wanted to love you in spite of everything. You must have wanted to love me too. Just a little."

"Yes, well . . . maybe." Garland was rather surprised to find it was true. Images swirled out of the dust, uncomfortable images that took away his concentration. Diana, a little girl again, stomping her foot with fierce concentration when she couldn't get her way. Diana, her chin up, a defiant little witch, flatly refusing to marry the man he had chosen. Diana, flying across the prairie, bold as a Comanche on a wildly unsuitable horse. His heart had stopped, like Cord's, when he saw her flying through the air.

Maybe he had loved her . . . just a little.

Anyhow, she was right about one thing. He didn't want to shoot her. He couldn't have shot her even if she turned her back. He didn't know why, but he couldn't. Maybe she'd been telling the truth before, about the sharing . . .

Diana saw the gun barrel dip, and she dared to hope somehow she had reached him. Maybe there *were* feelings between them after all.

She would never know, for just at that instant a shot rang out, then a second—as if by reflex—and the gun flew out of his hand.

"Surprised to see me, old man?"

28

"SURPRISE" was not the word for it. Garland's jaw dropped as an illusory shape materialized ghostlike from the storm. With the eerie yellow light behind, he seemed to loom, an earth giant, hair and skin and habitual black garb stained the color of the desert.

"Ryder?" Garland's voice was hoarse with dust and shock. "What the blazes are you doing here?"

"You didn't really think you could get rid of me so easily, did you?" came the drawling reply. Teeth and eyes gleamed unnaturally out of the sand tones of his face. "Leaving a man to die like that . . . a nasty habit. And stupid. Next time, check his boots for concealed weapons. Or better yet, pull the trigger when you point your pistol . . . though that's a lesson you still don't seem to have learned."

He turned slowly toward Diana, making her skin crawl. It was hard to tell where his lips left off and his face began, as he indulged himself in a rakish leer.

"I'm real sorry, honey, you weren't a little friendlier. We could have had fun, you and I. Too bad there isn't time to change your mind, but the area's going to be real crowded soon, if the signs I've been picking up are any indication. So I guess the three of us will be saying *adiós.*"

His hand tightened on the gun, finger curling almost instinctively around the trigger. As if he liked the feel of it, Diana thought, horrified.

It *had* been a reflex before. That second shot, when only one had been needed. His finger had moved of its own accord. She wondered if he was even aware he had done it.

"You're going to *shoot* us?" she said, struggling to keep her voice even. "Why?"

"Maybe just for the hell of it." He grinned. "Or maybe I'm thinking that ten percent of even the fattest fortune isn't what it could be."

"Ten percent? Of the *silver?*" Garland started laughing, funny little hiccups, like before, his face puckering beneath the mask of dust, gnomish and grotesque. Diana sensed he was laughing, not at Ryder, but at himself, the kind of despairing laughter that welled up in a man when he knew he had reached the end and had nowhere to go. "But there isn't any silver left. Look around you, man. Use your eyes! You want a hundred percent? Hell, I'll give you a hundred percent! I'll give you five hundred. A thousand. But a thousand percent of nothing is still nothing!"

"Well, shit . . ." Ryder looked singularly unperturbed as he cast a cool eye over the remains of the cave. "Now, isn't that a turn? But then, we always knew there was a chance someone would get here before us. A good chance. Anyhow, it was never the silver that was the real stake, was it? The real prize comes with the baby."

"The baby?" The words popped out of Diana's mouth.

Garland was speaking at the same time. "That baby thing's off. I've changed my mind. Besides, that has nothing to do with you. I only cut you in because it was partly your idea. I can bring the baby back and say it's my daughter's and get the courts to appoint me guardian. But you? They wouldn't even *look* at you."

Ryder tipped back his hat, a gesture that seemed faintly familiar, though Diana couldn't place it. The wind had stopped for a moment; the silence was almost uncanny.

"You were never very bright, old man, but I think this dust must be clogging your brain. It was a sixty-forty shot at best. You're only the kid's grandfather. The courts might have entrusted him to you, they might not. Especially if the lawyers were against it. It would be different if someone else showed up . . . say, the baby's natural father."

He looked so smug, Diana forgot to be cautious. "That baby's father would be Cord Montgomery. A man whose boots you aren't fit to polish! If you're going to try to pass the child off as mine, then you're stuck with the details of *my* life. And my marriage to Cord is a matter of public record."

"So much the better. Begging your pardon, ma'am, but it looks like you're your daddy's daughter after all. And here I thought you were smarter. Of course Cord Montgomery's the kid's father. And Cord Montgomery is going to claim his inheritance."

He saw the bewildered look on her face and smiled slowly.

"It hasn't occurred to you that there's a certain, uh . . . resemblance between your husband and me? Build, coloring, facial structure. I've even managed to get down a few of his gestures . . . like the way he tips back his hat."

"Oh!" Diana gasped. He *had* looked like Cord, just for a second. "You think you can make people believe you're my husband? But that's insane! Cord spent too much time in Missouri. St. Louis first, then Independence . . ."

"As a wagon master. Your daddy's hireling. No one pays attention to hirelings. Besides, he had a beard when he was there. I'm going to look real debonair with a beard, don't you think? And of course, I'll just be passing through. Just long enough to reestablish my identity."

"You have it all worked out . . ." Diana stared at him with loathing and the beginnings of the most overwhelming fear she had ever known. "But aren't you forgetting one thing? You're from those parts yourself. And you're not a wagon master. Aren't you afraid of running into someone you know?"

"Not particularly." He shifted the gun in his hand. "You may have noticed, I always dress in black. It's become a kind of idiosyncrasy. Funny things, idiosyncrasies. That's all people see after a while. A man can change his clothes, his hair, his way of moving, and folks'll walk right past him on the street."

Diana felt her heart sink. He really *had* worked things out. This was not some spur-of-the-moment impulse.

"You'll never get away with killing us—"

"You're damn right he won't," Garland growled. "Particularly if I don't get back on schedule. You see, there's a certain envelope in safekeeping . . . with a paper in his father's handwriting, found by an old family retainer . . ."

"*Written* by the retainer, actually." Ryder drawled it out, slow and easy, taking his time. "Poor Albert. He never forgave me for getting rid of him after my father died. I'm afraid you've been taken in, old man. You should see some of the versions he penned for the authorities. Really demented, I'm afraid. Everyone stopped taking him seriously long ago."

The gun was leveled at Diana now. A Colt, she thought, unable to take her eyes off it. Cord had shown her all about guns on the trail. This particular model was a new invention. It had a revolving chamber that held five shots, which could be fired one after another.

Five . . . and he had already used two. Diana sucked in her breath. Had she been right before? Had he fired that second bullet without being aware of it?

"I really think you forgot *two* things," she said slowly. All she could do now was keep him talking, try to work out something in her head. "That 'kid' you're counting on is in El Paso. With Cord's friends. I don't know what instructions he left, but I'd be willing to bet they didn't include turning the boy over to you."

His eyes crinkled at the corners. Blast him, Diana thought. He sees what I'm doing—and he's amused!

"You think I want *that* baby? Shoot, he's Rosalie's kid too. He'll probably end up with flaming red hair . . . and be the spitting image of her. No, the baby I'll be toting into the lawyers' offices will be considerably smaller. About the right size for someone who wasn't showing yet in Santa Fe. Twenty bucks ought to get me my choice of black-haired brats with skin that's not too dark. But I'll be sure to let someone know about the little Howard orphan in El Paso. Wouldn't want to leave any loose ends, now, would we?"

He adjusted the gun again, cocking the hammer. The wind was rising, but still only a soft, low, mournful wail.

"Well . . . ladies first, as they say. A real pity we don't have a little more time. I suggest you say your prayers, if you know any. But then, I suppose they taught you all about things like that in those fancy schools you went to."

Diana didn't even have time to be frightened. Everything happened too quickly. The shot was muffled, half-lost in the storm, and Garland was shouting—"No!" it sounded like, and "Damn you!"—and suddenly he was in front, his shoulder taking the bullet that had been intended for her.

Diana could only stand there, horrified, as he reeled around. A second bullet caught him in the stomach. An awful gurgling sound came out of his throat; then he was down on his knees, collapsing, writhing, and a dark stain was spreading across his shirt.

Two shots, she thought numbly. Four in all. She tried desperately to concentrate. That meant there was only one left—but one was enough. Garland might not be dead, but he was fatally wounded. No reason to waste a shot on him. Not until she'd been taken care of.

But to her amazement, Ryder lowered the gun slowly, calculatingly, pointed the barrel at her father's gaping wound—and fired the last bullet into his gut!

He *had* forgotten that second shot before.

She had no idea where her father's gun had fallen; she doubted Ryder did either. It would take a minute for him to find it or reload his own.

She inched backward, toward the slightly mounded rim of the ledge, feeling with her feet to keep from stumbling. Just a little more, she thought. It couldn't be much farther.

She had nearly made it when he saw her.

"No good, honey. I can shoot as well at twenty feet as five."

"I think you forgot *three* things," she said. "That's a Colt rotating-breech pistol. It holds five shots."

"Of which I have used four. That gives me one—for you. Or do you think I'm going to miss?"

"Of which you have used five." She was almost there now; she could feel the difference in the ground. It was going to hurt, sliding down the hill—jagged stones had dug through her boots on the way up—but she had to move fast.

"Four." He shook his head, smiling, as if enjoying her fear, the bastard! "Three for your daddy, just now. And one before. To knock the gun out of his hand."

"*Two* before. That second shot was automatic, wasn't it? You couldn't just leave it at one."

She saw the doubt in his eyes, and she knew a second before he did that she was going to get away. *Now!* she thought, and leapt sideways over the low ridge separating the hill from what was left of the cave. The faint click of an empty chamber sounded behind her as she half-skidded, half-rolled down the slope.

The storm was worse. Much worse than it had been—how long ago now?—when she scrambled up that stony bank. Sand blew in her mouth and nose, stinging, stifling; her eyes burned so badly she had to keep them half-shut.

Somehow she had to find the place where she had left her horse. She skidded again, sending a cascade of rocks down the hillside. Not that she would be able to ride. The storm was too violent. She was going to have to lead Brutus until it let up.

But the same conditions that made it dangerous for her were also blinding her pursuer. As long as she kept quiet,

Ryder could only guess where she was. As soon as it cleared, even a little, she wanted to be on horseback, ready to make a break for it.

She winced as a rock jabbed her thigh, cutting though her denim pants and starting another slide. So much for quiet! Would Ryder be keeping his horse close too? Would it be faster than Brutus? She tried but could only barely call it to memory. A huge black animal . . . he had kept it with the remuda most of the time, riding instead on one of the mules.

An unknown quantity. . . . Diana shuddered as she reached the bottom and felt her feet slide into the water. Typical of Ryder. No showing his strengths . . . or his weaknesses. But she had a feeling the horse was as powerful as it looked. And swift.

But Brutus was swift too. If only she could get to him . . .

She waded into the water slowly, agonizingly, terrified every second she was going to make a noise. She strained her ears, but all she could hear was the awful screaming of the wind.

Was it really taking so long to load the gun? Or were the seconds just dragging because she was so afraid?

She had to be close now. Everything seemed different without sight to guide her. She wished she dared whistle through her teeth, her signal to Brutus. There was a kind of cove, gouged out of the cliff, a short distance from where she had left him. Would he have gravitated toward that when the gusts grew fiercer?

A sudden crashing of rocks sounded behind her. Diana nearly let out a cry as she jumped, startled. Ryder. He had readied his weapon. He was coming down.

God help her, what was going to happen when he got to the bottom? Would he continue thrashing, stumbling along the shore, cursing as he searched for her through the turbid haze that cut visibility to almost nothing?

Or would he turn sly, slipping stealthily over rocks and sand? No clue to tell her where he was, what he was doing . . . whether a hand would come out and grab her from behind.

She reached the cove. The storm was somewhat less savage here. She could see several feet ahead, enough to tell her it was empty. Wherever Brutus had gone, it was not here.

Tears filled her eyes, sharp and burning. She hadn't re
alized how much she was counting on finding her horse
Just having him close would have given her hope.

And there was a knife with her gear. Diana could have
screamed with frustration. Only a camp knife, not much o
a weapon, but it would have been something. She could
have had it ready in her hand, a surprise for Ryder if he
leapt on her in the wildly blowing dust.

"You haven't got a chance," his voice called out, drifting
and ebbing with the wind. "Play all the games you wan
. . . they won't do any good. I'm faster . . . and stronge
. . . and I have a gun."

Oh, God . . . Diana nearly panicked. He sounded so near
She hadn't realized the cove was that close to the base o
the hill.

She froze, afraid to move, even more afraid to stay where
she was. Oh, please, she prayed—please, *please*, don't le
him come this way.

But his next words dashed even that slim hope.

"You're looking for your horse, aren't you, honey?
should have told you. He spooked when he saw me. He'
probably halfway to San Antonio now."

He was laughing! Diana heard the brittle sound, ever
above the storm, and fear swelled into anger. He was en
joying himself! He was so sure he was going to succeed
sure he would get her in the end. He was *enjoying* the thril
of the chase.

It was all she could do to keep from calling out a defian
retort. But that was exactly what he wanted. He was trying
to goad her into speaking. Her voice would give her away.

She eased out of the cove as quickly as she dared. A gus
of sand blasted her in the face, nearly knocking her down
He knew where she had left her horse—he guessed she would
come looking for it. Not that he'd expect her to linger afte
that obvious taunt, but she couldn't afford to take the chance

She forced herself out into the stream. The water felt like
ice, shocking her feet and legs. Despite the storm, the af
ternoon was hot and she was drenched with sweat. If she
hugged the banks, protected from the worst of the wind, he
would be able to see her. In the center, she'd be lost i
swirls of dust and sand.

Keep the water to your waist, she told herself, remem
bering the way the river had looked when her father wade

ut. That means you're still in the middle. Let it get lower,
nd you'll be too close to shore.

But which way should she go?

Diana hesitated, not even daring to breathe. Forward—
oward the settlements Garland had hinted at. Or back the
vay they had come?

Which way would he expect?

Fear closed in, horrible and debilitating for one awful
econd. Forward, probably. Instinct always propelled one
orward . . . didn't it?

And back might actually be safer. At least that way she'd
now the terrain. She'd be better off if she had an idea where
he was.

Yes . . . back. She started moving, slowly, making only
he tiniest ripples. She hadn't realized how hard it was,
valking in water when one didn't dare swim. How long
vould the storm keep up? She knew nothing about the des-
rt, the climate at that time of year, the tendencies of the
vind. And how long before the sun went down?

She squinted into the sky. The dust was so thick, it was
ll she could do to keep from coughing. There was a slightly
righter spot in the direction she sensed was west. But it
vas still relatively high. Well above the horizon.

Three, then. Maybe four. At least a couple of hours until
lusk.

She tried to go faster, but the riverbed was slippery.
Nothing for her boots to grip onto, and she fell with a terrifyingly loud splash. Righting herself, she stood absolutely
still, listening, but there was nothing.

Did that mean he had gone the other way, as she had
hoped? Or was he somewhere just behind? Slipping through
that murky veil, as silent as she. Maybe in the water too.

Before, all she had wanted was one brief respite so she
could leap on her horse and gamble everything on a wild
gallop across the plains. Now, on foot, she could only pray
that the storm held until night set in.

With a gun, Ryder would have the advantage . . . as long
as he could see her. In the darkness, they would be equal.

She had no idea how long she continued like that. Time
seemed to be suspended, but at least she was going faster.
She had begun to gauge the wind, swimming when it picked
up enough to cover the sound, gliding through the water.

Maybe an hour . . . maybe two. That faint patch of bright
ness was lower in the sky.

Her father had said they would follow the river for five o
six miles, but it hadn't seemed that far to her. More lik
three. Four at the most. If so, she must be getting close t
the spot where they had come down the bank.

She tried desperately to call it to mind. Why hadn't sh
paid more attention? The river had seemed a muddy ribbon
both the shores comparatively wide. The banks had bee
steep, almost perpendicular, with one path angling down.

If she could just find it . . . if she could make her wa
back up . . . The sun was bright enough to judge direction—
was the storm easing? She was almost sure she could fin
the way back to one of those ravines. Maybe Brutus ha
gone that way too.

There was a chance, of course, she'd run into Juan Jos
and his desperadoes, but that was a chance she was mor
than willing to take. It seemed ironic to remember how
terrified she had been of them, frantic to cover her tracks.

She was beginning to wish she hadn't made such a goo
job of it. With Ryder stalking her, she'd be almost gratefu
to be taken captive again!

The wind was dying away, not a howl anymore, but
dull whine. It was a moment before Diana realized she wa
staring at the bank some distance away—and seeing it!

Horrified, she scrambled out of the water. Half-runnin
now. No point worrying about making noise. If Ryder wa
close enough to hear, he could see her too.

She pressed into the sheer bank, clinging as she hurrie
along. What had been dangerous before was now the safes
course. She was as dusty as the earth itself. As long as th
storm continued to blur the landscape, however slightly, sh
would blend like a desert lizard into the cliff.

She was startled to see a boot print, clearly visible in
protected bend of the steep rock wall. Small. It must b
hers. She was on the right track, then! How odd that it ha
escaped all that blowing sand. How many other little cor
ners of the desert were untouched by the violence of th
storm?

She stopped for a moment, breathing heavily. She hadn'
realized how exhausted she was. She didn't know how muc
longer she could go on.

There was almost no wind now. The air was strangel

heavy and she could see all the way to the next turn. If Ryder was anywhere around, she wasn't going to have to think about going faster! The dust was settling, visibly. Diana could see it drifting down, brown next to the earth, a purplish haze above.

It was then that she spotted the path. Just a few yards away, but she had almost missed it. Softened by a layer of fresh sand—no footprints there—but she was almost certain that was the way she had come down.

And the way she was going to have to go up.

She hesitated, her heart suddenly beating madly. It had been level on top, open for miles. Only one low butte jutting out of the sand, and that so far it would take a couple of minutes at a fast run to reach it.

But there was noplace to hide here, no crevices, no vegetation thick enough to conceal her. All Ryder had to do was saunter over to the edge and peer down—and she was as good as dead!

At least on top, she might be able to burrow into one of the shifting dunes and wait it out until dark.

Taking a deep breath, she started up the path.

She half-crept, half-slithered on her belly the last few feet. Emerging slowly, very cautiously, she eased her head above the ground and scoured the landscape.

Nothing to the west. That was where he'd be coming from. No figure silhouetted against the flaming orange sky . . . no puff of dust that might indicate a horse.

The first feelings of relief were beginning to stir as she turned her head in the other direction—and found herself staring at a pair of dusty boots.

She raised her eyes to see dusty knees, a dusty gunbelt, empty . . . a dusty shirt. And on top, leering down, was Ryder's dusty grin.

"Smart, honey. Real smart . . . and predictable. Now, how did I know you were going to come this way?"

Diana raised herself to her knees, then sank back in rage and fear and frustration. So close. She had come so close! Now, here he was, grinning down at her, that evil pleasure on his face, and there was not a thing she could do.

Too late, she realized what had happened. He hadn't been following her at all. All that time she had tried so desperately to be quiet, he hadn't even been there! He had seen the tracks she and her father had made—that was how he had found them—and guessed she would come back the same way. He had simply returned there. And waited.

And she had walked into the trap. Numb with terror, she watched as slowly, very slowly, he raised his gun. Now she was going to pay for her stupidity.

The barrel had just begun to angle upward when she heard the shot. Sharp and somehow unreal. Ryder's arm twitched violently, the gun discharged in the sand, and suddenly his face was going into all sorts of hideous contortions.

Diana thought she had never seen such hate and fury before his eyes went blank and he dropped to the ground.

She could only sit there trembling, not registering anything except that she was alive. She didn't even hear the hoofbeats until they were almost there and someone was reining in beside her.

She looked up to see a familiar figure with a rifle slung across the front of his saddle.

But the voice was not familiar at all. Not with that Texas drawl.

"J. J. Montgomery at your service, ma'am." The *sombrero* was coming off with a broad, sweeping gesture. "Sorry about all this coffee-colored hair. I'm really quite a dashing redhead."

29

DIANA WOULD NEVER remember the details of the next half-hour. Vague impressions stood out, an image here, a sentence there, but everything else was lost in a dizzying haze, like the terrible dust storm now finally over. Juan José had dismounted—no, not Juan José; what was it he had called himself before?—and was coming over, squatting beside her. She knew that he was asking questions, making sure she was all right, and she was answering, but she had no idea what either of them said.

Somehow a blanket found its way to her shoulders. It was even hotter now that the dust was settling—the sun was a brilliant orange blaze sinking in the west—but she was shivering uncontrollably and it felt good to clutch it closer. Ryder's body had been dragged off someplace, and men seemed to be riding in from all directions. The *bandidos*, so coated with dust she could barely recognize them, only not sinister now, their faces more grave than threatening.

Hoofbeats drummed suddenly, a bold, almost desperate gallop, skidding to a stop so close she could feel a spray of sand on her cheek. Diana was on her feet, the blanket cast aside, heart thumping wildly even before her eyes confirmed what she had only dared to hope.

Cord!

She would never know how he got down from the horse, how she came to be in his arms, but she was crying, and he was crying too, and they were laughing at the same time and clinging and both talking at once. "You're alive!" she was saying—or was that his voice? "You made it!" "I was so afraid." "I thought I'd lost you forever."

Then his mouth was on hers, hard and hungry, claiming her, and she was claiming back. All the promises they had never been able to make, all the vows were sworn at that moment, without words. He was telling her that he loved her, that he had been frantic with fear, that his life meant nothing without her. And she was telling him she loved him too . . . and would love him until the day she died.

"My God, Diana, what a fool I've been," he cried when he finally released her. "I had everything I wanted—everything!—and I almost let it go. More than a fool. A raving idiot! What kind of madness gets into a man?"

Diana snuggled closer. "I don't know," she said, too happy to think about anything except that he was here and she was actually touching him. "But I'm glad it's over. You can't imagine how I felt when I found those buttons and knew you had been taken by Indians."

"Yes, I can." He was clasping her tightly, holding on, as if somehow the winds might pick up again and blow her away. "One of those damn savages found the scarf you left for me, and I went half-crazy. If anything had happened to you . . ." He kissed her again, even more deeply this time, satisfying himself that this was really her, that she was really safe in his arms.

It was a little disconcerting to let her go and hear a light giggle.

"You look so funny!" Diana did not even try to control herself. It felt so good to be able to laugh again. "Your eyebrows are all pale, and your scratchy whiskers . . . even your mouth, except where I kissed it clean. You look like a ghost."

"So do you, love . . . so do you. But you're my own sweet, precious ghost, and I'm never going to let you go again."

He was settling her back on the ground as he spoke, the blanket wrapped protectively about her shoulders again, and they sat beside each other for some minutes. Not speaking. Not needing to speak, just content to be close.

When they were interrupted, it was by a reluctant Juan José, or whatever he was calling himself now. Cord rose, and the two men moved a short distance away, speaking Spanish again, in an undertone, though words drifted back. Bits and snatches here and there.

Diana thought about telling them she could understand, but she was so tired suddenly, and it didn't seem to matter.

Pulling her knees up, she rested her head. It sounded urgent, whatever they were saying, but she couldn't imagine anything being urgent now. Something about bringing "him" in a few minutes ago. And "he" was still alive, but wouldn't last long.

"You didn't finish him off?" Cord was saying—or something like that. The other man's voice was clearer. "No," he was saying, "I left him for you."

Cord came back a second later to crouch beside her. Diana was too preoccupied with the amazing turns her luck had taken to notice the slight stiffness in his manner as he told her he would have to leave for a while.

Just a short time, he assured her. He would be back soon. His cousin would look after her in the meantime.

"You're Cord's *cousin?*"

Diana's eyes had recovered some of their spark as she turned to face the man Cord had left with her. That show of spirit did not seem to intimidate him, however. There was nothing even remotely resembling contrition in his manner as he ambled over.

"Cousin John—J.J. to my friends, of whom I hope you count yourself one." He sprawled casually on the sand beside her, the resemblance to Cord almost uncanny at that moment. "Or are you going to tell me again how dreadfully I deceived you, tripping you in the plaza so I could get to know your husband?" His eyes crinkled at the corners. "But I already knew your husband. I had known him since the day he was born. It was your acquaintance I was trying to make. It is much easier to keep an eye on someone if you can do so openly."

"But you *did* lie to me," Diana reminded him, somewhat but not totally mollified.

"How so?" Her old friend seemed to return for a moment as he lapsed into his comical accent. "By saying to you that my name is Juan José? But it is. John Joseph—in translation. Or that I have a fondness for the bourbon of Kentucky? It is one of the passions of my life! One of the *many* passions," he added with a sly wink.

"I have no doubt." In spite of herself, Diana smiled. Juan José was hard to resist. "But that isn't what I meant. I was talking about later. When I woke up and found myself surrounded by ruffians. You told me you were *bandidos* looking for the lost silver of Antonio Vargas."

"I did not. You said that yourself. I merely said it was as good an explanation as any for why I was there. And it was."

Diana studied him curiously. "It seems to me," she said, "an even better explanation would have been the truth."

"What truth, *turquesa?*" He turned solemn for a moment, looking for the first time almost regretful. "That we were searching, not for the silver, but for your father? That when we found him, he was a dead man? He was not very good to you, but it occurred to me you might have had an attachment all the same. I thought it wiser to keep you in the dark."

"You were wrong," Diana said quietly.

"Yes, well . . ." He got up and wandered off a few feet, gazing toward the butte as if something were happening there. "I have been wrong before. And there is just the slightest possibility I may be wrong sometime again. I was, for instance, wrong not to have kept a closer eye on you. I thought you were reconciled to staying with us for a while."

He was talking faster. Almost as if he wanted to distract her, Diana sensed. Kindly, perhaps. So the time would pass more quickly until Cord came back.

"It wouldn't have made any difference. I'd still have gotten away—you would just have made it harder. But how did you find me?"

"I almost didn't. That was a clever trick, leaving a false trail. It worried me when I saw only *your* hoofprints. No sign of your father's horse. There might have been a dozen explanations, of course, but I decided to have one of the men search the ravine, just in case. He came tearing after us half an hour later."

"I'm glad he did!" Diana shivered as she thought what might have happened. "And I'm glad the storm didn't obliterate the real trail." A faint popping noise came from somewhere nearby. Like a muted gunshot. She looked up, startled, but John Montgomery didn't seem to have noticed. At least he was talking fast again.

"It very nearly did. We found only a couple of prints, just enough to tell us which way you were going. Fortunately, I'm familiar with the area. I guessed you'd be heading for the river."

"So you came charging after, like a posse to the rescue."

"Posses don't rescue. They chase people. But yes, 'charging' is an apt description. We held back only long enough to leave a few signs for Cord. I did tell you he was resourceful—I knew he'd get away. There were several likely spots along the riverbank. We fanned out, each taking a different one. I just happened to get stuck at that butte over there when the storm hit its peak.''

''And you just happened to hang around afterward . . . like you just happened to go hunting when the Comanche attacked.'' Diana raised one brow, but the ironic effect was lost in all the dust on her face. ''And you just happened to be there when Ryder showed up.''

''Actually, I was leaving. He almost caught me when he staked his horse on the far side of the butte. It occurred to me it might be interesting to prop my rifle in a convenient niche in the rocks and see what he was up to.''

Diana looked back at the place where the path came up to the top of the bank. ''Interesting'' was not quite the word she would have chosen, but it would do. The area was empty now, nothing but a few scratches in the sand to show where the body had been.

''The silver was gone,'' she said softly. ''When we got there. It must have been gone a very long time.''

''I know. Some of my men just got back. I'm sorry, *turquesa*. Does it matter so very much?''

He was not speaking of the silver. Diana knew that as she turned and saw the pity in his eyes. And she knew suddenly what it had been, that popping sound she heard before. And whom they were talking about, the man still clinging to life . . . but barely.

''He was not all bad, you know. He couldn't shoot me when it came right down to it. I think he must have cared. He stepped in front of me just as Ryder was firing. The bullet that got him was intended for me. Surely that means something.''

''Perhaps he did care,'' John Montgomery agreed kindly. ''Stranger things have happened than that a father should come to have feelings for his very beautiful daughter.''

Stranger, indeed! Diana rested her cheek on her knees again. Nothing could be stranger than the events of the last few hours. But it was over now. All over. She was safe, and nothing could ever hurt her again.

Cord stood at the edge of the cliff and stared across the muddy river at the shimmering outline of hills in the distance. He had always loved the desert, the clean sweep of the sand, the great empty silences that came with dawn and dusk, the smell of dust and dryness and scrub, untainted by the smoke of the city; loved the vast barren spaces that tried a man's skill and nerve and made him feel like a man.

Today he hated it.

He became aware that he was still holding the gun, the pungent odor of powder still clinging to it, and he slipped it back in his holster. The bloated face of the dying man came to him, haunting him, as he knew it would haunt his nightmares for years.

He had thought he wanted to kill him. God, how he'd thought he was waiting for this moment! He had thought for years that it would give him the deepest, fiercest, most intense pleasure to point his pistol between those greedy eyes and let go.

Instead he had felt only the detached coolness of someone who knew what he had to do. The man's guts were half-spilling out; he couldn't have lived for long. He was barely conscious, writhing on the ground, whimpering in pain. You wouldn't leave a dog to suffer like that.

It was with no more emotion than he would have felt for a wounded wild animal that he had pulled the trigger.

He turned slowly from the bank and started back, taking the long way round, avoiding the butte where two corpses now lay wrapped in blankets, more for convenience than compassion, as they awaited his final instructions.

He had thought he was living for this day, thought his hate was enough, thought somehow it would see him through. But he knew now that hate was as destructive as brutality and greed. Hate was a consuming emotion. It gnawed a man away, from the inside out, until nothing was left but a shell.

It was love that healed where hate wounded. Love that had filled the terrible empty spaces that hate had carved inside him. Love that had made him whole again, for the first time since he'd stood on the banks of a swollen stream and gazed at long dark hair floating like shadow-ripples beneath the water.

It was love he wanted now, with all his heart . . . and he was bitterly aware that it might be too late.

He had lied to Diana, and lied again. Not half-innocently, as she had with him, getting in deeper and deeper. But knowingly and deliberately. And now he was being called to account.

Diana looked up as he returned, the brightness in her eyes
fading when she saw his expression.

"I think it's time," he said grimly, "that I told you what
I'm doing here. And who I am."

30

"BUT I KNOW who you are," Diana protested as she burrowed deeper into a nest of heavenly-smelling fresh straw. They had ridden for several hours, silently, and now it was dark, though as usual their Mexican escort had managed to find an open-fronted stable in the middle of nowhere, rustic, but surprisingly sturdy. "You're Cord Montgomery. You are my husband . . . and you adore me to distraction."

"Well . . . that's partly true." Cord rammed a blazing pine torch into the dirt floor and came over to sit beside her, one long, lean leg stretched out in front of him. Flickering light played on the crags and hollows of his darkly rugged features, clean-shaven now, for they had stopped at dusk to wash and change. "I do adore you . . . beyond distraction. And my name is Cord Montgomery. But that's not my full name. It's really Cordero Montgomery."

"Cordero?" Diana frowned slightly. Where had she heard that before? It felt strange to be wearing a dress again, one pretty outfit she had rolled up in her saddlebag. Pale blue muslin, his favorite, simple and flattering . . . the color deepened in the shadows, hugging and accenting every curve of her body. "I'm not sure I understand what you're getting at. Is it that important? Your given name?"

"Not the name itself, no . . . but what it means. That is extremely important."

"Then I really *don't* understand. If it's so important, why didn't you just tell me before?"

"Why, indeed?" A rustling came from one of the stalls, drawing his gaze for an instant. Brutus had shown up just as they were leaving the butte and was snuffling contentedly through the straw. Outside, the desert was almost unnaturally silent, all the little creatures still burrowed away from the violence of the storm.

When he looked back, his eyes had turned dark and strangely disturbed.

"I think it would be easier, love, if you let me tell the story from the beginning. It's not a very pretty story, but I'll try to keep it short. I had a cousin once too—a very beautiful cousin . . . and I was hopelessly in love with her. A childish crush perhaps, but it doesn't feel like that when you're on the brink of manhood. Maybe that's why I was able to be so sympathetic when you told me how you felt about your cousin. And what had happened to him.

"Not that it was quite the same thing. She was much older than I—at least she seemed much older then—and I must have had something of the mien of a spaniel, always following her around. Anyway, we were *first* cousins. There were never any fantasies she might return my affection. But I was at an age when passions run deep. I was shattered when she died."

"She . . . died? How awful, Cord!" Diana longed to reach out, assuaging the pain, but he looked so impassive, so drawn into himself, that she didn't dare touch him. Whatever he had begun, she was going to have to let him finish it, alone and in his own way. "But she must have been very young. How did she die?"

"By her own hand. She threw herself into the river. . . . I told you this wasn't a pretty story. She was pregnant and couldn't face the consequences. The man was a kind of drifter. He'd been hanging around for weeks. I was too young to understand what was going on, or maybe I'd have been able to do something about it. I only knew I was fiercely jealous of the attention she was lavishing on him."

He jumped up and paced over to one of the stalls, restlessly, every muscle coiled and rippling, like an animal in a cage. "I never found out if he knew she was pregnant. Maybe he did, maybe he didn't . . . it didn't matter. He just drifted on. And she died."

"Oh, Cord . . . that must have been heartbreaking." Again she wanted to touch him, and again she held back. "I don't blame you for not wanting to talk about it. But I still don't see . . ." She broke off suddenly, remembering. "That name—Cordero. I knew I'd heard it before! If I weren't so tired, I'd have recognized it right away. That's the name of the people who own the house we rented in Santa Fe."

"Actually, *I* own it." Cord's mouth twisted into a wry half-smile. "You didn't think I could afford an elegant *casa* like than on a wagon master's pay? My mother was Margarita Cordero—Margie, my father called her. It was she who painted the landscapes you admired. She was very talented. She might have been an artist, but she chose marriage instead."

He paused, studying her intently in the eerily undulating light.

"Her sister's name was Luisa. She married Antonio Vargas."

"Oh." Diana's eyes widened. She was beginning to see. And she wasn't at all sure she was going to like what came next. "That was the uncle you went to live with. After your parents were killed. No wonder you acted so funny every time the theft of the silver came up! But what made you go after my father? How did you know he had had something to do with it?"

"Because, *querida*, your father was the man who seduced my cousin."

He came back and squatted beside her, his face solemn, brooding, hating the things that could no longer be left unsaid. "I'm sorry. I know you don't want to hear this, but I'm afraid it's true. Carla—Carlota—may have been weak, but she was not a bad woman. And that bastard just walked away and left her! I found out later his wife—your mother—was still alive. He couldn't have married Carla if he wanted to, but marriage wasn't what he had in mind. He was just *using* her to find out about the silver."

He saw the horror on her face, the sheer disbelief, and raised a hand to silence her.

"There's no possibility I'm mistaken. There never was. You see, I knew—like Esteban Olivares—that my uncle was no thief. Once I started exploring the possibilities, it didn't take long to figure out who the real culprit was. I traced your father to St. Louis, quite easily—he'd been using his real name—and a little sleuthing turned up the fact that a large amount of silver had just come on the market. Melted down."

His voice turned hoarse, almost savage, taking on undertones that made Diana suddenly feel cold all over. "It wasn't hard to total it up. He'd disposed of everything in the same place. Give or take a little, it came to about half of what my uncle had been carrying.

"I knew then that for some reason, he hadn't been able to get it all out. And I knew it was going to eat away inside him until he went back for the rest."

"So you just . . . *waited* for him?" The realization of what he was saying came out in a gasp of shock and dismay. She had thought she finally knew this man, thought she knew what he was capable of. "All that time, you were waiting? Plotting a trap? Deliberately luring him to his death?"

Cord did not spare himself. "It took nearly fifteen years, but I managed. With a little help from my cousin, John. Or should I say my 'co-avenger'? Tío Antonio had staked him a couple of times. He even lived with us for a while. . . . And, of course, Johnny's always been a bit of an adventurer.

"We split up, those early years. It fell to me to follow the trail, pick up what I could, start building a reputation. When the time came, I wanted to be the best damn wagon master around.

"I don't say I didn't enjoy it. I loved the hard work and the challenge, even the dust, the camaraderie around the campfire in the evening . . . I loved taking on something and knowing I was doing it well . . . but I never lost sight of the objective.

"Of course," he added grimly, "I had a natural advantage. I was a 'white man.' Given your father's past, he was understandably leery of Mexicans. When he went looking for someone who knew the language and the territory and didn't have the blood—or so he thought—there I was. Ready."

He leaned back against the post behind him, conscious every second of the warmth of Diana's body, barely a few feet away, but not allowing himself to look at her. He had not missed her reaction before, and he had understood it—better perhaps than she understood it herself. Any normal human being would be appalled by what he was saying.

"After that," he went on, "everything fell into place. Cousin Johnny had taken to stopping by Santa Fe every couple of months, establishing his identity—and having the time of his life! The stage lost an actor when he hit the road. I had deliberately taken on a young crew, hoping at least a few would fall by the wayside, though the Army of the West was an unexpected bonus. If you have to take on a Mexican, who better than good old harmless Juan José, the amiable town drunk?''

"And the others?'' Diana asked. Her voice was low and expressionless. Cord had no idea how she was taking it. Did she understand better now that she had had a chance to think it over? Or was she hardening her heart against him?

"All friends of Antonio Vargas. The foreman of one of his *haciendas*, a couple of business associates, a devoted *vaquero*, another cousin—distant this time. The oldest would have been a neighbor, but he fell ill at the last minute. His son—Roberto—took his place.''

There was a long silence after he finished. Still Cord could not bring himself to look at Diana. The desert was coming to life again—coyotes keened in the distance—but here the silence was so heavy he could almost feel it.

"You must have been very disappointed,'' she said after a moment, "when you learned that the silver was gone.''

Cord felt his heart catch. Still no hint of what she was feeling. "No.'' He shook his head. "We never expected to find it. Whatever you may think of us, Diana, we were not greedy for the silver. All we wanted was to prove Antonio Vargas' honor. And restore his good name. There was plenty of evidence for that . . .''

He hesitated, not wanting to mention the body that had been found under a blanket, clearly shot in the back. She had been through enough horrors without that. There had also, surprisingly, been a few bars of silver, revealed where someone had been scratching in the dirt.

A timely bit of luck, since the Comanche who'd been trailing him would probably get there in the morning—and they wouldn't have taken too kindly to going back empty-handed.

"It was an obsession, Diana,'' he said slowly. "That's the only way I can describe it. The more I thought about the past, the more I lived in it again. I just hated and hated . . . until there wasn't room for anything else. I couldn't let go. Cousin Johnny tried to warn me, once in Santa Fe. He said there was still time to go back. But I couldn't.''

He stared out into the darkness that swallowed up the world beyond the open front of the stable. He knew he was going to weep if she didn't forgive him, and for the first time, in his life, he was not afraid of tears. He was afraid of losing her.

"God help me, I *couldn't!* It wasn't until I was riding through that damned blowing sand, not knowing where you were, what had happened to you, that it finally came to me. Carla was gone, and the uncle I could never bring back with all my grief and rage. You were here—and *you* were what mattered! All I wanted was to know you were safe. Fifteen years of imagining the taste of vengeance in my mouth, and I was choking on it."

The night seemed even darker. Cord was aware of the silence behind him—much too long—and he sensed she had already made up her mind. His own fault, but he felt as if someone had cut out his heart. It was a devil of a thing, finding out you couldn't live without a woman just as she was preparing to leave you.

He waited, expecting the anger, the recriminations, the awkwardness. Expecting anything but what she did.

She laughed.

Cord jerked his head around, sure he must have misheard. Must have misunderstood that light but very distinct sound. But there she was, laughing. And with a decidedly mischievous glint in her eye.

"So that's why you married me," she said tartly. "Not because your chivalrous instincts were roused by my terrible plight. Not because you were so charmed you couldn't resist, despite all that masculine bravado. And not, heaven forfend, because you were beginning to fall in love with me. You did it because you wanted to see my father's face turn purple!"

"In part, perhaps." Cord could feel the tension draining from his body. A sheer physical sensation. Somehow in the past minutes she had come to terms with what he had done, and she was not going to hold it against him. It was a generosity he did not deserve, and he was conscious of an uncharacteristic sense of humility as he went over and half-crouched, half-knelt beside her. "I must confess it was extremely satisfying. But I think even then, I *was* beginning to love you. I could, after all, have found a chaperone—or another boarding school—until matters could be settled with the attorneys. I had transferred a considerable sum to provide for any contingency."

"You have money of your own?" Diana blushed, realizing how that must sound. "I mean, I wondered how you arranged for the carriage and all those new clothes."

"Did you think I was dipping into your great-grandfather'
trust? I would have been the clever one, wouldn't I, to hav
gotten my hands on it so soon? I have, in fact, an inheri
tance of my own, from both my father and my uncle. Yo
haven't exactly gotten yourself married to a pauper. Tha
is . . ." He hesitated, suddenly unsure again, afraid he wa
taking too much for granted. "That is, if you still want t
be married."

He started to take her hand, then dropped it clumsily
"You had to ask my forgiveness once—for considerably les
devious lies. I gave it, but not very graciously, I fear. Dar
I hope for more mercy from you?"

Diana lifted the hand he had just released and laid it o
his cheek. The beginnings of whiskers were growing again
faintly rough beneath her fingertips. Were men always lik
this? she wondered. Brash swaggerers one minute, insecur
little boys the next? Or was it just this one?

She *had* been shocked by his obsession, by the horribl
twists his need for revenge had taken. But when the shoc
had worn off, she had remembered the one thing she woul
always remember. That her feelings for him ran deeper tha
anything else in her life.

"I think, my dear, I have already answered that."

"Maybe," he said, "I need to hear the words."

"Well, then . . . yes, I am merciful. Yes, I love you ver
much. And yes, I do forgive you for lying to me . . . thi
time. But do it again and I'll bit off your ear!"

"My *ear?*"

"It's all I can say," she said sweetly, "and still be
lady."

The laughter was healing. The pain washed away, all the
agonizing doubts, and Cord felt whole for the first time i
memory as he drew her into his arms. The warmth of he
body, molding supply, sensuously against his, kindled
responsive heat which spread from his groin until every cor
ner of his being seemed to blaze with longing.

This was what he had been searching for, all those years
without knowing it. This was what had awakened him o
restless nights in all those nameless places beneath the stars
This was what he had needed. Not love*making,* not anothe
body beside him in the darkness—but love. The sweet, ach
ing passion that consumed not just the flesh, but the hear
and spirit as well.

The straw was yielding, soft, and smelled of the pungent cleanness of the outdoors. He laid her back gently, feeling no pressure to hurry now, despite the urgency that throbbed through his body. They would have many more nights, a lifetime of nights, and mornings, and sweet sultry afternoons. There was no need to grab the passing moment. She was his, truly his, and he was hers, as he had never belonged to anyone before.

All the ghosts of the past were finally laid to rest as he drove himself deeply, satisfyingly into her. The long, slow, plunging thrusts and withdrawals, the answering gasps that slipped from her lips, were the balm his soul had been hungering for. Carla was at peace on her hill far away. Antonio Vargas' body would soon be returned to be buried beside her in the land he had loved. And Cord Montgomery was free to live at last.

"You are my heart, my hopes—all the dreams I never even knew I had," he said as they lay, satiated and content, in each other's arms. The torch had nearly burned down; shadows were brooding and thick. "You are my wife . . . and you are very beautiful."

She looked up with the blue-green eyes that would drive him mad till the day he died. "Even with straw in my hair?"

"Especially with straw in your hair."

He drew her closer, protectively, wrapping the blanket around them both as the torch gave a last feeble sputter and went out. He would fall asleep soon; he sensed that she was already, curled up like a kitten against him, but he needed this last minute to hold her in his arms and think what a miraculous, amazing, unexpected thing love was.

A year ago he hadn't even known who she was. Now he couldn't imagine his life without her.

He felt his eyelids growing heavier. The darkness closed in, not menacing, but comfortable, enveloping. Diana stirred slightly as he settled her head on his shoulder and let his lips rest briefly on her forehead.

"Sweet dreams, my love. . . . Sweet dreams."